# Never Fall for Your Fiancée

MERRIWELL SISTERS, BOOK 1

# NEVER FALL FOR YOUR FIANCÉE

### VIRGINIA HEATH

**THORNDIKE PRESS**
A part of Gale, a Cengage Company

LIBRARY OF CONGRESS CIP DATA ON FILE.
CATALOGUING IN PUBLICATION FOR THIS BOOK
IS AVAILABLE FROM THE LIBRARY OF CONGRESS.

ISBN-13: 978-1-4328-9635-5 (hardcover alk. paper)

Published in 2022 by arrangement with St. Martin's Publishing Group

Printed in Mexico
Print Number: 01        Print Year: 2022

For Greg, the long-suffering Mr. H
Who is always there to lend me his
shoulders to stand on every time he
pushes me to reach for the stars

# CHAPTER ONE

*Late November 1825 . . .*

The trouble with lies is they have a tendency, if not well managed, to catch a man out. Hugh's out-of-control, grossly overembellished falsehood was like a snarling, rabid dog about to sink its foaming teeth into his behind, and there was not a damn thing he could do about it.

He stared at the letter again, pathetically hoping he had misread his mother's flamboyant, sloping handwriting — but alas, he was doomed. She had booked passage from Boston to leave on the first and, if the tide and the current and the trade winds complied, intended to be in Hampshire for Christmas. Which meant he had received her blasted letter far too late to put a stop to it, no doubt on purpose, as his mother, stepfather, and a whole heap of trouble were currently bobbing somewhere ever closer on the Atlantic Ocean. Worse — if indeed things could get worse — there was only one purpose to their spontaneous and wholly unwelcome trip.

They were desperate to meet and become better acquainted with his fiancée now that she was finally out of mourning.

The fiancée who didn't exist.

"Let's face it, you're done for." His best friend, Giles, the unenthusiastic heir to a dukedom, was an eternal pessimist. He popped his eighth biscuit into his mouth and chewed thoughtfully as he stared at his ceiling. "Perhaps now is a good time to run away? Take an extended tour of the Continent and only return once they have sailed back. Your stepfather is a businessman, is he not? In my experience, all businessmen are so dreadfully dull they cannot bear to leave their business alone for prolonged periods of time."

"If I run, I might as well tell my mother everything. Unsupervised, she will dig and dig until she has fully excavated the whole truth and then I shall never hear the end of it. Might I remind you, I only invented Minerva in the first place because she threatened to come home and help find me a bride. You have no idea how tenacious that woman can be. She has become quite obsessed with my happiness since she went and married for *love.*" Hugh screwed up his face with distaste. "She has it in her head I will never be truly happy unless I am shackled to the woman of my dreams. If that woman is not *Minerva,* then she'll find me a replacement quicker than you can say 'I do.' "

"Well, at least your lone surviving parent wishes for you to have a blissful union. My father is determined to foist a duty bride on me, and despite my repeated assertions to the contrary, presents me with a suitably uninspiring candidate at least once a week. I've developed an irrational fear of Hyde Park now, as he has sucked all the joy out of my riding there. And Rotten Row used to be such a fruitful place to meet like-minded ladies."

By "like-minded," Giles meant discreet, open to a dalliance, free and easy with their favors, and desirous of no permanent complications. One of the many reasons he and Hugh had always been such good friends was their similar taste in women and abhorrence of permanent attachments.

"You know I sympathize — but can we please focus on the most pressing problem in hand. *My* problem. What am *I* going to do?"

"Well, if you are not prepared to run, you

are going to have to face the music, old boy. I hear confession is supposed to be good for the soul. Unless you can conjure up a fiancée in the next few weeks."

Not at all helpful. "Because there must be at least a hundred proper young ladies in Mayfair who would be delighted to be my temporary betrothed and dragged across the country to spend Christmas in dreary Hampshire."

"Why does she have to be proper?"

"Because Minerva is proper! That's how I created her. My mother wouldn't settle for anything less, and frankly, seeing as she is a figment of my imagination, crafted to serve a necessary evil, I purposely made her the sort of paragon which every mother would want for their son."

" 'Oh, what a tangled web we weave, / When first we practice to deceive!' "

Hugh glared at his friend. "Must you quote the theatre while I'm in the midst of a crisis?"

"I adore the theatre."

"I came to you for help. Some guiding words of wisdom because you are supposed to be my best friend. So far, all you've done is eat an entire plate of biscuits and tell me I'm done for."

"You are done for." Giles waved a fresh

shortbread at him. "I gave you my infinite words of wisdom when you started this mockery of a sham two years ago and you blithely ignored them all."

Even more unhelpful. "You agreed Minerva was a stroke of genius at the time!"

"Indeed I did. Because it *was* a stroke of genius and it made me very jealous. If only my father lived across an ocean so I could invent a fiancée . . . And I must say, you have a flair for effusive prose, which I lack. Those poignant letters you wrote during her long battle with consumption, where you stalwartly sat at her bedside and read to her, silently praying for a cure while cursing the fickle finger of fate, brought a tear to my eye, I don't mind telling you." The remnants of biscuit number nine disappeared before his friend wagged a chastising finger. "But you must also recall I was *all* for her tragic death. By then she'd more than earned it, the poor thing. Consumption is such a romantically lingering disease and you could have played the heartbroken hero. That would have bought you a few more months at the very least. Yet you dragged it out interminably. Expressly against my good advice that all good things must come to an end."

"I couldn't kill her then! If I had, I'd have

been right back where I started and vulnerable to my mother's rampant matchmaking again. She was about to buy passage on a ship to help console me at the end!"

But Hugh knew he was right. Despite meticulously projecting a flippant and shallow exterior to the world, Giles was annoyingly right more often than he was wrong. Hugh huffed out a breath in surrender. He'd overdone it, and now his precarious house of cards was in danger of collapsing in a heap. "All right, the miraculous recovery might have been a bit far-fetched."

"Not as far-fetched as her father's untimely death in the Cairngorms last year! Didn't I caution you against writing to your mother when drunk?"

"You did, and you were right, but Mama caught me unawares with her insistence on coming back to help plan the nuptials, and I panicked. I had the devil of a job convincing her of the truth of my lie." More folly piled upon nonsense, and all so that he didn't have to witness the inevitable disappointed look in his mother's eyes. An irony that wasn't lost on him now. "It quite spoiled my visit to the Americas last Christmas." Perhaps conciliation would make Giles more sympathetic? "I *should* have listened to you. Are you happy now?"

"Isn't hindsight a wonderful thing? Although clearly she wasn't convinced, old boy, or she wouldn't be coming now. With precious little warning, too. Anyone would think she's come to trap you." Giles grinned, obviously enjoying himself immensely.

"Again — hardly helpful." Hugh stood, affronted. "If you can think of nothing better than criticism, then I shall leave and consult my sensible friends."

"We don't have any sensible friends." And there Giles went again, being annoyingly right when it was unwelcome and infuriatingly unpalatable. "But if you're off, can you ring the bell on your way out?" He lifted the empty plate from his stomach and held it aloft. "Somebody appears to have eaten all of the biscuits."

Hugh took himself to White's, which served to depress him further because it was devoid of his friends but filled with all the sad, old, crusty bachelors who had nothing better to do with their time than sit with each other in the comfortable wingbacks and grumble about the state of the world. So he left, only to wander aimlessly down a decidedly chilly Piccadilly rather than go home. He'd never been good at introspection because, despite the crushing guilt that always seemed to plague him, he was an optimist at heart. Introspection made him either maudlin or remorseful, two emotions that had plagued him ever since Payne, his trusty butler, had placed his mother's blasted letter on the breakfast table this morning next to his two soft-boiled eggs — and Hugh realized he was about to break his mother's heart.

Again.

Exactly like his father.

The missive — and the unavoidable comparison — had quite put him off food in general. In fact, he hadn't eaten a thing all day. Was it any wonder his brain was struggling to find a solution? Momentous decisions and important plans probably shouldn't be made on an empty stomach. He decided to visit the Lion and Lamb in Conduit Street, an inn where he was guaranteed a hearty meal while being blessedly spared the presence of anyone who was anyone in society, so he could consider his dilemma in private. He took the narrow backstreets for speed and pondered his problem.

What to do?

He wished he had killed off Minerva long ago exactly as Giles had said. His fake fiancée was only ever meant to be temporary — a way to stall his mother, avoid falling

14

out with her and hurting her feelings yet again, and to give himself some time off. He hated arguments more than he hated introspection, and he hated disappointing people. And he particularly hated hurting people. Especially his mother.

Aside from her irritating habit of match-making, he adored the woman. She didn't deserve any of this. All she had ever wanted was the best for Hugh, and she had sacrificed herself tirelessly for the sake of his happiness. He'd practically had to force her to marry the love of her life, because she was so dedicated to Hugh — something that doubtless drove her to push for him to do the same. She felt guilty for snatching some happiness of her own; ergo, to lessen her guilt, she needed to see him happy, too.

Which in her book meant marriage, although heaven only knew why. Despite the apparent success she had made of her second trip up the aisle, the legacy of her first still lingered in Hugh's mind and always would. How could it not when he and his father were two peas in a pod?

Or almost two peas.

Dear Papa, like his father before him, had managed to sleep at night whilst Hugh knew he never would. To be the cause of all that hurt . . . Unconsciously, he shuddered and found himself shaking his head as he marched forward. Unlike his philandering father and grandfather, he had standards. A man should only enter into a marriage when he had every intention of honoring his vows. Such a noble undertaking obviously required two attributes that, thanks to his ancestors, Hugh was fairly certain he didn't possess: eyes that didn't wander and a heart selfless enough to be capable of great love.

He had *loved* a great many women in his thirty-two years on the earth, and not one of them had ever made either of those fickle organs work as a good husband's should. Besides the Standish male's penchant for deceit, that wayward, womanizing Standish blood ran through his veins and always would. No indeed, the path of matrimony wasn't for him.

As much as he didn't want to end up like one of those sad, old, crusty bachelors who only went to White's because they had nobody to go home to, Hugh was resigned to his eventual fate. He would inevitably be in a wingback at White's next to Giles, and the pair of them could moan about the state of the world together. Until one of them died . . .

And there he was, being all maudlin again, mapping out a sorry future for himself when he wasn't anywhere near his dotage and was still a carefree young buck enjoying sowing his wild oats.

Or at least he had enjoyed it. The bloom had faded off the rose a little in the last year, and he often had to force himself to go out purely to keep up appearances amongst his friends who were still dedicated to the sport. That worried him. It signaled his dotage was doggedly shuffling ever closer despite his fear of those depressing wingbacks at White's.

Hugh had promised himself he would make more effort to enjoy his bachelorhood fully; however, more often than not, he made excuses nowadays. He tended to avoid the hells he'd been so dedicated to when he had first invented Minerva and hadn't made any effort to chase any game women either. He'd dallied — of course he had — but the awkward truth was his carefree bachelor lifestyle wasn't quite as carefree as it used to be.

Deep down, in the most cavernous, honest recesses of his soul, which he liked to pretend didn't exist unless he was forced into introspection, he knew he had clung on to the idea of Minerva to avoid admitting to his mother that he was too much like his father to ever consider settling down. A tragic truth that would break her heart. He was very mindful of breaking hearts. Broken hearts healed over — they did not mend fully. Hugh knew this firsthand because his had been ripped in two when he had finally discovered that the father he worshiped and had always emulated wasn't quite the great man he had always assumed him to be. And while he had accepted that he shared all of those same flaws, he was damned if he would use them as weapons to wound others as well.

But in clinging to his self-righteousness for too long and avoiding the conversation that would make the need for Minerva obsolete, he'd made a mess of it. He hoped the solution miraculously materialized once his belly was full; otherwise, he truly was doomed.

He was halfway down Sackville Street when he witnessed the altercation.

"I'll pay you when I am good and ready, madam, and not before." The older gentleman stood on the top of the short stack of steps outside a front door. Judging by his attire, he was either on his way out or had just arrived back. Below him, on the pavement with her back to Hugh, was a woman. Like the gentleman, she wore a heavy winter coat, although hers had seen better days and

18

she had paired it with a thick woolen scarf and mismatched knitted mittens. Both looked homemade. Her head was swamped in an enormous velvet bonnet.

"Mr. Pinkerton — I earned that money." She had a nice voice, confident and mellow. Mature even. She was also very well spoken, something that surprised him in view of her outfit. From the style of her coat, easily ten years out of date, he assumed she was a widow of somewhere between thirty and forty, perhaps left with several children she had to feed all by herself. The world could be a cruel place for some — something he often pondered long and hard when he worried about the world during his most introspective moments.

Her spine stiffened, and she pulled her slim shoulders back proudly. He could imagine her looking down her nose at the fellow and found himself approving of her stance. "I have already waited four weeks, sir, and I flatly refuse to leave *this time* until you pay me."

The older gentleman noticed Hugh staring, and his face colored. "How dare you accost me on my own doorstep and cause a scene!"

"How dare you employ me to do a job and then avoid paying me for doing it. It's been a month, Mr. Pinkerton. A cold one. I have waited long enough."

Hugh felt his blood boil. The scoundrel! The poor woman was clearly in dire need of the money. She shouldn't have to resort to humiliating herself on the street to receive what she was clearly due. "May I offer my assistance, madam? It looks as though you could use some." For good measure, he glared at the man with haughty disdain.

She turned, and he realized she wasn't a madam at all but a miss. A very pretty miss. Very pretty indeed. So much so, she took his breath away.

"Why, thank you, sir. What a gentleman you are." Her eyes flicked back to the miser who had swindled her, and she gave him a thoroughly disgusted look that could have curdled milk. "Mr. Pinkerton here engaged me to create an illustration to accompany an advertisement, and whilst he has published the advertisement in *The Morning Advertiser, The London Tribune* — twice — and in today's *Times,* I am still to receive the funds we agreed upon for my labors. He owes me nine shillings and threepence."

Hugh had to tear his wandering Standish eyes away from her lovely face. "And what do you have to say on the matter, Mr. Pinkerton?"

"I shall pay her when I am good and ready and not before."

"Were you unsatisfied with the lady's work?"

The older man bristled at being challenged. "I've seen better."

"But you deemed it good enough to place in *The Times, The Morning Advertiser,* and *The London Tribune?*"

"Twice," added the bewitching young lady decisively. "And I daresay the advertisement has garnered him lots of new trade. Far more, I suspect, than the nine shillings and threepence he has neglected to pay me, because it is a very striking illustration."

Out of her reticule she pulled a torn square of newspaper and handed it to Hugh. In the center of the picture was an intricately drawn medicine bottle with "Pinkerton's Patented Liver Tonic" emblazoned on the label. To the left of the bottle was a haggard-looking man who appeared ready to keel over from exhaustion at any moment, to the right the same man invigorated and in fine fettle after just one week on Mr. Pinkerton's patented potion. The bold banner across the top of the advertisement proclaimed "Purge Fatigue Forever with Pinkerton's." Very catchy.

"It is a very striking illustration. So much

so I am tempted to invest in some of the stuff myself. You are a talented artist, Miss . . . ?"

"Merriwell. And thank you for the compliment, sir."

"I am no expert on the subject, Mr. Pinkerton, but it would seem to me that this splendid illustration is well worth nine shillings — and some." Hugh purposefully looked down his nose at the fellow. While it was obvious Mr. Pinkerton was a gentleman in the most basic sense, it was equally as obvious that Hugh was from the aristocracy.

"This has nothing to do with you, sir."

Perhaps it wasn't that obvious. "It is 'my lord,' not 'sir.' "

Hugh had never called anyone out for not using his title before, because he hated upsetting people, but Mr. Pinkerton deserved knocking down a peg or two. "Do you refuse to pay because you cannot afford it? Are you financially embarrassed, sir?" He purposefully allowed his voice to carry, mindful of the curious passersby who had slowed their pace to eavesdrop. "In which case, maybe Miss Merriwell will allow you to pay your outstanding debt to her in installments?"

The insult had the most splendid effect

on Mr. Pinkerton, who turned positively purple. "How dare you!" But he had already pulled out his fat purse and began to rummage in it, keen to get the pair of them off his doorstep. Hugh couldn't resist holding out his gloved hand and audibly counting each coin as it was slapped in his palm.

"There! Devil take you! Nine shillings." The older man went to shove his purse in his pocket.

"And threepence." Hugh winked at Miss Merriwell. "Don't forget the threepence, sir."

The coins were practically thrown at him. "Good day to you both! I shan't be using your services again, Miss Merriwell!" Mr. Pinkerton then wrestled with his key in the lock before running back inside and slamming the door.

Left alone on the pavement, Hugh smiled. "Here you are." He dropped all the money into the center of her mitten. "We got there in the end."

She beamed back, and it was like being bathed in liquid sunshine. Her face turned from exceedingly pretty to beautiful in a heartbeat. She had the loveliest eyes. Deep green, a little feline in shape and ringed with long, dark lashes.

"I am indebted to you, my lord. Thank

you for your timely interference. It was very kind of you."

"Think nothing of it. I have a particular weakness for damsels in distress." Much as he tried to ignore it, Hugh had a weakness for all distressed things, from damsels to stray dogs, from the forlorn and the feckless to all the world's foundlings. A weakness he would never admit to. Carefree, rakish bachelors about town didn't waste time worrying about such nonsense. "I've always fancied myself as a knight in shining armor." Damsels were one thing, a rampant social conscience was quite another. Hugh would become a laughingstock if his philanthropic nature were made public.

"Well, you were certainly mine." For some reason, that made him feel ten feet tall. "I've tried everything to get him to pay up. Accosting him today was my last resort. One which would have failed if you hadn't turned up when you did."

"Oh, I doubt that. You did seem rather determined."

"Nine shillings is nine shillings." She shrugged dismissively as she said this, as if it were the principle that mattered more, but he knew differently. Her clothes had seen better days, her boots were old and down at the heel, and nobody would be seen dead demanding payment in even this unfashionable part of Mayfair unless they really needed the money. "If word gets around I allow a debt to go unpaid, then I might as well work for free." She carefully put her money in her reticule and smiled again. "Thank you once more, my lord knight. I wish you the pleasantest of good days." She was going to leave, and he didn't want her to.

"So you are an artist?"

"I am hardly an artist. I create woodcuts."

"Woodcuts?"

"The little blocks with pictures carved into them . . . you know . . . that printers use in the presses." She mimed what he assumed was a printing press with her arms. "I'm an engraver of sorts, I suppose. Bespoke designs to the client's specification — flowers, banners . . . liver salts."

"That's a fairly niche occupation."

"It is." Her smile seemed resigned. "Very niche."

"Well, I've certainly never met an engraver, and it's Hugh, Miss Merriwell." He offered his hand. "Hugh Standish, Earl of Fareham."

She shook his hand, which bizarrely wanted to hold hers forever.

"I have never met an earl before, so we

are equal. And it's Minerva."

The world seemed to stop. Surely not?

"Minerva?"

"I know . . . it's a little pretentious. My father fancied himself a scholar. He named all his daughters after Roman goddesses. Mine is the goddess of wisdom and the arts, so I suppose it is fitting in its way."

"I've never had the good fortune to meet anyone called 'Minerva' before today." Hugh felt himself grin as the tiny shoots of salvation instantly bloomed. "How positively, perfectly serendipitous."

# CHAPTER TWO

"What happened to the real Minerva?"

She hoped her expression appeared understandably suspicious rather than pained as she tried to ignore the frigid slush seeping into her shoe. It wasn't every day a peer of the realm offered to pay you to pose as his fiancée for an entire month at his grand estate in Hampshire. In fact, it was such a bizarre request, only an idiot wouldn't be wary of such a proposition — and Minerva was no idiot. Especially as far as men were concerned. She was less wary than common sense dictated, however, because he had offered her twenty pounds for her trouble.

Twenty whole pounds!

A king's ransom.

Certainly more money than she had ever held in her hands and more than the hard-earned nine shillings and threepence currently nestled inside her battered old reticule. Not that those nine shillings would last long. She owed five of them to her landlord for the rent to prevent her imminent eviction and another shilling for the next month up front. The seventh would have to be spent in Ackermann's Repository of Arts in the Strand because a woodblock engraver, even an occasional and impoverished one, needed pens, inks, and sharp little chisels. That left just two shillings and threepence for luxuries like food until another commission came along, which, in the current climate, might take weeks.

Despite working for half of what her rivals charged, Minerva lacked the contacts necessary to get regular work. Her own fault. For years she had worked exclusively for the same printer near St. Paul's. Old Mr. Morton threw plenty of commissions her way because his well-heeled society customers, especially the ladies, had adored the designs she created for calling cards.

There was more money in the intricate pictures used in posters and advertisements, but those commissions had been few and far between, while the simple calling cards had been her bread and butter. At the time, when bread and butter had been plentiful, she had failed to nurture a broader clientele because there had been no need. Until Mr.

Morton died and his thriving business had swiftly closed nearly a year ago. Since then, she had been scrabbling around for work with no respected sponsor to recommend her.

If only she could afford to advertise, then she was certain she would double her income overnight. People took advertisements very seriously, especially if they were eye-catching — which hers always were.

"There is no *real* Minerva. I made her up." Her knight in shining armor looked delightfully sheepish at the admission. Sheepish suited him, although in fairness, everything probably suited him. He had the face and physique to carry off sackcloth.

"Whatever for?" Surely a man who looked as attractive as he did, an earl no less and one clearly in possession of an impressive fortune if his impeccably tailored clothes were any gauge, wouldn't have trouble finding a woman who would happily be his real fiancée rather than an imaginary one. He certainly did not have holes in his shoes. If anything, with his height, gloriously broad shoulders, sandy-blond hair, and twinkling blue eyes, he looked exactly like she imagined a real knight in shining armor would. If she ever had reason to draw one, Lord Fareham would undoubtedly be her muse.

In a greatcoat he was impressive; in chain mail he would be devastating. If she were being honest, that was another reason why she was still lingering in his presence. Her artist's eye was drawn to manly perfection.

He sighed and then winced. "You will think me pathetic, but I am afraid I made her up to put an end to my mother's incessant matchmaking."

"That seems a little extreme." Why on earth would he need a matchmaker? Surely women threw themselves at him? Simply walking alongside him was playing havoc with her pulse, and it was not just her. Minerva had clocked at least three admiring glances from other women in the last five minutes. That was an average of one smitten female every ninety seconds — and the street wasn't particularly busy. In a crowd, he'd probably get at least one a minute.

"Extreme?" He stopped dead and faced her. The not-sensible smitten female inside almost sighed before she remembered she did not trust any man as a principle and hadn't for many years for good reason. "Do you have family, Miss Merriwell?"

"I do indeed. Two younger sisters." And she assumed she still had one errant father somewhere. He could be dead for all they knew. A part of her hoped he was, because at least that gave him an excuse for abandoning them, but a bigger part expected nothing less and never had. Her father had never been a particularly reliable parent. He had preferred the Dog and Duck pub beneath their miserable rooms, only climbing the dank, rickety stairs home if he had run out of money or someone carried him up.

"Do they drive you to distraction?"

Constantly. Most days, she could cheerfully murder the pair of them. "Occasionally, my lord. As families are prone to do."

"Then you will understand how the closest family members can push you to the very edge of your patience and make you act rasher than you would normally. My mother is such a person. I adore her. . . . Obviously I do. She is a wonderful woman. Kind, generous, well meaning. She brought me up single-handedly after my father died and I owe her everything . . . but sometimes I could . . ." He sighed, vastly put upon.

"Strangle her?"

He grinned then, showing a row of pearly white teeth and introducing her to two very charming, rakish dimples on either side of his mouth. Gracious, he was handsome.

Dangerously so. She would need all her wits about her with this one.

31

"Indeed. She is a formidable woman, and used to getting her way, who seems to think I'd be happier with a wife by my side."

"And you are entirely opposed to the idea?" She started walking again in case the peculiar effect he had on her pulse showed on her face, and because standing still allowed the slush to find its way past the piece of oilskin she had used to plug the hole in the sole of her left boot.

"Obviously!" He seemed surprised by her question. "My life is wonderful as it is. Why on earth would I want to shackle myself to a woman who will only nag me?"

"Not all women nag, my lord."

"Very true — but I am the sort of man who would try the most even-tempered woman's patience and would ultimately turn her into a nag. It is as inevitable as night following day." That mischievous smile was doing the strangest things to her insides. "My mother never used to be a nag. I take full responsibility for driving her to it. I'm too frivolous, you see . . . too selfish. I'd be a complete disappointment as a husband and a father."

"In my experience" — which was extensive — "many men are disappointing husbands and fathers." As well as disappointing sweethearts. "It doesn't seem to be a barrier to them becoming husbands and fathers."

"Again, very true . . . However, unlike those men, I am keenly aware of my short-comings and suffer horrendously from guilt. I'd never forgive myself for making my poor wife's life miserable, never mind what sort of example I would be for any offspring." For a moment he seemed sad, but the emotion faded so swiftly she might have imagined it. "Any sons are bound to turn out the same and I'd make any daughters jaded well before they should be."

It was an unconventional perspective. In many ways, a refreshing one. "You avoid all responsibility." She wished she could.

"Wherever possible." At the admission, he paused as if he greatly disappointed himself. The twinkle in his deep blue eyes dimmed, and instantly she missed it. Then, in a flash it was back, and they sparkled with mischief again. "And they do say all work and no play makes Jack a very dull boy — and I would loathe to become dull, Miss Merri-well. I am simply not cut out for marriage. It takes a level of commitment and selfless-ness I am not capable of. I am far too shal-low and happy to be so." He paused and slid her a troubled sideways glance. "I sup-pose I sound like a thoroughly spoiled and self-indulgent chap to you."

"It is not my place to judge you."

He grinned, and once again it set her pulse fluttering. "Then you will be the first woman who hasn't. It's very decent of you."

She smiled back. She couldn't help it. Despite his many self-confessed faults, he had also selflessly come to her rescue when nobody else had in a very long time.

Not that it would tempt her to accept his ludicrous offer.

"As a rule, Lord Fareham, I believe nobody has the right to judge others until they have walked a mile in their shoes."

Although she pitied whoever was fool enough to want to walk a mile in her leaky boots or experience her daily hand-to-mouth existence. Unfortunately, she suspected it would take more than twenty pounds to change it. "I don't blame you for wanting to avoid responsibility. Responsibility can wear a person down."

As it had her. But the responsibility of two younger sisters and all that entailed had been foisted on her. Thanks to her feckless sire, she had been both mother and father to those girls since the day after her nineteenth birthday. She had had no choice other than to shoulder it and do what was necessary until the girls were safely married.

As much as she loved her sisters, at least once a week Minerva fantasized about how nice it would be to be solely responsible for just herself. Wouldn't that be a luxury? New shoes, a few new dresses, better-quality pens and chisels for her woodcuts. A place of her own to sit and be at peace. A few hours of solitary tranquility every day . . . Was that too much to ask?

Instead, they were all bundled together in three tiny rooms, and every penny went to necessities. As if to remind her of one of those necessities, her stomach growled in protest at the absence of the breakfast she couldn't afford to buy this morning. Or yesterday morning either, thanks to Mr. Pinkerton. With twenty pounds, she could buy breakfast, lunch, and dinner for all three of them for a year . . .

Good gracious! At this rate, she'd be biting his hand off to accept his outrageous proposition, seduced by just his presence and the alluring thoughts of toast and butter.

Minerva schooled her features into an unimpressed and slightly dubious mask. "You were explaining how your mother's matchmaking became intolerable?"

"Intolerable *and* suffocating. I endured it for as long as I could. For years, she shoved

35

young lady after young lady under my nose. Wherever I went, whatever I did, there would be someone there — eyelashes fluttering. Even my own house became a torture chamber." She caught a whiff of his cologne and was sorely tempted to lean closer to inhale it. "I suffered through endless teas and interminable dinners, making small talk with determined young ladies all too eager to sink their claws into me. And some of those ladies were *quite* tenacious, I can tell you. They resorted to all manner of devilments, Miss Merriwell. Unimaginable machinations which my mother was often fully complicit in. That I managed to remain single is, frankly, nothing short of a miracle. Just shy of two years ago, on the spur of the moment while at my wits' end with dear Mama, I invented Minerva to put a stop to it."

"I see."

Although she didn't. Inventing a fiancée, even under such trying conditions, seemed a bit extreme. Maintaining the ruse undetected for a prolonged period of time seemed highly implausible. Especially as his mother obviously wanted to see him wed. Surely, she would have investigated his claim? Sought out his imaginary fiancée?

"I take it your mother lives exclusively in

Hampshire?"

That might explain why she was yet to meet his Minerva. Unlikely, but possible, she supposed. And there she went again, believing the unbelievable. Why did she keep giving him the benefit of the doubt when bitter experience had taught her that men usually were that shallow? A silly question, when she already knew the answer: twenty whole pounds and an aesthetically pleasing broad set of shoulders. Two shameful truths that probably made her shallow, when she had always prided herself on her substance.

"She resides in Boston. The one in America, not Lincolnshire. Did I mention my stepfather is American?"

"She continued matchmaking all the way from America?" Now, that really was quite a feat and did not help to give credence to his story despite the shoulders.

"My mother is a determined woman, Miss Merriwell. And a romantic. It is her sole mission to see me settled and she wasn't the least bit deterred by the distance. At least when she was here, I could keep an eye on things or escape well in advance if I got wind of her plans." He pulled a face. "After she left, her scheming became much more unpredictable. Her campaign to see me shackled continued with a vengeance via correspondence, and thanks to her wide circle of acquaintances here in town, she was able to recruit an army of minions to continue the work she had started. Within a few months of her departure, I found myself inundated with invitations and daily surprise visits from every society matron or social-climbing gentleman eager to marry off a daughter. I was accosted at entertainments and harangued if I ventured outside."

"Poor you." How the problems of the rich and entitled differed from hers. Minerva would give her back teeth to swap. Living in his world certainly held more appeal than living in hers. Fancy clothes. Comfortable furniture. Servants there to serve your every whim . . .

"When that failed, my mother threatened to return alone, sacrificing her own happiness until *we* found me the perfect bride together. She knew the guilt I would inevitably feel would become insufferable. And she also knew I would loathe the enforced proximity which such a self-sacrificing visit would undoubtedly entail. As a point of principle, a gentleman should always rebel against a parent — don't you think?"

"I suppose a little rebellion ensures you are your own man." How wonderful would it be to have the luxury of rebellion! Her wandering father hadn't given her the option.

"Exactly! Except . . . I'll admit, in my case the principle got rather out of hand, and at the imminent threat of her booking her passage, I panicked. I invented Minerva — a young lady of gentle breeding who dragged me out of my shallow, self-indulgent existence and showed me there was more to life."

He gestured to her person as if she fitted the bill exactly, then winced again. "Like you, Miss Merriwell, I have a talent with the pen — except mine is with prose rather than drawing. Knowing my mother's penchant for romance, I declared there was no need for her to rush home, because Cupid's arrow had finally pierced me and my heart was hopelessly lost. In *gushing* detail, I told her I'd rescued a beautiful damsel in distress from a runaway carriage, and immediately fallen head over heels in love with her the moment I stared into her intoxicating eyes. It was a most convincing and, if I might say, touching tale but not one I am particularly proud of."

"Minerva was an act of desperation?" She knew all about desperation. Desperation tempted down-on-their-luck young ladies to seriously consider posing as a gentleman's fiancée for twenty measly pounds.

"She was — and one which was only meant to be temporary. But, at my mother's delight and the immediate cessation of all her matchmaking, I rather allowed myself to get a bit carried away. I embellished the lie to maintain the status quo."

"For two entire years?" There must be something intrinsically different in the makeup of men and women, she decided. Something that allowed them to act selfishly rather than do the decent thing.

"I was seduced by the freedom, Miss Merriwell. Freedom is a *heady* drug." He stared off into nothing, giving her an opportunity for her easily swayed artist's eye to stare at his magnificent profile a tad more longingly than she should have. She huffed out a withering sigh at her momentary lapse of good sense. The last time she had been swayed by soulful eyes and a pair of broad shoulders, it had ended very badly. "But alas, with all my embellished stalling, my intrepid mother has now decided enough is enough. She has booked passage home to help with the wedding preparations. I feel positively wretched about it all. If she discovers I've been lying to her all this time, it will break her heart. I never intended to hurt her . . ." He looked genuinely sad. Charmingly lost. Minerva was staggered that still called to her. "That is why I need you. If you pose as my fiancée, she need never know the awful truth of my deception."

"Surely you are simply prolonging the agony by perpetuating the lie?"

"I have no intention of perpetuating it. I only need you to be *my* Minerva for a few weeks. A month at most, so my mother can meet you, see that wedding plans are in place and then" — he shrugged his shoulders, frowning in a very nonreassuring sort of way — "then we'll find a convincing way for our prolonged engagement to be immediately terminated and my mother will be there to comfort me in my heartbreak."

And there it was, the unpalatable reality of the situation. The reminder that those twenty pounds came from something totally disingenuous.

"You want me to play the villain while we both lie to her?"

"I haven't worked out all the details yet."

"Clearly."

Despite the seductive allure of twenty pounds, a lie was a lie no matter how you dressed it up. The Merriwells might be on the cusp of destitution, but they had morals. Or at least some of them did. "I cannot do something so grievous to a complete stranger, Lord Fareham. Your mother has done nothing to hurt me, yet my actions will undoubtedly wound her if she discovers our duplicity. I will not be party to that."

Minerva turned, lofty decision made, then remembered he had aided her with Mr. Pinkerton. "I thank you for your kind assistance earlier. I wish you good luck with your predicament and a very good day."

And goodbye to the errant dream of twenty whole pounds. It had been lovely while it had lasted.

As had he.

For a little while, strolling beside him and daring to dream of all she would do with his money, she had actually felt four and twenty.

"What if I made it forty pounds?"

Her step faltered. Forty pounds would pay their rent for at least two years and give them plenty to spare for a few luxuries. Or they could move out of the depressing rooms in Clerkenwell and start afresh somewhere nicer. Somewhere larger. Somewhere with prospects in a better part of town. With forty pounds, Minerva could advertise her talents in the newspapers herself, extend her clientele beyond her small corner of the city, increase her ability to earn a decent living from illustrating.

Forty whole pounds opened up possibilities. Possibilities that might well change their lives.

# CHAPTER THREE

"I still don't like it." Diana had uttered the same sentence at least twenty times since they had left London. "It's all a little convenient. Potentially dangerous and, frankly, wrong, if you want my opinion."

Minerva didn't. She wanted to read or gaze out of the window at the lush green countryside rushing by. Anything to avoid thinking about the ludicrous, yet undeniably lucrative, scheme she had got them involved in until they arrived at his house.

She was going to pose as a peer of the realm's fiancée to prevent him from being caught out in a monstrous lie. Minerva didn't need Diana's scowl across the confined space of the carriage to feel uncomfortable about what they were about to do, because she was thoroughly ashamed for agreeing to it. Although, in her defense, she had only done so because things were dire.

The direst, in fact.

If her unexpected knight in shining armor hadn't turned up when he had to prize the nine shillings and threepence out of Mr. Pinkerton's pudgy hands, at this precise moment they could all be sleeping on the street. Participating in his little white lie would ensure they remained off the streets for years, and the brief interlude of living in the lap of luxury didn't hurt either.

Diana folded her arms and glared. "When exactly, Sister dear, did we stoop so low?"

*When you got sacked from the lending library for biting back at a customer and we could no longer afford the rent!* Minerva petulantly thought, but didn't say it. It was hardly fair in the grand scheme of things to solely blame Diana. Had she been in her sister's worn-out shoes when the gentleman had called her a brainless idiot, she'd have probably done the same before common sense had kicked in. They were all too outspoken and stubbornly proud. When life left you nothing else, you had to be. And despite being the most recent nail in the Merriwell sisters' coffin, Diana's outburst was hardly the only thing responsible for their rapid descent further down the slippery slope of poverty toward destitution. Nor was it Diana's fault Minerva had sold her integrity to a handsome but dubious man for the princely sum of forty pounds.

Forty pounds that she hoped would alleviate the shame she inwardly felt for having to sell her integrity in the first place.

Vee chewed on her lip nervously, reminding Minerva that her youngest sister, no matter how mature and studious she appeared on the surface, was still only seventeen. "Not to mention highly improper — three single, unchaperoned girls staying on the country estate of a bachelor." Vee was a stickler for the genteel propriety she devoured in books, although the Lord only knew why, considering their reduced circumstances and distinct lack of hope for any worthy suitors. She stared down at her gloved hands. "We only have his word and that servant's that he is the Earl of Fareham."

"He had the bearing of an earl." Not that Minerva had ever met one before, of course. Earls were few and far between in their part of London. Clerkenwell was the home of a declining number of watchmakers and reputable shopkeepers, a few more ne'er-do-wells and pickpockets, and a large proportion of the great unwashed. But it was cheap, and beggars couldn't be choosers. "Regardless, whether he is or he isn't, he is wealthy enough to afford this splendid carriage — and this is his *spare* carriage at that!"

Minerva realized she might be in danger of appearing a tad overwhelmed by the trappings of his wealth rather than being the usual sensible, level-headed oldest sibling in charge — albeit one who had been privately pondering Lord Fareham's soulful eyes a little too much. She stared levelly at her sisters and presented some cold, hard facts. "I appreciate you both disapprove of my decision. I disapprove of it myself. However, considering our ongoing and miserable situation, frankly, only a fool would have turned down his lucrative proposal."

Vee frowned. "I just wish you had allowed us to meet him first, Minerva. Then we could have made our own judgments about his character. Perhaps you should have invited him home for tea . . ."

She felt herself cringe at the thought of him seeing her in her true environment, with its shabby thirdhand furniture, peeling paint, and the lingering aroma of the slums outside. "I could hardly bring him home, could I?" Inviting his butler in had been bad enough. The man's eyes had been everywhere before finally coming to rest on hers with pity. "Lord Fareham lives in Mayfair!"

Vee immediately forgot to be seventeen again and glared through her spectacles, appalled. "There is no shame in poverty, Minerva."

It was a saying their erstwhile father often uttered while they were growing up and one that she might have believed had he not cheerfully abandoned them when things got too much for him. Which just happened to coincide with Minerva reaching an age where she could step into his worthless shoes. The scoundrel had trained her for it!

"There is no joy in it either, Vee. Only misery — as we well know." With each passing season, it got harder and harder, and like her sisters, Minerva was old beyond her years.

Old, tired, and slowly being worn into the ground by the relentless drudgery of life.

A sad indictment of her four and twenty years on the earth. "We all work as hard as we can, day in and day out, and yet still barely manage to scrape enough to make ends meet."

If their stars didn't dramatically change, even Vee would have to work all the hours God sent to earn her keep. Minerva had shielded her as much as she could from the depravity of their situation, allowing her to continue studying in the hope she might have a better future, but that would come to an abrupt stop once she entered the transient and despondent ranks of the workforce. Vee would have to grow up very fast, or her gentle, bookish, sensitive little sister would be grossly taken advantage of.

"I appreciate all your misgivings about Lord Fareham's proposition, really I do, for it is peculiar and exceedingly out of the ordinary. I am well aware that what I am doing is morally debatable, but I shall tell you now up front — I will happily pose as his fiancée until Easter if need be. I fail to believe it is possible for life on an earl's country estate in Hampshire, pretending to be someone else while being paid handsomely for it, to feasibly be as hard as our lives now. High morals won't put food on the table nor will they keep a roof over our heads!"

"I suppose." Vee was still understandably concerned, and really, who could blame her?

The past few days had been a bit of a whirlwind. On Wednesday her oldest sister had left home to reason with Mr. Pinkerton to keep a roof over their heads. On Thursday, that same sister had practically forced her into a strange man's coach headed for the south coast on the basis of little more than a promise, to live under another roof.

49

An ever-so-slightly scandalous, thoroughly charming bachelor's roof. Had Vee or Diana come home and announced to her they were all to pose as a potential scoundrel's fake betrothed's family, she'd have hit the roof. That they were both here, albeit begrudgingly, was a direct result of Minerva's unfortunate position as head of the family, one they respected and pitied her for in equal measure.

"I just wish we knew more about his character."

"Perhaps he's a murderer?" Diana was always the most fanciful of the three of them. "And perhaps this is all a convoluted ruse to feed his unquenchable thirst for killing?"

"You spend far too much time at that newspaper." Her sister was forever attempting to submit articles in the hope one would someday be published, but the proprietor of the rag paid her a pittance to correct the spelling and the grammar of his less talented male reporters each week before his tawdry publication went to press. "You are convinced everyone is up to no good." At just twenty-two, Diana was more cynical about the world than even Minerva was.

"I simply prefer to look at life through a clear, unobstructed lens rather than through the presently naive rose-tinted one you are clearly using. What has happened to you, Minerva? Do you honestly think the grass is greener as a rich man's *paid companion*? I still cannot fathom what you were thinking to agree to such a preposterous falsehood." Diana had taken it upon herself to do some hasty investigating at the newspaper before they left, and her account of Lord Fareham's reputation was, Minerva couldn't deny, a great source of worry. He had made several appearances in the scandal sheets both for his *leisurely* lifestyle and his alleged philandering. So much so she doubted he was overly burdened with the responsibilities of being an earl, as he had so convincingly claimed. As a result, he needed to be relegated to a flawed knight in her mind — and perhaps not even a knight at all. More a knave or perhaps even a scoundrel. That would be more prudent than contemplating his dratted soulful eyes! She was better equipped to deal with a scoundrel. An expert, in fact.

"Your earl is nothing short of a rake. A rake who consorts with other rakes and does rakish deeds." Diana pointed a quaking finger. "He's lured you to Hampshire to seduce you, mark my words. You'll be thoroughly ruined."

"That seems a lot of unnecessary trouble for something he could do just as easily in London." At her sisters' widened eyes, she hastily clarified. "Not me, of course! I have no desire to be seduced by him and nor would I stand for it."

Aside from her healthy distrust of all males — aristocratic or otherwise — she was no fool. An earl would never consider a woman like her for anything beyond a quick tumble. Minerva might not be much of a catch, but she had too much respect for herself to ever allow that to happen. Not that she was tempted. He was far too shallow, and despite her wayward artist's eye, she had high standards. Of course she did. Or she was simply jaded. Either way, men in general held little real appeal anymore. "The only relationship I want with Lord Fareham — and he with me — is a *business* relationship.

"As for ruination — I hardly think anyone gives two figs about my reputation regardless of what I do. Or either of yours, for that matter. We might consider ourselves a gentleman's daughters and therefore a cut above our unfortunate neighbors, but we've only ever had Papa's word he *was* a gentleman and we all know nobody could spin a yarn better than *dear* Papa."

She smiled at her sisters to soften the necessary blow she was about to deliver. "As far as the entire world is concerned, we are nobodies. Nothings. Three more struggling, faceless, downtrodden souls in a city filled to the brim with them. No one cares what we do, nor will they remember our misdeeds any more than they recall our good ones."

Vee pouted. "That's a very cynical summation and one I don't happen to agree with. Something will turn up. Something always does."

"Do you seriously believe a proper gentleman will one day happen to be in Clerkenwell, and see past the frayed and patched clothes on your back to the *genteel* lady beneath? If you do, then I am happy to be the one to shatter your silly romantic notions, because you will be disappointed, Vee. Real life is not a fairy tale."

Minerva used to dare to dream such nonsense until she realized dreams never came true — they got crushed instead. It was funny how becoming a parent overnight had made her view the world pragmatically. Some people were destined to live difficult lives, and theirs was so difficult even their own father couldn't stomach it. Nor could the young man she had foolishly thought herself in love with. Faced with three Merriwell girls for the price of one, he had hastily severed all ties, too. She wasn't bitter about that any longer — it still hurt from time to time when she felt miserably all alone — but she had learned her lesson well.

"All we have is us." She squeezed her baby sister's hand, feeling cruel and frustrated at having to be so. "That is why I am doing this awful thing — for *us*. Because Lord only knows, if we don't help ourselves, nobody else will. I couldn't turn down forty pounds! Just think of all we could do with it. Decent food, a better roof over our heads, new shoes. Pretty new spectacles for you, Vee, and perhaps even a new dress or two each."

"Unless we are murdered." Diana's pessimistic streak put Minerva's to shame. "A man who can maintain an outright lie to his own mother for nearly two years is, in my opinion, capable of anything. After all, who would suspect an earl of murder, especially so far from London? As you rightly said, Minerva, we are nobodies. Nothings. Faceless and easily forgotten. The perfect target. He probably approaches distressed and impoverished young ladies all the time, being all chivalrous and charming and helpful, lures them into his vile world with the promise of easy money, and then" — she sliced her finger across her neck — "mutilates you in your sleep before he buries your unidentifiable remains in his garden. Or his woods. Fancy country estates all come with their own woods. Those poor grouse and deer the aristocracy shoot have to live somewhere. I bet this den of iniquity we are headed to is positively surrounded by woodland. And it will be conveniently remote."

Vee frowned. "How does remoteness make anything convenient?"

"Because nobody will hear our screams."

Minerva glared at Diana and, feeling defensive, pulled rank in the hope the pair of them would stop badgering her, when her unease and her conscience were doing that quite enough already.

"Girls — I don't mean to be flippant about the peculiarity of the situation or its potential dangers. Nor do I want to sound mercenary or callous, but dismal facts are facts nonetheless. *We* are in dire need of money and *he* has pots of it which he is clearly happy to share in exchange for a brief bit of dishonesty. I confess, I didn't really consider much else beyond the forty pounds when I agreed to assist him. The forty pounds and the promise of greener grass." And perhaps his eyes and the odd way he made her feel also had some bearing on it. It had been rather nice to be the one rescued for a change. "I dragged you both along because I knew you'd only worry about me if I didn't. If you would prefer not to be part of it, I fully understand. Say the word, and I shall have you dropped at the next inn and you can take the post home."

She reached into her reticule and took out the two silver shillings and the two dirty pennies, holding the paltry amount in her outstretched palm as a reminder of the full extent of their current wealth. They all stared at the coins in silence for a moment. "Or perhaps you have a better idea to get us so much money swiftly, because Lord only knows if things continue as they are, we'll all be destitute and sheltering under bridges before winter is over."

Of course, neither sister did.

"Now, kindly stop moaning and criticizing and let's make the best of things. If nothing else, at least the actual grass is greener in Hampshire."

The coachman's knock on the roof above their heads punctuated her outburst with the stamp of finality. "Standish House!"

Then the fancy carriage turned, its well-sprung wheels suddenly crunching on the gravel of the driveway. There was no turning back now. Minerva inhaled a slow, deep breath, hoping it would calm the butterflies in her stomach. It didn't work. She glanced out of the window and saw nothing but thick, dense trees lining their route.

"I told you there would be woods." Diana was like a dog with a bone. "Nobody knows where we are, so nobody will come to our rescue." She slowly sliced her index finger menacingly across her neck again.

"Papa will save us if we need rescuing." Vee's cheerful assertion brought her other sisters up short. "I left our forwarding address at the Dog and Duck in case he comes home for Christmas and asks after us."

Diana shot Minerva a look. It was the usual look when their youngest sibling deluded herself into believing their wastrel father would return. The look that said, "You can deal with this because I'll only put my foot in it." Which was true. Diana was reliably blunt, and that bluntness would only upset Vee, who always felt things far too deeply.

"Darling, he's not coming home for Christmas."

"How do you know? Has he written to say he isn't?"

It was tragic to listen to, but Vee had been very young when he had left and still had enough childish hope to believe he had meant what he said in his final letter to them all those years ago. She had taken "See you soon" as a promise to return rather than a means to sign off his blunt missive telling them he was going away for a little while — something he often did — before he made it permanent. It was the main reason they stayed in Clerkenwell, in the cramped, damp rooms they had lived in with him. Vee wouldn't hear of moving in case their father decided to venture back to the horrid place he had abandoned them to. Yet moving was one of Minerva's first priorities once she had the forty pounds. The hopelessness of Clerkenwell was killing them. As much as they had cosseted and protected Vee as the youngest, it was long past time they all moved on from the awful legacy he had saddled them with.

"He hasn't written in five years, Vee. Perhaps it's time you faced the fact he's never going to."

"Of course he will. Just as soon as he's able." The youngest Merriwell turned her head stubbornly to watch the scenery go past, her way of terminating the unwelcome conversation. All at once her eyes widened.

58

"Oh my goodness! I can see the house! It's huge!"

All three of them pressed their faces to the window to get their first glimpse of their home for the next few weeks or so.

"Isn't it beautiful?" Even Diana couldn't stop herself from grinning at the spectacle. "It's practically a palace."

It was indeed. A vast, symmetrical Palladian mansion made of white stone stood in stark contrast against the twilight sky, its sparkling windows already glowing with candlelight, illuminating the soaring columns. Minerva had never seen anything quite like it. Or felt quite so out of her depth. When he had said he had a country estate, never in her wildest dreams could she have imagined this. It was another world. A world she had no understanding of and little in common with. Yet soon, she would have to pretend all of this didn't intimidate her in the slightest and that she was betrothed to its handsome, charming, and titled owner in front of an audience made up of his nearest and dearest.

*Oh dear.*

Instinctively, she gazed down at the skirt of her best dress. It was old and faded despite the new ribbon she had recklessly bought to liven it up for this charade. No amount of ribbon in the world could turn this old thing into a gown fit for Standish House. The butterflies in her stomach turned to panicked, flapping birds as she forced herself to face the reality she had been avoiding ever since she had sold her soul for forty pounds.

What in God's name had she been thinking?

# CHAPTER FOUR

Hugh heard the carriage arrive and ignored the fizzing nerves that had plagued him since he had proposed his plan to Miss Merriwell.

"She's here." He found himself standing and straightening his coat because he had no earthly idea what to do with his hands. "We should greet them."

"I don't see why I have to move. They're your guests, after all. Just as this entire mockery of a sham is yours, too. I have already logged my protest at this madness." But Giles slowly unfolded himself from the chair he had occupied for most of the day and grinned. "Although, I am curious to see if she is as pretty as you painted her. For if she is, then she has me intrigued. What sort of attractive young lady consents to pretend to be a scoundrel's fiancée for the miserly sum of forty pounds?"

"Forty pounds isn't miserly." It was probably more than Miss Merriwell earned in a year, if the shabby coat she had been wearing was any gauge, and it was one of the main causes of the guilt that was currently keeping him awake. He had made her an offer she couldn't refuse. A positively scandalous offer, truth be told, and all to save his own sorry skin. Poor Miss Merriwell had to be beyond desperate to have accepted it. He felt ridiculously bad about that.

Payne, his butler, had also reported she and her two sisters lived in a very sparse and spartan set of rooms in a very depressed part of town, and that bothered him, too. Clearly she was in the most reduced of circumstances — but she had also been well spoken, had carried herself with genteel confidence, and was obviously very intelligent as well as inordinately pretty. How the family had fallen on such hard times was something his social conscience was keen to get to the bottom of. Already, he suspected she would leave with significantly more than forty pounds. Knowing she wouldn't starve might alleviate some of his worries about her situation. "And might I remind you that you leapt at the chance to offer your services and I'm not paying you a farthing."

"Of course I did! I love a good farce, and

this one is bound to be a complete shambles. I wouldn't miss it for the world!"

"That's hardly reassuring."

"As your dearest friend, it is my job to tell you nothing but the honest truth, old boy. Though obviously, for those same reasons, I shall stand by your side regardless of the inevitable consequences. I'm sure you can rustle up an idiot from the rest of our irritating circle to offer you blind reassurance if that is what you desire. But somebody diligent needs to point out the pitfalls, and who better to gaze judgmentally at the ruined mess of your life with you once this nonsense has run its course than me? You know nothing gives me greater pleasure than telling someone 'I told you so.' " His friend retrieved the last bonbon from the bowl on the sideboard and popped it in his mouth. "And on the subject of 'I told you so,' why did you never tell me that your dreary house in Hampshire is, in fact, a thriving estate? I thought we were friends."

"The fact that it's thriving doesn't stop it from being dreary." Not that Hugh actually thought it was dreary. This was his sanctuary — although from what, he couldn't say. "As your friend, all I have done is spare you from it." *And keep it private.*

"Still, you . . . with tenants and crops

and . . . actually managing things responsibly . . ."

All too personal and potentially too revealing, when Hugh preferred to let sleeping dogs lie, so he shrugged and trotted out the answer Giles would expect. "I just sign things."

By his perplexed expression, his canny friend was not convinced. "Then you clearly sign a lot of things, old boy, as your estate runs rings around my stodgy father's crusty old pile in Shropshire. This place is modern." He eyed him suspiciously. "Impressively so . . ." This was not a conversation he could cope with when his nerves were bouncing all over the place. Fortunately, Payne magically appeared at the door in the nick of time, saving him from explaining that he had been trained to care about those things and couldn't seem to stop. Something his incorrigible friend would doubtless find hilarious.

"The Misses Merriwell are here, my lord. Shall I show them in?"

"Yes!" Suddenly everything was overwhelming, and this entire idea felt foolhardy in the extreme. Why had he dragged them all to Hampshire, when home always awoke the past? "Yes, of course."

Three wide-eyed young women soon

entered the drawing room, but Hugh only fixed on one. Minerva really was as lovely as he had remembered her. Today perhaps more so because she had already removed her bonnet and he got to see her hair for the first time. It was so dark it was almost black, the thick, coiled knot at the back suggesting it was very long. Bizarrely, his fingers itched to touch it. Loosened, slightly curling tendrils framed her face, highlighting the alabaster paleness of her skin and the stunning contrast of those beautiful green eyes.

Eyes that held his with a boldness he admired.

Eyes that called to him in a way none ever had before. What the blazes was that about?

Without the shapeless, chunky coat, she had a fine figure. A compact but delightfully rounded bosom, a slim yet not petite frame, and — from what he could ascertain from the way her plain skirt grazed her curves — a wonderfully long pair of legs. He liked that she was taller than average. Liked more that she was unfashionably dark haired when society favored blondes. All in all, she was nothing like any young woman he had ever seen before, yet exactly as he'd pictured his Minerva to be. Unique. One of a kind. A woman any man would be proud to have on his arm.

Or in them.

But he was staring. Openly. Perhaps even longingly.

Off-kilter, Hugh turned to his friend and saw the appreciation in Giles's eyes and had the sudden urge to poke his fingers in them to stop him from looking at her. Which was hardly fair to Giles but panicked Hugh in the extreme. He wasn't usually possessive. "Miss Merriwell — I am so glad you are here. Allow me to introduce my good friend Giles Sinclair, Lord Bellingham."

"Heir to the Duke of Harpenden?" One of her sisters frowned as she said this. "I've read all about *you* in the papers. There was a story about you only last Friday, in fact."

Obviously, that delighted Giles. "Really? Did they paint me the scoundrel?"

"A complete scoundrel."

"How wonderful. I am a great believer in both the press and gossip and do like to do my bit to keep the masses entertained."

"You should be ashamed of yourself."

Minerva squirmed and shot Hugh an apologetic look. "Diana has strong opinions regarding everything and feels the need to voice them often."

"I applaud that." Of course Giles did. "What is the point of having an opinion if

66

you never share it?"

This seemed to please the prickly sister immensely. "My sentiments exactly, Lord Bellingham."

Before her outspoken sibling said anything else, the eldest Miss Merriwell interrupted, looking embarrassed. "We are delighted to make your acquaintance, aren't we, Diana?" She glared at the younger woman, who couldn't be too far from her in age. Whilst also very pretty and dark haired, to Hugh's eye, Diana lacked the luster of her sister. The invisible pull that compelled him to stare.

"Miss Diana — named after the goddess of the hunt, no doubt." Hugh bowed and turned to his friend. "Mr. Merriwell named them all after Roman deities. Isn't that fun?" Then he turned back to her sister. "Does the name suit you as much as it does Miss Minerva?"

"I should very much hope so, Lord Fareham. For I am a warrior at heart."

"What is your weapon of choice?" Lord Bellingham took Diana's hand and lingered shamelessly over kissing the back of it.

She snatched it away and glared. "Cutting words and pithy setdowns, my lord. If they fail to suitably wound, whatever sharp or heavy object is closest at hand."

"I like her." Giles nudged him hard in the ribs. "Miss Diana, I believe we shall get on famously so long as you promise never to mince your words with me."

"Of that you can be assured, sir." Already Hugh could tell Diana was going to be trouble.

"And this is my youngest sister, Miss Vee Merriwell."

Minerva looked ready to strangle her outspoken sibling but hid her annoyance under a brittle smile, although her glare at Diana was quite frightening. Giles was, of course, enjoying himself immensely and looked intent on continuing to spar with the outspoken sister, as did she. To spare them all from it, Hugh stepped forward and shook the youngest Miss Merriwell's hand. Unlike the other two, she was fair, yet had the same feline green eyes behind her unbecoming spectacles, eyes that looked thoroughly overwhelmed and troubled.

"I don't recall a Roman goddess called Vee. Or anyone called Vee, for that matter. What an unusual name." Hugh smiled at her, attempting to put her at her ease.

"Vee loathes her name," said Diana with more than a hint of mischief. "She thinks it improper. So we call her Vee for short . . ."

Minerva glared. "Thank you, Diana . . ."

"But really it's Venus. The goddess of beauty and lo—"

"I said, *thank you,* Diana." Again Minerva intervened before the outspoken sister could finish, as their youngest was too mortified to do anything other than blush, something she did with crimson aplomb, the poor thing. He had to rescue her.

"I sympathize on your being saddled with a name you despise, Miss Vee. My middle name is Peregrine. How dreadful is that? But where are my manners? Come . . . sit." Hugh smiled, offering his arm, and the youngest sister smiled shyly in return as she took it, allowing him to maneuver her out of the line of fire. "Payne is rustling up some refreshments for us all. You must be exhausted from your travels. London is so inconveniently far from Hampshire."

Once they were all seated, the heavy veil of awkwardness descended on the proceedings. Small talk felt inappropriate. However, so did bluntly tackling the topic of the planned deception. Exactly how did one converse with one's fake fiancée and her family upon their first meeting? There was so much to do and potentially so little time to do it in. He wanted to get started straightaway. Just in case.

"How was your journey?"

"Very pleasant, my lord. Your carriage was very comfortable."

"Splendid." Hugh's eyes took in the sisters' tatty frocks and well-worn boots. "Excellent news." There was another awkward conversation that would need to be had. Anticipating their wardrobes would not be up to scratch, he had already engaged a team of seamstresses who would arrive tomorrow to measure them all for acceptable new clothes and produce them with haste. And new clothes weren't the only things Miss Merriwell and her sisters would need. He had done a great deal of planning in the last two days. He'd made lists, issued countless instructions, and even prepared notes on everything his temporary fiancée would need to know. Seeing as he had anticipated all that, why the blazes hadn't he worked on a few tactful sentences to broach difficult subjects? Or preempted his odd and overwhelming reaction to Minerva? "And the inn you stayed in last night . . . Was it to your satisfaction?"

"It was lovely, my lord." Minerva forced a smile. "And very comfortable, too."

"Excellent." He racked his brains for something more erudite. Anything . . .

No.

Depressingly, there was nothing else. The

ormolu clock on the mantel ticked more loudly than it ever had before. "Excellent." That was apparently the full extent of his vocabulary today. His toes began to curl inside his boots, so he looked at Giles in the hope he might take pity on him. But his friend stared back with deliberate blandness, his eyes dancing with amusement.

Excellent.

"Is this your first visit to Hampshire?"

"Indeed it is, my lord. The scenery was very lovely from the carriage window."

Well, that was another inane question answered as fully as could be expected. Hugh wanted to die. Miss Merriwell didn't appear any more comfortable, but bless her, she was trying. Her outspoken sister was glaring, the shy one staring at her lap as if her life depended on it, and Giles was barely holding in a laugh. When Hugh heard the rattle of teacups in the distance, he almost cheered out loud. "The refreshments are coming! Excellent." He was coming to loathe that bloody word. He resisted the urge to greet his butler like the prodigal son. "Step lively, Payne. The ladies must be starving."

His butler rolled his eyes and set about organizing the distribution of the delicately cut finger sandwiches with a pair of tongs

71

while they all watched the maid pour the tea with much more scrutiny than the task warranted. They then unanimously focused on nibbling on them the second the servants left them alone. Only Minerva resisted tucking in, preferring to stare at her plate mournfully.

"Egg sandwiches," drawled Giles, eyeing one with relish before winking at Diana. "How very fitting. Do you suppose the kitchen kept the eggshells? Because if they did, perhaps you can call Payne back and have him scatter them liberally over the carpet so we can all walk on them?"

"Might I speak plainly, Lord Fareham?" Minerva had steeled her shoulders.

"Hallelujah!" Giles again. "I wish you would. Somebody needs to."

She ignored him to stare intently at Hugh, those stunning green eyes swirling with an emotion that he couldn't fathom but which managed to make him distinctly uneasy nevertheless.

"It occurs to me we are all embarrassed at the Great Unsaid, therefore, I shall be the one to say it so we can all breathe again." She seemed to stare directly into his soul. "You are currently mortified to have been silly enough to get yourself into such a predicament you had to resort to hiring me

— a complete stranger — to pose as your fiancée. And I am mortified I am in such dire need of money that I agreed to it." She exhaled loudly and relaxed her shoulders and threw out her hands. "There! It's done. Now we have acknowledged the awkwardness, I'm sure we'll all feel much better about it." Although she didn't look better, she looked agitated. Very agitated. "Actually, Lord Fareham — might I have a word . . . in private?"

"Yes . . . of course. Follow me." With a sense of impending doom, he led her from the drawing room and into his study. In an attempt to put them both at ease, he sat in one of the wingbacks and gestured for her to do the same. She didn't sit. Or stand still. Instead, she paced in a haphazard circle on the Persian rug.

"Is everything all right?"

"No, Lord Fareham! Absolutely nothing is *all right*. I've made a dreadful mistake in coming here." She suddenly stopped and gesticulated passionately at the paneled walls. "I have no experience in *this* sort of life, my lord. None. I've never seen such grandeur let alone pretended I am comfortable with it. I am completely out of my depth and you have made a dreadful mistake in hiring me to help you."

For some inexplicable reason, he wanted to pull her close and murmur reassurances against her hair.

"I disagree." Hugh tried to keep the panic out of his voice. He couldn't allow her to back out, any more than he could risk sniffing her seductive hair. The ramifications didn't bear thinking about. "My mother is expecting to meet a genteel lady rather than a blue-blooded aristocrat, and you certainly have the voice and bearing of a genteel lady. In fact, I think she would positively approve of the lack of aristocratic blood in your veins. Since she married an American, she has developed exceedingly liberal ideas about class and claims to detest snobbery. They are a very egalitarian lot, the Americans. Not that my mother was much of a snob in the first place. She's very down-to-earth. Just like me."

She stared at him as if he were mad.

"Lord Fareham, whilst you strike me as a very personable man, I can assure you there is nothing down-to-earth about all this." She spun a slow circle on the rug. "I've never seen anything like this before. To think you live in this? *This!*" Her expression was suddenly distraught. "I never would have agreed if I had known I was to impersonate a woman destined to live in a *palace.*"

"I appreciate upon first sight Standish House might be a little overwhelming . . . but it's just a house at the end of the day. Made of bricks and mortar like any other."

"Just a house?" She didn't seem convinced. "Then look at me! Do I look like I could be an earl's fiancée?" As she was holding out her skirts, he supposed he should be looking at her clothes, but his eyes didn't want to leave her face. A face he had the sudden urge to touch. In case he succumbed and sent her screaming for the hills, he clasped his hands behind his back, then, realizing he probably resembled a stern admiral inspecting the fleet, unclasped them and held his palms out.

"My dear Miss Merriwell, I am not entirely sure what you see when you look in the mirror but I see a very beautiful, intelligent, and confident woman." Too beautiful. The siren was scrambling his wits. "It was one of my first impressions when we collided — even before I heard you speak. You have an air about you, Miss Merriwell. A certain something that makes you stand out from the crowd."

"I do?"

"Indeed. In fact, you are exactly the sort of woman I would want a real fiancée to be like, if I had a mind to have a real fiancée."

Alarmingly, that clarification seemed to be more for him than her. "The fundamentals are there. All the rest is merely window dressing. And window dressing is easily achieved. There are seamstresses coming first thing in the morning and I have meticulously planned the next few days to ensure not only you but also your sisters are all fully prepared."

She was wavering. He could see it in her expression. Yet Hugh was thoroughly ashamed of himself. "It is late and you are tired. Everything, in my experience, always seems worse with fatigue." The soothing words were for both of them. "After a decent meal and a good night's rest, I doubt this will seem half as daunting."

"Perhaps . . ."

"There is no 'perhaps' about it. And there is no hurry. Why don't I have Payne show you to your rooms? He can send up trays of food, have hot baths drawn, and the three of you can relax tonight. Then we can reconvene in the morning when you feel more yourself." Her teeth were gently worrying her bottom lip; whilst it was very distracting, he saw her indecision as a very good sign — then instantly felt guilty for it.

"How about we see how you feel after a few days here, when you are more comfortable with this house and the people within it? We have a fortnight until my mother arrives, *at least.* And that is assuming the trade winds are uncharacteristically ferocious. In truth, we probably have three. Which gives us ample time to make sure you are all fully prepared and used to all the grandeur." He was prepared to beg if it came to it. "Please — stay for this week and if at the end of it you still feel you cannot carry it off, then you can go with my blessing *and* the forty pounds."

"Oh — I couldn't take the *whole* forty." She blinked rapidly, clearly embarrassed she couldn't allow herself to look a gift horse in the mouth. "Not for failing to honor our agreement . . ."

"Half then. One week. Twenty pounds and no hard feelings."

"I suppose we have come all this way, Your Lordship . . ."

"If we are supposed to be engaged, you must call me Hugh . . . *Minerva.*" How lovely that sounded on his lips. Even more unsettled by his uncharacteristic reactions, he stuck out his hand for her to shake in case she changed her mind and then instantly regretted his decision. Without the barrier of gloves or mittens, her hand felt perfect in his. He could feel the heat of her fingers everywhere, but particularly along his spine, where something odd, almost tingle-like was happening. In case the tingles spread, he quickly withdrew and tucked his hands behind his back, not caring that he might resemble a crusty old admiral, clenching his fists in the hope the odd sensation would quickly subside and his bouncing nerves would return to normal.

They didn't.

He decided to politely focus on her eyes, then found himself drowning in them, so he dropped his gaze to the plump bottom lip she was still worrying with her teeth and almost groaned aloud at a bolt of lust so intense he could barely breathe. In desperation he took several steps backward, supremely conscious that he was still staring but powerless to stop.

When she finally blinked, he was able to suck in a calming breath, then forced it back out via his peculiarly strangled vocal cords to choke out one hideous, cringeworthy word into the painful void.

"Excellent."

# CHAPTER FIVE

"You will probably need this. For research. In case my family asks about your illness."

"My illness?" Minerva took the book and stared down at the cover — *The Complete Treatise of Diseases of the Lungs* stared back. "Gracious . . . What did I have?" They were over an hour into her first "Being Minerva" lesson, and she was already overwhelmed. Hugh hadn't told a few lies. He had constructed an entire world.

"Consumption."

"Consumption!"

He nodded sheepishly. "I was going to kill Minerva off, and a lingering death seemed appropriate."

"You want me to feign consumption?" She blinked at him, stunned. "This is your great plan for terminating the engagement? I must say, you are putting a great deal of faith into my acting abilities if I am to die whilst your mother is here."

"Of course not. That would be preposterous." His mouth struggled not to smile. He had such an easy way about him — one that made her completely forget he was an earl. But as he had pointed out, they were supposed to be not only engaged but madly in love. Therefore, her initial formality had no place in their relationship. Although Minerva suspected he wasn't one for formality at the best of times. "You made a miraculous recovery just before Christmas last."

"I recovered." She stared at him, incredulous. "From consumption. The disease that kills everybody."

"Not *everybody* . . ." He tapped the book and winked. "I did my research. To be a convincing liar — which I must warn you Standish males always are — it is imperative all lies are founded on fact. There are a few cases where the patient defies the odds. Granted, not many, and I hinted we suspected your initial physicians might have misdiagnosed your condition. The new chap I engaged from Switzerland was a godsend. I credit him with saving you from the snapping jaws of death. In fact, once you began his treatments, the change was almost immediate. I have another idea about how to end our engagement which you will be relieved to know doesn't involve you dying."

"I am all ears."

"You are going to elope with Giles."

Minerva opened her mouth to speak and closed it again when nothing came out. He saw her dumbfounded expression and grinned. "And best of all, nobody will see it coming, so neither of you will have to act smitten. A few days into my mother's visit, you and Giles will leave in the dead of night. I will awake to a heartfelt letter, written in your hand, which outlines your utter turmoil, your overwhelming feelings for my rakish best friend, how you both tried to fight the attraction, but — and this is the best bit — because of your recent brush with death and the loss of your father, you have come to the conclusion life is too short and too precious not to live it to its fullest with the man your heart desires."

"Will Lord Bellingham and I also be eloping with my sisters?"

"That would be daft. Who elopes with a crowd? No — with you gone, a shocked Diana and Vee will be dispatched hastily home in a carriage so I can mourn the betrayal alone."

"The archetypal tortured hero. Completely absolved of any wrongdoing."

"I know! Brilliant, isn't it? Abrupt. Sad. I adore the pathos. It draws a decisive line under the whole relationship."

"Relationships."

"Pardon?"

"Your mother will expect you to terminate your friendship with Giles on the back of his betrayal."

He waved that away. "Oh, I'll think of something on that score."

"This is utter madness. You do know that?"

He nodded with a good-natured smile, the sort that probably got him out of a great deal of trouble all the time. "I did tell you I gilded the lily."

"I think you did more than gild it, Hugh." Minerva glanced down to her copious notes and exhaled slowly. Why should she care how ridiculous his plan was or how convoluted his lies? The financial reward seduced her like a Siren's song. Forty glorious pounds if she could prevail, a healthy twenty if she only lasted the week. Regardless of the circumstances, it would be the easiest twenty pounds she would ever earn. She had promised him a week at least of her undivided attention, and she intended to give him his money's worth.

If he was happy to continue with this

nonsense rather than fall on his sword and beg his mother for forgiveness, then so be it. When it failed, which it likely would, it wouldn't be because she hadn't given it her all.

"I suppose it's as good a solution as any." She dipped the pen in the ink and held it poised. "For the sake of continuity, what were the approximate dates of my illness?" Just like a good woodcut, the devil was always in the detail.

"You began to deteriorate in the spring of '24. By the autumn, I feared the worst."

"But then I made my miraculous recovery just in time for Christmas."

"It was around the beginning of November, as I recall, because you were well enough for me to risk leaving your bedside to visit my mother in Boston."

"And how long were you away?"

"Three months. You wrote to me every week." He slid open the drawer to his desk and removed a bundle of letters tied with ribbon. "In case you are wondering — Giles was the author and he did take my request for a weekly love letter seriously." He grimaced as he placed them before her. "And typically, he had fun at my expense." Intrigued, she slipped the top letter from beneath the ribbon and opened it.

My dearest Hugh —
Oh! How I love you!
Your mere presence sets me all a-quiver
I want you back home
I am tired of being alone
Your absence gives me pains in my liver

"Please tell me you never showed any of these to your mother."

"Not directly . . . Although I confess, I left one or two of them lying around in my bedchamber. In case my mother was curious. Which I am pretty sure she was. On occasion." He grinned and patted her hand in reassurance. Thankfully, his touch didn't send her pulse rocketing as it had last night. It quickened slightly, but not in an alarming way. "Not all of the letters rhyme and not all of the poems are as dreadful as that one. I never would have left *that* monstrosity lying around. Just skim this pile to get the gist and then you never need sully your eyes with it again."

She placed the bundle on top of the weighty tome on lung diseases and concentrated on his face, something that was much easier than digesting his epic fairy tale. He did have such a compellingly handsome face.

Excellently proportioned features. Those

twinkling blue eyes . . . *Focus on the forty pounds and not his obvious enticements!* Enticements that had distracted her far too much since their odd moment last night when, doubtless overwhelmed, overtired, and overawed, one simple touch from his hand had rendered her speechless. And perhaps a tad off-kilter — because surely an innocuous touch shouldn't be that profound? But after a stiff internal talking-to that allowed her to rationalize the odd moment and dismiss it for what it was, she went to bed on a much more even keel. Only nerves about the task ahead had stopped her from sleeping soundly — not thoughts of him. Curiosity about the house rather than the host had sent her exploring, not realizing her host was an early bird, too — something that surprised her given his reputation. But now, rested, calmer, and more herself, his proximity wasn't having such an extraordinary effect. Minerva could blithely admire his handsome face while still being in full possession of her wits. "You arrived back in January?"

"Yes. Late January. Obviously, while I was away you were convalescing."

"Obviously. Then what happened?"

"I had barely been back a few days when my mother suddenly wrote to me suggesting a June wedding. She must have written the damn thing the second she waved me off on the dock, and she declared she was on the cusp of booking her passage."

"Oh dear. Why do I sense another setback?" All these lies, all this effort, must come from a very shallow, selfish place, yet despite having no sympathy for the predicament he had got himself into, she couldn't help but like him.

Hugh had no concept of what the real world was like, no concept of the sorts of problems real people had to deal with on a daily basis. For him, everything could be solved with money — which he clearly had no true understanding of the value of either. It wasn't his fault, any more than being poor was hers, but in her world he wouldn't last five minutes. That she had lasted several hours in his was testament to her superior strength of character. He smiled again, which made his eyes dance much too charmingly, and she found herself smiling back. Because he was, despite all his shortcomings — which she needed to keep reminding herself of — eminently personable in a scoundrelly sort of way. "Already you know me so well."

"What did you do, Hugh?"

"Your father died while I was still on the

ship, and any prospect of a summer wedding died with him. There was the obligatory period of mourning to consider . . ."

"Which coincidentally ends shortly after Christmas. Clearly your mother isn't stupid." Something that didn't bode well for Hugh's plan. In many ways, if she really couldn't cope after a week of these lessons, Minerva would be doing him a favor by terminating the charade before his mother arrived to save him from his own folly.

Or perhaps she should see it through till the bitter end, watch it all fail catastrophically and pat herself on the back when he finally learned a proper lesson about life. In which case, it would be a nobly earned forty pounds.

"She is not known for her patience."

"I suspect she has the patience of a saint to put up with you. Were you always this challenging?"

"Don't you dare hold her up as a candidate for sainthood. The woman is a menace, and believe me, I was driven to it." He sighed for effect, pretending to be vastly put upon, then spoiled it with another smile that sent her pulse galloping. There was something disarming about a man who was keenly aware of all of his shortcomings — yet made no apology for them. "And before you say it yet again — yes, I do know this is all nonsense. And no, I don't fancy my odds at this working."

"You don't?"

He shook his golden head with resignation. "Giles has it at three to one against. But what can I say? I'm an eternal optimist. It has to be worth a try . . . and already I am heartened you are such a fast learner."

"I've always had a talent for digesting information quickly and retaining it. It's the more physical accomplishments, rather than the temporal, which are beyond me. I am dreadfully uncoordinated and clumsy."

"How can you say that when you are such an excellent artist?"

The lovely compliment warmed her. "I have one dexterous talent but I can assure you it is the only one . . . on the subject of which, I must warn you I cannot dance, so ensure I am never asked to do so. I have two left feet and appalling balance, absolutely no ear for music, and lack all grace. I blame my height. My limbs are so long, when I move with the beat it takes forever for the end of the appendage to catch up."

He threw his head back and laughed. The deep, rich sound did odd things to her insides. "Duly noted. Although I cannot think of a reason why you would need that skill here." He picked up his empty cup and frowned into it. "Do you think we could squeeze in some more tea before breakfast?" After a cursory glance at the clock on the mantel, he stood decisively and yanked the bell. "All this talking has left me parched."

"Speaking of bitter ends — how did my dear papa pass?" Minerva sat back in her chair and folded her arms, knowing the tale would be vastly entertaining. For all his faults, Hugh was a brilliant storyteller.

"He was walking in the Cairngorms."

"In January."

"Yes indeed — and against all his loving family's advice. But he was a stubborn man, as Scots are prone to be. . . . Did I mention you were half Scottish?"

"Like so many things, you neglected to apprise me of that detail." Only a day in and already she thoroughly enjoyed sparring with him — but obviously only in a benign and platonic way. Sparring wasn't flirting. It might sail a bit close to the wind on occasion, but she was much too sensible nowadays to allow her head to be turned by a man like him, or by men in general, for that matter. Forewarned was forearmed, after all, and even if Hugh hadn't forewarned her of his lack of substance, she had had ample experience on the subject in her twenty-four years. Enough that there was a limit to how much she would allow herself to be charmed. "Is it pertinent?"

"Only inasmuch as he was there in January to visit his family. The Scots do love to gather for Hogmanay and he always saw the month out with the Landridges."

Apart from Payne, the Merriwell family had been introduced to all the servants as Landridge — the name Hugh had given the fictional Minerva on the day he had supposedly rescued her from the runaway carriage. "Landridge doesn't sound like a typically Scottish name. In fact . . ." She riffled through her notes to find the niggling detail, then jabbed at it with her finger. "You stated I came from the Chipping Norton branch of the Landridges because — and this is a direct quote — 'nobody who was anybody ever ventured to Chipping Norton on purpose so nobody will be able to properly question your lineage.' "

"And believe me, that *pertinent* detail is something I lost a vast amount of sleep over until I found a fascinating book on Scottish history in the library. Thanks to that, I made your father the son of an English Landridge and a Scottish lass from clan Macpherson — a clan, I might add, whose ancestry is genuinely rooted in the Cairngorms." Even

Hugh was chuckling at the ridiculous twists and turns of the story he had woven. "My mother is a stickler for such details."

"What happened in the Cairngorms?"

"It was a bitter January. The fresh snow lay thick on the ground and more was expected. Despite the grim forecast, your father still ventured out for his daily constitutional, convinced he would be back before the threatening storm started, but alas . . ." Hugh shook his head, those twinkling blue eyes alight with humor. "They found his body three days later once the blizzard passed. Buried under several feet of snow. Frozen solid. Such a grave, *grave* tragedy."

"I am starting to think you might be a lunatic." But she was laughing. How could she not? He might be an incorrigible rogue — but he was an entertaining one.

"That's simply because you are hearing all this in one go and the abridged plot is not dissimilar to a Mrs. Radcliffe novel . . ."

"Mrs. Radcliffe's books are more believable than *The Trials and Tribulations of Miss Minerva Landridge.*"

"But imagine those chapters gradually dripping out over the course of the past year and a half." He blithely glossed over her interruption, pretending he hadn't heard her. "Trust me, the tale flowed seamlessly.

As in all good works of fiction and in life, I might add, there were short periods of great drama and longer months where not much happened at all. I am simply giving you the highlights."

"Of which there are an unrealistic glut."

"However *and* most importantly, regardless of the glut of trials and tribulations fate threw at poor Minerva — my mother is completely convinced of *my* sincerity."

"Because the Standish male is such a convincing liar?"

He nodded, and for a second appeared resigned and a little lost again. Something she was undoubtedly imagining to make herself feel better for taking his forty pounds. Or for liking him irrespective of his acknowledged faults.

"I blame heredity." Then he grinned smugly, making her think she had definitely imagined it. "She asks about you in every letter."

"Oh dear."

"Only a pessimist would say 'oh dear.' "

Hugh paused as the tea tray arrived and watched intently as Minerva poured. His scrutiny unnerved her. The mundane task of pouring tea seemed like a test. Not that he was looking at the pot — more he was looking at her. She had never felt so self-conscious in her life. Was she pouring wrong? Was he assessing her speech? Her etiquette? Her woefully inadequate best dress? All she had to save herself from cringing was her own stubborn pride. "Poor Papa. And poor me. To escape the jaws of death only to lose a loved one so rapidly afterward. Fate can be so cruel."

"I know. But despite all that, you were magnificent. Brave. Stoic."

"Perhaps I should also be considered a candidate for sainthood? After all my suffering, I still have to put up with you . . ."

"Honestly, it is a mystery to me you haven't. You were a rock for your family this past year. An absolute brick. Without your strength, your mother would never have coped with her grief."

"I have a mother? Interesting. What is she like?"

"Fortunately, I've always been hazy on the details concerning your family."

"That's very unlike you." She blew on her tea before risking a sip.

"I know! But clearly I had some foresight. At least now, once we meet her, we can take her as she comes."

Minerva choked on her tea.

"Meet her! Surely you haven't hired me a mother?"

"I told you I meticulously planned every-thing." He seemed inordinately proud of himself. "She's a professional actress, too! Giles is a huge fan of the theatre. He personally recommended the woman and propriety dictates you need a chaperone." Something that hadn't bothered either of them so far. Downtrodden young women from Clerkenwell didn't have time for the luxury of propriety.

"Should you take recommendations from a man who wrote the words 'pains in my liver' and is proud to be a complete scoun-drel?"

This seemed to bring him up short. "Giles wouldn't intentionally sabotage me. . . . Or at least I don't think he would." He took a moment to consider it and then brushed it away like a fly near his face. Another vast difference between them. Minerva had learned to expect the worst from people, and he had never needed to learn that les-son. "Either way, she arrives next week, so if she fails to pass muster, we can issue her marching orders well before my mother ar-rives."

"You really are the eternal optimist." She envied him that. She had once been one before life had shaken it out of her.

"You say that like you disapprove."

Minerva shrugged, unrepentant. "A little optimism is all well and good — in its place. But I'm more of a realist." One who still liked to dream from time to time but realized the dreams were futile from the outset.

"Why?" He regarded her with interest. Almost as if he actually cared. It prompted her to be more honest with him than she was comfortable with.

"Because in my experience, fate, like life in general, is nearly always cruel. Not everyone enjoys a carefree life like yours."

Whatever reaction she had expected, it wasn't his. His features suddenly turned serious, and he gazed deep into her eyes as if trying to see her world as it truly was outside of this gilded cage, then serious turned to troubled. "Oh, Minerva . . ."

His hand reached out and found hers, the contact oddly both reassuring and unnerving at the same time. She found herself staring into the sympathetic depths of his eyes, supremely aware of how his touch warmed both her skin and her heart.

For a moment, just that made everything all right.

Then, exactly as it had last night, one simple touch became profound. Almost as if there was a connection between them, intense and strangely loaded. Minerva did not recognize the emotion. It felt new.

Precious.

Kinship . . . tinged with undeniable attraction, desire, and something else . . .

"What's going on!"

At the sound of Diana's voice, she snatched her hand back and, floundering, hid behind her teacup, hoping she was doing a convincing enough job of looking decidedly unmoved by the strangely charged and poignant moment as she took a sip — but she was anything but.

What was that about?

She wasn't usually a hapless dolt around men, not even on that one imprudent occasion when she had foolishly allowed her heart to become engaged, nor did she ever find herself gazing at one as if the sun rose and set in his eyes. She was certain that had never happened before. Her sisters stood staring a few feet away, yet she had heard neither enter.

The room, the furniture, and all common sense had evaporated the second his skin had touched hers.

"Hugh was apprising me of some important details I need to know."

"I think he was apprising you of more than that." Diana positively glared at him.

"I have read about *you* in the papers, too, Lord Fareham, and I am not at all impressed. I will tolerate no *funny* business." Her sister turned to her in accusation. "I thought this was merely a business relationship?"

"It *is* a business relationship!" Minerva could feel the tips of her ears redden. "And as usual you have jumped to ridiculous conclusions based on nothing. Exactly as you did in the carriage when you accused Hugh of being a murderer!" That was a low blow, but under the circumstances, better to put her sister on the back foot rather than continue to cringe under the weight of her stare. So much for last night's reaction being a one-off. Going forward, she decided it would be prudent never to touch Hugh again if her current state was any gauge.

"You thought I was a *murderer*?" At least it distracted Hugh.

"Diana has a vivid imagination." Although clearly so did she if she could read so much into one innocent touch. Because she could still feel it, she tucked the offending hand under her leg in the hope the peculiar sensations would go away.

He laughed, thank goodness. "Allow me to put your suspicious mind at rest, Miss Diana. To the best of my knowledge, I have never killed a soul and have no immediate intentions to alter that state of affairs. And for the record, there really was *no* funny business. We *really* were discussing my fictitious fiancée's past." If holding her hand had any effect on him, he hid it well, which only served to make Minerva feel more foolish because it still had an effect on her. Only sheer willpower stopped her face from glowing like a beetroot. "I can assure you, nothing untoward occurred, nor will it."

"And I can assure you, *sir,* you may have charmed my usually sensible older sister, but you haven't fooled me!"

"Then I shall endeavor to impress you with actions and deeds, Miss Diana, and perhaps, in time, you will concede I have no intentions of killing any of you."

"Don't make promises you can't keep, Hugh." The words escaped Minerva's mouth before she could stop them. "Give it a few days and you'll regret that hasty assurance. Diana — apologize to Lord Fareham. You cannot go around accusing people of goodness knows what." Especially earls — even easygoing ones — when they held the purse strings.

Her sister's expression conveyed absolutely no remorse. "I apologize."

"And I accept."

"Are you coming to breakfast, Minerva?" Always the diplomat, Vee offered an olive branch to end the suddenly awkward situation, her eyes darting between them. "Payne says it is almost ready, my lord."

"Excellent." Hugh stood and reached out to help Minerva up, then thought better of it under Diana's intense, suspicious scrutiny. Instead, to her utter relief, he tucked both his hands uncomfortably behind his back and pasted a polite smile on his face. "Shall we?" He gestured for the girls to go first. "The four of us have much to discuss."

Vee gratefully scurried away, but Diana had to issue one last mortifying setdown to their host.

"Be warned, Lord Fareham, I have appointed myself my sister's guardian for the duration of our stay here and I intend to watch you like a hawk. There will be no flirtations or seductions on my watch."

"Diana!"

He grinned at Minerva's outrage, looking ridiculously handsome and thoroughly naughty.

"Is that a challenge, Miss Diana? Because I do *love* a challenge."

# CHAPTER SIX

"The spoon with the round bowl is used exclusively for the soup." Payne was wielding Hugh's best silverware like a sword. "Regardless of whether you want to eat it or not, it is *never* acceptable to refuse the soup."

"Who doesn't know the difference between a soup spoon and a dessert spoon?" Giles's whisper distracted Hugh from watching Minerva, something he had done unhindered from the fireplace for the last ten minutes. "Are you sure they are a gentleman's daughters?"

"I think she's doing well." As she had for the last five days, Minerva was taking it all in her stride. And as to her claim she lacked grace or the ability to do anything practical, she certainly didn't need lessons in how to navigate a typical table setting. She looked every inch the lady and moved with a subtle fluidity he enjoyed watching. The fact she had insisted upon this particular lesson was more to help her sisters. "The woman has a mind like a steel trap. She never needs anything explained twice."

He liked that about her. He also liked that he was never quite sure what was going to come out of her mouth next. She was quick-witted and outspoken. Hugh couldn't recall another woman who had ever made him laugh more, despite all their interactions now occurring under the watchful eye of the more outspoken Diana. He didn't enjoy that so much. He had a million things he wanted to ask Minerva if they were ever left alone again.

"Not Minerva, you idiot! I knew you were staring at her — not that I blame you." Giles glanced back at the three women sitting in the middle of the long, formal dining table. "She is as pretty as a picture and a delight to be around. Minerva holds herself well. So does that prickly vixen Diana, for that matter. It's the youngest who bothers me. Since she arrived, she's resembled a permanently startled deer. Your mother will never be convinced by her."

Giles had a point. Vee was struggling.

"She's young. Practically still a child. But if she is anything like her sisters, she's sharp and she'll catch up." Except no matter how well she did during their lessons, the second she had to perform, the poor thing froze and seemed to forget everything.

As if to prove it, Payne's instructions wafted across the room. "Tilt the bowl thus, Miss Vee." His white-gloved fingers carefully guided hers on the delicate handle of the bowl and inclined it slightly toward the center of the table. "And using the outer edge of the spoon *only,* carefully submerge it into the broth just deep enough to fill it." Clearly enjoying his new role, he watched each of his willing pupils mimic his actions. "That's it, Miss Diana! Splendid work, Miss Minerva! A little less exuberance, Miss Vee . . . There is no need to panic. It is only soup. . . . We'll get it out of the linen. . . . Perfection, ladies . . . Now bring the utensil carefully to the lips and sip from it. Slurping, even quietly, is wholly unacceptable. The sipping of the soup should be a silent affair."

"Why is it never acceptable to refuse the soup?" Diana had already mastered the mystical art of the soup and was obviously bored — ready to move on and clearly impatient with her younger sibling's nerves. Whereas Minerva spent far too much time behaving like Vee's mother. At this rate, they would waste another hour, maybe more, on nonsense. "When we practiced the main course, you said we could pick and choose what we wanted and nobody would judge us. Why is that not the same for the soup course?"

"Who knows? Suffice to say, the soup is sacrosanct. However, if it is not to your liking, then it is acceptable to swish it around with said spoon like so." Payne delicately wafted the cutlery within the Sèvres bowl with exaggerated airs and graces. "His Lordship, for example, loathes white soup and simply stirs it for the duration of the entire soup course."

Three similar pairs of green eyes instantly flicked to his across the room, but Hugh's only wanted to lock with one of them. He didn't want to think about why that was. Not deeply, at any rate. Just what lay on the surface.

Attraction.

Palpable, visceral, and carnal.

He recognized the signs but would never act on them.

Despite Miss Diana's half-accurate assassination of his character the other day and despite the mischievous, rebellious side of him that saw her threat as a challenge, she had no concept of the deep seam of nobility that ran straight through him and guided his blasted principles. Nor did Giles. Miss Minerva Merriwell might well be a delicious temptation and be thoroughly delightful company — but she was also here because he had asked her to assist him. Whatever happened with their charade, he would never betray her trust by abusing it. He couldn't bear to disappoint or hurt her in that way. This was a business arrangement, and he would not be one of the contributing factors that made fate, and life in general, cruel to her.

Those words had haunted him since she had spoken them, and he had felt compelled to reach out and hold her hand before he'd been caught holding it. Hugh had not yet had a single private moment with Minerva to ask her what had prompted them. Whatever had happened, he wanted her brief stay here at Standish House to be a fond memory. In a life he suspected was largely devoid of much joy, she deserved that if nothing else.

Her beautiful emerald eyes were regarding him with amusement. "Is it soup in general you loathe, Hugh, or merely the *white soup*?"

"Merely the white." He sighed dramatically, poking his nose in the air like one of the snooty patronesses of Almack's who always disapproved of him, making the youngest Miss Merriwell giggle. "It tastes of nothing but blandness. But one *simply* has to serve it."

"Why?"

"Because white soup is currently *de rigueur* and therefore expected."

"And French phrases like *de rigueur* are also *de rigueur,*" added Giles for good measure in his trademark bored tone. "And they must be tossed around liberally in all conversations, in order for the speaker to sound suitably *au fait* with current linguistic fashions. The dullest conversationalists nowadays are nearly always fluent in French."

At Vee's widened eyes, Hugh smiled kindly. "Pay him no mind, Miss Vee. He is pulling your leg. You do not need to speak French. Nor do you need to be dull. Simply be your normal charming self, and your dining companions will be enchanted."

"Isn't serving food you dislike merely a waste of good food? When a great many of the less fortunate are starving?"

Once again, Diana appeared ready to wade into battle with him. For some inexplicable reason, she was determined to dislike him no matter how much he tried to charm her. However, he had to concede her point, one that gave him uncomfortable pangs of more overprivileged guilt. It was something that plagued him more than ever since he had discovered both fate and life in general had been cruel to Minerva. The rescuer inside him wanted to fix that because she deserved to be happy.

"The servants know only to give me a dribble of the stuff. Out of politeness." Hugh did his best not to look embarrassed while inwardly vowing to strike the unnecessary extravagance of white soup from the menu henceforth. "Most guests seem to enjoy the white soup. As to wastage — it is something we are very mindful of here at Standish House. Most of the kitchen scraps go to feed the pigs. On the rare occasion the chef has made too much food, for a ball or banquet" — Good grief, that sounded even more privileged! — "the excess is always distributed amongst the tenants or the needy in the parish." The truth did not make him feel better. Who knew a simple lesson in table etiquette would make him feel so bad about owning the table? "I think the ladies have mastered the soup, Payne. Shall we move on?"

The butler removed Minerva's bowl first. "Thank you, Payne."

"And thank you for thanking me, Miss

Minerva. However, it is not done to thank the servants during dinner."

"Whyever not?"

Payne shot Hugh a withering look, pleased she had played into his capably insubordinate hands, then pretended to whisper, making sure his voice carried. "Because our *betters* like to tell themselves servants are invisible rather than acknowledge the fact that they are simply being rude by ignoring them."

Hugh took the criticism as he took all of his irascible butler's criticisms — lightly. Underneath all the bluster, he had a massive soft spot for the wretch and admired his spirit. "Rude is admonishing your *betters* in front of guests, Payne. In any other household, he would be dismissed on the spot. The fact he has survived, and is paid handsomely despite his rudeness, is testament to *my* generosity as an employer."

"The fact he hasn't dismissed me in the ten years I have had the *displeasure* of serving him is testament to the amount of nonsense I am privy to — or the poppycock I am expected to miraculously rectify. And I include this debacle in with that nonsense. It's enough to turn a man to drink. Lying to his mother! For two whole years, no less. His Lordship and I both know I am paid handsomely in case I am tempted to direct my loyalties to *better* employers elsewhere." Payne collected the rest of the bowls, then positioned himself back at the head of the table. "Now — to the correct knives and forks again. This is your meat knife and this is your fish knife. Never use the wrong knife, ladies . . ."

"The only conceivable way I see this mockery of a sham working is if you dispose of the youngest Merriwell." Giles possessed the enviable talent of whispering without moving his lips. "Can't you send her somewhere? Home, perhaps?"

"Minerva wouldn't hear of it." She had been quite specific from the second he had propositioned her. It was either all three of them or none of them. However, poor Vee's strangled performance was a concern. A very real concern. If she behaved like that in front of his eagle-eyed mother, all his plans would be shot in the paddock before the race started.

"She's what? Nineteen?"

"Seventeen."

"Seventeen! Send her home to her family, Hugh. If nothing else, it would be a kindness. I daresay the child would be relieved."

"I don't think there is anyone at home for her to go back to." Which rather complicated matters. "I get the impression the sisters are all alone in the world." Payne had certainly not seen any other family on his visit to their humble lodgings in an unsavory part of London. Nor had they mentioned any . . .

"You 'get the impression'? What sort of an answer is that? Why the blazes haven't you asked? I thought you prided yourself on your meticulous research? Surely you didn't base such an important decision in choosing a suitable *Minerva* based solely on her name actually being Minerva?"

"Of course not!" It hadn't been solely on her name. Mr. Pinkerton had played a part. And there had also been something about her. The way she held herself. The way she spoke. The way she called to him.

"Oh good grief!" Giles looked toward the heavens for strength. "You *did* choose her based solely on her name! Good God, man — are you even certain they are a gentleman's daughters?"

"They have the bearing of a gentleman's daughters." That was apparently yet another question he couldn't answer. Hugh needed to rectify that immediately because he wanted to know. About her. She intrigued him. Consumed him. Far more than she should.

"You're doomed."

"So you keep saying."

"I've a good mind to wash my hands of this shambles immediately."

"But you won't. You're enjoying it too much."

"I shall enjoy telling you I told you so." Giles folded his arms belligerently, then gestured to the door, where an unobtrusive footman hovered, trying to attract their attention. "I think she's here."

"You see — another piece of my plan is falling neatly into place. Come on . . . let's go meet Minerva's new mother."

"It's easiest if you call me Mrs. Landridge and the girls call me Mama, as I am already immersed in her character." The actress was the right age, looked suitably genteel but motherly at the same time. The perfect choice to play Minerva's mother. She suddenly clutched Hugh's arm and leaned closer. "I do that with every role I take on, my lord. Every. Role." She also liked to roll her *r*'s.

"Er . . ." Hugh knew next to nothing about the theatre or theatre types. Perhaps such theatricals were the norm. "That is very good to know."

"In my humble opinion — and in the esteemed opinions of some of my most ef-

110

fusive critics — complete immersion gives a superior portrayal."

The hand gripping his sleeve released him to waft in the air. For some inexplicable reason, her voice was excessively loud, almost as if she were projecting it from the stage to the gods now rather than sitting on the yellow-striped sofa in his drawing room barely two feet away. "When I played Lady Macbeth, for instance, during a hugely successful extended run at Drury Lane, I went quite mad for almost three months. I even took up sleepwalking."

"You did?" *Surely that was a bit excessive?* "How very dedicated of you."

"Acting is an art, my lord, one which takes a great deal of dedication if one wishes to receive the sort of accolades I do." She smiled wistfully at what she clearly saw as a happy memory rather than complete lunacy. "It was universally agreed by everyone who saw the play, they had never seen such a tragic, twisted, and *utterly convincing* portrayal as mine — and to the best of my knowledge, nobody has come close to playing her better since. Yet none of them truly understand the very essence of my performance." Lucretia DeVere shuddered and clutched at her ample bosom. "You see . . . I *became* her, Lord Fareham. . . . In every

111

sinew, every hair, every fiber of my being . . .
I was the misunderstood wife of Macbeth
himself! *That* is my secret."

"I see." Hugh turned to Giles and blinked,
not entirely sure what to make of any of
that while wondering if his friend's recommended choice was intentionally as mad as
a hatter purely for his own amusement.
However, Giles was nodding sagely rather
than smugly, appearing more than a little
bit smitten with the odd matron by his side.

"It was a triumph. I saw the play four
times in quick succession. Your performance, Mrs. DeVere, moved me to tears."

"You sweet boy." The peculiar woman
squeezed Giles's arm as if he had just given
her the moon. "But it's Mrs. Landridge,
dear. Widowed mother of three charming
daughters. Still keenly mourning the loss of
her beloved husband." Actual tears formed
in the woman's eyes. "But delighted the
good Lord spared my darling Minerva and
that she has found the happiness she deserves."

Her watery eyes fixed on Hugh while her
bottom lip quivered. "What a treasure she
found in you, sir! All those months you sat
diligently by her bedside . . . all those
months where you refused to give up! Never
have two souls deserved each other more

than my precious Minerva and the man I shall soon proudly call my son." Her chubby hand cupped his cheek, and even Hugh felt a little emotional. "I *adore* you!"

"I say."

"I told you she was convincing."

"Indeed. Very." Even the rapid rise and fall of her substantial bosom somehow conveyed both pathos and joy simultaneously. "I've never seen anything like it in my life." He felt the beginnings of a smile play at the corners of his mouth. "I think it might actually work."

"But only *if* we can sort out the Vee problem."

# Chapter Seven

"The gentlemen are awaiting your presence in the drawing room, ladies." Payne shared a pointed look with Minerva. "I believe there is someone there who His Lordship is eager for you all to meet."

She had liked the wily old butler the moment she met him, and since the second they had arrived at Standish House, he had been an absolute godsend. He helped her navigate this enormous and confusing house while preparing her for whatever lesson Hugh and Lord Bellingham were intent on teaching her, and he had an uncanny knack of being close by at times when the correct etiquette was beyond her, subtly giving her cues and then blending into the background. For some reason she wasn't going to question, Payne wanted her to succeed. Thanks to him, she was able to paste on the façade of confidence. Enough to give her siblings confidence in what she had dragged them into, too.

Payne seemed to have a particular talent for appeasing Diana, who had almost entirely behaved herself for five whole days since the embarrassing setdown she had given Hugh upon catching them innocently holding hands — not that it had felt particularly innocent at the time. It had felt . . . worryingly delightful. And while she did her best to glue herself to Minerva's side, Diana also took the lessons seriously and was taking it all in stride.

Vee, on the other hand, was a worry to both of them. She had not settled well into the grandeur of Hugh's house nor was she coping with the new demands made upon her to become a Landridge. But she was only seventeen. Barely. Seventeen was such a difficult age. Neither a child nor a woman, yet struggling to be independent and to have her voice heard.

"Do you need some time, Miss Minerva, to prepare your sisters?"

Clearly Payne knew she hadn't broached the subject of their fake mother yet. She hadn't dared. "Yes, please, Payne. Tell His Lordship we will be with them shortly."

Alone in the enormous dining room, Minerva took a deep breath and smiled brightly. "I think we are all doing brilliantly.

Isn't this fun?"

"It beats real work." Diana's fingers unconsciously touched the lace on the cuff of her new blue day dress. A dress she had been thoroughly overwhelmed by this morning when the first batch of their pretend wardrobe had arrived fresh from the modiste. Wool, in deference to the season, but of a gauge so fine and soft it might as well have been linen in the way it fell in soft folds to the floor. Like Minerva's boldly striped confection, Diana's snugly fitted bodice bore a scooped neckline, which did wonders for their figures. Vee's was similar, in a gentle pastel color, but high necked. The new spectacles perched on her nose were much more becoming than the ugly ones Minerva had struggled to pay for. "The grass apparently is greener and the food is to die for."

"I don't care about the stupid grass! We don't belong here. I'd rather be home." Vee had uttered the same thing since the first night.

"We'll be home soon, darling . . . a few weeks at most . . . but we'll be returning significantly richer than we've ever been. Just think of all the books you'll be able to buy?"

"I suppose . . ."

"There is no 'suppose' about it! In the meantime, I am thoroughly enjoying being someone else for a change. This reminds me of the little shows we used to put on for Papa. Do you remember?"

"I suppose it does." Vee's expression brightened. Any mention of the past always cheered her, not that their selfish father had ever watched one for longer than five minutes before disappearing again to drink at the Dog and Duck or play cards somewhere — or spend the night with whatever light-skirted woman he happened to be sniffing around at the time.

"You were always so good in those. I'd make masks out of paper and Diana would always manage to drape the sheets to look like whatever costume we needed and we'd rehearse for hours. Just like we are now. Except now we have all the props and scenery, and guess what — there will be more characters."

"There will? Who?"

"Because *Hugh's* Minerva has a mother, he's hired a genuine actress to play her." Something she had only confided thus far to Diana, knowing Vee wouldn't cope well with too much at once. "Isn't that fun?"

"I take it that is who we are meeting now?" Diana, for once, beamed at Vee, trying her best to support Minerva. "How exciting! I wonder what she'll be like?"

"I don't want to meet her." Her younger sister's face was appalled. "We had a mother. She died. Calling anyone else 'Mama' would be disrespectful to her memory."

Not that Vee had any true memories of the real woman. She had been two when their mother had died. Minerva had been barely nine, so even her memories had faded over time. She could just remember their mother's face but not her voice, odd recollections recalled in stark relief, but so many were hazy because she had lived more years without her now than with. She remembered a fragile woman worn down by life. One who cried a great deal and bickered constantly with her husband. One who claimed to have been a gentleman's daughter, too.

"It's just pretend, Vee . . . not at all disrespectful. She is the fictional Miss Venus Landridge's mother, not yours. You are playing a part. I've told you the story Lord Hugh made up. Our *pretend* father recently died . . ." She had made the mistake of omitting the word "pretend" yesterday, and her sister had immediately burst into tears. "Leaving just us and our *pretend* widowed mother. He could hardly convince his mother we would all be here unchaperoned, when she expects us to have a mother. You are a stickler for propriety, Vee. . . . You *know* that would be the case."

"I won't do it!"

"You never batted an eyelid when I told you our pretend father was dead."

"That's because I knew I would never have to mention him by name if I chose to. I could nod and look sad, which I am, but I would never have to call another man 'Papa'!"

"Then perhaps we manage to navigate all this without you ever having to call this woman 'Mama'?" Not ideal, but as it was unlikely Vee would be capable of much more than sitting in Hugh's mother's presence without looking like an overwhelmed child, it was a way forward.

"That's an excellent idea!" Diana wrapped her arm around Vee's shoulders. "Only speak when directly spoken to and never say the word 'Mama'! Come on, Vee . . . you can do this. We've come this far and Minerva is right. Without Lord Fareham's money, we could be destitute within the year."

"I'd rather be destitute than call a stranger 'Mother'!"

"Oh, for pity's sake, Vee!" Diana's new-found patience was short-lived. "Stop being a baby! Sometimes, a person just has to strap on their stiff upper lip and grin and bear things!" Exasperated, she settled her eyes on Minerva, the message in them clear. *Stop mollycoddling her!*

"Vee, I promised Lord Fareham I would give him at least a week, during which he would have our full compliance. Please do this one thing, Vee — simply because I *need* you to."

"I won't!"

Out of the corner of her eyes, she caught Diana's look of complete frustration at the pair of them, and her temper flared, both at Vee's continued belligerence and her own inability to discipline her properly.

"Oh yes you will!" As much as Minerva had never wanted to be a parent to her sister, let alone a strict one, it was obvious Vee needed one today. For all their sakes. "Because as much as you might prefer destitution, I can assure you, your only two remaining family members do not! And until our feckless father returns — if he *ever* returns — I am burdened with being the head of this family and therefore, whether you like it or not, what I say goes!"

"He's not feckless!"

"Then where is he, Vee?"

Minerva didn't wait to see if her words hit the mark and flounced out of the dining room expecting her sisters to follow, pausing once she arrived at the door to the drawing room to turn around. During that short walk, remorse at her flash of temper had begun to replace the anger. Behind Diana stood Vee, clearly on the verge of tears, and her heart wept for her. But it couldn't be helped. While she hated hurting Vee's tender feelings, her sister needed to learn the world didn't revolve entirely around her. Vee might have been a child when their father had left, but Minerva had barely been a woman and had no clue how to raise his other daughters. Necessity had meant she had had to learn fast. If she could do that and give up her own life in the process, surely it wouldn't kill Vee to do this one thing?

Without saying another word, Minerva knocked on the door and sailed in. Hugh instantly sprung to his feet. He always sprung to his feet when she entered a room. She liked that tiny, thoughtful gesture.

"Ladies! I'd like you to meet Mrs. Agatha Landridge — your widowed mother fresh from Chipping Norton."

An older woman with silver strands in her blond hair and a plump face beamed at them and rushed toward Minerva. "My dears! What a pleasure to meet you. And what beautiful daughters I have!" She turned to Hugh and nudged him. "You neglected to tell me they were quite so lovely, my lord. I presume their green eyes and stature come from their father." For some reason, her bottom lip quivered the second she mentioned him. "I miss him dreadfully."

"Your new mother likes to *immerse* herself *fully* in every character she plays." Hugh's twinkling blue eyes locked with Minerva's. "Therefore, for the duration, she has announced she will be Mrs. Agatha Landridge at *all* times. Newly widowed and still grieving."

The strange woman enveloped Minerva in an exuberant, perfumed embrace, which left her blinking back at Hugh, a little bewildered. "But I thought he'd been dead a year?"

"What is a year when one has lost the love of her life, Minerva? The loss of my husband has left me broken. I doubt I shall ever fully recover." Her new mother released her and similarly engulfed Diana. "My darling . . ." She stepped back and held her at arm's length. "And look at you! Just as beautiful as my dear Minerva!" Teary eyes traveled to

Vee, who stood warily near the door and appeared ready to bolt at any moment. "And you must be my Venus . . ."

"I am not your anything!" Vee actually stamped her foot before breaking into a run and disappearing down the hallway.

Their new mother looked shocked at the outburst, her small hand flapping near her breast. "I knew she was sensitive about her name . . ."

"It's not her name." Diana huffed out an irritated breath. "It's the situation. She feels pretending to have a mother is disrespectful to our real mother's memory."

"I am so sorry. I should have told her about this sooner. I did just spring it on her, and Vee needs time to adjust . . ." And Minerva was going to wring her sister's neck when she got hold of her if she continued to be so childishly stubborn. "I'll go speak to her now. She'll be better once she's calm."

Hugh and Lord Bellingham exchanged an odd look. One that didn't suggest they had much faith.

"No . . . let her digest things for a little while on her own. You and Diana can catch her up on this afternoon's lesson later. We'll probably get more ground covered without her anyway. . . . Perhaps she's missing home? The rest of your family?"

"What rest of the family?" Diana answered before she could. "It's just the three of us."

She watched Hugh's handsome face fill with sympathy. "Your father is gone, too?"

"Long gone." The wastrel. But Minerva did not want to discuss that now in front of an audience. Instead, she turned to her strange new mother. "I suppose we should get to know one another . . ."

Whoever originally said "clothes maketh the man" had plainly not known the first thing about women. Minerva looked like a princess, hardly recognizing her own reflection in the mirror, but she still felt like an imposter regardless. An imposter about to face her worst nightmare.

"Are you ready, Minerva?" Vee, on the other hand, couldn't contain her excitement. After her rude outburst yesterday and the subsequent tense discussion the sisters had afterward, the youngest Merriwell had dug her heels in — until three stylish riding habits had arrived in the second batch of new outfits from the modiste. The impressive garments came with a message from Payne, who informed them His Lordship thought they had been cooped up inside long enough and should ride to the village later in the morning on horseback. With that exciting prospect, Vee was on board again and vowed to make more of an effort not to be offended by everything, because she had always wanted to learn to ride.

Minerva, in stark comparison, had never wanted to learn to ride.

In fact, she had never wanted to be nearer than twenty feet to a horse her entire life and had deftly managed to avoid being so without the sturdy security of a carriage and an able driver protecting her person.

Horses were big, unpredictable, and fast creatures who, frankly, terrified her. Sitting on the back of one was Minerva's idea of complete hell. Perhaps if she possessed the skills necessary to be a horsewoman — namely balance and the graceful athleticism required to stay on top of one — today's trial wouldn't be a trial at all. However, with her gangly long limbs, complete lack of co-ordination, and genuine fear that her innate clumsiness might cause her to fall and break her neck, she would rather face the Spanish Inquisition than an hour on horseback.

"Hurry up, Minerva! The gentlemen are waiting!" Now even Diana was chivvying her. "Lord Bellingham says once we've mastered the basics, we are going to ride the mile to the village afterward. An actual quaint English village! I am dying to see it. I always fancied myself living in a village over smelly old London. Parts of it are supposedly medieval."

Clearly only Minerva was dreading their outing, but with Vee finally smiling for once and nothing tart or pessimistic coming from Diana's lips since yesterday's dinner, she could hardly be the one to spoil their fun.

"Go on ahead. I shall meet you down there."

She needed a minute alone to calm her bouncing nerves. With any luck, Hugh would have selected a squat, docile mount for her, or one so old and slow a tortoise would give it a run for its money — one low enough to the ground that the inevitable fall wouldn't hurt.

Much.

With a sense of impending doom, she poked another of her new hatpins into the strange, feathered confection on her head. It wasn't so much a hat as a decoration, but it was exceedingly pretty and had been made to match the magnificent burgundy riding habit she was sporting. At least that was something she could appreciate. The heavy velvet skirt was longer at the back than she was used to, but the fabric was stunning, and the cut sublime. Especially the tight bodice trimmed with an homage to military braiding and twenty shiny brass buttons. And it was new. She had never owned anything before that wasn't second-hand.

She stared at her reflection and inhaled deeply. Of all the challenges she would have to face as an earl's pretend fiancée, this was hardly the most challenging. As Hugh had reassured her last night, any activity that kept them occupied during his mother's visit would make the time pass more quickly, along with diverting his mother's attentions elsewhere. The more diverted she was, the easier their brief time together would be.

Whilst out riding, Minerva wouldn't have to lie, pretend to be anyone else, or remember an elaborate backstory — as all gently bred ladies knew how to ride, and he'd told his mother repeatedly how the pair of them enjoyed nothing more than galloping across the fields together. But at least he had faithfully promised there would be no galloping or even cantering. All she had to do was place her bottom in the saddle and keep it there.

How hard could that be?

# CHAPTER EIGHT

Vee and Diana didn't appear to need his help with their mounts, because Giles had talked them through the basics and a thoroughly immersed Mrs. Landridge had sandwiched herself between the girls' gentle horses to instruct them on the noble art of riding like a lady. Minerva was yet to arrive. Hugh was about to send a groom to fetch her when she suddenly appeared at the edge of the stable yard, looking so gorgeous his breath caught in his throat.

Good heavens, the woman had a splendid figure! A figure the bold velvet habit clung to in the most magnificent way.

He bounded over a tad too eagerly, before he checked himself and slowed his pace in case Giles was watching. His friend had enough ammunition on him already without learning Hugh found Minerva devilishly attractive and harbored scandalous fantasies involving her that had the annoying habit of coming alive when he slept. "There you are! I was about to send a search party."

She looked nervous. More nervous than he had ever seen her, those feline green eyes filled with trepidation as they took in the horses. "Which one is mine?"

"The chestnut mare over there." He pointed to the pretty filly waiting patiently on the cobbles. "Her name is Marigold, and before you ask, no, I didn't name her. My mother did. Come and meet her." He took Minerva's elbow, expecting her to follow, but she remained rooted to the spot.

"Isn't she a little on the . . . um . . . large side?" He watched her eyes wander to the neat gray pony he had assigned Vee, then back to Marigold.

"You are a tall woman, Minerva, anything smaller and your legs will be trailing on the ground."

Her gaze was rooted to the horse. "You say that like it's a bad thing."

"It is a bad thing — for the horse."

For the first time since her arrival, she finally looked at him. "Are you suggesting I will squash a smaller one?"

"I wouldn't dare." Hugh smiled and wrapped her arm around his, tugging her reluctantly forward and trying to ignore how pleasant the seemingly innocuous contact was. "My dear Minerva, it is perfectly natural to be a little wary of a horse when you have never ridden one, but you have my word that Marigold, despite her *gargantuan* size, is as docile as a horse can be. Why — you could fall asleep in the saddle without a care in the world should you fancy it."

"*If* I can stay in the saddle! I have no center of balance and . . ."

"And you are making this into more of an ordeal than it needs to be. Riding a horse isn't like dancing. It largely requires you to sit — something I daresay you have done without consciously thinking about for most of your life. Let's get you *seated* and you'll see for yourself."

They'd had a long conversation about this last night after dinner, although he had thought her more reluctant than scared when she had grabbed him in the hallway and tried to come up with as many reasons as she possibly could as to why she didn't need to learn to ride. Judging by her pinched features and widened eyes, his intrepid fake fiancée was actually more scared than reluctant. Perhaps more petrified than scared. It was the first time he had ever seen her flounder, and it made him feel . . . peculiar. "You will amaze yourself at how quickly you get the hang of it. It is simply a case of sitting upright. Just look at your sisters."

Almost as if he had paid her to perform on cue, Diana nudged her equally tall mare into a trot, her pretty face breaking into a grin as she easily maneuvered a quick circle around the exercise paddock. Then Vee swiftly follow suit. "They have both been riding less than five minutes and look at the pair of them. Honestly, Minerva, there is nothing to it. Think of Marigold as a tall, robust stool if it helps. Once you are in the saddle, you hold on to the reins and use them to direct the horse. All my horses are fully fluent in the subtle language of the reins." Hugh reached out and stroked Marigold's muzzle. "Go ahead . . . pet her. She won't bite."

Tremulously, she copied and gave the horse a perfunctory pat. Marigold didn't so much as blink. "There . . . you see? As docile as they come."

A waiting stable boy rushed forward with the block and placed it on the ground. Minerva decisively placed one foot upon it, then the other, and froze. "Aren't sidesaddles a lot harder to master — what with the rider dangling precariously over the side rather than on top?"

"Not at all. You are not dangling, because your . . . um . . . bottom is still atop the horse." Hugh grabbed the pommel and gave it a hearty shake to demonstrate how sturdy it was as he thought about her bottom. "It is perfectly safe. Trust me."

"Says the man who has probably never ridden sidesaddle in his life."

She had him there, so he glossed over it. "Once you are saddled, you also have the reins to help steady you. It's probably best to demonstrate them once you are up." He gestured to the saddle with a flick of his head. "So gather your skirts in your right hand and . . . up you get."

She bundled up the fullness of her heavy habit in one hand, cocked her leg awkwardly, almost tripping in the process, then spun back to face him, bewildered and more than a little panicked. "Exactly how *do* I get up?"

"Why don't we leave mounting the horse for another time and I'll simply lift you today?" Hugh didn't wait for an answer, and instead briskly put his hands around her waist. The feel of her womanly curves brought him up short. Her arms suddenly looping around his neck brought him up shorter. She was gripping him so tightly he had no choice but to feel the soft press of her bosom against his neck as it rose and fell in time with her rapid breathing; his eyes were level with her lips, unable to look elsewhere thanks to the bundle of burgundy velvet wedged against his cheek. Not that he paid much attention to the velvet when his big hands nearly spanned her waist and he could smell her sultry perfume where it lingered on the pulse of her throat.

The incendiary effect on his body was instant, and despite the chilly winter morning, his skin burned. "You might need to let go for me to lift you."

She released her grip only slightly.

"Perhaps put your hands on my shoulders?" His voice came out strangled, not because she was strangling him but more because their intimate position was suddenly giving his body inappropriate ideas. Her long legs were plastered against his torso. If he didn't act swiftly, something of his would be inadvertently and mortifyingly plastered against her thighs.

"I'm sorry. I've never been lifted before. As you rightly pointed out, I'm hardly slight. Do you promise you won't drop me?"

"My dear Miss Merriwell, while the Standish male is untrustworthy in nearly all things and should never be trusted as a general rule of thumb, we would absolutely never drop a lady. Even a less-than-slight one. Please trust me in this."

Finally she put a little distance between them, placing her palms flat on his collarbones and staring deeply into his eyes, making him yearn to kiss her anxious frown away. "This is all very new to me."

This was all very new to him, too, and it certainly wasn't fun. His heated skin didn't feel like it fit his skeleton any longer, his heart was hammering a fevered tattoo against his ribs, and his hands wanted to go roaming on an extensive journey of discovery. For the sake of his own sanity, and in case he forgot to be noble, Hugh didn't linger over the task and practically threw her up into the air in his haste to release her.

She gave a little squeak as she landed on the saddle, then nearly fell off the damn thing in her hurry to grab the reins, forcing him to use his body to hold her upright as she fought for balance. As she had said, she wasn't slight. She was a tempting armful he was only too aware of. He didn't bother trying to explain how to hook her leg around the pommel and arranged the limb himself as dispassionately as he could with uncharacteristically clumsy fingers, trying to imagine it was any other leg than her ridiculously long and shapely one and failing miserably. Since when had he been drawn to legs? Or perfume? Or silly little hats?

"Now shove your other foot in the stirrup."

The spare leg flayed about ineffectually in the air, displaying the merest glimpse of silk-clad calf. He lunged and gripped the offending thing firmly around its booted ankle and stuffed it unceremoniously where it needed to be before jumping back, more than a little flustered and confused as to what exactly was going on.

They were just legs, for pity's sake. Hardly warranting such an effusive reaction when he saw legs every single day. Most people owned two of them. Nor was he some green youth who had never touched a woman before! He had touched dozens of them, all over the place, seen copious pairs of naked female limbs and never once experienced a reaction like this to any of them.

Perhaps he was ill?

That had to be it.

All the stress of his mother's impending visit and this complicated damned charade was obviously taking its toll. Either that, or the circumstances had unsettled him. For so many reasons, she was forbidden fruit; ergo, it stood to reason the wayward, womanizing Standish blood flowing through his veins wanted to take a bite. It was all heredity. That had to be it if even the bloody woman's calves were alluring!

It was best to just accept it and move on without too much inner scrutiny. "Fetch me my horse!" And best to do something swiftly to take his mind off it all.

The groom brought Galileo around, and Hugh heaved himself onto the animal's back while Minerva sat stiffly atop Marigold with unnecessarily widened eyes. "Allow me to demonstrate the reins . . ."

When she had said she lacked a talent for anything physical, she hadn't lied. Hugh had never seen such an ungainly, cack-handed attempt at horseback riding in his life. It would be laughable if it wasn't so crucial. His mother was a vehement horsewoman. He'd told his blasted mother that Minerva was also a keen horsewoman. And there wasn't a hope in hell his mother wouldn't suggest a daily ride to get the blood pumping.

That Minerva had not fallen from poor Marigold was a miracle in itself — but at least she was upright.

Almost.

And at least her general demeanor had

moved from terrified to simply startled. For a woman who normally moved with an achingly hypnotic economy of motion, who could bring to life the rejuvenating qualities of Pinkerton's Patented Liver Tonic with nothing but a brush and some ink in her talented, graceful hand, this Minerva might as well be a hat stand in comparison. Her posture was so rigid, all four of her limbs were locked at odd right angles as the group plodded laboriously toward the village. Worse, she still didn't understand the concept of bouncing in time to the horse's gait. Instead, she bounced intermittently but stiffly, her lush bottom jarring with each apparently alien motion.

Giles and the others were long gone — at Hugh's insistence. His friend was enjoying the bizarre spectacle of Minerva in the saddle much too much for his liking while Hugh had patiently walked her in circles around the exercise yard, hoping against hope she might eventually get the hang of it. But alas — a ramrod straight, slightly panicked hat stand was all she was capable of.

Now they were blessedly alone but picking their way cautiously down the lane to the village. With any luck, they would arrive before the shops closed, but he wasn't going to hold his breath.

"I told you I was useless at things like this." Her voice was despondent and apologetic. "We should probably just turn back."

"Nonsense. You are doing splendidly." He smiled encouragingly. "Perhaps if you concentrated less, you would relax more."

"If I relax, I'll fall off." Marigold swished her tail impatiently, and Minerva wobbled precariously for a moment, then looked so miserable he felt dreadful. Who knew something as simple as riding a horse would defeat her? "This horse clearly hates me."

"She doesn't hate you. The thing is . . ." Hugh took in her granite posture and sighed. "Horses are sensitive creatures who take their lead from us. You need to relax for Marigold to relax, too."

"And how, exactly, does one relax on the back of a skittish horse!" The snippy tone made Marigold snort and chomp on the bit.

"For a start, you could think about loosening your arms. Look at me." Hugh made sure he was practically lounging in his saddle. "As you can see — I have a firm hold of the reins should I need to quickly take command." He shook them for effect. "But the muscles in my arms and wrists are soft. Galileo doesn't need to feel the bit tight at the back of his mouth to know I am in control, because we trust each other." To prove his point, he used his left hand to tug gently, and his mount instantly responded by moving a little farther away from Minerva on the narrow lane. "*Relax your arms,* Minerva."

She took a deep breath. "Is this better?"

Not even slightly. "A little — however, you do still resemble a woman with a couple of sturdy broomsticks shoved up her sleeves."

She looked down at her arms, ruler straight and raised almost horizontal from her body, and made a conscious effort to bend them. "Will the terror lessen, do you suppose?"

Maybe it would if he took her mind off what she was doing?

"It occurs to me I have been very remiss in my attentions. I've been so wrapped up in teaching you how to be *my* Minerva, I've hardly learned anything about the real one. All I know is your parents are no longer alive and your father was a scholar."

She frowned, her eyes never leaving the road ahead as she concentrated too hard at relaxing. "I said he was gone, not dead." She risked flicking him a quick glance. "And I saw no evidence of him actually being a scholar, although he frequently claimed to be one. But then my father often claims to be a lot of things."

"He's alive?"

"Who knows?" She shrugged, then wobbled some more. "He wrote us a letter one day saying he was going away for a little while and we haven't seen hide nor hair of him since."

Hugh was appalled. "He never came back! Even after your mother died?"

"My mother died when I was nine. My father abandoned us promptly after my nineteenth birthday. He left no forwarding address." She said it so matter-of-factly. "I cannot say I miss his presence much. He was more hindrance than parent, especially in the later years."

"That is outrageous!" For some inexplicable reason, he wanted to turn his horse toward London, hunt the wastrel down, and then beat the bounder to a pulp. "What sort of a gentleman behaves like that?"

"I never said he was a real gentleman either." She looked troubled. "Again — he claimed to be. He was an engraver — like me. Oh dear . . . Is that why you asked me to pose as your fiancée? You assumed I am a proper gentleman's daughter?"

"It was an easy assumption to make. You are well educated, well spoken. You have a genteel bearing."

"Those come from my mother, who also claimed to be a gentleman's daughter." She winced. "But again, I have no proof of that either. They were estranged from their respective families."

"It makes no difference to me in the grand scheme of things." He liked her exactly as she was. "So long as you can convince my mother you are a tiny bit genteel . . ."

"There may be some tenuous link somewhere — although I sincerely doubt from my father's line." She looked thoughtful for a moment, then shrugged. "He was as convincing a liar as anyone I've ever met, and I wouldn't put it past him to have made it all up." She risked another quick glance sideways and offered a pained half smile. "He was quite clever that way."

"But he lacked the moral fiber to do his duty by his family?" Such a thing seemed unbelievable to Hugh. A chap did not shirk his responsibilities!

"He was a terminal wastrel with questionable morals who preferred an easy life to hard work. He managed to make the minimal effort while we were younger — or at least I assumed he did because he just about managed to keep a roof over our heads. He was a woodcutter, too. A reasonably good one. He taught me, actually. Which ironi-

cally freed him to spend more time social-
izing in the local public houses or with his
lady friends as I got older — until he
abdicated all his parental responsibilities
entirely."

"And left it all to you." She nodded.
"That's unconscionable."

"Yes, it is — but that was Papa. He ran
with a very bad crowd by then, and in the
final days, and the weeks after, several
unsavory characters and more than one
Bow Street Runner came looking for him.
Clearly he was running away from more
than just his familial responsibilities." She
shrugged, resigned, and barely wobbled at
all. "The Standish male does not have the
monopoly on untrustworthiness, Hugh. In
my experience, most men are untrustworthy.
It's in their nature, but my father was in a
league all his own. In fact, I would go as far
as to say that whatever misdeeds any man
in your family has done in the past, I'll
wager my *dear* papa probably did worse."

Not a wager he was prepared to risk. "For
all their copious faults, a Standish would
never leave his family in the lurch." They
would lie, cause enormous heartbreak unre-
pentantly to said family, do exactly as they
wished, betray all trust, and ultimately
disappoint, but they never ignored their

responsibilities. Even the most scandalous ones.

# CHAPTER NINE

"Enough about me." The village was blessedly close, and Minerva was done with dredging up her depressing past. "Tell me something about you a devoted fiancée should know."

"My favorite color is red. It's daring and bold and just the tiniest bit naughty. Like me."

"That's hardly the enlightening revelation I was hoping for." She'd repeatedly tried to tease something personal out of him for days with little success. Every question was answered with something flippant or amusing, to such an extent she was starting to think he was purposefully being flippant. Which suggested, as she suspected, there was more to him than he wanted the world to see. Something she was also well aware she might be conjuring to justify her peculiar reactions to him, and yet there were distinct flashes of something else. She couldn't deny that.

Like the odd look in his eyes that first morning when he had held her hand after she had confessed her life wasn't as carefree as his was. There had been empathy there. As if he immediately understood her situation somehow and felt responsible for it. He kept that Hugh firmly under wraps most of the time, but it was that man she was curious about. So curious, she'd had to resort to pumping Payne for information.

"I suspect you've already worked me out and know all you need to. I am exactly as I seem. A gentleman of leisure. Charming . . . quite spoiled and selfish and incapable of any meaningful purpose above what dreaded duty and my birthright force me to do."

She risked taking her eyes off the road and the reins to glance at him, and something about his expression bothered her, confirming all her suspicions. "I don't believe you."

"It's true. In view of everything you've just told me, I am ashamed to say, I'm as shallow as a puddle. What you see is what you get."

"Yet I still suspect you have hidden depths. There is something about the whole carefree bachelor exterior which doesn't quite ring true." Because he *was* kind and thoughtful. She had seen that. He also undoubtedly had the patience of a saint. A man with those qualities couldn't be entirely selfish, and moreover, Minerva liked him a great deal and she wouldn't be able to do that if he were as shallow as he claimed.

"I'd like to hear your evidence for that grievous accusation."

"You are an early bird — like me. And usually people don't get up in the morning unless they have a good reason to."

"I like to have first dibs on breakfast."

"Liar. You work in your study. You start every morning at six. Payne told me."

"Payne *thinks* I'm working and I've never done anything to dissuade him from thinking it. But the truth is I go to my study at six because I've usually just arrived home from a night of debauchery and I grab a quick forty winks in my study to ensure I am in a fit state to be seen at breakfast."

"I think your wily butler would know if you'd been out all night."

"He's not that wily." Hugh was smiling as he maneuvered his horse around a pothole with a confidence she envied. "For years I've been pretending to go to bed, purposefully rumpling the bedcovers so they look slept in, and then I climb out of my bedchamber window to do unspeakable things with highly questionable associates."

"Unspeakable things? Really?" She couldn't help but smile at the flagrant lie. "What unspeakable things can you possibly get up to in this sleepy corner of Hampshire?"

"Gambling, mostly. Drinking and carousing." He ticked them off his fingers. "And philandering, of course. I'm a slave to hedonism in all its many forms." Then he winked at her flirtatiously, looking every inch the dashing scoundrel, and the feminine part within Minerva inwardly sighed at the sight. "Fortunately, after darkness has fallen, the village transforms into a den of iniquity."

"Payne says you meet your estate manager every day when you are in Hampshire, and when you are not in Hampshire, insist on weekly letters from him and travel down at least twice a month to oversee things." The wink had made her pulse quicken exactly as it had when his strong arms had lifted her effortlessly onto Marigold earlier. "He claims, despite appearances, you are fastidiously diligent when it comes to estate matters, therefore I must conclude you are a *very responsible* gentleman after all — against all your vehement claims to the contrary."

He didn't deny it. "You and Payne suddenly seem very cozy."

"You are not the only curious person with questions. At least Payne answers mine honestly."

"*Honestly.* Good grief! I don't like the sound of that. What else has the tattler said?"

"That you haven't increased any rents for the last five years because of the difficult economy and that your tenants universally love you."

"If they love me, it is because of my acute and universal *lack* of business acumen, of which they can easily take advantage." He gestured to the church now only a little ahead of them. "That's Saint Mary's. William the Conqueror built it. He set up home in Hampshire for a while — back when Winchester was still the capital."

He really didn't want to talk about himself, or at least the less frivolous side of himself at all, but she decided she wouldn't be swayed. The more time she spent with him, the more he intrigued her. Yes, he was handsome and charming, witty and addictively likeable, but those twinkling blue eyes of his saw more than they let on, and she was coming to believe the mischievous rogue he played so well covered up a very different sort of man. The sort who rescued damsels in distress and knew exactly what to say to prevent a situation from being awkward. Shallow men weren't intuitive. Nor were they so alluring. "Payne says you are an excellent landlord who looks after them and treats them with respect. He says you always take the time to listen and frequently heed their advice."

"I *pretend* to listen to them. It's one of my few talents. I can appear completely engrossed in a conversation whilst avoiding hearing any of it at all. My tenants *think* I listen to them. Payne *thinks* I listen to him and you wrongly assume I'm listening to you now, when in reality, all I am thinking about is lunch. You see? As shallow as a puddle. Here you are, trying to have a meaningful conversation, and all I can think about is myself."

Something told her he thought about everyone, which was an admirable trait. It made no sense he would try to deny it. "Yet your estate is thriving — largely thanks to all the modern farming techniques you have implemented. I've seen all the new books on the subject in the library. And they have been read."

"Not by me."

"Payne says you are a better landlord than even your father was, and everybody apparently loved him, too. He says despite your best efforts to the contrary, you are actually very much like your father. Peas in a pod, in fact. Is that true? You've never really mentioned him."

Something suspiciously like despair skittered briefly across his features before he masked it with dismissal. "What is there to mention? Like you I was young when he died. Talking about him only makes me feel maudlin, and why would I want to be intentionally maudlin?" He nudged his horse to trot a little beyond hers and then pointed to the bustling market square as he blatantly avoided her question. Too blatantly. "Ah — look. I see Giles's horse tied up over there. The others shouldn't be too far away, or they better not be. I'm starving."

Clearly she had hit a raw nerve, as he didn't wait for her, leaving Minerva to navigate the cobbles and a few pedestrians all by herself, something that took more concentration than keeping her horse walking in a straight line.

By the time she reached the inn, Hugh had dismounted and handed his horse over to a groom. He shook his head and huffed out a withering sigh as he grabbed her horse's halter. "That was barely ten yards.

What kept you?" Another groom rushed forward with the block, and Hugh waved him away. "Believe me, it will only end in catastrophe. I'll help the lady down." He held out his arms. "Give those white knuckles a rest and let go of the reins, Minerva."

Reluctantly, she did and clumsily gripped his shoulders. They felt reassuringly solid and disconcertingly wonderful . . . and she really needed to stop thinking nonsense like that about a man who was paying her to do a job.

In case he noticed the odd effect he had on her, and because it seemed like the quickest way off the beast, she lunged toward him, realizing too late that she should have taken her stupid foot out of the stirrup first. As it twisted, Marigold stepped sideways to escape her flailing, and the ground loomed.

"I've got you!"

Mortifyingly, he did. His strong arms were wrapped tight around her ribs as she hung suspended above the ground. Her foot still tangled in the stirrup, and her face sprawled against his chest as he engulfed her, her breasts scandalously flattened against his stomach. Minerva could do nothing but cling to him, inhaling his fresh, clean, manly scent as the groom wrestled her foot out of its stirrup prison, then suffer the indignity of having Hugh haul her upright in the intimate cage of his arms the second it was free.

For a long moment they stood pressed together, something that her body seemed to enjoy far more than it should, until he abruptly broke the contact, holding her at an appalled arm's length as he blinked down at her.

"Good grief, woman! When I held out my arms, I didn't expect you to launch yourself into them at that second. You might have given me some warning you were about to take flight. You'd have flattened a lesser man."

"I am so sorry. I did warn you I was clumsy." The collar and lapels of his coat were awry. They gave her wayward fingers an excuse to touch him as she straightened them, and then their eyes locked.

And held.

As if they had a mind of their own, her palms smoothed his lapels flat, and beneath them she felt his heart beating. Sure and steady but as rapidly as hers. In that second, she realized the heady, magnetic, dangerous pull she felt wasn't one-sided. He felt it, too.

Why didn't that worry her? When her attraction to him wasn't wise?

She watched his eyes drop to her lips before slowly returning to hers in question, felt her body leaning to meet his . . .

*"Hugh?"* Beneath her fingers, Minerva felt the muscles in Hugh's shoulders tense the second he heard the other voice, and he instantly stepped back. "I thought it was you!"

His head whipped around to face a very beautiful blond-haired woman on the arm of a very dashing-looking man, and he smiled. It was an odd smile. A strained one. One that never touched his eyes. "Sarah . . . Captain Peters . . . hello . . . You are back, then?"

"Only temporarily. Teddy has leave and we won't rejoin his regiment till January." If the blond woman was aware of Hugh's discomfort, she didn't show it. She beamed at him. "But the best news is the regiment is returning to Aldershot in the New Year, so we'll be permanently stationed in Hampshire and much closer to home. Mother is thrilled." Hugh looked the exact opposite despite his rigid smile. "She's missed spoiling her grandchildren."

"That is *excellent* news." He didn't seem to know what to do with his hands. To stop fidgeting, he clamped them behind his back.

"Excellent." She had never seen him so awkward. "I trust your mother is well?"

"Indeed she is. We are all in fine fettle."

"Excellent." That single word was like a nervous tic. What was it about this woman that made the normally confident Hugh so stilted and uncomfortable? Unless her reckless lapel smoothing had started it? That had been a mistake that she should be grateful had been interrupted — but wasn't.

"How *are* you? It's been . . . what? Two years since we last collided?" The blonde's eyes flicked to Minerva with curiosity. "Are you still the merry bachelor about town?"

His eyes finally stopped staring at the blonde to find hers, and that seemed to shake him out of whatever odd place he had gone to. For a moment he seem horrified she was still beside him, then he winced. Minerva had no earthly idea if he was wincing because of her — or the situation.

"Good gracious, where are my manners?" He grabbed her hand and wrapped it around his arm, his hand resting on it possessively — or perhaps he was clinging to it desperately to prove a point? "Allow me to introduce you to my fiancée. Minerva, this is Mrs. Sarah Peters and her husband, Captain Peters. This is Miss Minerva . . ." He stared at her blankly as if he had forgotten the new alias he had given her.

"Landridge." She politely inclined her head as Payne had taught her to do with others of a similar rank. Curtsies were for nobles only. The more noble the noble, the deeper the curtsey. *Look them in the eye. Smile. Act nonchalant.* No mean feat when her mind was whirring. "I am delighted to make your acquaintance, Captain and Mrs. Peters."

Now the blond woman who had tied her fake fiancé's tongue was looking her up and down with interest, and for some reason everything about her, and most importantly the effect she had on Hugh, seemed to grate. Minerva snuggled closer to him as if she were besotted rather than inappropriately flustered by his shoulders and their oddly charged moment before this vixen interrupted it. "We have been engaged these past eighteen months." And she didn't care if she sounded proprietary. Fiancées were supposed to be possessive. It was merely part of the act.

"I must have missed the announcement in *The Times.*"

"There was no announcement." Finally Hugh seemed to have found his voice. "We've managed to keep it quiet. Minerva didn't want a fuss and she's not really one for London society. We met out of town when . . ." He was floundering again. Badly.

"He rescued me from a runaway carriage." She gazed up at him with what she hoped was adoration rather than what felt alarmingly like the sudden onset of jealousy. "And more recently an uncooperative sidesaddle." A mishap this graceful and beautiful creature had probably witnessed — alongside the wholly inappropriate and unguarded lapel smoothing. Although now that she thought Minerva was Hugh's fiancée, that was probably a good thing. Fiancées were allowed to smooth lapels, and she could use it as a believable excuse later if Hugh brought it up, a prospect that already had her toes curling inside her smart new riding boots. Minerva beamed to cover her mortification and tried to remember she was playing a character. "Hugh is my constant knight in shining armor. I would be thoroughly lost without him."

The awkward silence that followed was dreadful, largely because Minerva got the distinct impression she was the only person out of the four of them who had no idea why it was awkward.

Hugh's hand was gripping hers like a drowning man on a piece of driftwood in high seas. Captain Peters was yet to say a word, and his too-pretty wife had pasted a smile on her face that was as false as Minerva's lies.

"How is your mother, Hugh? Is she enjoying life in America?"

"Very much."

"It's so brave of her to have moved across the world."

"You know my mother." Something Mrs. Peters clearly did. "She is made of stern stuff." Beneath his sleeve, his forearm had gone quite rigid. Minerva could sense that he wanted to escape. Just as she could sense Hugh and the pretty Mrs. Peters had a past. One she fully intended to get to the bottom of once she got him alone.

"Well, it has been a pleasure meeting you both, but alas we must away." She squeezed his arm and felt some of the tension ease. "My mother, sisters, and Lord Bellingham are loose in the market and I fear for his sanity if we leave him alone with them for too long."

"Yes . . . poor Giles." Hugh bowed politely. "Do send my regards to your mother."

"And send mine to yours." A delicate, gloved hand lightly touched Minerva's arm. "It was lovely to meet you, too, Miss Landridge. I am *so* glad Hugh is finally settling down. Seeing as you are not fond of town, perhaps you can convince him to reside more frequently here in Hampshire? Then I could call upon you both . . ." Lovely blue eyes locked with Hugh's. Minerva couldn't read the stark message in them. "I believe I should like that a great deal."

# CHAPTER TEN

Hugh hated the past creeping up on him unawares. He hated more that it happened in front of Minerva. As they walked aimlessly around the market with the others, he had felt her eyes on him as all those distressing buried memories came unbidden to the fore.

He could still feel them on him, despite purposefully placing Vee on the chair between them in the inn's dining room and largely ignoring Minerva throughout the meal. Over a decade on, and it still hurt as much to see Sarah as it had that first time. Instantly, he was that heartbroken and floundering boy again. Lost and anchorless as his whole world and everything it was built on crumbled around him. He had smothered it with false politeness just as he always did, but Minerva wasn't stupid. She knew something had been amiss. He'd been on tenterhooks the entire meal hoping she didn't ask outright in front of everyone. What was the best way to explain away Sarah without admitting how much her very existence pained him? An hour on, and he was still at a loss.

Therefore, he decided to tactically avoid the questions. However, avoiding them was easier said than done when the group was ensconced in the inn's private dining room, where there were no other distractions to explain his uncharacteristic lack of conversation.

But there was no getting away from the fact her unexpected appearance had caught him completely off guard and had destroyed his good mood — a mood that had begun to deteriorate when Minerva started comparing him to his father, sending his thoughts scattering to all the dark places he avoided like the plague. That had been before she'd thrown herself in his arms, smoothed her palms over his chest, and sent his body hurtling into a different and entirely unwanted direction, too. Now his emotions were all over the place and much too close to the surface. So much so, he was barely keeping them in check.

"Are you sure you don't want some wine, ladies?" Giles held the bottle up, ready to pour. "It's very good."

"Neither I nor my girls would ever touch the *demon* drink, Lord Bellingham." Lucretia frowned when Diana held out her glass rebelliously, so instead, the mad actress turned to Vee. "Keep your elbows off the table, dear." She had been giving the girl motherly pointers all day and seemed oblivious to the youngest Merriwell's increasingly bubbling hostility. To her credit, Vee hadn't retaliated. She had ignored all the cloying fake mothering through gritted teeth while she still used all the wrong cutlery. "Tables are for plates not for elbows."

"The plates have been *cleared.*" If looks could kill, then Vee's was in danger of bludgeoning the actress to death.

Out of the corner of his eye, he saw Minerva's hand pat her sister's leg beneath the table, and reluctantly the elbows were removed. "Are you looking forward to the ride back, Vee? You looked like a natural horsewoman born in the saddle."

"Oh, she is!" said Lucretia, clutching her bosom dramatically. "It was poetry in motion." Vee blossomed at the compliment. "She takes after me on that score." Then fresh daggers shot out of the young girl's eyes. "I've always had a way with horses."

"Well, thankfully she doesn't take after me." Minerva was like a diplomat overseeing a tense treaty. "I think we can all agree my horsemanship was a disaster." Her eyes sought his for support. "As Hugh will attest, I couldn't get off or on without incident."

"True." Sensing she wanted more than a nod, he choked out the longest sentence he had managed in over an hour. "She practically flattened me on the dismount." His nose had been in her hair. She had smelled of roses. He had felt the soft press of her breasts against his rib cage. The sultry curve of her hips beneath his hands. Had almost succumbed and kissed her in the intoxicating heat of the moment. Was it any wonder he hadn't seen Sarah until it was too late to escape?

"I did warn you I was uncoordinated."

"If it's any consolation, what you lacked in coordination, you more than made up for in entertainment. Watching you in the paddock gave me my first thorough belly laugh of the morning." Giles toasted her with his tankard. "I'm devastated I missed the dismount. It sounds magnificent."

Hugh wasn't devastated. It was bad enough Minerva had had to witness the stilted meeting with Sarah. Thank goodness nobody else had. The very last thing he needed was Giles sticking his intuitive nose in and laying all his sordid past secrets bare.

"It will be better next time. I hope. Now that I know one needs to release the foot from the stirrup before vacating the saddle. Although I think my riding improved toward the end — before the catastrophic dismount."

Her eyes sought his again for affirmation, and Hugh nodded while struggling to smile. It felt false on his face. Damn Sarah for opening old wounds when he had enough on his plate already. "Much improved. By the end you showed genuine shoots of co-ordination."

"Only shoots?" Her mock despair made her youngest sister smile. "Oh dear. And I thought I was doing so well."

"It's a mystery why you are so uncoordinated, Minerva." Lucretia was fully immersed in Mrs. Landridge. Her eyes had gone predictably misty, signaling another heartfelt, fabricated recollection from the past she had created inside her theatrical, baffling, slightly scary mind. "Her father, God rest him, had a fine seat. We used to ride together every day when we were first married . . . before the children, of course . . ." Her hand sneaked across the table, grabbed Vee's. Squeezed. "I miss your dear papa so dreadfully! Why did he have to die?"

Vee's tenuous hold on her emotions finally collapsed, and she shot up like a firework, angry tears already leaking from her eyes and her chair falling noisily backward in the process. "He's not dead! Stop talking about him as if you knew him!" Her palms slammed down on the table, knocking over two thankfully empty cups, then she stormed out of the room.

"Vee!" Minerva was out of her seat just as fast. Then she, too, bolted, no doubt to placate her sullen sister yet again until the next immature tantrum exploded.

"Did I go too far?" Lucretia seemed stunned by the outburst.

"I think we galloped past *far* about an hour ago." Diana stood and tossed her napkin on the table. "I suppose I'd better go and support Minerva. She mollycoddles Vee far too much otherwise." She stomped out, leaving Hugh with his evil best friend and the contrite, blinking actress.

"Well, this is all going swimmingly." Giles toasted Hugh with his tankard again. "I predicted a total shambles and now my prediction has come true."

"Enough."

"But at least I am right and I do so love

164

to be right."

"Should I go and apologize, do you think?" The actress was wringing her hands.

"Well, it certainly couldn't hurt." His friend patted Lucretia's arm. "Although if I might be so bold, you might consider allowing *Lucretia* to do the apologizing and retire Mrs. Landridge for the rest of the day."

She nodded. "If you think that's best."

"I do. And on your way out, can you ask the maid to bring in some more of that cake? I'm still a little peckish." Giles waited for her to leave the room, then shuffled over a few chairs to sit in the one dead opposite. "I hate to labor my point, old boy, but you really do need to send Vee home. She's going to ruin everything before the best of the fun has started."

"I can't. There is nobody there to send her to."

"Then give her a maid, or hire the chit a governess if it makes you feel better, and dispatch her on a little *sojourn* to the coast for the duration. I'm sure she'll be delighted. She's in over her head, Hugh."

"I'll talk to Minerva."

"Yes. That's the answer. Ask Minerva's opinion and then suffer the inevitable consequences when she says no. Even Diana concedes she mollycoddles the girl too much." Giles paused and masked his frustration while the maid hurried in, bobbed a curtsey, and deposited a huge slice of cake in front of him. Only when she was gone did he resume. "Open your eyes, man! As much as it pains me to say it, with Minerva, Diana, and that bedlamite, Lucretia, there is the minutest chance you might just pull your ridiculous plan off. But currently Minerva is directing too much of her energy to placating the child. Vee seems to come first, last, and always in her eyes."

"She's practically her mother and has been since their useless father left them to fend for themselves five years ago!" Hugh was still angry about that, too.

"That's very noble of her and a dreadful travesty to be sure — but how exactly does that help you?"

"It doesn't."

"You employed Minerva to do a job, not rescue her and her family."

"I'm not rescuing anyone."

"Really? From where I'm standing, it seems as if Minerva has developed some sort of a hold on you which has diverted you from your purpose."

"What utter rot! I am neither rescuing Minerva nor infatuated by her." Although they had shared a moment just before Sarah ruined his day. A strange, charged, wonderful moment when she had looked into his eyes and he found himself drowning in hers. Happily drowning in hers. Surely that was only curiosity? And perhaps a healthy dose of lust?

"Did I mention anything about infatuation?"

Damn!

Before Giles had a field day with his friend's unfortunate choice of word, Hugh nipped it in the bud. "You insinuated it. Do not deny it. I can read you like a book."

"I am delighted to hear it. Actually falling for your fake fiancée would be an utter disaster — one that would only end in catastrophe. You are in grave danger, old boy, of starting to care about her feelings."

"Balderdash." Hugh brushed it away, trying to ignore the way Giles's warning set his mind reeling. "I am simply trying to keep everyone happy in order to get on with the job in hand. And clearly failing." Hugh felt his heart race, adding panic to the seething cauldron of uncomfortable emotions churning in his gut, because he *did* care about Minerva's feelings. "To be honest, I'm at my wits' end!"

"Then put your foot down!" His friend took a huge bite of cake and waved his fork at Hugh. "Sometimes you are too nice for your own good."

*"Nice?"* That was almost as bad as "infatuated."

"Yes. Nice. That's why you have reached the end of your tether." The fork wafted in the air. Hugh considered snatching it out of his hand and stabbing it into Giles's forehead. "You spend far too much time pussyfooting around others rather than putting them in their place. Which ironically is what got you into this ridiculous predicament in the first place. You should have told your mother to stop interfering in your life . . . but, *no!* You created a convoluted buffer to avoid the confrontation. You'd be a fool to avoid it this time. Stop allowing Minerva to pander to Vee. Demand your money's worth! I'm sure you can do it subtly if that's more palatable to your namby-pamby sensibilities. You're a charming fellow and a rich one. Engage a chaperone for the chit and send the pair of them to stay in your house in Mayfair. Vee will be safely supervised in one of Berkeley Square's finest houses, Minerva will be placated and able to focus solely on the role of your fiancée, and if the gods are in your favor, a miracle will occur and your mother will sail back to Boston none the wiser."

As a plan, it made sense. Miss Venus Merriwell was the weakest link. And he wanted to punch Giles in his annoyingly smug face for being right again. "How can you eat more cake now?"

"I'm starving." The fork jabbed again. "But cease trying to change the subject, because I will not allow it. Vee's emotions are too close to the surface and her efforts at pretending to be a lady fall woefully short."

"I know."

"Then the time for avoidance is done. You are master of this house. Be masterful, Hugh! You know I'm right."

"I know!" Yet it didn't make him want to pummel his irritating friend any less.

"Splendid." The last piece of cake disappeared into Giles's mouth. "I'll ride on ahead with the girls and Loony Lucretia and you find a way to hang back with Minerva."

"That shouldn't be a problem. She really is useless on a horse." Another thing he was irrationally furious about. Who couldn't sit on a blasted horse, for pity's sake?

Some sort of truce had occurred by the time they rejoined the ladies in the stable yard. Lucretia was standing awkwardly on the opposite side of the cobbles with Diana, while

Minerva and Vee sat together on a bench. It was obvious the youngest Merriwell had been crying, but once again her sister had managed to placate her, judging by her overbright smile as he and Giles approached. She nudged Vee, who looked miserably up at Hugh with watery eyes. "I apologize, Lord Fareham. I overreacted."

"Apology accepted." Despite his own black mood, he still felt sorry for the girl. He remembered that age only too well. It had been a horrible, confusing time filled with pimples, and he had only suffered through the traumatic loss of one parent, not both of them. "You'll feel better after a good gallop across the fields." As would he. Not that he could, thanks to her vexing older sister and the awkward conversation that couldn't be put off any longer.

He avoided Minerva while the horses were brought around.

Much as he loathed Giles's being right, Hugh needed to take charge. He needed to be resolute in what *he* wanted because this was *his* foolhardy plan, and he couldn't allow the delicate feelings of a child to destroy it. This was a business transaction, plain and simple, and he was paying Minerva to give it her full attention. He would put his foot down if the need arose. Stop being so *nice*

— what an insultingly insipid word! — and cease all carnal thoughts that clouded his mind and muddied the water. And he needed to put all the tangled feelings churned up by Sarah back in the dusty corner of his mind.

Having a plan and executing it were two different things, and as they set off toward the house, Minerva naturally lagged behind Hugh, who rode a little ahead of her because his control on his temper was hanging by a thread and not all of that was her fault. But every time he turned back and had to slow his horse for her to catch up, his temper simmered more. Even Galileo was becoming annoyed at the sedentary pace and, like Hugh, wanted his legs. Hugh went around a bend, looked over his shoulder, and then had to stop yet again when she wasn't there. As the seconds ticked by and there was still no sight of her, he had no choice other than to turn Galileo around and angrily retrace his steps.

"What the blazes are you doing?"

She was stationary, hanging at an odd angle from the saddle, yanking at her skirts, which had wrapped themselves around her legs. "I'm getting down!" She glared at him, her face scowling. "I've had enough! I hate riding! I told you I'd be useless at it, yet

171

you forced me to do it regardless! And then you galloped off!"

"Galloped? The chance would have been a fine thing."

"Trotting then! Or cantering! All I know is it was at a pace significantly quicker than you promised!" The heavy burgundy velvet finally gave way, giving him a very unwelcome show of her silk-clad legs all the way to the knees as she awkwardly slithered down to the ground and glared again. "I'll walk Marigold back and then I'll never sit on a stupid horse again!" With exaggerated haughtiness, she marched to the front of the horse and grabbed the reins, then shooed him away with one imperious gloved hand. "Go! And while gone, you can use that vivid imagination of yours to conjure up a good reason why *Miss Landridge* regrets she is unable to ride when your mother asks!"

It was the shooing that ultimately did it, sending all the morning's frustrations careening out of his mouth in one sarcastic snarl. "*Miss Landridge* is unable to ride because she doesn't listen to a damn word I've said! You sit on the poor horse as stiff as a board, choke the poor thing on the bit, and then expect it to walk along compliantly at the speed of a snail! *Poor* Marigold is bored senseless!"

"Don't take your bad mood out on me!"

"Why not? You're the one responsible for it!"

"How dare you!" She had the nerve to look down her nose at him. No mean feat when he still sat on Galileo and a good six feet off the ground. "I've been nothing but pleasant to you all day, despite your having a face like thunder throughout luncheon." Then off she went. Nose in the air, distracting hips swaying as she stomped, the very picture of outraged self-righteousness.

"And that was your fault, too!" Because looming over her didn't feel right even when he was rightly fuming, he jumped off his horse and trailed after her.

"Oh yes! Of course it was! It had absolutely nothing to do with *Mrs.* Sarah Peters, did it?" Minerva turned to wag her finger. "Just admit it! You've been in a sulk since we collided with her in the square." Her hands went to her hips as they stood, now practically toe to toe. "And it hasn't escaped my notice you were absolutely no help during that nonsense over dinner. That actress is a menace!"

"At least *that* actress is doing exactly what I'm paying her for!"

"Surely you are not suggesting I haven't?

On what grounds?" For a woman who had no idea if she possessed any blue blood at all, she displayed indignation like a snooty duchess. "I have done absolutely everything you've asked. *Absolutely. Everything.* Why, I even sat on this stupid horse when I expressly told you I had no talent for it." She shooed him again and stuck her self-righteous nose back in the air. "How *dare* you!"

"Oh I dare, Minerva!" The lid finally exploded off the seething cauldron of emotions, and they all spewed out in a rush. "You and your bloody family have pushed me to the very edge of my patience and I'm done with it!"

"Don't bring my sisters into this . . ."

"Why not? You did. In fact, you insisted upon bringing them and I have been nothing but patient with the pair of them. Diana is rude, convinced I am a debaucher, and cannot keep her big mouth shut, and Vee is a petulant child who frankly cannot cope with any of what I expect her to do!"

"Vee's outburst had nothing to do with coping and everything to do with Lucretia! The woman is mad! All her bosom clutching and expostulating. *Oh my dear husband.*" She clutched her own bosom with one hand, dragging his eyes there before the back of her other hand went to her forehead. But the damage was done, and the unwanted lust reared its ugly head again. *"Why, oh, why did he have to die?"* Then as if she had made her point, she dispassionately shrugged. "Get rid of her, Hugh. She's spoiling everything."

"Actually — it's Vee I'm getting rid of." Her mouth fell open. "She's the one spoiling everything and it *cannot* continue."

"I beg your pardon?"

"I shall assign her a responsible maid as a chaperone, and she can sit out my mother's impending visit in my house in Mayfair, where she cannot cause any more trouble!" Hugh ignored the urge to stamp his foot. "In fact, she can leave tonight."

"Over my dead body!"

"Oh, be reasonable! She's a child and she's taking up far too much of everyone's time. Especially yours. When I agreed you could bring your sisters to Hampshire, you made no mention of the fact she is so young or so . . ." Was "whiny and irritating" too harsh? "Needy."

"She is seventeen!"

"She can't even master cutlery, for pity's sake. She wanders around looking permanently startled and overwhelmed, and then rewards us with regular bursts of histrionics when anyone dares mention a parent of any sort — even a fictional one! And you" — his own finger had started to wag of its own accord — "indulge her every whim. The cutlery debacle yesterday is a case in point! You mastered a table setting in under five minutes on the first day. So did Diana. But because poor, sensitive Vee didn't know her soup spoon from the carving knife, *you* made Payne waste a blasted hour teaching her *again* while all she achieved was a giant soup stain on the tablecloth!"

Haughty disdain was replaced with wounded dismissal. "She will improve. . . . I will help her."

"I am not paying you to help *her,* Minerva. I am paying you a very generous fee to help *me!*"

"That is very mercenary!"

"Mercenary be damned! You seem to have conveniently forgotten I am paying you to do a job and I deserve my money's worth. From now on, I insist you give that task your single and undivided attention until the job is done. *That* is what we agreed."

"If Vee goes, then so will I. On Saturday. As we *also* agreed."

"If you think I'm paying you twenty pounds because you deign to stay till Saturday on sufferance like a martyr — think again. It's Friday and by *childishly* stating your intentions to leave a day before you actually do, *you* have rendered our bargain null and void. If you choose to renege on our bargain, I won't pay you a single penny! How's that for mercenary!"

It was Hugh's turn to spin on his heel and storm off. He'd said his piece. Perhaps not quite how he had intended — he wasn't particularly proud of himself and hated the fact he'd had to hurt her feelings in the process — but it was said, and that was the end of it.

Mercenary! This wasn't charity, this was business! He grabbed Galileo's reins and was about to haul himself back onto his horse when he suddenly stopped. He could hardly ride away and leave her walking all alone, no matter how furious he was. His blasted good manners were too ingrained and his conscience too sensitive. Nor was there a cat's chance in hell he was going to hoist the vixen back into her own saddle. He didn't need the reminder of the smell of her perfume or the feel of her womanly hips, and he certainly didn't need all the nonsense from his errant body that went along with them. He was done with the blasted *hold* she had on him. Instead, he tugged his horse to follow him as his legs ate up the ground between her and his house.

Unfortunately, thanks to her wonderful, shapely long legs that he wished he hadn't seen and couldn't seem to get out of his mind, she managed to catch up with him as he approached the stable, grabbing his sleeve and hauling him to face her with a strength that surprised him. And she didn't look the slightest bit contrite either, damn her.

Her jaw was set. Her green eyes had hardened to emeralds. The feather on the silly little hat perched on her irritating dark head quivered with indignation.

"Keep your stupid money! And I wish you good luck! Although frankly, if you think Vee behaves like a petulant child, you should take a good look in the mirror. What sort of a man invents a fiancée because he finds responsibility too daunting and is frightened of his own mother!"

# CHAPTER ELEVEN

Insufferable man! There really was no depth to him, just as he'd repeatedly said, but Minerva had tried to convince herself there was, despite knowing he was bound to be exactly like every other man she had met. Probably because crediting him with some substance made her feel better about agreeing to his ridiculous proposal in the first place and justified the unwelcome effect he had on her pulse. He was selfish and shallow and heartless. As mercenary a scoundrel as she had ever met! No better than her father and no better than that lily-livered coward of a sweetheart she had given her foolish tender heart to! Men inevitably put their needs first, last, and always.

As if she would countenance him dispatching her baby sister back to the capital with a complete stranger! When she knew poor Vee was simply suffering from nerves — as seventeen-year-old girls were prone to do. Nerves that she would conquer, because despite Hugh's lowly opinion of her, Vee possessed the same grit, fortitude, and stubborn determination as all the Merriwell sisters. Life hadn't given them a choice to be otherwise. Not that he was capable of comprehending any of that either. As if he would last five minutes on his own in Clerkenwell!

She slammed the back door hard as she charged through, not caring if it knocked his perfectly straight, perfectly white, perfectly superficial teeth out. As much as she needed his money, Minerva was too furious to regret telling him to go to hell. No doubt remorse would come soon enough, although hell would have to freeze over before she allowed him to see how much his twenty miserable pounds meant to her.

"Thank heavens you're back!" Payne appeared in front of her, blocking her path. His harried eyes flicked over her shoulder to where his wastrel, disappointing master was rapidly bringing up the rear. "Your mother is here."

"But she can't be!" Hugh came alongside, taking up more of the hallway than was necessary. Further proof if proof were needed he was intrinsically selfish. "She can't possibly be here for at least a week."

"Well, I can assure you she is, my lord. And what is worse, she is currently ensconced in the drawing room with a fresh pot of tea, her husband, Lord Bellingham, the actress, and the younger Misses Merriwell."

She felt Hugh deflate beside her as her own stomach dropped to her toes. "Bloody hell."

"Bloody hell indeed, my lord. As I greeted your mother at the front door, everyone else came through the back and they met in the middle. There was absolutely nothing I could do to prevent it."

Out of the corner of her eyes, she saw Hugh rake his hand through his hair as he frantically looked toward her, and quashed the charitable urge to feel sorry for him. He had every bit of this coming, and she would enjoy watching it. She was done with being such a soft touch. "I'm doomed."

"Not necessarily, my lord. While I will admit she seemed shocked to see them, once Lord Bellingham had concluded the introductions, she appeared delighted. From what I have witnessed in the half an hour since, they are all having a perfectly lovely visit. Minerva's *mother* is currently recounting what happened to Mr. Landridge in the Cairngorms and your own mother is on the edge of her seat, thoroughly engrossed in the tale. However, I do recommend you make haste in case Mrs. DeVere gets *too* carried away." Payne grabbed Hugh and pushed him forward. "The sooner she sees you, the sooner we can send everyone to their rooms to rest and change for dinner."

Minerva trailed after them, her mind reeling, and her heart beating too fast in her chest. She felt sick, scared, panicked — obviously still incensed at the selfish, shallow, mercenary clod Hugh — but beneath all that was the unmistakable glimmer of hope. She could still earn her forty pounds and not have to dispatch Vee in the process. When Hugh stopped dead, she almost slammed into the back of him.

"I can't. Not yet. I need to think . . ." But it was too late.

"Hugh?" An older woman turned the corner and beamed. "My darling!"

Arms outstretched, she rushed toward him and hugged him tight. Whatever Minerva had imagined his mother to look like, this petite, pretty, surprisingly young woman was not it. She barely reached Hugh's chest.

"Are you surprised to see me?"

All color had drained from his face. "Very . . . I didn't expect you for at least a fortnight."

"We got an earlier crossing at the last minute, by which time it was pointless writing to you about it." Her deep blue eyes, so like her vexing son's, peeked around the shielding wall of his big, vexing body and took in Minerva with barely disguised curiosity.

In that moment, she realized one very pertinent thing. Hugh's mother was as surprised to see Minerva as he was her. Which suggested she hadn't believed he had a fiancée and was here to put an end to all his nonsense. "And this must be Minerva?"

Hugh turned, his expression uncertain, obviously waiting for her to decide his fate. He knew she could destroy him in one fell swoop. He also knew only she had the power to save him. The boot was now firmly on the other foot, and this boot had no leaky holes in the sole.

Power . . .

What a triumphant, heady feeling.

One she had never had cause to experience before. No wonder the rich enjoyed it. "Indeed I am, my lady." Minerva stepped forward and bobbed a surprisingly graceful curtsey. "It is so wonderful to meet you." She was oddly proud of her ambiguous and noncommittal answer. Some devil inside her had taken over, and she realized she would rather enjoy making Hugh sweat.

The older woman took her hands, holding them tightly as she examined her from top to bottom, smiling. "I must say, you are not at all what I pictured. Hugh neglected to mention you were tall or dark haired. He did, however, describe one thing correctly. You are inordinately beautiful . . . and from his letters, come across as eminently sensible. Which beggars the obvious question." Those wily eyes flicked back to her son for a second before twinkling back at Minerva. "What on earth do you see in Hugh?"

"What an excellent question." She could tell he was holding his breath, could tell he was willing her to rescue him. If she did, it wouldn't be to save his sorry skin. "When I first met him, I suspected he had hidden depths."

"And now?"

"Now . . ." Minerva allowed her gaze to settle on Hugh, allowed several painfully loaded seconds to tick by as she smiled at him. "Now, I know with absolute certainty my initial assumption was" — she threaded her arm around his and stared up at him with adoration, secure in the knowledge the forty glorious pounds were now hers — "absolutely correct."

His hand came up to cover hers where it

rested in the crook of his elbow, and he squeezed his thanks. She wanted to snatch it away and stamp on his foot, but she didn't. "I take it you have already met my family, my lady? I am devastated I couldn't be there to facilitate the proper introductions."

"We managed well enough without you, dear. What a charming bunch they are. And your sisters — so like you. I see that now. You must all get your height and distinctive coloring from your father."

Annoyed by the way his touch still had the power to lay siege to her nerve endings, Minerva untangled herself from Lord Selfish and took his mother's arm instead as they started toward the drawing room.

"Indeed we do, ma'am. He was tall like Hugh." The truth. "And we all have his eyes."

While Vee was a tad wooden throughout most of the tea, she was performing admirably. Even when their effusive fake mother went on and on about the loss of their father, Vee endured it all stoically, giving Minerva a smug sense of satisfaction. Although in fairness to Lucretia, she dominated so much of the conversation with her impassioned monologues, the rest of them were spared. Even Diana was behaving — or almost behaving. But thankfully, as most of her pithy interjections were directed at Lord Bellingham, who more than held his own, their dialogue was more entertaining than jarring, and Hugh's mother and her delightful husband, Mr. Peabody, laughed and seemed vastly relieved throughout.

Minerva repeatedly felt Hugh's eyes on her but ignored them, knowing if she didn't, hers would only shoot daggers at him and make his mother suspicious. There would be plenty of time to allow those daggers to fly later, and she would let him feel the full force of each and every blade. He deserved nothing less. But for now, she was being the perfect Minerva he was paying for. She wouldn't give him the satisfaction of questioning either her effort or his dratted value for money.

It wasn't only the weight of Hugh's stare she could feel across the room. His mother was doing her fair share of staring, too. Understandably, she supposed, as Miss Minerva Landridge had been an enigma for the past eighteen months, and if she were in the other woman's shoes, she would have plenty of questions.

"Are you looking forward to being mistress of Standish House, Minerva?" His mother stared over the rim of her teacup.

"More daunted at the moment, my lady." She reasoned the more she stuck to the truth, the better. "I am not used to anywhere near so grand or so vast. In the absence of a map, I still have to rely heavily on the servants to navigate myself around it."

"I felt the same way when I came here as a young bride. It took about a year, as I recall, before I felt I knew the whole house and the grounds sufficiently to not get lost. Although getting lost in the gardens was no chore. I've always loved them."

"They are lovely." After living in a grotty corner of London, all of Hampshire seemed beautiful. "I have made a start of exploring the grounds on my afternoon walks." The only time she could snatch for herself during the busy lesson-packed days, thanks to the lord and master. "I found the folly yesterday quite by accident because I had taken the wrong path."

"Have you seen the cave yet?"

"You have a cave?"

"We do indeed — but alas, the hermit who used to live in it is gone. Gruff Godfrey . . . Do you remember him, Hugh?"

"I do. He had a pointed hat and the longest beard I've ever seen." She could sense him daring her to look at him and was only too happy to ignore the plea. It was about time Hugh learned the world didn't revolve around him.

"I never understood why he was called 'gruff.' I rather liked him and always found him very pleasant. But alas . . ." Hugh's mother sighed, her face a picture of regret. "Lord Tiverton, the wretch, pilfered him in the summer of '96."

"He was stolen?" What sort of monster stole another human being? "That's dreadful."

"She means he was lured away, Minerva. Lord Tiverton doubled his wages." Hugh smiled kindly when she had no other choice but to look at him or appear horrendously rude. "Having a hermit in your garden was all the rage back then." She realized then and there she would never understand the aristocracy. Her world and theirs were just too different.

"It was hardly a passing fad, darling. I'll have you know some of my friends still have their hermits to this day and wouldn't be without them. But Hugh's father thought having a hermitage was an unnecessary extravagance, as does his son, so now it is just a cave — although a very pretty place to wander to when you need a little fresh air. Do you walk *every* afternoon, Minerva?"

"I confess I am not very good at resting after luncheon and I do so enjoy the fresh air."

"A rest sounds wonderful, doesn't it, Mother? You and Jeremiah must be exhausted after your long journey. A good nap and perhaps a nice long bath is exactly what you need. I am sure Payne will have your rooms ready by now. We'll serve dinner late."

"That does sound good." Mr. Peabody's American accent was like nothing she had ever heard, but Minerva liked it immensely. His mouth seemed to draw out the vowels and soften the consonants. "Nearly three hours in that carriage has certainly rattled these old bones." He couldn't be much more than fifty and was still a handsome man, very much in his prime.

"Then I'll have Payne draw your baths immediately." Hugh gestured to the butler. "Two hot baths. Quick sharp."

"If I didn't know better, I would say you are trying to get rid of us, Hugh darling." His mother made a point of leaning forward and pouring herself more tea before settling back in her chair. "Why don't you tell me about the day you first met my son, Minerva? Hugh said for him it was love at first sight."

"Well, I am ashamed to confess, it wasn't

for me." She might as well have a bit of fun at his expense. It would make suffering his presence until this charade was over much more bearable, and Hugh wasn't the only one who could embellish. Minerva was an artist — albeit in a very tenuous way — and embellishment was an artist's stock-in-trade. "It took a little while for Hugh to grow on me."

"Really?"

"Really." She did her best to look troubled. "I read the papers, you see, and as I am sure you are only too aware, my lady, they hinted at such a . . . *dubious* reputation."

"Dubious? What a wonderfully polite way of putting it, Minerva. You do not need to sugar the lemon for me, my dear. Let us always be honest with each other and call foul where necessary." Hugh's mother rolled her eyes before skewering her son with her stare. "I am well aware of what they printed and am only relieved they didn't print the half of it. He was a *complete* scandal, Minerva. A complete scandal . . . although not as bad as Giles, of course."

"I should think not." Lord Bellingham took mock offense at the suggestion. "Nobody is more of a scandal than me. I am the dictionary definition of the word 'scandal.' Just ask my father . . ." He winked at Hugh's mother, who couldn't completely hide her smile. "Could somebody pass me the biscuits? If Minerva is about to launch into the gripping story of the day they met, I shall need sustenance to survive it."

"I love this story, too." Like Lord Bellingham, Diana was enjoying herself far too much. She smiled at her partner in crime and helped herself to one of the biscuits on the plate he now cradled. "It is *so* romantic." Minerva was going to strangle the Judas as soon as she got her alone.

"Well, after we met, he called upon me . . ."

"Oh, don't start it there!" Hugh's mother seemed crestfallen. "I want to hear the whole thing from your perspective, especially now I know my son's version of events cannot be entirely trusted. Let us not forget he told me you fell in love with him the second you saw him. If he got *that* pertinent detail wrong, heaven only knows what else he has. I think we should start with the carriage, don't you? The one my son apparently rescued you from."

"Yes . . . of course . . ."

Hugh came to her aid. "It was a high-perch phaeton. Your father's . . . in Chipping Norton." His mother glared at him with narrowed eyes.

"I asked Minerva to tell me the story, Hugh — or am I to assume she doesn't know it?"

"I had taken my father's phaeton against his knowledge and, as it turned out, against my woeful skill at driving it. I was going down the lane a tad too fast and something spooked the horses . . ."

"What spooked them?"

Hugh had neglected to tell her that bit. "I am not entirely sure. It could have been anything. Horses are difficult creatures at the best of times. All I can say for certain is they went off like a shot and there was nothing I could do to stop them. I dropped one of the . . . er" —What was the stupid word? — "*ribbons*. . . . While I was scrambling about trying to reach them, the carriage started to rock quite alarmingly on its axle. As it hurtled toward a dense copse of trees, I thought I was done for, then out of nowhere appeared Hugh on the back of Galileo . . ." A nice believable detail she was quite proud of. "He galloped alongside and tried valiantly to grab the ribbons himself. When that didn't work, he leapt into the carriage."

"From a speeding horse? About to career into a dense copse of trees?"

"It was quite a feat of derring-do. Very

heroic . . ." And Minerva was in danger of over-egging it and losing her audience. "But thankfully, he managed to grab them and then he wrestled the horses to a stop in the nick of time. My very own knight in shining armor." A comment that would be laughable if it wasn't so tragic. That it hurt was her own stupid fault. She knew better than to expect anything from a man. Knew, too, her taste in them couldn't be trusted. Once again she had had her foolish head turned by a fine pair of shoulders and a twinkling pair of eyes, and worst of all, she couldn't really blame Hugh for being like all the rest of them, because he had warned her what he was.

Repeatedly.

She took a fortifying sip of her tea, both to calm her bouncing nerves and to avoid huffing in frustration at her own stupidity, then smiled at Hugh, hoping she appeared sincere rather than fuming. "And that, as they say, was that."

"But I thought you just said it wasn't love at first sight?" There were obviously no flies on Hugh's mother.

"It wasn't." How on earth did Hugh keep track of all his lies, when Minerva was already struggling? Because he was shallow and selfish, the wretch, and she had substance. Or at least she did — before she had stupidly allowed him to mine through her defenses! The false smile began to slip, so she ruthlessly nailed it back in place. There were forty pounds up for grabs, and there would be time aplenty to castigate herself for the mistake later. "After he stopped the carriage, he escorted me home, and unbeknownst to me, asked my father's permission to call upon me again before he left Chipping Norton."

Hugh's mother sipped her own tea a little too casually for Minerva's liking, then turned to her son. "You never did explain how you came to be in Chipping Norton in the first place, dear."

"Oh yes I did, as well you know it. You just want to see if Minerva knows all the gory details." He took a sip of his own tea, his even stare never leaving his mother's. "But Minerva *does* know all the gory details. There are no secrets between us. She knows I was at a questionable house party in Long Hanborough hosted by Lord Ashby."

The older woman turned her nose up. "I have always disapproved of Lord Ashby. I especially disapprove of his questionable house parties."

"Which is exactly why I always went to

them. And it was a jolly good thing I did, too, else I never would have met Minerva and fallen instantly in love — and would probably still be at a highly questionable house party as we speak."

"How long did it take for Cupid's arrow to strike you, Minerva?"

Hugh had said they were inseparable immediately, but it suddenly galled her he never had to work for anything. Life came too easily to undeserving men like him.

"Several visits over many, *many* weeks." She took another sip of her tea and smiled winsomely over the rim as if remembering it all fondly. "He even proposed before I agreed to allow him to court me."

"He did?"

"Indeed. Twice." She held up two fingers. "I turned him down on both occasions." She had the satisfaction of seeing his normally twinkling eyes narrow. "I didn't want to rush into something I might *bitterly* regret afterward. Marry in haste and all that . . . and I needed to be sure he wasn't the man I read about in the scandal sheets. I knew I could never love — or even particularly like — a bounder that . . . *mercenary.*"

"What a sensible girl you are, Minerva." Hugh's mother seemed impressed. "Most young ladies would have jumped at the chance of being a countess. In fact, I'll wager they wouldn't have looked past his title."

"Perhaps they wouldn't — but wealth and status alone have never been enough to impress me. I believe in judging a man by his measure rather than the size of his purse." And like every other man who had disappointed her, Hugh now fell woefully short.

"I raised all my daughters with a strong moral code." Lucretia nodded sagely, shamelessly taking the credit for Minerva's pragmatic restraint. "I always told them never to settle for anything less than the very deepest, most abiding, all-consuming love. The sort I shared with their father . . ." Her voice caught, and her eyes clouded convincingly. Minerva had to give her that. "God rest him . . ."

"Well, anyway." Unchecked, they'd have to suffer through another one of the actress's emotional monologues, and they had suffered through at least three already. There was only so much Vee could take, and it would be prudent not to test her limits after what happened at the inn. "After he rescued me so selflessly, then *diligently* courted me despite my blatant indifference, Hugh gradually wore down my justified reservations and I began to see his true worth."

That made him sound almost noble, drat it. "The poor thing was quite desperate by the time he proposed for the third time. He was so persistent and *so* hopeful I came to realize he truly did love me if he was prepared to put himself through endless torture simply to win me, and I came to believe he did intend to change his selfish ways."

"And thanks entirely to you, he turned over a new leaf." Hugh's mother sighed and nodded, then beamed at her son. "How very romantic."

That little devil inside her couldn't resist one final dig. "Besides, I couldn't bring myself to turn him down again, could I? He was so besotted, I firmly believe another rejection would have crushed him."

"Oh, it would have!" She found an unlikely ally in Lord Bellingham. "He couldn't eat, couldn't sleep. Could barely function in those dark days after Minerva refused his second proposal. It was tragic to watch. But I told him — Hugh, old boy, nothing good comes without hard work. *Prostrate* yourself on the altar of remorse and *beg* that girl to take a chance on you."

"Hugh begged?"

"On bended knees." Minerva smiled at

him then. "His voice choked with emotion . . ."

Payne reappeared and coughed politely, spoiling her fun. "The hot baths are ready, my lord. I took the liberty of having the maids draw one for *everyone.*"

"Excellent." Hugh sprung to his feet, no doubt grateful his time in the pillory was at an end. "Excellent!"

Everyone, barring his mother, also stood.

"Go." She shooed them all with a flick of her wrist. "I shall have my maid draw me a fresh bath later. For now, I think I need fresh air, so I shall take a little turn about the garden. And as Minerva isn't one for relaxing in the afternoons either, perhaps she will join me. *Just* the *two* of us." Her gaze shifted quickly to her son as if gauging his reaction. "I can show you the cave I was telling you about and we can have a proper chat. I should like to get to know my future daughter-in-law better." Canny blue eyes so like Hugh's regarded her steadily. There was an undeniable challenge there. One she couldn't escape without arousing suspicion. "I believe there is much I still need to know."

"That would be lovely." Minerva knew it wasn't going to be. She wouldn't be able to drop her guard for a second.

"You have interrogated the poor girl enough for one afternoon, Olivia. There'll be plenty of time for walking tomorrow and I daresay Miss Minerva needs a good lie-down after all your questions." Mr. Peabody winked at her.

"I am a *bit* tired."

"Then that settles it! I am going to enjoy grabbing an afternoon nap. After weeks on that boat, I'm looking forward to stretching out on a proper bed. Those bunks aren't made for men like me."

Like Hugh, he was tall, but that was where the similarities ended. Jeremiah Peabody had jet-black hair threaded with a little silver, and dark, laughing eyes. Almost as if he found everything about life — or perhaps this particular situation — vastly amusing. He took his reluctant wife's arm and tugged her toward the door. "And to that end, we shall bid you a pleasant afternoon and look forward to seeing you again at dinner."

"By which time, I shall have thought of a million questions, I'm sure." And with that, she sailed out, closely followed by everyone else, leaving just Hugh and Minerva. He waited till they were all out of earshot before he dared speak.

"Thank you for . . ."

"My fee just went up to sixty pounds."

The unplanned words tumbled out of her mouth. Clearly having some power had gone to her head.

"I'm sorry?"

"You heard me. Sixty pounds and I will have the first thirty pounds by tomorrow morning. There will also be no more talk of dispatching Vee — or we leave as planned first thing."

As his mouth hung slack, she sailed out of the room herself, not quite believing what she had just done but feeling oddly proud. Did that make her mercenary? Probably. And a tad vengeful. But in view of Hugh's disappointing shallowness, she decided not to allow it to bother her.

# CHAPTER TWELVE

Hugh was sick and tired of pacing the floor of his study. He'd paced it all afternoon because the minx only emerged from her bedchamber for dinner, predictably flanked by her annoying sisters and refusing to leave either of their sides or his mother's afterward, to enable him to speak to her alone. The only communication had been the pointed glares she shot in his direction when she was certain nobody was looking, and those were so cold, they left no element of doubt as to the way she was feeling.

Minerva was seething.

Whereas Hugh's anger had abandoned him when raw, visceral panic had taken its place upon learning his mother had arrived home early. Panic that his now-renegade fake fiancée seemed intent on cruelly fueling. Just as she had enjoyed twisting the carefully constructed backstory he had woven for nearly two years to make him a laughingstock in his own damn house! The way Minerva told it, Hugh had been a pathetic and ardent suitor from the outset. One she had been training to be a better man since. Silly Hugh. Unreliable Hugh. Self-centered and self-important . . . Thank goodness she had come along at the right time to fix all his myriad of faults before they became so ingrained, he was a lost cause.

His mother, of course, lapped it all up because Minerva was purposefully echoing all the things she had nagged him about for years. No doubt simply to torture him, she had just gone to bed on his mother's arm, too, the pair of them gossiping like fast friends.

Meanwhile, Hugh was being left in the dark, forced to watch his meticulously orchestrated charade play out from the stalls rather than from the center of the stage, and he didn't like it one bit. After their altercation this afternoon, the new Mercenary Minerva might well be royally stabbing him in the back — yet while she was being guarded by her loyal coven, he had no possible way of finding out.

It was all a huge mess, one that was making him so anxious he couldn't concentrate on anything else.

Payne scratched on the door and let himself in, still plainly carrying the note he had sent to Minerva in an attempt to call a desperate truce to the hostilities.

"She refused to take it, my lord. She told me to tell you she still wasn't speaking to you, which, she argued, included reading anything you have written."

"Blasted woman! What does she think she is playing at?"

Payne simply shrugged, his expression deadpan.

"Do you think I am in the wrong?"

"I think the version of events you gave me is a bit different to the one Miss Minerva just apprised me of. In your version, you neglected to mention you were in high dudgeon well *before* your altercation with her."

Of course she would have told him about Sarah, although Payne would have the good sense never to mention her directly. "I confess, I was in the highest of dudgeons after her sister threw another tantrum." There was no denying Hugh hadn't been himself when he had embarked on his necessary conversation with Minerva. "Vee would try the patience of a saint."

"And you, my lord, were of course an angel."

"I lost my temper, Payne, as anyone would when faced with unreasonableness."

"Miss Minerva said you galloped off and almost caused her to fall from her horse, when you knew perfectly well she was a novice rider and lacked the confidence to cope well with that speed."

"It was barely a trot."

"She also called you a selfish, shallow brute."

*"Brute?"*

"The lady's exact words, my lord, and you will be pleased to know I challenged her comments."

"Thank you, Payne. . . . I am a lot of things, but a 'selfish, shallow *brute*' isn't one of them."

"Indeed, my lord. I said to her, 'Selfish and shallow I will grant you, because he is both in spades, but I have never known His Lordship to be brutish. Such a trait would take far too much effort.' " The butler smiled at Hugh's narrowed eyes and dropped the note on Hugh's desk. "If I might be so bold as to offer some advice, my lord."

"As if I could stop you."

"You had a tiff and are both still too aggrieved to be reasonable. Therefore, I suggest you both sleep on it and then discuss it in the morning. Rested, I am sure she will be in a much better frame of mind and more receptive to your apology."

"I am not apologizing!"

"For a man who has such success with the ladies, it always surprises me how little you know about them." Payne turned to leave.

"*Et tu, Brute!* You *do* think I am in the wrong."

"In all honesty, my lord, you are both stubborn people. It is frankly a miracle you haven't fallen out before today. Until now, you have both displayed impressive restraint and an admirable facility to compromise. I am strangely proud of you. But you are the man and therefore you must be the one to apologize. That is the law."

"Which law?"

"The law of women, my lord. Believe me, as all married men will doubtless readily attest, your life will be much easier if you throw yourself willingly on your sword. Or do you wish to spend all of tomorrow frozen out of the proceedings, too? I am afraid in this particular situation, you need Miss Minerva much more than she needs you. Best to keep her on your side, don't you agree?"

His smirking butler bid him a good-night,

then left Hugh to ponder. It was true, the wench had him over a barrel. He was still smarting at her demand for more money. It wasn't so much the money he had a problem with, because he had plenty of that, it was more the manner in which she presented him with the ultimatum. She had wanted to put him in his place, and by Jove she had. Then she had thrown him in purgatory and seemed only too delighted to leave him to languish there for the duration. As much as it pained Hugh to admit it, perhaps Payne was right about one thing. There was nothing he could do about it tonight. Better to tackle it with fresh eyes and hopefully a more conciliatory mood tomorrow.

Defeated, he took himself up to bed and dismissed his valet. He was done with feigning politeness when all he really wanted to do was kick the furniture around. But instead of shattering his toes on the unforgiving old oak bedstead, he settled for balling up his waistcoat and cravat and furiously tossing them at the wall before he took a deep breath, tugged off his boots, and stretched out on top of the covers to ponder some more.

This really wasn't how he wanted his dealings with Minerva to end. In light of his mother's impromptu arrival, he and Giles had already deemed it necessary to bring the elopement forward, too. She and Giles would flee tomorrow night. It seemed the most prudent way of limiting the potential catastrophe and, ironically, the awkward frisson between Hugh and his beloved all day, combined with Minerva's lackluster and lukewarm recollections of their courtship, did play in their favor. If it was apparent to his mother and Jeremiah the affection between the besotted couple was more one-sided than they had been led to believe, they wouldn't be completely surprised if Minerva's head had been turned elsewhere. All they had to do was get through one more day together. Just one more paltry day and their charade would be done.

Not that the vexing Minerva knew any of this, because she hadn't read his blasted note!

And if she awoke in a snit tomorrow, and avoided him again, he would have to get Payne or Giles to explain it all to her. And get them to say goodbye.

For some reason, that made him feel both sad and furious in equal measure. Sad, because despite her recent betrayal and flagrant blackmail, he liked her. A great deal. He had from the outset, and he couldn't bear the thought of her disappearing when he knew he would forever worry about how she was faring on her own again. And he was furious because she would leave still unjustly assuming he was a brute, while absolving herself of all blame for his supposed brutishness.

That hardly struck him as fair.

Why did she get to have the last word when there were important things to be said? The logistics for tomorrow, for example? The need for her to continue to behave as if she was peeved at him. The fact he needed her to know she could come to him if life or fate was ever cruel to her again? She was denying him the right to continue to be her knight in shining armor, when he was resolutely committed to continue being it.

He jumped off the bed and began to pace again, annoyed with himself for still being annoyed and annoyed at the thought of her enjoying the blissful sleep of the self-righteous when he wouldn't sleep a wink. So much for being master of his own house. What sort of master had to resort to pacing the Persian?

Not this one.

Something inside him snapped, and Hugh was striding across the landing toward the east wing before he thought better of it.

If she wouldn't read his note, then she would hear it in person!

As he turned into her hallway, he saw the thin strip of light bleeding beneath her door.

Good.

She wasn't asleep. He hoped she was feeling as remorseful and frustrated as he was by today's unfortunate chain of events. He stalled his clenched hand before it pummeled on the door, realizing in the nick of time that without stealth, her sisters would dash to her aid and he'd have to try to hold one of the single most important conversations of his life in front of an overprotective audience. Instead, he tapped lightly once and then strode inside without allowing her the opportunity to tell him to go to hell.

"Minerva, we need to . . ." The rest of the words died in his throat. She stood at the window in nothing but a billowing nightgown. A nightgown the firelight rendered translucent. Her dark hair was loose, hanging almost to her hip, a breathtaking silken curtain that shimmered in the dim flame of the single candle.

"What the . . . !"

He winced at the shriek and motioned with his hands for her not to scream as she scrabbled for the shawl hanging on the mirror and held it against her, thoroughly spoiling his splendid view. "I am sorry for barging in — but it cannot wait. I really do need to speak to you."

"Here? How dare you come here!" Her eyes then raked the length of him, taking in the loose untucked shirt and bare feet and calves poking out of his breeches. "You're not even dressed!"

"It was a sudden decision . . . and in the spur of the moment I forgot myself. I'm sorry." But he wouldn't be deterred. Nor would he be seduced. "Would it help if I apologized for part of what transpired earlier?"

"Only part!" Instead of placating her, his words only served to get her dander up further, and Hugh sighed, remembering his butler's advice.

"I am sorry for being in a bad mood earlier and for taking it out on you." He owed her that much of an apology. "And I am sorry for galloping off and leaving you to struggle with Marigold alone. That was ungentlemanly."

Still clutching the shawl in front of her like a shield, she looked down her nose at him. "It was. Very."

"In light of what happened subsequently, I also regret falling out with you over Vee."

"That doesn't sound the least bit like an

apology."

"It is a partial one. One which when combined with the other two acknowledges I am three-quarters to blame for this morning."

"I suppose you expect me to take responsibility for the remaining quarter?" He decided to take the fact she was not shouting as a positive sign.

As tempting as it was to moan about Vee, he wouldn't. Her sisters were her Achilles' heel, and mentioning that wouldn't release him from purgatory. "Not all of it." He held up his finger and thumb an inch apart. "Just the bit where you were mean to me and then tried to blackmail me as revenge for my shoddy behavior."

"It was shoddy."

"My behavior or your attempt at blackmail?" He offered her a tenuous smile as an olive branch.

"Both." Contrition replaced the affronted outrage. "I shouldn't have stooped to your level. You don't have to pay me sixty pounds."

"I will and gladly. You saved my bacon today and for that I am truly thankful. Do you accept my apology, or shall I get down on my knees and plead as I did when I *begged* you for your hand?"

The beginnings of a mischievous smile tugged at the corners of her mouth. She wasn't the least bit sorry for making him sound pathetic and lovelorn in front of his mother, and he admired that. "As tempting as that is, I shall accept."

"Thank you." He reached for her hand and brought it to his lips, then had a very odd moment when he realized it wasn't only her hand he wanted to kiss.

It was all of her.

Off-kilter yet again, Hugh stepped back awkwardly and tried to look unaffected as she blinked back at him. Lord, she was lovely! Too lovely. All that hair, the nightgown. The shadow of the long legs he could see beneath it. Realizing he was staring, he looked away, only to be confronted with the large bed that dominated the room. Its covers turned down in invitation. "Then I declare a truce." His heart was racing. Beads of nervous perspiration seemed to multiply along his spine as images of the pair of them in that bed skittered vividly across his mind. "Now can we talk?"

"You didn't just come here to apologize, then?"

As he was in danger of awkwardly bouncing on the balls of his feet, Hugh sat on the chair by the dressing table and, after casting another frantic glance around the room, had no choice but to gesture for her to sit on the bed or continue to stand like Eve tempting Adam before him. "There is much to discuss and I haven't had a second with you alone since you told me to go to hell outside the stables."

She sat, rearranging the shawl primly around her shoulders and forcing him to notice some alluring female jiggling beneath the nightgown. Then the jiggling reminded him that the diaphanous nightgown was the only flimsy barrier between his eyes and her nakedness. More unwelcome images writhed erotically in his imagination, more than he feared he was capable of coping with. Rather than groan out loud at the visceral effect they had on his body, he crossed one leg over the other and tried to imagine he wasn't alone in this intimately lit bedchamber with a woman who had no idea how much he wanted her. He tried valiantly to picture Lucretia in that seductive garment instead — short, stout legs and slightly crinkly graying hair unbound. He clung to that unappealing image like grim death. "What were you and my mother whispering about after dinner?"

"Your mother wanted to go through your entire story with a fine-tooth comb. How

213

we met, our courtship, my illness, and my father's death." Her pretty face became pained. "I did my best to answer every question, but I am not entirely sure she is convinced, Hugh. She asked the same things over and over in different ways. All very cordially, but I got the distinct impression she was trying to trip me up."

"She excels at that."

"If I say so myself, I did a good job of distracting her. I asked a great many questions about Boston and Mr. Peabody."

"Jeremiah has always managed to distract her."

"It's obvious she adores him." Minerva's face softened, and she had a faraway look in her green eyes that made him want to go far away with her. "She lit up whenever she talked about him."

"They married entirely for love."

"How lovely . . ."

"I know . . ." With her before him doing odd things to his heart, he sincerely wished he was capable of it. But it wasn't to be. He might be able to behave himself in the short term, but like his cheating sire and grandfather before him, he wasn't capable of the commitment such a lofty undertaking entailed. Even if she was willing and he tried to fight his wayward blood, he'd end up breaking her heart. Because that's what Standish men did. "After being shackled to my father, she deserved some happiness." What had possessed him to admit to that? Being too canny and intuitive for her own good, Minerva noticed. Sympathy clouded her green eyes.

"Was he not a nice man, then? That comes as a surprise. I've not heard a bad word against your father in the time I've been here. Even Payne seems to admire him — and he is thoroughly devoted to you."

"*Payne?* Devoted? If that's devotion, I would hate to see what disdain looks like." Nightgown or no nightgown, Hugh was not going to talk about his father. She hadn't scrambled his wits that much. "Ironically, it was my father who introduced my mother to Jeremiah." Or perhaps she had, seeing as he apparently *was* talking about his father. "Jeremiah was a good family friend for many years before she was widowed, he was my mother's rock during my father's illness, and then it wasn't long before friendship turned into more. I was best man at their wedding. I have a great deal of respect for Jeremiah. He is the only person who has ever made my harridan of a mother see reason."

"Your mother isn't a harridan."

"You have only endured one tea and one dinner."

"Perhaps — but it is obvious she adores you and only wants what is best for you."

"And you learned all this during two interrogations in which she tried repeatedly to trip you up?"

"We did talk about your scandalous lifestyle — before I came along and rescued you from it." She failed to hide her amusement as she tried to look appalled. "Opera dancers and married ladies, Hugh? Your mother says they were a predictable choice considering your irrational fear of falling in love."

"I am not the least bit afraid of falling in love." Although just saying it aloud made his insides tighten. It wasn't an irrational fear, it was a genuine one. Love wasn't for the fainthearted and it certainly wasn't for the easily distracted. Because the other side of the coin to love was heartbreak and, inevitably, loathing. Ergo, it was best avoided.

"Then I suppose that is why you . . . How *did* your mother put it?" She paused and then giggled. He wanted to catch the infectious sound in his fist and keep it forever. "Actually, I cannot repeat it. It's too scandalous."

"But clearly very amusing. Go ahead. Say it. It's cruel of you to laugh at me to my face but refuse to say why. At the very least, I should have the right of reply."

"Very well. If you insist . . ." A very becoming blush stained her cheeks despite her attempt to appear bold. "Your mother says you deftly avoided falling in love by . . . heavens! I cannot believe I am going to say this . . . hopping from bed to bed before you had time to warm the sheets." She forced herself to meet his eyes and folded her arms across her chest. "Let's hear your defense, then, Hugh? Is she right? Do you purposefully conduct your affairs based on their transient nature?"

Yes.

The more transient, the better.

"I believe my mother has exaggerated my conquests greatly to illustrate her point, but as usual, she has the wrong end of the stick." Hugh folded his arms, too, acting bemused rather than overthinking the bullet she had sent flying straight through the bull's-eye. It was hardly a bombshell, more of a considered choice he'd made. He knew his limitations and wasn't prepared to suffer the inevitable crushing remorse that would follow each mistake. Just imagining hurting Minerva was already causing an ache in his heart. That pain would be unbearable if he actually did hurt her. "The sad truth is — and you must never repeat this outside this room — despite giving it my best shot, I have never found a single woman I have wanted to spend more than a few nights with." Apart from her.

"Your best shot? That suggests you have tried and failed. You could hardly spend a prolonged period of time with a married woman, Hugh! That is a road to nowhere. Perhaps you should give one of the many single ladies a go? A nice young lady who has kept her sheets pristine and is waiting for a handsome and charming fellow like you to sweep her off her feet. Have you never courted a single lady?"

And now Minerva was beginning to sound like his mother. She used to come out with exactly that sort of reasonable rot all the time, when she of all people should know the Standish male was not to be trusted.

Of course he had never courted a single lady!

The one thing he *hadn't* inherited from his wayward ancestors was his blasted conscience — a grave burden that had certainly never plagued either his father or his grandfather, and very probably nary a great-great-grandfather before that. Therefore, Hugh flirted shamelessly with certain women, and they flirted shamelessly back. That wasn't courting, it was a dance. One both parties knew would end in the bedroom but would never stray further than that. "When I told you I wasn't the marrying kind, I meant it. I am fairly certain I am not capable of falling in love — or not completely, at any rate." And suddenly, because of her, that flaw depressed him.

He saw her disbelieving expression and decided to clarify the point rather than hear her inevitable counterarguments. "That elusive, all-consuming, selfless feeling poets and hopeless romantics like my mother go on and on about simply isn't in my arsenal of human emotions. It is a defect in my bloodline."

She stared at him, and he realized he had once again said too much. "Oh, Hugh — have you considered you simply might not have met the right woman? You are far too thoughtful and nice to be incapable of love."

" 'Nice'?" She had inadvertently given him the way out. He scowled with mock affront. "That is the second time I've been called 'nice' today, and frankly I am outraged by it! 'Nice' is such a nondescript and uninspiring word. Wallpaper is nice. As is a new hat which looks exactly like the old one. Are you sure you didn't mean 'debonair'? Charming? Irresistible? There is a dictionary full of adjectives far more suited to me than 'nice.' "

"Well, you are nice. You are also irritating and far too confident for your own good. And secretive. I've always suspected there was more to you than meets the eye, but every time I try to take a peek beneath the surface, you batten down the hatches and brush away my questions with charm."

"See — you admit it! I *am* charming. I shall take that compliment as a replacement for the insipid 'nice' you just foisted upon me."

"There you go again . . . deflecting, leaving me to once again wonder why you feel the need to immediately deflect. What are you hiding?"

"Absolutely nothing." He opened his arms, wishing he wasn't a carbon copy of his father. "This is me."

"You are a conundrum, Hugh Standish."

"Now, I do like *that* word. 'Conundrum' suggests a man of mystery. I hear the ladies love a man of mystery."

"Deflecting again."

"Always." He shrugged, trying to ignore the constant, nagging emptiness this conversation had highlighted. As much as he wasn't looking forward to her leaving, because he knew already she would leave a temporary void in his life, there was no point dwelling on it. Because ultimately, he wouldn't. Just as soon as another willing woman came along to distract him, he would be distracted. That was the Standish way — damn it. A fait accompli. "If my mother is unconvinced by our betrothal, it's probably just as well we will finally end this charade tomorrow."

"Tomorrow?" Was that disappointment he saw swirling in her stormy eyes? "So soon?"

"I think it's for the best, don't you?" He willed her to disagree. To make him revise the sudden plan. "The longer we draw it all out, the more holes she will find in our story."

"I suppose . . ."

"It is actually the main thing I came to talk to you about tonight." He had needed to say goodbye as quickly and as cleanly as possible. "Let us get through tomorrow and then sometime around midnight, Payne will come and fetch you, so make sure you've packed a bag, and you will leave with Giles in his carriage." Just saying it aloud made him miserable. Empty. Lonely. "I will dispatch your sisters, your belongings, and Lucretia in my carriage early the following morning, and you will rendezvous at a coaching inn midway between here and London."

She digested it all for several moments, staring at her hands in her lap, before she finally nodded. "Yes . . . I suppose it does make sense."

Then her lovely eyes lifted to his, and he saw something else there. Something that looked a great deal like a sadness that mirrored his. He quashed the urge to go to her. "It is just so quick . . . so sudden. I wasn't expecting it all to end so abruptly."

"It's for the best." Hugh stood, fearing if he didn't escape promptly, he might do something he would regret. Something wholly stupid and dangerous — like postponing the elopement to spend more time with her, something the persistent voice in his head was screaming at him to consider. "I shall have more of the details tomorrow. In the meantime, I think your lack of devotion for me against my absolute devotedness gives our tragic tale of heartbreak more credence, don't you? After all, who would choose a rakish earl over the more rakish heir to a dukedom? It probably couldn't hurt to cast the odd longing gaze at Giles tomorrow." Which would be utter torture to witness.

"Yes . . . I shall try to appear intrigued by him."

"Don't try too hard." Not what he should have said at all. "Giles's head is quite big enough already." There was nothing else to say, despite there being so much still unsaid. "Thank you for hearing me out."

She walked alongside him to the door, but before he could open it, she touched his arm. It was an innocent and gentle brush, but like all her touches, one so potent he felt it burn through the thin sleeve of his shirt and sear itself onto his soul.

"Thank you, Hugh. For everything. These last few days have been . . . rather lovely. I shall always look back at my time here fondly."

He nodded, feeling oddly emotional, then gripped the door handle. It was time to sever their unexpected acquaintance. "Good night, Minerva."

"Good night, Hugh." She looked sad. So sad. As was he. It was ridiculous, really, when they barely knew each other, but he already knew he would miss her. He wouldn't have to fake that emotion for his mother. "And thank you for coming to talk to me. I've never been able to sleep on an argument. I am glad we get to part as friends."

Friends.

As insipid a word as "nice" if ever there was one. "Me too. And because we are friends — please know if you ever need help, I will always be there. You know where to find me." Leaving an open door was easier than a goodbye, because this goodbye hurt too much, even though he knew already this proud, vexing, and stubborn woman would never use it.

"More proof you are exceedingly nice. In fact, you are the *nicest* man I have ever met."

If only . . .

Hugh made a face of disgust as he was expected to, depressingly shallow and unworthy to the last. He had one foot out the door when he turned and did something very stupid. Possibly the most stupid thing he had ever done in his thirty-two years on earth. He listened to the screaming voice in his head, gave in to temptation, and kissed her.

# Chapter Thirteen

His lips were soft. His touch achingly gentle as he cupped her cheek. Yet the emotion both conjured was as intense as it was unexpected. As his mouth brushed over hers, his free hand sought hers at her side. That touch, too, felt profound, their laced fingers an acknowledgment of the strength of their feelings in a way no mere embrace ever could be, but also an admission that they both knew that whatever this was between them was never meant to be.

Neither of them hurried to increase the contact. The moment was too special for that. Instead, they strung the poignant kiss out, marveling at its intensity while mourning the cause of it.

Goodbye.

So final, yet . . .

Minerva sighed against his mouth, then melted against him, needing to deepen it, needing to feel his body against hers just this once before she had to let him go. Slowly, she traced her fingers over his face, searing it onto her memory for all the empty years to come. Then, because it was necessary, she did the same with his shoulders, then his arms and chest, while his hands toyed with her hair.

Beneath her flattened palms, she could feel his heart beating again, a sure and steady rhythm that seemed to echo the sound of her own beating erratically in her head. His skin radiated warmth through the thin linen, the muscles in his chest too intriguing not to explore with her fingertips. She felt them tremble a moment before he moaned her name against her mouth and his arm snaked around her waist, tugging her closer still until their bodies touched from ribs to hip.

Time had no place. She lost all concept of it as his lips slanted against hers, oblivious of everything except the way he made her feel. She had been kissed before, and more than once. Yet those chaste, innocent, brief touches of lips all those years ago fell woefully short of Hugh's. His was a wholly different and potent experience, which opened her eyes to all manner of things she had not really understood before.

This kiss was both physical and temporal.

Both passionate and painful. Making her body yearn while her heart wept.

Who knew a kiss could say things no words could? Filled with longing, sadness, regret, joy, understanding, and gratefulness all at the same time. Or that the line between tender and heartfelt, and passionate and all consuming was so fine or so precarious it could change in an instant? Like the world shifting on its axis, this kiss had the power to alter everything immeasurably, and she knew nothing would ever be quite the same again.

When his tongue teased hers, she welcomed it, plunging her fingers into his hair to anchor him in place, not caring that the blatant need in her breasts would be obvious, flattened as they were against his chest, or that her greedy hips had pushed themselves wantonly toward his so that she could feel his desire.

Entwined, they stumbled back into her bedchamber, and one of them must have kicked the door shut, because she felt the cold wood against her back while his hands smoothed unhindered down her shoulders and rib cage before he filled them with her bottom.

She didn't recognize the bold woman whose hands burrowed beneath his shirt, who was suddenly impatient with the barrier of her nightgown, whose palms raked over his bare skin as if her life depended upon it. Her body now controlled her mind, reacting in a way it had never reacted before — even when she had thought herself in love.

It welcomed him. Wanted him. Molded against him, until she could discern the full size and shape of his hardness, reveled in it and ached to feel it inside her. Then his hands found her breasts, and she had moaned into his mouth. Moaned and writhed because it felt so glorious. Then all at once his was gone.

Hugh had broken the contact and now stood breathless, blinking and stunned. "That was . . . unexpected."

She had no earthly idea if that meant he regretted it, but the distance between them made her suddenly self-conscious, so she reached for her shawl.

"No . . ." His raised hand stayed her. "Please don't. Let me have the memory of you exactly as you are now." His eyes, still darkened with passion, dropped to her lips, then greedily raked her body before they changed and swirled with something else. Something deep and complicated that she didn't understand. He took another step back, shook his head, and smiled with regret. "I shall miss you, Minerva."

"And I shall miss you, too, Hugh."

As the door opened, he turned, stared deep into her eyes as if searching for something, then sighed. "For what it's worth, I have adored having you as my fiancée."

Minerva stared down at her tea. Had she sugared it already? If she had, she didn't remember, so she spooned some in to be sure and stirred it idly, returning to the same thing she had been mulling over all night.

*That kiss.*

Thank goodness she had the breakfast room to herself, because all these hours later she was still not fully over it or fit to be seen in company.

Obviously, it had been a goodbye. A thank-you. An acknowledgment that the attraction between them had been mutual. Bittersweet, too, tinged with regret that their enjoyable interlude was at an end but also accepting of the fact that they could never be more. Under all normal circumstances, a carefree earl who owned this palace and a cynical girl from Clerkenwell would never have met, let alone spend almost a week ensconced in one another's company. She was in no doubt, life for them would move on — but oh my goodness! That kiss had been something!

Thanks to Hugh, she now knew a kiss was not just about lips — but teeth and tongues, bodies and hearts as well.

Somewhere she had offered him both and gave them freely, expecting nothing in return. Because what was there to expect? He lived in his world and she lived in hers, and never the twain should meet. There was no future, no past, only that moment. A moment she had lived in fully.

In truth, if he hadn't been the one to tear his mouth away, she realized she would have given him more. Allowed him greater liberties, Lord only knew how many, because her body had craved them and in that moment it had felt right.

She smiled and added more sugar to her tea. Because Hugh had been as stunned as she at the spontaneous passion that had erupted like a volcano between them. Wonderful, poignant, perfect but as impossible as it was impractical. As soon as her door had clicked quietly closed, she had staggered to the chair at her dressing table. And there she sat for a good ten minutes before she allowed her eyes to finally focus on her own reflection in the mirror, and barely recognized the wanton creature who stared back.

Her hair was a tangled disaster. Her lips plump, swollen from his kisses, while the proper nightgown she had dressed for bed in had somehow undone itself at the neck and had slipped down, exposing one entire naked shoulder and an improper amount of flesh between her chin and the upper swells of her breasts. If that hadn't been scandalous enough, two very erect, very greedy nipples were prominently poking through the filmy linen, the dark shadows of them something he had to have seen when his eyes had possessively raked the length of her just before he left.

Hours later, those same nipples kept pebbling each time she remembered how she had craved his hands on them — so persistently, she had wrapped her thickest new shawl around her upper body in case they announced her shameless behavior and carnal desires to the entire household with their blatant erectness.

"You're up early."

Minerva jumped, then felt her face heat guiltily at the sound of his mother's voice. "I am an early bird by nature, my lady." Hugh's mother was the last person she wanted to see in her current state. Not when she was still in the undeniable throes of residual lust for her son. Self-consciously, she checked the shawl around her shoulders and gave the sturdy knot she had tied a tug in case it shifted and gave the game away. "I have never been very good at sleeping in."

"Me either — and please, call me Olivia . . . until we are officially family, at least."

"Very well . . . Olivia." It was very hard to appear normal when her bosoms felt so heavy and she was in the midst of guiltily recalling every scandalous moment of that eye-opening embrace.

"Is everything all right, Minerva?"

Good gracious! Was it obvious she had been thoroughly ravished and had enjoyed every second of it? She had no choice but to brazen it out. "Yes, of course. Why wouldn't it be?" To prove it, she took a sip of her tea and nearly gagged at the sickly-sweet taste of it. Exactly how many sugars had she put into it whilst mooning about Hugh? It was like treacle. But for the sake of appearances, she had to choke it down regardless.

"I am probably imagining it, I am sure, but I thought I sensed a bit of an atmosphere yesterday at dinner. Have you and my son had a falling-out?"

232

Minerva almost sagged with relief that her heavy, wanton bosoms hadn't given her away. "I confess, we had a little tiff just before you arrived. Nothing serious."

"Serious enough for you to shoot daggers at him down the table all evening when you assumed nobody was looking."

"Ahhh — you saw that, did you?" *Brazen it out.* Hugh wanted her to be less enamored of him to give credence to tonight's elopement. "I had thought I was being subtly peeved."

"Oh, you were subtle, my dear, but not much gets by me. I see you have tea, so I shan't offer to pour you another." Minerva frantically choked down more tea in a bid to be rid of it as Hugh's mother fixed herself a cup from the sideboard. It tasted worse than the first sip. "Hugh was trying too hard to engage you. You were the perfect hostess, chatting away to everyone but him."

"It was only a little tiff. I am too headstrong and he can be . . ."

"Maddening? Stubborn? Selfishly unreasonable?" The older woman smiled, evaluating her openly over the rim of her cup. "To be frank, my dear, I was heartened to see it. It shows he cares. I have never trusted those couples who claim never to argue. I think it shows a lack of depth in their relationship and a grave imbalance. People who love one another argue. People who are indifferent don't." Then she grinned, displaying the exact same mischievous dimples as her son. "Jeremiah and I have had some stinkers over the years. I once threw a hairbrush at him."

"And it hit me here." Right on cue, Mr. Peabody sauntered in tapping his temple. "The darned thing was made of solid silver, too, so I had to suffer the indignity of a giant, purple bump for a good week afterward."

"It wasn't giant." His comment was regally waved away. "He is exaggerating. It was barely the size of a quail's egg."

"You say quail's egg, I say more duck egg. Either way it made me a laughingstock." He winked at Minerva. "Good morning, future daughter-in-law. You look well today."

"I feel well." If a strange throbbing in the nether regions and obscenely pointed nipples were the definition of "well." "I see you are an early bird, too, Mr. Peabody." Where was everyone else? Suddenly, being Hugh's *Minerva* all alone made her nervous.

"Hardly. But as my wife is determined to learn all about you as quickly as possible, I hurried down to save you. Seven o'clock is far too early for an interrogation."

"That is very kind of you, Mr. Peabody,

but I didn't need saving. We were having a perfectly lovely chat."

"Never be fooled by that, young lady. The pleasant chat is merely the preamble. Think of Olivia much like a spider. She'll build an innocuous, almost invisible web, lull you into a false sense of security, and before you know it, she's lured you into her trap and then she'll eat you alive."

"Are you trying to put her off me, Jeremiah?" Although, by her amused expression, Hugh's mother didn't appear to have taken offense at the gibe.

"I am merely stepping into the breach until Hugh arrives — to shield the poor girl from the worst of your incessant prying." He sat directly opposite his wife and then handed her his cup, grinning. "I cannot help but notice this is empty, my darling."

"Something which is just as well, or you would presently be wearing it, *dearest.*" Blue eyes, so like Hugh's, twinkled. "You see, Minerva — devoted couples argue all the time."

Mr. Peabody rolled his eyes as she got up to fix his drink. "I knew she wouldn't be able to leave it alone despite my repeated warning it was none of her business. She bored me to sleep last night speculating on what she believed was the peculiar atmosphere between you and Hugh."

"And I was right. They had a tiff. But it is over now." She plonked his cup in front of him, and he gave it a tentative sniff before taking a sip and sighing.

"There is nothing like the first cup of coffee in the mornings, is there?"

"I wouldn't know. I'm a tea drinker." A fresh cup of tea appeared in front of Minerva, and she almost sighed aloud, too. She pushed away the cooling cup of treacle and measured just the one scant spoon of sugar into the new cup with more precision than it needed. "Coffee always tastes so bitter to me, Mr. Peabody."

"Gracious girl, we are about to be family. Please call me Jeremiah. . . . And coffee is not for the fainthearted. It's a strong drink. A man's drink . . ."

"What he means is, it's an *American* drink. My husband is radically opposed to tea. On principle."

"Of course I am! My grandfather was a revolutionary. He was there at the Boston Tea Party, standing up for fairness and patriotism. He risked his life for it! He'd be spinning in his grave if he knew I allowed that British muck past my lips."

"Assuming he isn't already spinning like a windmill in a gale because you conveniently

236

forgot your proud revolutionary heritage when you chose to marry an English-woman." Hugh strode in looking effortlessly handsome, and her lips, alongside other parts of her, started to tingle with abandon. "Somehow, I think he would find the occasional cup of tea more palatable than a blue-blooded daughter of the British establishment. Good morning, everyone."

His eyes flicked to hers only briefly before he kissed his mother's cheek, but this morning they looked at her differently. They dropped for just a second to Minerva's lips before they pulled away, and she knew in that instant he was having recollections about last night's kiss, just as she was.

"How is everyone today?" As his eyes kept darting to hers, Minerva answered.

"I am well, thank you." She wasn't well at all. She was all over the place, completely at sixes and sevens and severely lacking sleep. That was all his fault. "I trust you are well, too?"

"I am. Excellent, in fact . . ." There was longing in his eyes, and once again they dropped to her lips. *"Excellent . . ."* Hugh rapidly turned to Jeremiah with an over-bright smile. "And how are you? Recovered from your travels, I hope?"

"Your mother is prying. Your fiancée is

237

politely tolerating it, and I wish I was still in bed."

"And what is she prying into, pray tell?"

He sat opposite her, forcing Minerva to smell his cologne. The spicy, obviously expensive scent had been mixed with crisp fresh air as if he had been outside. There was something about the combination that made her want to bury her nose in his neck and sniff. "Our little argument yesterday." Why was it so hard to meet his eyes? Probably because only a few hours ago, she'd allowed her wandering hands free rein on his body and made no secret she had craved his on hers.

"It was hardly *little,* dear, if it lasted throughout dinner. What exactly did the pair of you argue about? Despite all my prying, Hugh, your fiancée has been annoyingly scant on details."

"It was nothing, Mother. Just as Minerva said. A tiny lovers' tiff." Their eyes finally met properly across the table, and his were amused. "All that matters now is that it's all sorted."

"Then if it's in the past, I see no reason why you cannot share it with us. Once finished with, silly arguments make such wonderful entertainment. What did my horrid son do, Minerva?"

His mother really was like a dog with a bone, one she was unlikely to let go of unless she was thrown a few treats to replace it. "If you must know, we disagreed about the wedding venue." Hugh's cup paused midway between the table and his mouth, which made her immediately feel stupid at her hasty fabrication, but she was committed now. Backtracking would be impossible.

"Hugh suggested he wanted us to marry in London while I thought I had made it perfectly clear I would prefer to marry here . . . in Hampshire. Saint Mary's is so beautiful . . ." His mother's eyes had lit up. Minerva apparently couldn't have picked a better topic to appease her, although she also recognized his long-awaited marriage was his mother's dream and his worst nightmare. "I thought his devoted tenants should get to enjoy the day . . ." Her voice trailed off, and she took a nervous gulp of her tea. It was so hot it brought tears to her eyes.

"Well, of course you should marry in Hampshire!" His mother glared at her son. "I am staggered you would even consider London, Hugh! I hope you conceded Minerva was right?"

"Of course I did. London was merely a suggestion."

"A stupid one. As well as unnecessarily complicated. It will be devilishly difficult to plan the wedding from such a distance." She patted Minerva's arm. "I am entirely on your side in this. No wonder you shot daggers at him throughout dinner. Had I been in your shoes, I'd have probably hurled the silverware." Then she shuffled her chair a little closer. "Have you finally set a date?"

"No . . ."

"Probably just as well, as there is much to arrange and until we know about the availability of Madame Devy, it would be silly to commit to a date."

"Madame Devy?"

"The modiste, dear. The very *best* modiste in the whole of England. She is highly sought after and a veritable genius with silk. She must make your wedding gown! I shall send word to her today and tell her it is an emergency. She owes me many favors. . . . But once she has all your measurements, I am certain she will be able to turn things around by Christmas."

"Christmas?"

"Well, obviously, this far from summer, it stands to reason in the absence of a June wedding you should have a Christmas wedding." She clapped her small hands together and beamed. "What do you say, Hugh?

Wouldn't a Christmas wedding be perfect?"

"Yes, *excellent* . . ."

"Have you thought about colors, Minerva?"

She opened her mouth to speak, and then his mother cut her off. "No! Silly me. We cannot discuss colors with Hugh present. It's bad luck for the groom to know anything about the dress. We shall talk about that later. . . . But we can talk about guests, can't we? And bridesmaids. I suppose you will want your sisters as your bridesmaids, won't you? And I shall assume that rapscallion Giles will be your best man, Hugh?"

It was as if Minerva had inadvertently opened a gate and allowed a flock of crazed sheep to escape. Hugh's mother was in her element, firing off ideas and questions she clearly expected no answers to. Her husband seemed to give up the ghost and withdraw into his coffee, while poor Hugh gripped the handle of his teacup so tightly, she wouldn't be at all surprised if he suddenly snapped the thing off.

She cast him a mournful glance, hoping he could see the apology in it. Then Lord Bellingham walked in, and she watched Hugh practically sigh with relief.

"Giles! Thank the Lord! You couldn't have timed it better. Please save me from this living hell. My mother is planning wedding dresses. Come! Sit! You must be starving!"

"I am not hungry."

"What? Has the world ended? I've never known you to not be hungry."

"Might I have a word, old boy?" He smiled to the table, then stared pointedly at Hugh. "In private?"

"Of course." The wretch was up and out like a shot, beyond eager to escape when he had only just arrived, leaving Minerva alone to deal with the rabid monster she had inadvertently constructed.

"We'll hold the wedding breakfast here, at Standish House, then have an evening feast for the village. . . ."

# Chapter Fourteen

"What do you mean you have to go?" Hugh gripped Giles by the lapels and seriously considered shaking him. "You can't!" Because Hugh had kissed her, practically ravished her, and the only hope he had of *not* kissing her ever again was if she left tonight. "I need you!"

"It's an emergency, old boy." He waved the note in his hand, then snatched it away when Hugh tried to grab it. "Ask Payne. It came by express fifteen minutes ago. I have to go."

"But Giles . . ."

"It shouldn't take long."

" 'Shouldn't take long'? What sort of a woolly answer is that? When will you be back, damn it?"

"A few days . . ." *Good grief!* "A week at most."

He did shake him then as blind panic took hold. "A week! A bloody week! What the hell am I supposed to do with them all for a week!" He had a million ideas what to do with Minerva, all of them wholly inappropriate. Each and every one had stopped him from sleeping last night, then necessitated an icy wash followed by a brisk gallop across the fields before the sun even rose first thing this morning. Neither had done anything to dampen his ardor. "You need to take her today!"

"Well, I can hardly elope with her now, can I? She's eating breakfast with your mother!"

"They are planning my wedding! Have you any idea how much *planning* my mother is capable of in a single week?" Hugh let go of Giles to pace, trying to focus on his own misery and not to notice his friend's suddenly gray pallor and fraught expression. Something was wrong. Very wrong. So wrong it stopped him from lusting after Minerva. "What is it, Giles? Can I help?"

"Nothing serious, old boy — rattling skeletons which urgently need my attention, that's all — but thanks for offering."

He could tell by his friend's closed expression he would hear nothing more. And Minerva accused Hugh of being secretive, which of course he was with good reason, but he'd known Giles for over a decade and sometimes wondered if he knew him at all. He frequently disappeared with little explanation, always claimed rattling skeletons but never confided what those persistent old bones were. "I shall be back as soon as I am able. You have my word. As I said, it shouldn't take long . . ." Although even Giles didn't look convinced by that half-hearted statement. "Or at least I hope it doesn't. In the meantime, try to avoid getting married, there's a good chap."

"Easy for you to say. My mother is doubtless writing the guest list as we speak. The banns will be read on Sunday . . ." Fresh panic gripped him. "Bloody hell, Giles! How do I stop the banns from being read?"

"They have to be read three times before they're official and I'll definitely be back before that happens."

"Hardly reassuring." Aside from putting off his mother, Hugh couldn't imagine being able to resist Minerva for one week, let alone three. She had been so passionate. So magnificently wanton. If her kisses alone made him lose his head, anything more didn't bear thinking about. Except he kept thinking about it. Those long legs, the gauzy nightgown, the dusky nipples beneath it he was now desperate to see properly. Touch . . . taste . . .

"Look on the bright side, while she is occupied with wedding preparations, she won't have the time or inclination to be suspicious. Just maintain the status quo, act besotted, let your mother have her fun, and before you know it, I shall be back to sweep your fiancée off her feet and scandalously steal her from under your nose." Giles attempted to smile, then shook his head in apology. "I *really* do have to go, old boy."

"Then go, damn it! The quicker you do, the quicker you can come back and the quicker this sham will be over."

If Hugh survived it — and that was a very big "if" indeed. If his mother didn't kill him for his duplicity, his lust for Minerva would. Perhaps, in this instance, death would be a blessing? He had never been so consumed by a woman before. So tempted to ignore all of his hard-and-fast rules about the sort of women he wooed. This morning, as soon as he saw her, he had wanted to flirt with her. Pick her flowers. Spend all day with her. Talking, kissing. Getting to know her in every possible way. He blamed the nightgown, the firelight, and all that seductive hair for his idiotic lapse in judgment. But unfortunately, last night his wayward Standish blood had fired his loins to such an extent, the pragmatic, reasonable, and noble part of his brain had stopped working and he had completely forgotten all his deeply ingrained principles.

So much for respectfully keeping his hands to himself. Thanks to his foolhardy and spectacular lapse in judgment, they had had a high old time thoroughly getting to know Minerva. He couldn't look at his palms without remembering how perfectly her delectable bottom had filled them. Or her breasts.

Giles left him to pace the study. A week didn't bear thinking about. Under the original circumstances, it would be a risky gamble that would be near impossible to pull off. But now he'd kissed Minerva! Thoroughly kissed Minerva and been thoroughly knocked sideways by his own incomprehensible reaction to it, rendering a single day in her company pure torture.

What he didn't understand, what he had been wondering incessantly since he'd left her last night, in between reliving the experience over and over again in his mind, was what was different about the way Minerva kissed from all the other women whose lips had locked with his over the years. He'd lost himself in it, poured all of himself into it, and then been left blindsided by the impact. Her kisses were potent, addictive, dangerous, and best avoided henceforth. He could barely look at her now without a new, strange, and frightening yearning taking over. A yearning he hoped to God was just carnal.

"Lord Bellingham's carriage has left, my lord." Payne hadn't bothered knocking — or perhaps he had and Hugh was so bewitched by the vixen he'd been rendered deaf as well as stupid. "Therefore, it would be prudent if you apprised me of the alternative plan."

"There is no alternative plan. And unless you can come up with something brilliant, we shall just have to make it up as we go along, Payne. Until Giles returns."

"Oh dear . . ."

" 'Oh dear' indeed, Payne. My mother has already made a spirited start on the wedding preparations and she hasn't been home a full day yet."

"Those will only keep her occupied for so long."

"But at least they will keep her occupied for the time being. I have no choice but to allow my mother to plan to her heart's content."

"But she is planning *with* Miss Minerva. Is it fair to load such a burden solely on her shoulders?"

"I suppose not."

Poor Minerva. All the money in the world wouldn't compensate her for that onerous task. Hours and hours together, his meddling mother gradually chiseling away at their flimsy story until there was nothing left to hide behind. "Damn and bloody blast, Payne! What the hell am I going to do?"

"Until a new plan emerges, might I suggest you attempt to be the model son and fiancé."

"I don't follow."

"Spend as much time with your mother as possible. Take her riding, visit her friends — whatever it takes to keep the woman busy. Accompany Minerva in all dealings with your mother, or at least as many of them as you can without arousing suspicion. That way you can better manage their interactions as well as mitigate any unwelcome surprises. And, what better way to distract your mother than by allowing her free rein to plan the wedding? At least it allows you to direct the inevitable meddling there, too."

"That is exactly what Giles said."

"Then we have our alternative plan. Shall I inform Miss Minerva once she is alone?"

"No, Payne. I will." Because Lord only

knew they needed to talk. Aside from the hastily cobbled together plan, Hugh needed to construct some boundaries between them, which were suddenly very necessary if he was going to survive till the end. "Can you find a way to occupy my mother and her blasted sisters so I can speak to Minerva after breakfast?" The last thing he needed was Diana realizing her prophecy concerning his supposed plans to debauch her sister had come true. And in less than a week. A very stark reminder indeed of what could happen in the coming week if he lost his head again.

"It is an unforeseen development, to be sure — but not insurmountable." Hugh was pacing the floor of the rarely visited portrait gallery like an expectant father, his errant hands clasped tightly behind his back in case they gave in to the overwhelming urge to touch her. Heaven only knew why he had chosen this place for their clandestine meeting, because now he felt the weight of all his ancestors' eyes on him as well as Minerva's. His philandering cruel grandfather and his philandering and duplicitous father both a stark warning of the hereditary weakness that flowed through his veins, and which would break her generous heart if he succumbed. "All we need to do is keep my mother occupied."

By the looks of her, she was as uncomfortable with their meeting as he was. Her hands were clasped tightly in front of her like a prim schoolmistress, when she hadn't been the slightest bit prim last night. Those hands had wandered as freely and as boldly on his person as his had on hers. Something he had enjoyed at the time but wished he didn't remember quite so vividly now. "She's already occupied, Hugh. Thanks to my clumsy comment." She stared down at her feet, her expression pained. "I am so sorry I brought up the wedding. I was trying to extricate us both from an awkward situation and yet have only made it more awkward in the process."

"It's all right. In a funny sort of way, it's the perfect distraction. So long as she is fervently planning our nuptials, she won't be watching the pair of us too closely. All we have to do is cheerfully play along."

"Even though she wants to take me to meet the vicar tomorrow?"

"There is no need to worry about the vicar. Reverend Cranham is a thoroughly decent chap. Besides, I shall be with you. We should become inseparable until Giles returns. It's the safest option for keeping our stories straight."

She nodded, still frowning. "It's not the vicar who bothers me, it's lying. In *church,* Hugh. Lying to your mother is bad enough, but I don't want to lie in church." She pointed heavenward and shuddered. "I don't want to be consigned to eternal damnation . . . not even for forty pounds."

"I thought we agreed it was sixty? Although I don't fancy eternal damnation either. How about I invite the reverend to tea after church tomorrow, then we can avoid outright lying in the house of God? I know it's not ideal . . ." None of this was ideal.

"Tea here would be better, I suppose." When she frowned, a little furrow appeared between her dark eyebrows. Hugh's lips desperately wanted to kiss it away. "But if I am honest, I am not happy with your mother planning the wedding at all. I'll feel dreadful allowing her to get all excited about something which is never going to happen. She has been nothing but lovely so far."

"Perhaps we can dampen her enthusiasm a little. Stall her from going all guns blazing."

"I fear she will be hard to stop now that I have set her off. I left her discussing the music with Lucretia and Diana. Your mother favors Pleyel, by the way, over the Mozart piece Lucretia feels would be more appropriate."

"That's because my mother *loathes* Mozart. She says it is overdone, trite, and sets her teeth on edge."

"No wonder the discussion downstairs has become so spirited. Lucretia is apparently in love with Mozart."

"Which do you prefer?"

"It hardly matters, does it?" She looked at him as if he had gone mad. "My point is, I have stupidly set a snowball rolling down the hill and already it is a speeding boulder."

"The first thing we need to do is slow my mother down and tell her we do not want a Christmas wedding because . . ." He flailed his hands about, seeking inspiration.

"Because . . . I want my father's relatives to come down and traveling in winter is always difficult in the Cairngorms?"

"An excellent idea! And hardly fair this close to Christmas . . ."

"And on such short notice . . ."

"They would be distraught to have missed it. As will you, of course. We *could* propose a February wedding."

"Valentine's Day?" She grinned and he grinned back, pleased their thoughts were so aligned.

"Exactly! My mother will adore the romantic symbolism — Valentine's is nearly three months away, thus preventing her from running too far ahead of herself. With any luck, Giles will be back well before the week is out and no real harm done. After all, even my mother cannot plan an entire wedding in a week and she will insist on doing it properly."

"But what about the modiste? She said she was going to write to her as a matter of urgency."

"I think it's best to let that happen, don't you? It adds credence to it all."

"But we'd be wasting the poor woman's time."

"Hardly wasting. Madame Devy is a canny businesswoman and will insist on payment for services rendered whether you wear her dress or not. Not to mention the fact my mother will thoroughly enjoy the whole process. That dress will keep her busy. Especially if you become quite particular. Everything else can easily be canceled well in advance of being made. All the accounts will be going through me anyway, so I can see to all that without her noticing. It is the sensation of purchase my mother enjoys, not the payment. So long as she thinks she is spending, she won't bother to check the receipts." He smiled in what he hoped was his most reassuring manner. "And I shall be with you — remember? We are in this together." He liked that part, at least.

"You cannot be with me all of the time, Hugh. However, if she happens to ask one of us something unexpected as she did this morning, we must ensure we are singing from the same hymn sheet. We are going to need to find a way to alert one another to ensure our stories are straight. It will need to be a better system than having Payne practically leap on me the second I left the room to retrieve my shawl from the breakfast room. I have been gone far too long. Lord only knows what the others must be thinking?" She made a face. "I hope they don't think I am purposefully avoiding them."

"They will assume you went to the retiring room regardless. Because nobody ever says that is where they are going. Ladies are always going to retrieve a shawl or a book or their lost handkerchief."

"That is even more embarrassing."

Hugh couldn't help but laugh at Minerva's awkward mortification. "So embarrassing, in fact, everyone will be at pains *not* to mention it, because nobody ever mentions such things."

"Apart from you. I do wish you hadn't mentioned it. Now I shall feel doubly self-conscious when I return."

"Knowing Lucretia, she's probably waxing lyrical and everyone will simply be too relieved you have finally returned to give your absence a second thought."

"Let us hope. But in future, let's not use any of that as an excuse to hold a covert conversation. I shall spend forever blushing." A very tempting image. She looked delightful when she blushed. "Perhaps we could have some sort of word we could casually drop into conversation? A code between us which necessitates a meeting. Something which won't sound odd in any context."

"How about an endearment? Two hopelessly in love engaged people would use endearments when conversing with one another, wouldn't they?"

"It will need to be something specific. Something we wouldn't accidentally say in the normal flow of conversation."

" 'My darling'?"

"No good." She shook her head dismissively, and he couldn't help but notice how the weak winter sunlight made the loose tendril of hair hanging near her ear shimmer. "I call Vee 'darling' all the time. 'My love' would be better. I never say *that* to anyone."

For some reason, Hugh rather liked the sound of that.

" 'My love' works well for me, too. I've never had cause to say that either." Nor had anyone ever said it to him. A suddenly depressing thought, which suggested he had missed it without realizing. His glanced to the walls as he cursed his ancestors for their bad blood. To make it wayward yet saddle him with a conscience was doubly cruel.

"All right . . . 'my love' it is." She was pacing now, and those long legs made her rounded hips undulate with every step. " 'My love' will be our emergency endearment . . . to be uttered only when we urgently need to meet. Then we shall quietly slip away as soon as it is convenient without arousing suspicion. Where shall we meet?" She stopped abruptly to stare at him, and Hugh realized he was still staring longingly at her legs.

"Er . . ." What had possessed him to kiss her? Now he couldn't get the damned thing out of his mind despite the need to focus on more pressing things. Like the survival of this elaborate charade. "Here is probably the most prudent place. It's out of the way, rarely visited, and we will have ample warning someone is coming long before they can hear us whispering. Besides, it negates the need to worry about the weather."

"Very well. Up here it is."

"And there is also a handy servants' staircase which allows one to avoid the main thoroughfare. Do you think we should meet here every night, too, once everyone has gone to bed?" Why had he asked that? Meeting her in the dark, when the house was quiet, was surely the path to serious folly. "To catch up on the day and to plan the next, perhaps?"

"I suppose it *is* a much more prudent place than my bedchamber." As soon as she said it, she blushed, and bizarrely Hugh did, too. "Although it would be better to meet here first thing . . . rather than when it's dark . . . because . . . well . . ."

"Because we cannot allow . . . um . . . what happened last night to . . . er . . . happen again?"

"Precisely. It was . . . a mistake."

"Brought about by exceptional and fraught circumstances. I've been meaning to apologize . . ."

She held out her hand to stay him, her lovely cheeks glowing crimson. "No

258

need . . . We must both take an equal share of the blame for what occurred. We had argued, made up and then I thought it was . . . well . . . a harmless goodbye."

"As did I." Hugh sighed and, in the absence of knowing what to do with his body, rocked on his heels. He felt intensely stupid doing it while wondering why he was also aggrieved Minerva was so sensible about it all. "The trouble with goodbyes is one doesn't usually need to consider the implications of them . . . or the subsequent awkwardness they can create when . . . they get out of hand."

"Well, we certainly did a very good job of making things awkward, didn't we? But I am glad we have spoken about it. Ignoring it and pretending it hadn't happened only seemed to make the discomfort worse." She peeked up at him shyly through her lashes while drawing her frustratingly kissable bottom lip through her teeth. "I think it would be easier if we simply blame the heat of the moment and say no more on the matter, don't you? I mean, it is not as if that kiss *meant* anything, did it?"

"Yes . . . I mean *no* — of course it meant nothing!" The urge to pace was now overwhelming because his toes were curling in his boots, and any moment they were likely to cramp. It had meant something, damn it! This wouldn't hurt so blasted much if it hadn't.

By tacit agreement they were now walking toward the door, both keenly eager to escape the other now that the awkward conversation had been well and truly had. *Blasted Giles! Blasted goodbyes! Blasted ancestors! Blasted, blasted bloody kiss!*

She turned toward the staircase gratefully, before looking back. His heart soared, because he hoped he would see she hadn't meant any of what she had just said, just as he hadn't truly meant his plausible denial.

"You have no idea how truly relieved I am, Hugh. . . . It really would have been very silly to let one unfortunate slip sour an otherwise pleasant and cordial relationship."

His silly heart plummeted to his cringing, almost-cramping toes. Pleasant. Cordial. Words as insipid and uninspiring as the dreaded "nice." And "heat of the moment"? An apt but depressing summation, as for her the heat had obviously since rapidly cooled while for Hugh it was still raging like a furnace.

"Don't forget to invite the vicar for tea."

"I shan't. It is imperative we avoid eternal damnation. I cannot imagine how awful hell would be if I was stuck in it with you, doubtless forced to be your riding tutor for all eternity as my punishment because the devil has a warped sense of humor."

She giggled, and the gloriously naughty sound sent all the blood rushing to his groin again. "A fate worse than death indeed. For both of us, I can assure you. Will Marigold be there?"

"Of course not. After yesterday, that poor horse is now Saint Marigold and like all members of the sainthood will be welcomed with open arms at the pearly gates when her time comes." Hugh wanted to stand there and talk nonsense with her all day. "You should go. Before they send a search party."

"Or summon the physician." She smiled, then sighed, making him wonder if she wanted to while away the rest of the day with him, too. "I shall see you in the drawing room soon."

"Yes. The drawing room. Presently. With my mother."

"And Mozart." Alongside Hugh's unrelenting and unreturned lust.

*"Excellent."*

# CHAPTER FIFTEEN

"It is most unfortunate you injured your shoulder the day we arrived. I was looking forward to riding with you, Minerva. My son has been most effusive about your equestrian talents."

Olivia — the informality of that name still didn't feel right on Minerva's lips — was doing a very good job of separating the pair of them from the gentlemen as they strolled along the meandering garden path in search of the elusive cave. "As in all things, I fear your son has greatly embellished my talents."

"I don't doubt it. So far, his version of things leaves a lot to be desired — although I am glad you had the good sense to make the scoundrel wait and court you properly. Everything comes to Hugh too easily." Something Minerva couldn't argue with. "Do you know, he neglected to mention you had siblings? Not once did I hear about Diana or Vee, yet I knew the quartet at the local assembly in Chipping Norton played so ill during your first waltz the pair of you struggled to dance through your laughter." A charming image that made Minerva smile. "And whilst that is a perfectly lovely anecdote which I enjoyed, I should have thought the details of a pair of sisters might have featured in at least one of his extensive paragraphs. Especially as the three of you are obviously so close and Hugh has always been such an enthusiastic and entertaining letter writer with an eye for minute details."

"Their omission was very careless of him." What else could she say? Thank goodness he hadn't described her sisters, else they would all have three complicated stories to learn.

"Careless? That is one way to describe it. 'Thoughtless' is better. I was dumbstruck when I encountered them in the hallway. I didn't even know their names. It was embarrassing." The older woman slowed her pace to thoroughly scrutinize Minerva. "Although, now I have seen you, I understand why you consume him so. He often raved about your beauty. No pertinent details, of course, despite his love of them. I imagined you to be one of those blond and ethereal sorts the ton favors. So fragile and delicate you'd evaporate in high wind. I could not, for the life of me, conceive of how you survived your illness. Yet now I see you . . ."

"It all makes perfect sense? As you can plainly see, I am not the least bit fragile — although I wouldn't mind being a little more delicate. Even Hugh struggles to lift me." Minerva had felt the large muscles in his shoulders bunch as he had heaved her onto that horse. "He hides it politely, though." She had seen the strain on his face as he had hastily stepped away.

"Men in love see little fault in the women they have given their hearts to, whereas women are always much more pragmatic, don't you think? We see the faults clearly, but learn to live with them. Not all women, of course. Some ladies, I am sorry to say, have little more than fluff between their ears. I am heartily relieved to discover you are not one of them. I should have loathed a silly daughter-in-law, and I suspect, had he picked such a woman to spend eternity with, Hugh would have come to loathe her, too. He has always been a deep thinker — not that he chooses to show that particular side of his character often — and those who think deep thoughts need an intelligent spouse to discuss things with. If he ever deigns to drop the charming rogue façade long enough for a deep discussion, of course. He does like to appear irritatingly superficial most of the time."

"Why is that, do you suppose?" Because of all the things that intrigued her about Hugh, it was this which interested her the most. He was happy for people to think him shallow, lazy, and selfish yet became coy to the point of guarded, which contradicted the image he was at pains to portray.

"Hard to say . . . He's always had a mischievous side and has always had the ability to see the humor in everything. Yet as a boy, he was also incredibly academic, with a tremendous thirst for knowledge. That studiousness drove him to learn as much from his father and his tutors as he could. There is no denying my son is exceptionally clever, although nowadays only those closest to him would ever realize it. He never used to hide his intelligence."

"Then why does he?"

"I first noticed the change in him after his father died. He worshiped his father. His death really hit him hard. It was so tragic, you see, and so pointless. Thirty-seven is no age for a man to be struck down and the decline was unbelievably quick. Cruelly quick. One day he was striding around the estate much as Hugh is now — the next he was wasting away." Olivia's expression was sad.

"He had a cancer." Her gloved hand brushed her throat below one ear. "Just a tiny lump in his neck. So tiny we all thought it insignificant. Then it grew. The physician tried to cut it away, but it had already spread and there was nothing to be done. It seems staggering to think such a small thing in such a robust man could wreak such extensive damage so fast. None of us expected it, but for Hugh it was a dreadful blow. At just seventeen, he had to watch the man he believed invincible die in front of him over a matter of months. He emerged from his grief a very different young man to the boy he was."

"Seventeen is such a difficult age at the best of times."

"It is indeed, as I am sure you well know." Olivia slid her a loaded sidelong glance. "Your sister seems to particularly struggle with it." Another reminder this tiny woman was a formidable one who was cannier than Minerva could have imagined. "I couldn't help but notice she chafes a little against your mother. Or notice that it is you who tries to mediate."

"My sister is shy and awkward in her skin. More so since she has needed to wear spectacles this past year. Whereas my mother does not possess an introverted bone in her body." She hoped her smile didn't appear as brittle as it felt. If Lucretia's constant attempts at motherly nagging continued unabated, Minerva feared for the worst. Vee would only tolerate so much when her emotions were so very close to the surface, although she was trying to behave. Which was more than could be said for the actress, who at best was trying and at worst drove all three of the Merriwells quite mad. "They are as different as chalk and cheese. I am afraid the pair of them do not understand one another at all."

"All parents are doomed to clash with their offspring. That is the way of things. Neither will ever fully understand the other despite the invisible bonds which bind them. I despair of Hugh constantly — and doubtless he despairs of me." Another pointed look was accompanied with a wry smile. "I'll bet he painted me quite the harridan."

"No . . . not at all." It was probably safer to stick to the topic of her sister. "He is much fonder of you than my sister presently is of our mother. It also doesn't help familial relations that poor Vee hates the name my parents saddled her with, and I cannot say I

267

blame her. Venus is a dreadful name with unmistakably awkward connotations. I hope she grows into it one day."

"Oh, she will!" The older woman patted her arm. "All her awkwardness will pass soon enough, then she will blossom like you and Diana. Even the most beautiful butterflies start as caterpillars first. It is character building. I daresay you were a caterpillar not so long ago yourself, Minerva. What were you like at the tender age of seventeen?"

"Very awkward and not the least bit even-tempered. I believe I did my fair share of chafing against my parents, too." At seventeen, she and her useless father had had some blazing rows. And eighteen and nineteen, for that matter — until he abandoned her. "Girls, in particular, are more belligerent at that age, I think."

"Oh, my son was belligerent at that age, too! Belligerent and stubborn. He is still as stubborn as an ox, only nowadays he does it with a rakish smile rather than a sulky snarl. He was also a sorry-looking specimen. His features were too large for his face. He was a painfully gangly thing with rounded shoulders, big feet, and even bigger hands. For the longest time I feared he would never fill out enough for those excessive appendages to be in proportion."

Minerva cast a glance at the man in question a few yards ahead of her. There was nothing rounded about his broad shoulders now, and while there was no denying his hands were big as they had easily held her entire bottom, he was perfectly in proportion. If anything, he was too perfectly proportioned.

"He is a handsome devil, isn't he?" His mother had caught her looking and was smiling knowingly. "Too handsome by far."

"He is." Although, to his credit, he really didn't display any of the narcissistic tendencies that plagued other perfect specimens. "It is hardly a surprise he has been so popular with the ladies." But it was his relationship with his father that intrigued her more. And perhaps Mrs. Peters? Although much as Minerva wanted to ask about the woman who had left Hugh monosyllabic, shaken, and angry, she wasn't sure a past sweetheart was something she should ask his mother about.

"But he has clearly met his match." Olivia scrutinized her again. "Between the pair of you, I should have the best-looking grandchildren in the entire county." Minerva managed a smile despite suddenly feeling very uncomfortable with the abrupt change in topic. "And doubtless all will tower over me, too. . . . Do you plan to start a family straight after the wedding?"

"Er . . . um . . ." Allowing herself to consider the statement, even superficially for the benefit of formulating a reply, instantly reminded her that to make any children with Hugh would require a greater level of intimacy than she had engaged in already. A level of intimacy her needy body had been scandalously only too willing to accept then, and still hankered after now.

"Why do I suddenly feel my ears burning?" Hugh couldn't have heard his mother's question, but he had turned around at precisely the same moment as Minerva's cheeks exploded crimson — he must have somehow sensed it.

"I was asking your fiancée if you planned to start a family immediately after the wedding? If the pair of you get cracking straightaway, I could have a grandchild by Michaelmas."

"Olivia!" Next to Hugh, Jeremiah rolled his eyes. "That is none of your business, woman!"

"Whyever not? Hugh is my only child, and therefore my only chance at grandchildren. I am not getting any younger and should like to enjoy them before my dotage. Minerva will soon be his wife, so it stands to reason she will have a say in the matter, too." She looked toward her son expectantly, not the least bit contrite. "Minerva only has *so many* childbearing years left and it's long past time Hugh did his duty."

"Have you not seen my ravishing fiancée?" His gaze suddenly locked with Minerva's, as the flirty Hugh decided to make an unexpected reappearance. Those twinkling blue eyes raked the length of her slowly. Possessively even. She could feel the heat of his gaze through all the thick layers of winter clothing to her sensitive, wanton bare skin, which still craved his touch. "For I would hardly call it a duty, Mother."

"There is no need to be crude, Hugh. You're embarrassing Minerva."

"You brought the subject up."

"In a proper manner. You decided to make it improper."

"That's because I am improper and always have been."

"You are *both* embarrassing Minerva!" Jeremiah came to her rescue, offering his arm and pinning them both with his glare. "Walk with me, my dear, and save yourself. Then I can list all the reasons why only a fool would want to marry into this family." Then he set off at a brisk pace, putting some welcome distance between the pair of them.

"I'm very sorry. . . . She means well. . . . She just cannot stop herself from interfering. And Hugh is reliably Hugh and loves to vex her when she does." He patted her hand. "You will get used to it."

"It is lovely she cares." Minerva doubted her father gave two figs about her life. "I know Hugh loves his mother, too. It's funny — we were just discussing parental relationships with children and how fractious they can be."

"Then they gave you a proper display of it to prove the point. They're always the same. Always butting heads and trying to outdo one another in who can be the more outrageous. I am trying to run interference — but Olivia is not easily swayed. Inexcusable grandchild questions aside, I hope she hasn't been too ferocious on her quest to discover all there is to know about you. She's been desperate to meet you for nearly two years."

"If Hugh had done a better job of informing his mother about my family and me, and not thwarting your previous attempts at visiting, then she wouldn't have so many questions."

"There is that." Jeremiah tossed a glance over his shoulder to where Hugh and his mother were now bickering several yards away. "Can I entrust you with a secret, Minerva?"

"Of course."

"Between you and me, my wife has been convinced for several months he'd been making you up entirely." He said it with a chuckle, but it confirmed her suspicions. Olivia had her son's measure, and Minerva would have to be careful. "Because it is such a convoluted tale . . ."

"They do say the truth is always stranger than fiction." She hoped her own smile appeared natural and not as tight as it felt. "And let's not forget, Hugh can embellish a story better than Aesop, with scant regard to the truth."

"That he can. He has a way with words."

"And uses them selfishly to distract everyone from whatever he wants to distract them from."

"Indeed, he does." Jeremiah looked back at his stepson affectionately, who was now pointing to something while his mother smiled. "But not always selfishly. He's always had a talent for using the right words to pour oil on troubled waters. A second ago they were arguing — but now his mother is laughing. Another potentially awkward moment already ironed over. He always hated confrontation, even as a boy, and went to ridiculous lengths to avoid being the cause of it."

"Did you know Hugh as a child?"

"Since about the age of ten. His father and I were friends. Good friends. He befriended me at a time when Englishmen hated Americans and vice versa, and we remained friends forever after."

"How?"

"Diplomacy, my dear. After the War of Independence and before the War of 1812, relations between our countries were hostile. For my sins, I was sent here as part of the United States Legation to London when tensions still ran high. It was a difficult time. Hugh was one of the peers assigned to the Foreign Office and he held out an olive branch."

"*Hugh?* Worked for the Foreign Office? When?"

"Not *your* Hugh. His father. Didn't you know he's named after his daddy?"

"I didn't."

"Now he's older, sometimes I swear it's like looking at the old Hugh in a mirror. Peas in a pod, the pair of them." He smiled, remembering. "Both had a way with words. Both thoroughly charming. Both born diplomats. Both worried too much about others."

"He never told me . . ." More pieces of the difficult puzzle that was Hugh slotted into place. She had sensed those qualities, knew they drew her, but had no proof. "Not any of it."

Jeremiah nodded, then sighed. "I'm not surprised. He doesn't like to talk about his father any more than he likes to talk about himself. I think it's still too raw." That certainly explained his reluctance to talk about him when she had asked.

"It's hard to lose a parent."

"Yes . . . of course." Jeremiah's expression was suddenly filled with sympathy. "You recently lost your own father. My sincerest commiserations. I should have said that before."

"We were not close in the way Hugh was with his father." Something about Jeremiah made her spill the truth without thinking. "The sad truth is, he was a selfish man who always put himself first and never really cared about the feelings of others."

She caught him studying her with interest and realized she was in grave danger of deviating from the original plan, because she was discussing her real father. "His solitary walk in the Cairngorms is a perfect example of his selfishness. His Scottish relations begged him not to go out, but he thought he knew best and lived to rue the day." A thoroughly stupid thing to say. "Or didn't . . . as it turned out." In case the flagrant lie was apparent in her eyes, she looked down at her feet. "It really is a convoluted story, isn't it? Consumption and the Cairngorms. No wonder Olivia had her doubts about it?"

His deep chuckle rumbled, and she looked up to see him nodding in agreement. "She came here determined to catch Hugh out — and caught your entire family instead. Her face was a picture, I can tell you."

"I'll wager it was. Perhaps almost as stunned as Hugh's was to find her in the drawing room a good two weeks before she had told him she would arrive. I suppose she took that earlier ship on purpose."

"Already you know my wife so well. I believe the pair of you will get on famously. Once she's ascertained you are worthy, of course." He winked, and Minerva was suddenly uncomfortable. Because she wasn't worthy. She was lying to two lovely people for money.

They rounded a copse of trees, and she saw a cluster of thatched roofs in the distance, their matching chimney pots puffing out cheerful smoke. In case her crush-ing guilt leaked and made Jeremiah suspi-cious, too, Minerva decided to change the subject. "Another village? I didn't realize."

"Not a village at all. It's much too small. That's Hugh's Hamlet. Or at least that's what the locals have taken to calling it."

"Hugh's Hamlet?"

"Your fiancé's revolutionary solution to the aging or widowed tenants on the estate?" At her genuinely baffled expression, he shook his head. "Most landlords kick those who can no longer work off their land. The good ones pay them a small pension to ensure they can afford to live somewhere else. Hugh decided to build them their own little cottages so they can stay here till the end of their days rent-free *alongside* their pensions."

"What a lovely thing to do." Something odd happened beneath Minerva's ribs. A little thud, like a bolt sliding into place, then her heart seemed to grow and swell. Hugh really was a nice man. Perhaps one of the nicest.

"I'm guessing by that stunned look, he never mentioned it?"

"Of course he didn't. And I sincerely doubt he'd have taken any credit for it if I had asked him, so thank you for enlightening me." The more she learned about her fake fiancé, the more she liked him — when already there was so much she liked. A dangerous state of affairs when they had no future.

"He wanted to reward them for their years of loyalty. Like his father, Hugh is also an unfashionably liberal man. And just like his daddy, he doesn't brag about it either. If anything, he's cagier about his philanthropic work than his day-to-day work and that's saying something when the whole of London thinks all he does is enjoy himself."

"I knew he is diligent with estate matters . . . but I had no idea he was philanthropic."

"Then, my dear, it would be my pleasure to enlighten you. Just don't tell Hugh I let slip his *dirty* little secret. He'd never forgive me for telling you the *shocking* truth."

# CHAPTER SIXTEEN

"Do any of you play the pianoforte?" His mother directed the question to all three sisters, pointing to the instrument in the corner of the drawing room, and Hugh kicked himself for not knowing the answer. Music was one of the accomplishments considered acceptable for all gently bred young ladies. Now that their second dinner was done, and they were moving past the getting-to-know-you stage and moving to the what-shall-we-do-to-while-away-the-next-hour stage, it was inevitable his mother would want to hear someone play.

"Sadly no." It was Diana who responded. "None of us have ever shown any talent with an instrument. But Minerva is an exceptionally gifted artist and Vee excels at sewing and embroidery. I dabble in writing short stories, my lady. I did try poetry for a while, but my efforts were a little too dark for the medium and they gave Vee nightmares. We all enjoy reading, although our tastes are vastly different."

"What sort of books do you prefer, Miss Diana?"

"Being a terminal cynic, with a curious penchant for the macabre, I tend to favor a good gothic novel. The more horrible, the better. I recently read a very disturbing book called *Frankenstein.* It is about a mad doctor who makes a monster out of bits and pieces of the many bodies he has robbed from graves, then brings it to life. Have you read it?"

"I cannot say that I have." His mother pulled a face. "And I must say, Diana, you are not really convincing me to read it either." She shuddered. "Monsters and stolen body parts do not appeal to me."

"Me either." It had taken a week, but now apparently even Vee had finally found her voice. "I prefer the classics. Milton, Shakespeare, Homer, Chaucer . . . I adore *The Canterbury Tales* and the *Iliad.* I am currently reading *Paradise Lost.* It is fascinating to think a man from so long ago could be so insightful."

Diana rolled her eyes at those choices. "Vee is the bluestocking of the family. She likes her literature old and crusty. The older and crustier, the better."

Vee surprised Hugh by taking this criticism well. "Diana is simply jealous I understand the intricacies of those texts and she doesn't. It must be galling to have a younger sibling with *superior* intelligence."

"What do you like to read, Minerva?" Jeremiah was pouring glasses of sherry on the sideboard.

"Minerva loves *romance.*" Diana clasped her hands to her heart and fluttered her eyelashes disparagingly. "Sickly Byron poems, damsels in distress. Knights in shining armor."

Hugh's gaze flicked to Minerva's just as hers flicked to his, before she turned away to sip from her sherry glass, pretending she wasn't blushing a little. It was obvious they were both thinking the same thing. She had referred to him as her knight more than once, and the main reason she was here was because she had been a damsel in distress. "Although she is less of a hopeless romantic nowadays, ever since her despicable first love cruelly broke her heart."

Beneath his fingers, Hugh felt the fragile stem of his port glass snap. "First love?" It was obvious from all three sisters' faces, Diana had inadvertently let something slip she shouldn't have.

"More sweetheart than love, truth be told.

For a little while they made eyes at one another across the pews at church." She waved it away with impressive nonchalance. "But we do like to tease her about it. As sisters do."

His mother was having none of it. "How did the scoundrel break your heart, dear?"

"He didn't break it." Minerva, too, was doing a good job of brushing it away. "It was my first foray into flirting. We exchanged a few meaningful looks over the course of several months — but he left Chipping Norton before they could develop into anything more. Which is just as well." Her gaze sought his once again, and he could tell she desperately wanted him to change the subject. "Else I never would have fallen for Hugh."

"A knight in shining armor always trumps a few stolen glances." His mother squeezed his fake fiancée's hand. "Especially when you have a lifetime of stolen glances ahead of you."

He should change the subject.

"What was his name?" Jealousy had apparently taken over his vocal cords.

"I don't recall. . . ." Minerva was lying. "It was a long time ago. I was what? Eighteen? Nineteen? It really was nothing. In fact, I barely remember the fellow's face."

More lies. She both recalled it and regretted the loss of it. The faceless fellow had meant something, had hurt her, and Hugh hated him regardless.

"Good grief . . ." His mother had a look of awe and wonder on her face as she pointed to him. "Look at his expression! Hugh's jealous!"

"Merely curious, I assure you."

"Does curiosity pinch the features quite so much, Hugh? Or make you grind your teeth and glare? I think not." She nudged Minerva. "I've never seen my son jealous of anything before. It is quite the sight to behold."

He was going to strangle his mother, just as soon as he could stop his teeth from grinding.

"It's *very* romantic, isn't it? And also *very* funny." She pinned him with an innocent stare he knew from experience was merely a precursor to a good skewering. "Hugh, darling — seeing as Minerva has come to terms with your shocking reputation, you can hardly be jealous of a few stolen glances on her part. Even the most sensible ladies are not immune to having their heads turned and she is a *very* beautiful woman." Something he was only too painfully aware of. "Therefore, it stands to reason many, *many* men would have previously tried to stand in your privileged shoes."

What was he supposed to say to that? "Their loss is my gain."

"Indeed it is, my darling. And that is what you should focus on. Try not to allow Minerva's past loves to consume you. And whilst a little jealousy flatters a lady's ego, too much is unbecoming."

"I am not the slightest bit jealous."

"Then relax your eyebrows, dear. A scowl like that will only bring about premature wrinkles."

"Some sherry, Mrs. Landridge?" Jeremiah purposefully placed his body between Hugh and the vile tormentor who had given birth to him.

"No, thank you. I rarely drink anything stronger than tea." Lucretia's theatrical voice filled the entire room, giving Hugh an idea that just might save him from his current predicament.

"Do you play the pianoforte, Mrs. Landridge?" *Please say yes.* "Or any other instrument, perchance?" He'd have a couple of sturdy footmen cart the enormous harp from the music room if it came to it.

Lucretia blossomed. "My *voice* is *my* instrument!" Of course it was. "If somebody plays the pianoforte, I should be delighted to sing a little ditty for you all."

"My mother plays. . . . In fact, she is a *virtuoso* on the pianoforte." He leaned past the barricade of his stepfather to offer her a sickly grin. "I am sure she would be *delighted* to accompany you."

"I should be delighted." Thwarted from embarrassing him, her returning smile was just as sickly. "I suppose I could play a quick song. Do you have one in mind, Mrs. Landridge?"

"Do you know any Mozart?"

He wanted to hug her. Without realizing it, Lucretia had become his unwitting accomplice. He suppressed the urge to grin. "My mother *adores* Mozart, Mrs. Landridge." She wasn't the only one who could give a good skewering. "In fact, she can play most of his pieces from memory . . ." Each and every one drove her mad. Especially the operettas. Dear Mama had a deep well of loathing for Mozart's operettas.

"I really can't. . . . It's been so long since I played, Hugh, I cannot remember any of them."

"No matter, Mother dearest . . . fortunately, we still have *all* the sheet music."

"I am *quite* sure we don't, dear."

"Oh yes we do, Mama! Don't you recall I

*bought* you the entire works several years ago?"

She had been livid. The month before she had departed for Boston, she had invited every single eligible woman from Land's End to John o'Groats to a ten-day house party at Standish House, which she had neglected to tell him about. He arrived home expecting a quiet week to focus on estate business and instead had suffered through the most interminable ten days of his life with the most rabid, most husband-hungry young ladies he had ever had the gross misfortune to meet. They simpered, they flirted. More than a few tried to kiss him, and one tenacious debutante had brazenly arrived at his bedchamber door in her nightgown offering him a free sample of the goods. After that, he had resorted to barricading his bedchamber at night for the duration in case he found himself ruined!

Hugh, obviously, had rewarded his mother for her treachery by sending a messenger to London to purchase every piece Mozart had ever written, then producing it with a flourish one evening, declaring he adored it, so she could play it while her gaggle of prospective daughters-in-law warbled out every aria directly next to her shoulder. It had been a magnificent piece of revenge. She had retired that night with a throbbing head-ache, and the very next day had ordered every page be burned on a bonfire. Not being stupid, Hugh had rescued them just in case he ever needed to torture her again. Clearly that day had come.

He gestured to his hovering butler across the room.

"Payne — fetch the Mozart from my study, would you? The complete works. It's in the bottom drawer of my desk. There's a good chap." He toasted his mother and the actress with his broken glass, gripping the stem with his little finger so that nobody would be able to see it was now detached. "I do love a bit of Mozart. *Especially* the operettas. And perhaps, if I may be so bold, Mrs. Landridge, you could honor us with *more* than the one song."

"I suppose I could sing a few of the arias . . ."

"Yes, the arias! Mother's favorites! Sing *all* of them! Wouldn't that be lovely?"

"Really?" Lucretia was beside herself with joy at the chance of a solo performance in front of a reluctantly captive audience. "Well, in that case . . . perhaps I will partake of a little sherry, Mr. Peabody . . . to lubricate my voice."

Twenty minutes later and Lucretia was

murdering yet another aria, this one from *The Magic Flute.* Her singing brought a new meaning to the term "soprano" because she certainly hit notes Hugh had never heard in his life and had no desire to ever hear again. Some brought actual tears to the eyes, and not tears of joy at the beauty of the music. It was so bad, Diana, Vee, and Jeremiah had stopped pretending not to giggle.

Not that Lucretia noticed. She was fully immersed and had become a frustrated opera singer with every fiber and sinew of her being. It was so bad, his mother had skipped several passages in the hope it would speed the actress up and was blatantly scowling more with each spirited stanza.

It was so bad, it almost stopped Hugh obsessing about Minerva's mystery beau who had cruelly left her brokenhearted. Not quite bad enough, though, because he couldn't seem to stop thinking about him.

For probably the twentieth time, he allowed his gaze to wander to her. For some unknown reason that spoke volumes about the strength of her character, Minerva managed to listen intently to the racket without grimacing or sniggering once. Occasionally, her concentration was so intense she seemed lost in it — unless the unexpected reminder of that faceless Romeo from her past had set her thinking about him to the exclusion of all else — including the exuberant Lucretia?

Did she miss him?

Had she loved him?

Had they been hopeful flirts, innocent sweethearts, or — and this one really stuck in his throat — lovers?

During Hugh's singular but memorable foray into intimacy with Minerva, he had not, he realized now, thought her kisses either clumsy or untutored. Which surely they would have been if Romeo hadn't introduced her to the sport first? Alongside the unstoppable surge of furious jealousy, this thought also beggared the question as to how Hugh had measured up. For if Minerva's had surpassed every other kiss in his extensive experience, it now seemed tragic his might not have had a similar effect on her. Something primal, wholly male, and visceral demanded his should have eradicated all future thought of Romeo's from her pretty head forever.

"Should we rescue your mother or make her suffer a little longer?" Jeremiah was doing another round with the sherry. "Bearing in mind we all get to suffer alongside her."

"I'm all for her suffering all night." And

he wouldn't feel bad about it. "She deserves nothing less."

"Fair enough. In which case, I call dibs on you carrying Minerva's mother up the stairs when she collapses in a heap on the floor." He waved the almost-empty decanter in front of Hugh's face. "That voice of hers apparently needs a lot of lubricating, and seeing as her performance is getting worse by the second, there is every chance she is now well on her way to being drunk."

"She is?" He took a long hard look at the actress for the first time since she had taken her place at the piano. Her face was flushed. There was a manic look to her expression. She was clasping her enormous bosom with more fervor than usual and leaning on the instrument in a manner that suggested standing straight was now much too much effort. "Oh dear." Sober, Lucretia DeVere lacked all social awareness; drunk, there was no telling what she might do. "Perhaps we should intervene?"

# Chapter Seventeen

They waited till the final verse before both erupting in simultaneous applause. "Mrs. Landridge — that was splendid." As the host and her employer, Hugh realized it was his job to extricate Lucretia from the piano. He strode across the room and grabbed her hands, practically yanking her from where she had taken root. Behind her, with impressive speed, his mother gathered up every sheet of music, her eyes shooting daggers at him as she did so, before turning to Minerva.

"Minerva — please. Indulge us in a song. I shall play anything *but* Mozart?"

"Oh no! Really. I cannot sing."

"She really cannot." Diana was quick to back her sister.

"Nonsense, my dear. Hugh raved about your voice last Christmas in Boston. He said you sang like a nightingale."

Now Minerva was shooting him daggers, too.

"As has been proved time and time again, Olivia, your son has grossly embellished my talents. Believe me, nobody wants to hear me sing."

"You can't be any worse than your mother," mumbled Jeremiah under his breath.

"I could sing another?" Lucretia yanked her arm from Hugh's.

"No! *No . . .*" His mother only just remembered her manners. "You have delighted us enough, Mrs. Landridge, and I don't want you to strain that marvelous voice of yours. Minerva will sing. I absolutely insist."

"I always did an encore at Drury . . ." Hugh rudely interrupted before the actress dropped them all in it.

"Please, Minerva. For me?" He pleaded with his eyes as he took another firm hold on Lucretia. "Your dear mother deserves a rest after her efforts."

"I really cannot stress enough how badly I sing . . ." Trapped, Minerva stood, as both Vee and Diana stifled unladylike snorts at the prospect and Hugh manhandled Lucretia to a chair. "We could play cards instead. What about whist?"

His mother wouldn't be deterred. "What

would you like to sing, dear?"

"I don't really know many songs."

"Seeing as it is almost December, what about a Christmas carol? Surely you know a Christmas carol?"

"Not many." Minerva was walking to the pianoforte like a condemned prisoner on the way to the gallows.

"How about 'Hark! The Herald Angels Sing'? Everybody knows that one." She played a few bars encouragingly. "What key?"

"Off," said Diana, earning her a jab in the ribs from the youngest sister before they both sniggered again.

"Any," said Minerva miserably. "It will make no difference."

The music began again, and his fake fiancée seemed to shrink into a shadow of her former self. *"Hark! The herald angels sing . . ."*

She was flat. Dreadfully flat. Her normally animated and lovely voice was nasal and unpleasant.

*"Glory to the newborn King . . ."* The "King" was off-key. Badly off-key. *"Peace on earth, and mercy mild . . ."*

"I will never understand the English sense of humor." Jeremiah sat heavily next to Hugh on the sofa. "But yours is even more warped than your mother's — and that is saying something." They both winced at Minerva's failed attempt at a high note. "I assume you knew your fiancée was completely tone deaf?"

"Of course I knew!"

Good grief, it was awful. So awful it bordered on the marvelous. He felt his lips twitching.

"But purely to torment your mother, you sacrificed the woman of your dreams to complete humiliation. Her sisters are openly laughing at her." Vee and Diana were practically hysterical. "She's going to strangle you later."

"No, she won't." He hoped. "She's stepping into the breach to save us from Mrs. Landridge." Who drunkenly believed she was back in a theatre in front of a paying audience. As if Minerva knew he was staring at her, her emerald gaze lifted to his. Those lovely eyes were narrowed, but her own mouth was curving into a smile. She knew she was awful, too, yet she had done it anyway to save him. Nothing seemed to daunt Minerva. He loved that about her.

"Can I pour anyone else some more sherry?" Lucretia had abandoned the safety of the sturdy wingback Hugh had put her in to top up her glass. She took a healthy swig, then tripped over her own feet. "Whoops! Silly me!" Although she managed not to spill a drop.

"She's definitely drunk." Jeremiah grinned at Hugh. "And she's definitely *your* problem."

*"Hark! The herald angels sing . . ."*

He managed to get to the actress before she tripped again, but as Hugh tried to grab the sherry out of her hand, she snatched it sideways and sloshed it all over Jeremiah, something that made Minerva stop midchorus.

"Brava, Minerva!" His mother practically slammed the lid of the piano down. "What a rare talent for music your family has."

"Oh, thank you, my lady!" Lucretia believed the compliment was for her, basking in it as if it were the sun. "Thank you!" Her hand fluttered near her ample bosom, then to Hugh's horror, she bowed. "Music has always been a passion of mine." She beamed as he tried to lead her to the doorway. "My dear Lord Fareham — did I ever tell you I played the Queen of the Night on Drury Lane?"

"*No . . .* really?" Hugh patted her arm as he tugged her along, before turning to the rest of the room, which had gone ominously quiet. He rolled his eyes, mimicking drinking with his free hand and mouthing the words "too much sherry" slowly in case anyone missed it.

"Yes indeed . . . It was a *triumph!*"

It was like watching knitting unravel, and there was nothing he could do about it.

She was now leaning on him like a dead-weight, making it difficult to maneuver her with any speed. "If you don't mind me saying, you look a little unwell, Mrs. Landridge. Perhaps the sherry was off?" Because she was wonderful, Minerva had come to assist him. Even so, the sizable Lucretia proved impossible to budge.

"Come, Mama . . . It's late. . . . Let's get you to your bedchamber."

"The critics called me 'mesmerizing' . . . said my performance completely stole the show. . . . Drury Lane" — she slurred the word "Drury" — "has never seen the like since."

"You performed at Drury Lane?" Clutching the now-haphazard stack of the complete works of Wolfgang Amadeus Mozart, his mother bustled over. "The *actual* Drury Lane?"

"I did indeed. Many, many, *many* times . . ."

"My mother was an actress in her youth." Minerva's expression was apologetic. "Before her marriage, of course. Since then she has been entirely respectable. Surely Hugh told you about that?"

"We don't tend to talk about it — for obvious reasons — but, alas, Mama is not used to sherry and has quite forgotten all her normal inhibitions," said Diana, stepping into the breach, too. "But it caused quite the scandal when Papa asked her to marry him, as I am sure you can imagine. Actresses are few and far between in Chipping Norton and country squires are certainly not supposed to marry them."

"You *did* tell her, didn't you, Hugh?" Minerva rolled her eyes in mock irritation.

Then his mother joined her. "Of course not. It is yet another interesting detail my son omitted to mention."

"But I *specifically* told you to tell her, Hugh." Minerva glared at him, exasperated, shaking her head, clearly getting her own revenge for his forcing her to sing. "You promised me! I wanted there to be no secrets from your family. Your mother deserves to be forewarned in case Mama's past causes another scandal." She then turned back to his mother, acting better than any thespian he had ever seen at Drury Lane. "I am so sorry this is how you had to find out, Olivia. What must you be thinking of us?"

"It is quite all right, dear. This family is quite used to its own share of scandals. My evil son is one of them." Without warning, she whacked him on the back of his head with the Mozart. "As I said earlier, during Hugh's *obvious* fit of jealousy over your former beau, the past is the past and best left there. Whatever Mrs. Landridge did before her marriage to Mr. Landridge is nobody else's concern except her husband's. And as he is no longer here, the topic is dead and buried with him."

"Dead and buried . . . my *beloved* Mr. Landridge!" Lucretia suddenly listed sideways, finally remembering who she was supposed to be. Her inebriated pointed finger waggled directionless. "My darling husband, *Mr. Landridge,* forgave me for my scandalous past because he loved me with all his heart. He was my soul mate . . . my one true love . . ." She screwed up her face and clutched the front of Minerva's dress. "Oh, why did he have to die?"

This was disintegrating quickly into a farce.

The sort of catastrophic farce Giles had predicted — and there was nothing Hugh could do about it.

"I think it is long past your bedtime, Mama." Both Vee and Diana simultaneously relieved him of his burden, and the three of them managed to propel her forward.

"That sherry is strong stuff. . . ." Lucretia swayed as they led her to the door. "It has gone straight to my head . . ."

"Good night, ladies." Jeremiah was holding the door. "Thank you for an . . . enlightening and entertaining evening."

"I am so sorry." Minerva winced at Jeremiah, then Hugh, then his mother as they bundled past. "This is all so mortifying." With impressive speed, they maneuvered Lucretia across the hallway to the staircase.

They were barely out of sight when he felt the full force of the now-rolled-up Mozart again across his cranium.

# CHAPTER EIGHTEEN

"It is such a shame your mother won't be joining us." Olivia daintily spread jam on her triangle of toast. "I do hope she feels better soon."

She was also being very polite about the root cause of Lucretia DeVere's absence at breakfast — the impressive consumption of almost an entire decanter full of sherry in a scandalously short period. It had taken all three of them to get her up the stairs. By the time they had dragged her to her bedchamber, she was singing again, and they had needed the help of both Payne and a maid to lift her bulk onto the bed.

This morning, she had been much as they had left her last night. Fully clothed and snoring.

"I wonder where my idiot son is?" Olivia had also been hideously polite about Minerva's cringeworthy performance last night, taking her to one side before they

300

reached the breakfast room and apologizing for her son's warped sense of humor and for unconsciously embarrassing her by insisting she sing.

"If he's not quick, he will have to leave for church without having any breakfast. Which will serve the scoundrel right. That reminds me, I need to speak to Cook before we depart for church. I want white soup served at every meal. Including breakfast. And there is to be absolutely no seasoning added to Hugh's. My son needs to learn I will not be trifled with."

"Payne — are you sure you checked *everywhere* for Hugh?" He was probably still waiting patiently for Minerva in the portrait gallery for their early morning rendezvous, unaware she had been intercepted by his mother on the landing.

"He is not in his rooms or study and the stable hasn't seen hide nor hair of him, Miss Minerva."

"Perhaps he's wandered to one of the *lesser*-used parts of the house." She was willing the butler to understand, although to be fair to him, he probably had no idea the pair of them were supposed to meet in the gallery covertly. "Maybe he has gone somewhere *quiet* to think?"

"My idiot son doesn't think. Or if he does,

he thinks only of his own amusement."

"But it was funny last night." Diana's lips had been twitching all morning. "Especially when Minerva delighted us." Next to her, Vee sniggered, which set Jeremiah off, too, causing Olivia to scowl at him.

"And do not think I have forgiven your part in last night's debacle either, Husband. You plied poor Mrs. Landridge with drink and embarrassed all her daughters in the process."

"I hardly *plied* her, Olivia. Don't you recall her summoning me over? And did you not hear her add the words 'Mr. Peabody, don't be stingy' to the opening bars of *Una Donna A Quindici Anni*?"

"Still — you should have applied some common sense! Especially when poor Mrs. Landridge is unused to alcohol."

"She didn't drink it like a stranger to the sport." Jeremiah snapped open his paper just as Hugh strode in, looking a little flustered but as effortlessly handsome as usual.

"Sorry for my tardiness." His eyes darted to Miverva's in question, confirming he had been waiting for her upstairs.

"Did you forget today was Sunday, too, Hugh?" Minerva smiled at him over the rim of her teacup. "Honestly, if I hadn't collided with your mother on the landing this morning, I would be late, too."

"Ah yes . . . I had forgotten. I had also forgotten my mother's zealous observance in attending the Sunday sermon."

"I might have known you would forget church this morning." Olivia pointedly turned away from him and rolled her eyes. "Hugh requires near constant nagging, Minerva."

"She never nags me, Mother."

"Whyever not?"

Minerva hadn't expected that question, which meant she told the truth rather than parry with a pithy setdown. "Because he is normally no trouble at all." Aside from being the charming conundrum who occupied far more of her thoughts than he should. The conundrum blew her a kiss down the table, and she couldn't help but smile at his nerve. "If one ignores his flirtatious tendencies, of course. I shall need to knock that out of him."

"I must say, Minerva, in view of his outrageous behavior yesterday, I am surprised you would even deign to speak to him today. You owe your dear fiancée a groveling apology, Hugh."

He sat in his chair at the head of the table and tried to look contrite. "Please forgive me, Minerva. As my mother was at great pains to tell me last night, I shouldn't have used you, your mother, or my own dear mother's deep hatred for Mozart for my own shallow amusement." The mischievous twinkle in his deep blue eyes called him a liar. "Do you forgive me?"

"I shall give it some thought." She took a casual sip of her tea. "Although forgiveness hangs on your actions rather than your words and shouldn't be rushed into. I shall expect some proper groveling today and will come back to you with my decision after dinner."

Olivia nodded in approval. "Very sensible, my dear. It is always best to start a marriage *stingy* on the forgiveness, as it encourages the husband to improve those aspects of his character which need the most work early on." Jeremiah's withering sigh behind his newspaper earned a glare. "My own husband is still a work in progress, of course, because he was *old* and too set in his ways when we married. But Hugh is young enough to train properly. So long as you are diligent, Minerva. Don't allow that boyish charm to distract you from his wicked ways."

Before Hugh could offer a rebuttal, Olivia shivered dramatically. "Is anyone else chilly?" The room was the perfect temperature. "Payne, could you throw another log on the fire, please?" A look passed between Hugh's mother and his faithful servant. Then he produced the *log* from under a cloth on the sideboard. It was the sheet music from yesterday, the entire works of Wolfgang Amadeus Mozart, tied in a roll with string and lying ceremoniously on a silver platter that he carried slowly around the table so he could parade it past Hugh before it was tossed on the fire. The paper instantly crackled and curled as it burned. "What a lovely sound! I cannot say I have ever enjoyed Mozart more."

Hugh toasted her with his teacup. "*Touché,* Mother."

"Do not think I am done with you yet, darling." Olivia smiled with mock innocence as a footman placed a loaded plate in front of her son. "Unlike your charitable and forgiving fiancée, I shall have no qualms about seeking further revenge. Sweet, swift, unexpected revenge . . ."

He stared down at the plate warily. "Have you poisoned my eggs?"

"As if I would do something so predictable, dear."

"Run, Minerva," Jeremiah's stage whisper came loudly from behind his newspaper.

"Run like the wind back to the sanity of Chipping Norton. Save yourself before it's too late."

Twenty minutes later and Minerva found herself squeezed into the same carriage as Hugh, his mother, and her husband, while her sisters had the one behind all to themselves. She was seated next to Olivia, the two gentlemen opposite, Hugh's long legs encroaching in the space needed for hers as they pulled up outside Saint Mary's.

"My lady . . . Mr. Peabody . . ." The vicar beamed. "How delighted I was to learn of your unexpected return. It has been too long. And you have brought Lord Fareham, too, I see. Saint Mary's has missed him."

This statement earned Hugh another glare from his mother as she took the reverend's proffered hand to exit the carriage. "I had hoped now that he was finally settling down, he would be more diligent in caring for his rotten soul in my absence — but alas, he is a terminal disappointment. Which leads me to assume you have not yet been introduced to my soon-to-be daughter-in-law either, which is very remiss of him, too. Miss Minerva Landridge, allow me to introduce Reverend Cranham."

The older gentleman took her hand, too,

bowing over it as he helped her down. "Miss Minerva, I have long despaired of His Lordship ever abandoning his carefree bachelor ways and I cannot tell you how happy it makes me to know he has finally found a bride."

"Thank you, Reverend." There was something about the white-haired vicar's cheerful smiling face that instinctively made her like him. "Hugh always speaks very fondly of you." Or at least he had on the one occasion he had mentioned him — when he had promised to invite the man to tea for the sake of her lying soul.

"Does he indeed? That is very gracious of him. Although I must confess that until this week, I knew nothing but hearsay about you, Miss Minerva. His Lordship has been very closemouthed about his lovely fiancée, which in turn has set the entire village abuzz, now that you are finally here in the flesh. The pews are filled today, and I suspect that is more to do with their desire to glimpse the woman who has finally stolen this rapscallion's heart rather than the scintillating nature of my sermons." He glanced toward Hugh and grinned. "I have had the family pews freshly dusted, my lord, in honor of your presence here today. They had accumulated quite a thick layer."

"Thank you, Reverend." The two men shook hands like old friends. "And might I congratulate you on the splendid job you have done of efficiently alerting both my mother *and* my fiancée to my laxness in attending. You seem to take great pleasure in maligning my good character."

"The more people I have praying for your soul, the better."

"I fear it is much too late but I appreciate the sentiment nevertheless." Hugh waggled his arm at Minerva. "Let's get this over with, then, shall we?"

She waited while Jeremiah and the reverend escorted Olivia through the ancient doors before asking the question that had kept her up most of the night. "Do you think we got away with it?"

"Thanks to your quick thinking, yes."

"Entirely?"

"She is too busy with her outrage at her menfolk to give Lucretia much thought. She's furious at Jeremiah for plying Lucretia with drink and she's more furious at me for the Mozart and for lying to her about your musical abilities simply to make her look stupid."

"I am *so* sorry about that." She squeezed his arm and quashed the urge to run her hands up and down his biceps. "I've never had an ear for music — but in my defense, I did try to warn you." Music, like the sound of the church organ wafting toward them as they sauntered down the path, all sounded like noise to her. Noise that simply varied according to the tempo. Pleasant but instantly forgettable. She could hear the different instruments, appreciate the skill it took to create, but could rarely identify the difference between the melody of the verse and the chorus.

"Which explains why you were the only one not wincing at Lucretia's caterwauling. And there I was thinking you were the consummate actress . . ."

"I feel most sorry for your poor mother. But bless her, she carried on regardless."

"As did you . . . and you did it for me."

"Well — you are *paying* me."

He shook his head. "You did it because I asked you to and I am humbled by your generosity. You are a very nice person, Minerva."

" 'Nice'? I thought you considered that word an insult. An insipid and uninspiring word."

"I believe I am coming to see one can be thoroughly nice without being either." He paused beneath the archway. "Are you braced for the curious stares and whispers?"

"Of course. How bad can it be?"

"Spoken like a true daughter of the city, used to the faceless thronging masses. But this isn't the capital, my darling Minerva, and the country folk really do have nothing better to do than speculate on the naughty Earl of Fareham's elusive fiancée." He patted her hand as if she were old and senile. "It is going to be torture. Hold your head up high. Smile. Try not to take anything you overhear personally. If we are lucky, the next hour will only feel like three interminable weeks."

He led her through the doors, and instantly she felt like a scientific specimen under a magnifying glass. The Reverend Cranham hadn't lied when he had said the entire village had turned out. Every pew, bar the family seats at the side, was stuffed full of people squashed together. In the aisles more were standing, and every face and pair of eyes were instantly glued to hers as Hugh led her toward the altar. Then, almost by tacit agreement, the whole congregation began to whisper, the noise not dissimilar to that of an enormous, agitated hornet's nest and, exactly as he had intimated, not the least bit subtle in their curiosity or their judgment.

*She's tall . . .*

*Not how I pictured her . . .*

*Unfashionably dark . . .*

*Old . . . best get her skates on if the mistress is to get grandchildren . . .*

*Unusual . . . pretty . . . sickly . . . consumption . . . He could do better . . . I heard they have to get married . . .*

Minerva had never felt so exposed and self-conscious in her entire life. When they reached their pew at the front, conveniently in full view of everyone behind them, Hugh opened the little gate that separated the Standishes from the masses, helped her sit in the seats behind his family and her sisters, then sat next to her, the ever-present twinkle in his eyes suddenly gone.

He reached out and took her hand, doubtless as a show of support or to show the curious onlookers he was suitably besotted, but the innocent contact instantly set her pulse jumping as the Reverend Cranham took his place at the lectern and smiled at his flock while he waited for silence.

"Today is the first Sunday of Advent. A time when we eagerly anticipate the celebration of the birth of Christ our Lord and pray for him to once again walk amongst us as he promised. The term 'Advent' comes from the Latin word *adventus* — meaning 'beginning, commencement . . . or arrival.' *Ar-*

*rival* . . . A fitting word for us all here today, I think. Although not being cynical by nature, I choose to believe you are all here in such *unusual* abundance to celebrate the true meaning and spirit of Advent — and not to shamelessly scrutinize the newest member of our flock."

The vicar stared pointedly at Minerva for a moment, then back out to the subtly chastised congregation. "But before we commence our celebration of the birth of Christ, let us celebrate another eagerly anticipated joyous occasion." He picked up a piece of parchment and positively beamed.

"Today I am delighted to publish the banns of marriage between Lord Hugh Peregrine Standish, the Earl of Fareham . . ." She felt Hugh's fingers tighten around her hand as all the air whooshed out of her lungs. Surely Olivia hadn't been able to orchestrate this so fast? "And Miss Minerva . . . Concordia . . . Merriwell" — her own hand gripped back at the sound of her real surname included alongside the alias — "Landridge." By his sharp intake of breath, Hugh also expected the Almighty to smite them at any moment, but being a gentleman he still held her hand so they would go to hell together.

*Merriwell!*

What a disaster!

Directly in front, both Diana and Vee also stiffened, but there was something about the way her baby sister's body immediately shrank in the seat that suggested she knew how this new, terrifying state of affairs had come to pass.

"This is the first time of asking." The vicar's voice was like the clanging chimes of doom. "If any of you know cause of just impediment why these two persons should not be joined together in holy matrimony, ye are to declare it now."

Both the Reverend Cranham and Hugh's mother smiled as the long silence stretched, so intense, not a soul seemed to breathe. All Minerva could hear was the rapid beating of her own heart in panic. She didn't need to hear Hugh's to know he was feeling exactly the same. They were gripping one another's fingers now for grim death.

After what seemed like forever, the reverend finally spoke. "Then as there are no objections, let us commence our Advent celebrations with an uplifting carol which also fittingly celebrates an arrival and a joyous new beginning. Hymn one hundred and sixty-six — 'Hark! The Herald Angels Sing' . . ."

# CHAPTER NINETEEN

"I cannot believe she arranged for the blasted banns to be read!" Hugh was in danger of wearing a groove in the parquet as he paced angrily in the portrait gallery that evening. "Behind my back! Behind your back! When we have both expressly told her there will be no blasted wedding until Saint Valentine's Day!"

His mother had seemed to take the postponement well, had even agreed it would be the perfect date for the wedding if they couldn't get Minerva's fake family from the Cairngorms to Hampshire by Christmas. But as usual, his mother was a law unto herself, paying her customary lip service to his desires while plotting her own agenda behind his back.

Hearing his name read in church, unexpectedly announcing his impending nuptials, had made him feel peculiar. Not queasy exactly, which still surprised him, but he'd had to hold Minerva's hand very tightly for the ground to steady, then keep holding it throughout the service in case he panicked some more. There was a finality about the banns and a stark reality he had never wanted to experience, like a death knell to all he held sacred banging in the distance. The suddenly foreboding sound of Giles's voice echoing in his mind like a prophecy. *They have to be read three times before they're official.*

One down.

Two to go.

But his bloody interfering mother had started the process, and unless his friend came back soon to steal his fiancée away, things would be even more official next Sunday than they were today.

"And they used my real name." Minerva was slumped on the marble bench, looking miserable. "Poor Vee is beside herself with remorse."

In her desire to have the deed done without his knowledge, his mother had caught the youngest Merriwell off guard in the library and prized the middle names of all three of the sisters out of her. The glaring inclusion of "Merriwell" had, according to Minerva, leaked out toward the end of the interrogation due to nerves. The mistake had, she had been assured, been quickly covered up as a traditional ancestral family name that all three of the sisters had been baptized with. He had to give Vee credit for coming up with something so plausible in a crisis — but the fact that Vee had waited until it had been said aloud in church before admitting to her mistake bothered Hugh immensely.

"Now your mother can trace my lackluster lineage, and she'll discover I've never been to Chipping Norton. I've never even set foot in Oxfordshire. I am a big fat fraud who never should have agreed to do this."

"If my mother had the slightest inkling there was anything incendiary in the name 'Merriwell' or had any doubt about Vee's explanation, she would have started her digging yesterday. Instead, she hasn't so much as mentioned it — and that is because she is too busy feeling smug at having the banns read when I least expected it. Remember — her only mission is to send me to the altar, and today's machinations have sent me several steps closer to it than I was yesterday." Minerva looked so wretched, Hugh had the devil of a job resisting the overpowering urge to envelop her in an embrace, and settled for patting her shoulder. "It's not your fault. Put the accidental slip of your surname into a little box marked 'revisit if required' and then store it away. I daresay it will never come up again."

"How can you be so blasé? Yesterday that mad Lucretia let slip she was an actress and it took some hasty explaining, a swift extraction, and some very humiliating singing to distract your mother. Today, Vee inadvertently revealed another secret. At this rate, your mother will soon know everything. We are living in a house of cards, Hugh — and the wind is blowing. It is only a matter of time before your mother puts all the pieces together and our flimsy house tumbles around our ears."

"Well, she hasn't put them together yet."

"But what if Vee slips up again? Or Lucretia? Or Diana?" She pointed to the pair of them. "Or either of us? And what if Giles isn't able to get back soon? Do you seriously think we can maintain this charade for another week, let alone two?"

Of course he didn't. Any more than he would be able to keep his hands off her for that long. "We have managed it so far." But he could see his false optimism wasn't helping. She'd had a pinched look on her features all day. She looked tired and worried and at her wits' end.

This was harder for her than it was for

him, and that truth shamed him. All Hugh had to do was pretend to be himself, keep a close eye on his mother, and herd her in a different direction if necessary. Minerva had to remember the complicated story of their courtship and her illness, and behave like a lady of the gentry. All while keeping her sisters in line, being the consummate diplomat, and forever thinking on her feet.

Feeling incredibly selfish, and phenomenally grateful for her persistent and selfless diligence, he raked a hand through his hair and sat next to her, then against his better judgment, wrapped his arm around her shoulders. As he expected, the contact was pure torture. "It will be all right, Minerva. . . . Whatever happens, you will have tried your best."

Instinctively, she rested her head against his, and he tried not to think of how lovely that felt. He had missed this. Missed it being just her and him. Fate and, more importantly, his mother, meant this stolen, midnight meeting was the first time they had been properly alone since yesterday. Yet so much had happened in the intervening hours, there was so much still waiting to be said. He hadn't broached the subject of the Romeo who had broken her heart. He hadn't slept a wink last night obsessing about that little love affair, and he wouldn't sleep tonight unless he did.

"I don't want to let you down, Hugh. You've been very kind to all of us."

"And you have been wonderful — I am still in awe of how you and your sisters were able to move Lucretia from the drawing room last night at lightning speed when I could barely budge her."

"The secret is to lift them slightly off the ground . . ." She shrugged, dismissive. "We have extensive experience of removing a drunk from the premises when they are no longer welcome." Yet another aspect of her life he didn't want to have to picture. "It was no bother."

"You take too much on yourself." And that needed to change. "But as grateful as I am for your interference, I recognize I have been remiss in relying on you too much these past few days when you have quite enough on your plate already." He kissed the top of her head. He couldn't help it. Minerva needed looking after. "Too many people — myself included — constantly take advantage of your good nature."

"You are not taking advantage, Hugh. Nor is anyone else."

He cuddled her closer and took her hand, the contact suddenly as necessary as breathing. "I have eyes, Minerva. The more I get to know you, the more I realize you pull yourself in every direction trying to be all things to all people. A mother to your sisters, a pretend fiancée to me, a gracious hostess, a good friend. Your intrinsic niceness is humbling . . ." It certainly made Hugh want to be a better man around her. "There is no need for you to run yourself ragged or worry yourself sick in the process. What will be will be . . . and I will be with you all the way."

"Except when I have to take tea with the Standish Ladies' Society tomorrow, or be measured by Madame Devy . . ." His mother *was* making a flurry of plans for Minerva that excluded him. More weight on her already-overburdened shoulders. "And then there's the local assembly she has committed us to attending. Where I shall be expected to dance — when I cannot — and everyone, including your mother, will know I am a fraud."

"I wouldn't worry about that. I can teach you to dance."

"Nobody can teach me to dance, Hugh, because I cannot hear the music like everyone else hears it — remember? Dancing requires a level of balance, coordination, and rhythm I simply do not possess. Look what happened when you tried to teach me to ride a horse."

He had forgotten all those things. The broomstick arms. The lack of empathy with the horse's movements. The wobbling. "Perhaps you could suffer another injury which precludes you from dancing?"

"Your mother is dubious of my torn shoulder as it is. She offered to have the physician look at it this afternoon . . . to see if I am fit to ride again, because it appears quite fixed. I've been attempting to wince each time I lift a teacup in the hope she will believe me. She will call him for sure if I feign a sprained ankle, and I am bound to forget I am supposed to have it at a crucial moment and start limping on the wrong foot. Or worse — not limp at all."

"And there I was, worrying about the inconsequential things — like our impending marriage." He was trying to lighten the mood but instead managed to make her look more miserable — if that were indeed possible.

"I suppose I could own up to not being able to dance. After all, it would hardly come as a surprise when I am so musically incompetent — but then, of course, it would mean calling you a liar again. Because you wrote to her in *great* detail about our first *magical* waltz . . ."

"I *could* teach you to waltz."

"Oh, don't be daft, Hugh . . ."

"No — I'm serious. You could politely refuse to dance with anyone at the assembly except me. It would be seen as perfectly acceptable and understandable that you should want to have as many conversations with your new neighbors as possible instead of dancing. You are to be the new mistress of Standish, after all. Your sisters can dance every dance. I'll have Payne and Lucretia teach them on the side. Then, the only dance people will expect you to dance will be with me and we will only dance the waltz. My mother will love the symbolism. It will look gloriously romantic."

"It will look ridiculous, Hugh. *I* will look ridiculous. Singing badly for your mother to avoid imminent catastrophe is one thing, making a complete fool out of myself in front of a room full of strangers is quite another."

"Will you at least allow me to try to teach you?" He stood, holding out his hands, and watched the charming furrow he always had the urge to kiss away appear between her dark brows.

"I cannot dance!"

"But this is the *waltz*. The waltz is entirely

different to all the other dances because it relies on the gentleman leading! If it all goes wrong, it is me they will blame. All you will need to do is count to three and be able to hold on tight while I twirl you around. Come . . . I'll show you."

"Now? It's late and I am not sure I have the patience yet. It's been a particularly trying day. Perhaps tomorrow . . ."

"There is no time like the present and we have the place all to ourselves." Which was probably a dangerous combination, but he couldn't summon the enthusiasm to care. Not when he needed her to smile again to make him feel better.

"This is pointless." Reluctantly, she allowed him to pull her up. "I take absolutely no responsibility for stepping on your toes. Expect them to be completely crushed."

It would be worth it if he could send her to bed happier than she was now. "And I take absolutely no responsibility for you falling helplessly, head over heels in love with me as I twirl you around — because the waltz is the dance of love and seduction, my dear faux fiancée . . . and I am sinfully wonderful at it. So sinfully wonderful I'm surprised they haven't made a law against it. Or me."

"And so modest." There was the smile he

missed. The saucy glint in her lovely emerald eyes as he arranged her arms into the correct pose. Both warmed his heart. Nothing kept his Minerva down long. "Have you forgotten you are effectively paying me to dance with you?"

"There is that." He slid his palm around her waist slowly, savoring the opportunity to hold her in his arms just once more. "Will flirting cost me extra?" The corners of her mouth began to curve upward. "Because to waltz truly well one has to flirt."

"Most assuredly. In fact, I can tell you now it will be very expensive. I shall have enough on my mind concentrating on the steps while simultaneously being *your* Minerva. Therefore, additional chores, like flirting, come at a premium. It will be so expensive I doubt even you could afford it."

He loved her like this. Funny and confident and bold. Unburdened. "I am a very rich man."

"True . . . but as you rightly pointed out, I do have rather a lot on my plate, so I must decline for now. Should I need another thousand pounds, rest assured I shall let you know."

"A thousand pounds? You put a great deal of stock in your capabilities at flirting."

"No more than you put in your capabilities at waltzing, sir." Standing in a perfect dance frame in his arms, staring along her nose at him in mock disdain, she let out a withering sigh. "Are we going to stand here like this all night? My arm is beginning to ache. I am not being paid to endure aching limbs either. They also come at a premium."

"Very well, Mademoiselle Mercenary. Try to follow my lead. Whatever I do, you must mirror. It's simple." He attempted a few steps, all of which she got entirely wrong and most of which resulted in her stepping on his foot.

"I told you this was pointless!" The light in her eyes had dimmed again as she tried to tug her hand from his. "I am incapable of dancing."

"It isn't you — it is me. I am teaching you poorly. Let's try it again. Mirror . . ." Then it occurred to him that likening the waltz to a mirror was the root of the problem and perhaps not the best instruction to a novice who lacked coordination — because each time Hugh stepped forward, so did she. He let go of her and demonstrated the steps again on his own, pointing at his feet. "Imagine together we are drawing a big box on the ground." She might not understand dance, but she understood art. "I will start on the right foot." Which was the foot *she* would need to begin with. "I step back on the right. I step to the side with my left. Then I bring my right foot together to stand beside the left."

"That is a triangle, not a box."

"Exactly right! Because it is only half of the dance. To complete the box, now I step *forward* on my right. To the side again on my left and . . ."

"Bring your right foot together with your left again to return to the point you started?" She drew a big square in the air with her finger.

"See — I told you it was simple. Shall we try it side by side?"

Without touching, they danced several tentative squares until Hugh was certain she understood the basics, while he simultaneously spoke the steps. "Back, side, together — forward, side, together — back, side, together — forward, side, together — one, two, three — one, two, three . . ." It took five minutes before she had it, but once she did, there was no stopping her.

"Squares . . . unbelievable." Minerva suddenly beamed at him in wonder. "Look, Hugh! We are perfectly synchronized! Have you any idea what an achievement this is for me?"

"I am starting to understand." And he felt

proud to have found a way for the waltz to make sense and for encouraging her to smile again.

"What do we have to do next?"

"Nothing other than what you are doing. No matter what I do, simply concentrate on drawing your box on the floor. Ignore my feet."

"I thought we were mirrors."

"I've smashed the mirrors. The mirrors were a stupid idea and I am an idiot for thinking of them. Now you are drawing a perfect box with your feet and I'm going to draw the same box with you."

"I really don't understand . . ."

"And that is the beauty of it, my lovely Minerva, you really don't need to." He took her hand in his and placed the other at her waist. "You just need to trust me and allow me to carry you for a change rather than vice versa." He held her closer than the dance required but nowhere close enough for him. "Draw your box, my darling. . . . Back, side, together — forward, side, together — one, two, three . . ." Miraculously, it worked and nobody seemed more stunned by it than Minerva.

"We're dancing!"

"I know."

"I haven't stepped on your toes!"

"That I also know. My toes thank you."
She giggled and he felt ten feet tall.

"When do we start twirling?"

"Not until we've practiced an hour of this at least. Let's not run before we can walk."

"An hour? But, Hugh . . . it's past midnight. Your mother has another packed day planned tomorrow and I don't want to face her tired." And he didn't want to spoil the moment by making her fret.

"Let us do another few minutes tonight to cement it in your mind and more first thing in the morning when we are both refreshed. And perhaps tomorrow night, if you continue to show promise, we'll commence the twirling."

# CHAPTER TWENTY

Minerva stretched contentedly before burrowing back under the covers to block out the early morning light. She had practically floated to bed after spending more than an hour dancing with Hugh in the portrait gallery. Then she had slept like a baby, dreaming sweet dreams of handsome knights in shining armor, candlelit ballrooms, and waltzing like the most graceful of princesses. And this morning, she would dance with him again before breakfast, something that already had her bubbling with excitement.

She couldn't believe that she, the tone-deaf and clumsy Merriwell, could dance so well and so effortlessly. But it was true. She had seen her reflection on the windows as he spun her past the enormous gilt mirror at the farthest end of the room. It had been a magical ending that wiped away all the stresses of the day and had left her feeling buoyed and hopeful rather than fearful and out of her depth.

Hugh had done that.

The only disappointing thing had been the lack of kiss at the end, when he had insisted on escorting her all the way to the door of her bedchamber and lingered over saying goodbye.

Which was probably just as well. Just the dancing had seduced her thoroughly enough. A kiss would have sent her over the edge. Especially one of Hugh's kisses. Because his made her whole body feel wanton. Wickedly ripe for the picking . . .

The tap on the door had her jumping guiltily and checking her shameless nipples to see if they were poking scandalously through her nightgown. Just in case they damned her, she pulled the covers to her chin. "Come in, Martha. I am awake." Her assigned maid knew she was an early bird.

"It's me, miss — Payne." The butler's voice was barely a whisper. "Could I have a word?" That didn't bode well.

"Of course. Give me a second." Hastily, she shoved her arms into the sleeves of her robe and gathered it closed before opening the door. Instead of looking pained as she expected, Payne was grinning.

"I have a message from His Lordship regarding this morning, Miss Minerva. A slight change of plan. He asks that you meet him at the stable in half an hour."

"The stable?" Despondency quickly followed her curiosity. Giles must have returned! There would be no more dancing this morning. No more flirting or twirling or laughing together. "Whatever for?"

"I have no idea, miss. All I know is I have been tasked with rousing you and informing you to dress up warm." The long carriage ride back to Clerkenwell . . . Instantly, she felt sick at the prospect. "And to tell you to hide if you happened to collide with anyone. That is *most* important. Your presence is apparently imperative and cannot be delayed."

As painful as that was to hear, it made sense. After all the potentially damning mistakes these past few days, prudence dictated she needed to elope as soon as was feasibly possible before their flimsy house of cards really did collapse. If nobody saw her before breakfast, once she was gone, it would be easy to claim she had stolen away in the middle of the night.

Tears pricked her eyes. She wasn't ready to say goodbye — but then again, would she ever be? Despite all her resolute intentions, Hugh had sneaked past her defenses and stolen part of her jaded and unhopeful heart regardless. Perhaps more than just a part of it, if the pain was this intense?

"Tell him I will be there as soon as I am dressed, Payne." Her throat had constricted, the sadness in her voice too obvious to properly disguise.

"Very good, Miss Minerva. Martha is on her way with some fortifying tea."

This was it.

The end.

Probably just as well.

If it hurt this much now, how much would it hurt next week or the week after?

With leaden feet, she went to the wardrobe and began to rifle through her new clothes to find something suitable to elope in. Dress warm, he had said. Although Payne hadn't told her to pack. Should she?

Her eyes fell to the tatty old bag she had brought with her, pathetically empty on the shelf. She would need her things once she got home. She grabbed the handles, then dropped them as if they were hot. She had no idea what to take because most of it had been provided by Hugh. Were all these beautiful clothes now his or hers? Miserably, she closed the wardrobe. It made no difference. She would never wear them again. Every stitch would simply remind her of him, and Payne would arrange to have whatever was deemed fit sent later alongside her sisters.

"Your tea, miss, and a bit of toast." Martha hurried in and deposited both on the bedside table. "You make a start on those while I sort out the rest." The kind-faced older woman nudged her out of the way and studied the array of gowns, quickly settling on the smart new emerald wool pelisse with its jaunty military-style braiding and matching dress, while Minerva attempted to choke down the food.

She lay the garments on the mattress, and hurried back to fetch stockings in the finest gauge of lambswool, soft leather half boots, and gloves. Next, atop those, came a beautiful green bonnet with silk ribbons and intricate velvet flowers. The same flowers encircled her reticule, in which the maid placed two delicate embroidered handkerchiefs. A pretty chemise, edged in tiny rosebuds, stays, silk garters. All the trappings Minerva had never dared hope to experience but had quickly become used to.

She would miss all this, too.

And this wonderful house. Her marshmallow eiderdown and goose-feather mattress. Those crisp, white sheets that crackled each night as she slipped between them. Tea in bed. The well-meant sparring between

Olivia and Jeremiah. Payne, the servants, mad Lucretia and her heaving bosom. Hugh's twinkling blue eyes over the dinner table.

*Hugh.*

She mourned each and every aspect of her unexpected temporary life, alongside the man who had given it, while Martha chatted and fixed her hair, then she stared dispassionately at herself in the mirror next to her fancy dressing table. Somewhere over the last ten days, she had turned into a lady.

"You look beautiful, miss."

"Thank you, Martha . . . for everything."

" 'Tis my pleasure, miss. Shall I have the striped silk pressed for tonight or the pink taffeta?"

"Whichever you think best, Martha." It wasn't as if she would be wearing it.

As if the entire house also understood her time was up, Minerva collided with nobody on her way out. Not a maid, not a footman, not even Payne, so she was denied the opportunity to say goodbye. To avoid the busy kitchen, she slipped out of the French doors in the morning room and crunched across the frost-covered lawn to the stables.

"There you are!" Hugh bounded toward her across the yard, beaming from ear to ear, obviously relieved his convoluted and meticulous plan had finally succeeded. "We need to be quick! The grooms tell me my mother has taken to riding early every morning with Jeremiah. We don't want to encounter her! That would spoil everything."

"I don't think she is up. The house was very quiet when I left."

"Maybe — but she is small and moves with surprising stealth. It would be just like her to suddenly appear." He took her elbow and practically propelled her toward a waiting curricle. Now the warm clothes made sense. There was no carriage, because this smart gig was much faster. They would fly along the road to London at top speed. He helped her up and then solicitously wrapped a thick blanket around her knees, reminding her he was the most considerate man she had ever met. "Step lively, Payne! The clock is ticking."

In her quest to drink in every last second with Hugh, she hadn't noticed the butler reappear carrying a huge basket. "Your mother is up, my lord, but fortunately I was able to intercept her. You will be pleased to know she is currently sipping chocolate in the breakfast room with Mr. Peabody."

"Excellent, Payne. You can break the bad

news to her in approximately twenty minutes."

"Where is Lord Bellingham?" Minerva craned her neck, but there was no sign of him in the stable yard.

"Still absent without leave." Hugh wiggled his hands into gloves. "Why do you ask?"

"Because I thought we were supposed to be eloping."

"Not today, you're not. Today you are running away with me." To her complete surprise, he hauled himself up onto the seat beside her and grinned. "We deserve a day off."

"Your mother will be furious." Payne looked unimpressed as he passed his master a second thick blanket. "She had plans for today."

"Which she will just have to follow without Minerva. Her sisters and Lucretia can accompany my mother to the Standish Ladies' Society — they have too much free time. Do inform my dear mama we shall be back in time for dinner. Probably." With that, he snapped the ribbons and the two spritely grays set off.

For several minutes Minerva was lost for words.

Aside from not entirely understanding what was going on, the palpable relief of not leaving had her feeling decidedly off-kilter — because the depth of her sorrow at saying goodbye to Hugh had felt like a death, one she had already begun to mourn. But the elation that followed, the way her heart seemed to swell inside her chest with the sheer joy of it, forced her to consider something she hadn't considered before.

She had feelings for Hugh.

Deep, romantic feelings for Hugh.

He turned to her, smiling, his mischievous blue eyes alight with excitement, golden hair mussed by the wind as they turned out of the long driveway of his estate and onto the winding country lane. "I thought we should have an adventure. I hope you don't mind."

"Why would I mind?" Everything with him was an adventure.

"You might have been looking forward to the Standish Ladies' Society and be annoyed at me for ruining your plans."

"They were hardly *my* plans."

"Which is exactly why I am stealing you away. It occurred to me last night, you have been doing everything for everyone, and absolutely nothing for yourself. Today shall hopefully rectify that. For the duration, you are relieved of the chore of pretending to be *my* Minerva, my mother's future daughter-in-law, mother to your sisters, and chief diplomat in any crises. Today, you just get to be you." She could feel her silly heart swelling some more, so much she feared it might burst. "Hence I have kidnapped you because you simply cannot be *you* back there."

"But Hugh — what if something happens while we're absent?" As lovely an idea as this was, there could be serious complications for him.

"Sometimes you have to embrace the fickle finger of fate and accept the what-ifs to let the cards fall where they may. We cannot predict the future, and more often than not, we cannot direct it either. In which case, why fight it?"

"A very lofty *philosophy* all of a sudden, but hardly practical." But wonderful nevertheless.

"*If* it all goes wrong in our absence, then I shall face the music like a man and do what needs to be done." He shot her a typically mischievous look. "Which means we shall both run as fast as our legs can carry us to the waiting carriage Payne will have had the good sense to organize, hightail it to Portsmouth, stow away on a ship to the Continent, and live out the rest of our days as exiled fugitives on a sunny beach somewhere in Italy. You could paint portraits to earn enough to keep us in wine and I shall work the land myself to grow our food." He nudged her, looking smug. "I really did read all those newfangled books on farming you saw in the library, so everything will work out perfectly well if we do have to make a dash for it."

It sounded perfect. "Well . . . if we have a contingency plan already in place, I suppose it wouldn't hurt to escape for a few hours."

"That's the spirit. Set all that other nonsense out of your mind for now and enjoy your day. When was the last time you had an entire day to yourself?"

"I don't remember." Years and years. Since before her mother died.

"A travesty which needs to be addressed. What would you like to do?"

"I have no idea. I've never had an entire day off."

"Are you prepared to entrust me with the itinerary?"

"As I have been kidnapped, what other choice do I have?"

"A very good point." He steered the curricle around a tight bend, and a long, straight road stretched tantalizingly before them in the winter sunshine. "Hold on to your bonnet, Miss Merriwell. Tightly. As I intend to drive you very, *very* fast. Adventures should always take your breath away."

He was true to his word. They flew as the scenery whipped past, the well-sprung curricle skipping over the bumps in the road and the frigid winter air buffeting their cheeks as they swiftly ate up the miles between them and Standish House. The speed and wind made conversation impossible, so she relaxed as much as she could into the seat and simply enjoyed the ride, snuggled under the thick blanket he had had the good sense to bring.

Eventually, after what had to be almost an hour, he slowed. "Are you hungry?"

"Starving." In her premature grief, Minerva had barely nibbled the toast her maid had brought her. "But we appear to be in the middle of nowhere." She scanned the horizon for any signs of habitation. "Is that a village over there?" She pointed to the faint wisps of smoke that could be seen emanating from its chimneys. "Perhaps there is an inn?"

"What a lack of imagination you have! Breakfasts at inns are too pedestrian. *Our breakfast* is packed in that basket and I know just the place to eat it." Although, it was clear he had no intention of sharing the destination with her. Instead, he turned onto another narrow winding lane that inclined slightly uphill as it wended its way through dense trees.

Eventually, the trees parted and the jutting ruins of an ancient building came into view, its vast arched windows festooned with ivy. "That's Netley Abbey."

"It's beautiful."

"Too beautiful, I am afraid, as it has been newly *discovered* by those prone to tour or needing inspiration to write poetry." Hugh made a face of distaste. "But at this unfashionable hour we are guaranteed to have the place to ourselves."

He pulled up alongside a tree, nimbly jumped down, and secured the ribbons to a low-slung branch before helping her down. "I hope you are wearing walking boots. It takes a bit of effort to get there."

Minerva picked her way over the uneven ground, following Hugh, who strode ahead carrying the enormous basket. When they finally reached the abbey, he left her to marvel at the lacy remnants of the roof, which seemed to be suspended above them with nothing but ivy. He then laid a cloth over the base of what must have once been grand columns that supported the huge structure.

"As this is the sort of place which demands a history lesson, I shall tell you it is medieval. Or at least most of it is. After the delightful despot Henry the Eighth dissolved the monasteries, it enjoyed a brief stint as a nobleman's grand house before it lapsed into rack and ruin."

"I can see why it inspires poets." She ran her palm over the cold, rough stone of a window frame, the stained glass long gone. "If I had my inks and brushes with me, it is exactly the sort of thing I should like to draw."

"I should have told you to bring them . . ." Hugh was immediately annoyed at himself. "It never occurred to me you would have wanted to, when it should have. I keep forgetting you are an artist."

"It never occurred to me to bring them from London." She didn't want him to feel bad. "And I can only dream of aspiring to be an artist one day or draw whatever I wish simply for pleasure. I make woodcuts and draw what I am told. But I shall store this lovely place in my memories and draw it for pleasure one day." Minerva turned toward the veritable feast he had laid for them. "In the meantime, you promised to feed me."

"That I did." She took his proffered arm and allowed him to lead her to it, laughing as he whipped out a handkerchief and draped it over the bare piece of stone he had reserved for her bottom to rest on. Then he produced two fine porcelain plates and handed her one. "As this is an informal meal, I shall allow you to serve yourself. However, I heartily recommend one of those little apple tarts."

"Apple tarts? For breakfast?"

"Well, I could hardly pack coddled eggs and bacon, could I? They would have been stone cold well before we got here, and eggs don't travel well. Besides, coddled eggs don't go with champagne." He winked as he fished out the bottle from the basket with a dramatic flourish. "But those strawberries do. Have you any idea how hard it is to come by strawberries in winter?"

"They came from your glasshouse, didn't they? So for you, not very hard at all. Did one of the servants pick them for you? What a *hideous* struggle."

"Semantics, my dear Minerva. You are supposed to be impressed."

"I am impressed. By everything. You always manage to impress me." Today, last night, that first time he had stepped in to rescue her from Mr. Pinkerton. A true knight in shining armor, when she had been convinced none existed.

"What can I say?" The cork popped, and the cold champagne foamed over the neck of the bottle. "I am naturally impressive." He poured her some in a beautiful crystal glass. "And much too modest for my own good."

# CHAPTER TWENTY-ONE

There was something intimate about eating together in the ruins of an abbey. The walls and the densely woven ivy enveloped them, protecting them from prying eyes, while the sun shone down through the huge chasm that had once been the roof. Hugh hadn't been prepared for the effect it was having on him. Her delight at simple pleasures like strawberries and apple tarts. His delight in simply being all alone here with her.

"I am glad there are no poets here with us. They would have ruined it."

"It's not just the poets who ruin this place. This is also Hampshire's most sought-after spot for courting couples. Nothing spoils the digestion quicker than a pair of simpering, cooing lovebirds. Nobody wants to see that at any time — let alone breakfast."

"True — but I am not surprised they come here. It is so very romantic." She stared at the walls with a faraway look. "I

wonder how many young men have proposed to their sweethearts here."

"Or stolen a kiss or two?" Or more. Not
that it was wise to think of anything like
that with her within arm's reach. "Another
apple tart?"

She shook her head and smiled. "How
many young ladies have you brought here
over the years? Several, I'll wager. Seeing as
it's the perfect spot for a seduction."

"None." Just her. "This is the sort of
hideously romantic place young ladies get
ideas in." The sort of hideously romantic
place he was getting ideas in. Some lustful.
Some worryingly poetic. Decisively, he
stood, hoping to swiftly banish them. "Come
— I can see you are dying to explore the
place." Like a fool, he held out his hand to
help her up and regretted it the second she
took it, thanks to the overwhelming feeling
of contentment the simple contact created.

"Surely, if one is about to embark on
seduction, the setting should be nothing if
not romantic?"

"There is romantic and then there is *romantic.*"

"There is a difference?" She let go of his
hand to run her fingers lovingly over a glass-
less window frame, yet he could still feel
her touch.

All the way down to his toes.

"Obviously . . . depending on the intended duration of the romance."

"I see . . ." Her mouth curved knowingly. "What you mean to say, but are being much too polite and gentlemanly to say outright in case you offend my delicate female sensibilities, is 'romance' implies love and promises and commitment, whereas *'romance'*" — she imitated his exact tone — "is simply passion. The sort which burns quickly and just as quickly fades. I am familiar with the concept."

As was he. He couldn't stop thinking about the passionate Minerva who had kissed him with abandon. Bold, confident kisses . . .

The specter of the suitor from her past loomed, royally spoiling his good mood and making him irrationally jealous all over again.

"Ah yes — I had forgotten about the scoundrel who broke your heart."

"My heart wasn't broken. It was disappointed, that is all."

Relief. Palpable and visceral. Worrying. "You didn't love him, then?" Because Hugh suddenly needed to know.

She clambered up some ruined stairs to nowhere and took in the view beyond, denying him the right to see her expression for the absolute truth. "It was naught but a silly infatuation."

He wanted to remain relieved but couldn't leave it there. "But it was more than a few stolen glances across the church pews, wasn't it?" Nor could he leave it there. "Diana implied he hurt you grievously."

Her shoulders stiffened. "He just left, Hugh — as men do. Not that I blame him for it." She twisted momentarily, as if to prove she was unaffected, then stared out at nothing once again. "He was barely twenty, I was just nineteen. We had been courting for less than a year and had never discussed the future, because we were both too young to settle down and too poor to seriously consider anything more than a dalliance. When an opportunity presented itself for him to take better employment elsewhere, he took it and naturally we parted ways with no hard feelings."

He didn't believe her.

"Naturally?" She was being too generous. "And I suppose the significance of the timing was purely coincidental?" Of their own accord, his feet followed hers up the steps. "Didn't your father disappear when you were barely nineteen?"

He watched her shoulders stiffen again

before she unconvincingly shrugged his comments off. "Taking on the responsibility of both my sisters at such a young age was an unreasonable expectation for any man — let alone a boy." By the time she turned around, all the emotion was hidden from her face, yet she struggled to meet his gaze, focusing instead on the knotted brambles choking the ivy on the ruined wall below.

"Do not make excuses for him." Hugh gently tipped up her chin, needing to see the truth in her eyes. Needing hers to see his were furious on her behalf at the weak coward who had deserted her in her hour of need. "If he had loved you, he would have stayed. No matter what."

"Then he clearly didn't love me enough, did he?" He heard the almost imperceptible note of bitterness in her tone within the flippant answer. "Despite his repeated and heartfelt declarations to the contrary."

"If he made promises, he should have kept them."

"What for? So we could both be miserable?" The flash of pain and acceptance cut him to the quick. She expected no better, when he knew she deserved everything and more. "Besides, where I come from, a few stolen kisses do not automatically equate to a solemn promise, and promises are like piecrusts anyway — pretty for a little while but easily broken. Nobody cares about a young lady's reputation in Clerkenwell, and fortunately, I had the good sense not to permit him more."

Hugh felt the breath he hadn't realized he was holding escape, and with it went most of his irrational jealousy, when he knew he shouldn't care. She mistook his relief as pity and pulled up her slim shoulders proudly, looking him dead in the eye. "With hindsight, I firmly believe he did me a favor."

"Desertion is a favor?"

"I needed to grow up, and despite everything I had witnessed firsthand from my father, I still harbored silly, romantic notions when I needed to realize men are fundamentally untrustworthy as a breed because they are allowed to be and are really not worth the woman's effort in the long run."

"A cynical view. Not all men are untrustworthy."

"True." Not that she appeared particularly convinced. "Although I have yet to find one I can trust further than I can throw him. And, to their credit, some gentlemen are honest enough to admit to their failings up front — like your good self." And with one pithy comment, she tossed him into the same lackluster league as her cowardly former sweetheart and her feckless, missing, shameful excuse for a father. "Which is admirable, for it gives a lady enough fore-warning to avoid any potential misunder-standing at the start. Only a fool would fall for a scoundrel she knew was a scoundrel." Her teasing tone did nothing to lessen the sharp sting of her words.

She gazed off into the distance again. "But enough of that . . . Is that the sea?"

Deflection.

Something he had always been a master of when people touched a nerve, yet until that moment, Hugh hadn't realized how frustrating it must be for others, because he wasn't done. He wanted to expose Minerva's nerve completely, get to the root of it and fix it. He wanted to argue against her cynicism but was furious that he couldn't. How could he when she had spoken the truth? He was also untrustworthy, and she deserved better.

"Not quite. It's an inlet."

"That's a shame. I've never seen the sea before."

At least that he could fix. "Another travesty easily remedied." If only they all were. "We are a few miles from the coast. Would you like to see it today?"

"Could we?" Her lovely green eyes were bright again, excited.

"Today is all for you. If you want to see the sea, then your wish is my command. And I know just the place." He held out his hand to help her down, and once again found he was unable to let sleeping dogs lie, despite knowing he had no right to be jealous and certainly no right to pry. "What was his name?"

"Why do you need to know?" Just her touch seemed to warm him from within.

"Because if I should ever collide with him, I know already I shall feel duty bound to tell him what a fool he was to let you go."

Which also made him a fool, too.

But what other choice did he have? If he hadn't been his father's son, and therefore exactly the sort of man to ultimately, albeit unintentionally, let her down, then Minerva was the sort of woman he could see himself spending forever with — and happily. She was smart and funny, generous with her deeds and her thoughts, passionate, persistent, wonderfully flawed in her own unique and comical way, and without a doubt the single most attractive and alluring woman he had ever gazed upon. From her unusual height to her inability to sing, he adored everything about her.

"He was a fool." She paused on the stairs, her features softening as she gazed down at him. "You say the loveliest things, Hugh." She smiled and he basked in it. "No wonder all the ladies love you."

"Except you." That reality hurt.

"Except me." Deeply hurt.

"Because only a fool falls for a scoundrel."

"Exactly." Her foot reached the bottom step. "I am a great many things, but I am certainly not . . . oh for goodness' sake!" She yanked the fabric of her coat to reveal the single tenacious branch of bramble that had attached itself to her skirt. Another yank did nothing to shift it.

"You are making it worse. . . . Allow me." Without thinking, Hugh reached behind her to untangle it. "Don't move backward . . ." Her hand came to rest on his shoulder as she steadied herself. Hugh tried to ignore it while he wrestled with the thorns and his own crushing disappointment because she didn't want him, and he knew she shouldn't want him. Because he *was* his father's son and incapable of being the man she deserved just like those others. But what if he could be . . .

There was no denying if he could be that man for anyone, he stood more chance with this amazing woman than any other.

*Madness!* This romantic place was clearly scrambling his wits.

"Almost done . . . there." He intended to smile, triumphant, then escape, regroup. Save them both from his ridiculous, impossible desires, but his eyes were suddenly level with her lips and the smile failed to form because her hand was still on his shoulder and she smelled of strawberries and champagne and she was all he had ever wanted.

*What if . . .*

His hand was just millimeters from her hip, desperate to touch her. The few inches of air that separated her lush body and his seemed to crackle expectantly.

Neither of them moved.

He could hear her breathing.

Hear the intimate silence enveloping them.

Hear his own heartbeat.

His own indecision. His fears.

His own hideously romantic ideas. Some lustful. Some worryingly poetic. Neither by any means hideous. In fact, at this precise moment, they were thoroughly . . . excellent in every single way.

*Excellent!*

The floor shifted beneath his feet.

Clearly coming here, at this time of the morning, all alone with just her had been a huge mistake. Acting on his desires would be another huge mistake. Both for Minerva and his niggling, damn conscience. It would kill him to hurt her. For the sake of his own sanity and to do what was right, he stepped to the side to sever the hypnotic spell of whatever strange, invisible web was wrapped around them.

"Right, then — onward and upward with our adventure." He had to force himself to walk back toward the breakfast basket rather than run for the hills in a blind panic, force himself to make meaningless small talk while he hastily packed the food away. Force himself not to give in to the urge to say to hell with it and kiss her anyway and be damned. Force himself not to be thoroughly annoyed that he couldn't. Shouldn't.

Wouldn't.

Force himself not to notice she seemed disappointed that he hadn't.

He helped her back in the curricle instead, then busied himself with reattaching the basket to the back, returning to his seat only when he felt composed enough to continue as if nothing was amiss at all, when everything was.

He was in pain.

Pain like he had never experienced before, because it was apparently his heart that felt it the most keenly, an organ that had never been thus affected before or one he had ever given much thought to. It forced him to face a reality he had never expected, one he had believed himself immune to and unable to feel. One that had crept up on him without him realizing, taking root and growing quietly stronger in a secret corner he never knew existed.

He had feelings for Minerva.

Affectionate, possessive, needy, and all-encompassing feelings, but for the life of him, Hugh had no clue what to do about them beyond ignoring them and hoping they went away.

"I thought we'd tour a few of the pretty villages, then have lunch at the Queen's Head in Titchfield. They do the most wonderful pies. Trust me. Pies to die for. And then we'll drive to Hill Head, where there are miles and miles of beach for you to finally see the sea in all its glory. How does that sound?"

"Excellent . . ."

Hugh did his best to be the perfect host for the next few hours, and to her credit Minerva also carried on as if nothing had happened, but the atmosphere their peculiar moment had created hung in the air regardless. He spent most of their luncheon pondering whether or not he should broach the subject, and once he decided he would, he spent the next hour procrastinating about how best to bring it up. Before he bit the bullet, they caught the first glimpse of the ocean on the horizon. Not that he paid much attention to it, he was too busy watching her face, trying to enjoy the look of awe she had as the vast expanse of water came closer into view. He couldn't spoil that by bringing up what Minerva would call the Great Unsaid — even if his foolish heart wanted him to say it.

"I can hear it!" Unsurprisingly, being almost December, the brisk sea breeze was doing its best to whip the water. Wave after wave formed way offshore and rolled to crash on the shingle beach before them, sending torrents of foam between the pebbles, which quickly receded. "It sounds exactly like the sound you hear when you put a shell against your ear. I never believed that before. . . . But it's true."

She didn't wait for him to help her down as he brought the curricle to a stop. Instead, she hopped down and rushed to the beach.

The wind plastered her skirts to her legs. She had to hold on to her bonnet with one hand, yet long tendrils of dark hair escaped unbidden as she ran, enthralled by the view.

Then she turned to him, laughing, the very picture of absolute joy, and he found himself caught up in it, smiling back, and his odd mood lifted.

"Come on, Hugh! You promised me a walk on the beach. And there is so much of it!"

There was probably a worn path somewhere, but she was too impatient to find it, so he helped her scramble down the bank and, still holding her hand, led her as close as he dared to where the water met the shore without risking a stray wave filling their boots. "This is wonderful, Hugh! Thank you for bringing me."

"Another splendid thing for you to paint one day."

"I doubt I could do it justice . . . all the colors . . . all the movement."

"They say the moon controls the tides."

"They do?" She stared up at the sky in wonder, not that any sign of the moon was visible. "How on earth does it do that from so far away?"

"Something to do with gravity, or so I've read. I can't say I understand it all, really."

"Some things aren't meant to be understood, they just are. That is enough."

"Very philosophical."

She bent to scratch a flat white shell out

of the wet sand, but turned her face to grin at him. "It's clearly the day for it. And what a lovely day it has been — embracing what-ifs and not understanding the things that just are." Hugh merely nodded, a little thrown that her statement seemed to sum up everything he was feeling. He held out his arm and she took it, making everything instantly right again, and they wandered the entire length of the beach. Minerva collected shells, examined seaweed, watched the gulls glide overhead, took in everything, and shared it with him with an almost child-like delight. When the wind stole her bonnet, and sent it rolling along the beach, she chased it, laughing, causing more unwelcome pangs of need and longing, more regrets.

More what-ifs . . .

He finally caught her bonnet and dusted off the sand with his hands. She took it and spun a happy circle. "It's beautiful, Hugh — just as you said. Are all beaches as beautiful as the ones in Hampshire?"

"Not all. Some more so. Some less."

"What about that beach in Italy? The one we might have to run away to later? Is that as lovely?"

"That is the most beautiful beach in the world." Because she would be on it with him. Anywhere that she was, was beautiful. "We wouldn't be running away there otherwise."

She stopped spinning and gazed at him, and Hugh saw everything he was feeling mirrored in her eyes. The longing. The yearning. The sadness. The million what-ifs that neither of them wanted to acknowledge, and something snapped.

Some things were not meant to be understood, they just were, and right here, right now was one such moment.

A perfect moment.

Perhaps the only one they had left.

He reached for her hand and tugged her against him, wrapping his arms possessively around her waist. Neither of them spoke. Words seemed unnecessary, because he was drowning in her intense emerald gaze and she had looped her arms around his shoulders and taken a step closer so they were touching from chest to hip.

He wasn't entirely sure it was him who dipped his head first, or her who tugged it down, but he sighed into her mouth when their lips finally touched, and poured everything he felt, every tangled emotion, every impossible dream, all his passion and all his fledging affection into the kiss.

The kiss to end all kisses.

But one that came with a million more what-ifs and not a single answer.

# CHAPTER TWENTY-TWO

Minerva had no idea how long they stood there entwined in each other's arms. Time stood still, and there was nothing but her and him and the distant sound of the sea. But as the crashing waves grew louder, once again it was Hugh who pulled away. He let go and stepped back, then paced, raking his hand through his hair, looking completely miserable.

For her, it wasn't just a physical severing of the kiss, but an emotional one. She could feel him distancing himself from it — from her. As if he regretted it.

"I'm sorry. . . . I shouldn't have done that. It was a mistake. A huge mistake. I am not entirely sure what came over me . . ."

"It *was* a mistake." She tried to appear blasé about it. Unaffected rather than wounded by the bitter remorse she could see in his eyes. Eyes that were now too stormy to twinkle with mischief as they usually did. Eyes that struggled to hold hers.

"You have to understand it is an impossible situation."

She knew it was an impossible situation. Knew it before she allowed him to kiss her. Knew it when she'd allowed herself to develop feelings for him, yet developed them regardless. That didn't make his rejection hurt less. "Pay it no mind. It was just a kiss."

Just a kiss.

One that had made her heart sing before it surrendered itself completely to him. What an absolute fool she was. He had never hidden the fact he was a scoundrel, and she had thought herself immune to scoundrels, but she had fallen for Hugh anyway. Seduced by his charm and his easy way. Somewhere over the last week she had forgotten where she came from, forgotten this wasn't her life at all. It was a fabrication. A construct. An intoxicating break from reality, that she, the proud realist, had lost sight of alongside all the harsh lessons life had thrown at her.

"We should probably forget it happened . . . shouldn't we?" Now he looked queasy, which was just plain insulting.

"Probably." Not that she had forgotten the last kiss, the one that had expediated her growing attachment to him. The one she thought about all the time. "We should also probably head back. It will be dark in an hour or so."

"Yes . . . of course . . . unless you want to discuss what just happened?"

"What is there to discuss? It was just a kiss. Let's not let it spoil our day." How she managed to smile, she would never know, when she wanted to weep and howl at the missing moon like a banshee.

"Yes . . . an excellent idea."

He held out his hand to help her up the steep bank, and she pretended she hadn't seen it. She didn't want to touch him now. Didn't want to be anywhere near him.

Fool! *Fool!* "Will it take long to get back to Standish House?" She couldn't wait to get to the sanctuary of her borrowed bedchamber and lick her wounds in private. What had possessed her to give her heart to another man who had no intention of staying for the duration?

"If the roads are clear, less than an hour."

*Fool!*

He was paying her. Paying her to keep him from the clutches of matrimony. There was a glaring clue if ever there was one as to the man's intentions. What had she been thinking? Had she thought she was the one to change him? Her? A downtrodden wood-block engraver from Clerkenwell, when all of society's finest beauties hadn't tempted him to change his ways before?

Of course not!

The sorry fact was, she hadn't thought beyond the romance of it all and had allowed herself to be swept away. Right from that first day, she should have told him where he could shove his money!

"I wonder how they all coped without us?" Her tone was light and conversational. She wouldn't allow him to see how much he had hurt her. If he regretted the kiss, she wouldn't deign to care about it. Let him think it didn't matter.

"I suppose we are about to find out." He came around the side of the curricle to help her in, and she thanked her tall ancestors for providing her with long limbs, so she was able to climb up before he could assist, and wrapped the thick blanket about her suddenly chilled body like a shield.

Redundant, Hugh climbed in beside her and began to steer the curricle around, the tension stretched between them like a barricade across the narrow bench seat. Neither said a thing. Minerva racked her brains for something, anything, light and inconsequential to convince him he didn't matter to her in the slightest, and when nothing came, she turned slightly away, watching the scenery rather than Hugh, grateful his expensive, sporty curricle was fast as the miles sped by.

They had been whizzing along for a good twenty minutes when he suddenly yanked on the ribbons and brought the little gig to a screaming stop. "We need to talk."

"We really don't."

"I am so incredibly sorry about that kiss. And I'm sorry about earlier . . . on the stairs. And that night outside your bed-chamber door." Beside her she felt him exhale slowly. Saw the tension in his fisted hand still gripping the reins. "To be perfectly frank, Minerva, I'm having the devil of a job *not* kissing you now despite knowing it cannot go anywhere."

*Cannot go anywhere.*

A very polite way of reminding her that engravers from Clerkenwell had no place forming fanciful attachments to earls.

"But I want to clear the air. Bring the Great Unsaid out into the open and find a way for the two of us to come to terms with the issue. We can't keep ignoring what is blatantly there between us."

"Between us? I see you are conveniently relieving yourself of all the blame for what just happened. It was you who kissed me. Twice. I do not recall asking you to on either occasion and am quite content never to do it again. Fear not, I have no designs on you, *Lord Fareham.* There *is* nothing between us. It was just a kiss. Not my first and doubtless not my last."

"It was more than just a kiss, damn it! It meant something. To both of us." He reached across the seat and took her hand in his while she digested his words. "Am I wrong? Or is it only me who is afflicted with odd, futile romantic feelings which refuse to go away?"

" 'Romantic' or *'romantic'*?" Her silly heart needed to know despite the fact that he called it futile.

"Both." All the color seemed to drain from his face, which took away most of the satisfaction of hearing him admit she mattered. "In the beginning I tried to convince myself it was purely a carnal attraction, but this goes beyond lust, Minerva. Is it just me who feels it?"

She made him wait several seconds before she sighed and flicked her gaze briefly his way. "No. . . . It's not just you." At least he was in turmoil, too. Somehow that made her feel less foolish for pouring her heart and soul into a futile kiss. "Shall we blame the forced proximity? The odd circumstances? The fact we are pretending to be an engaged couple to all and sundry? The beautiful atmospheric abbey, the deserted beach . . . ?"

"You could blame any and all of those things. . . . However, for me, I shall call it what it is. Attraction . . . passion . . . undeniable *affection.* Something which could be much *more* if we both took a chance on it."

Her silly heart soared again, buoyed with forlorn hope. *"You . . .* have an affection for . . . *me?"*

"Well, it should hardly come as a surprise. You are inordinately nice."

He smiled without humor and stared at their interlocked fingers. "But I have too much affection for you to indulge my feelings with no consideration of the potential consequences. The Standish male makes for an exceptionally bad husband and I was resigned to never be one. I will not make promises I am unlikely to keep, Minerva, as much as I want to. Not to you. I care for you and respect you too much to pretend to be anything other than what I am. Another untrustworthy man, who will probably ultimately disappoint you in the long run — just like your father and that good-for-nothing Romeo who deserted you."

"What are you saying?"

"That I am not in a position to offer marriage. Just myself for the time being . . ."

And there it was.

The offer doubtless many an unsuitable woman received from an aristocratic man — the temporary, insecure, and unbinding commitment of becoming his mistress. She should have expected it, just as she always expected to be disappointed by a man, but it hurt nonetheless — because the disappointment came from him. Her knight. When clearly her knight, like every fairy tale, had been entirely a flight of fiction.

"And I dare not ask you to take a chance to wait and see if I might change as our relationship develops . . ." He paused and stared at her intently as if he expected her to say something, agree to his insulting offer.

"No." She forced the word out as she removed her hand from the cocoon of his. She wanted a better life. One independent from the financial and social shackles that bound her. Becoming a rich man's mistress, as well as belittling all she was and all that existed between them, was as transient and unreliable as her piecemeal woodcutting. In fact, it was worse. With woodcutting there was always hope amongst all the uncertainty. As a mistress, there was no hope, just the certainty that eventual abandonment was inevitable. "Please do not ask me that again."

He stared down at his lap. "Of course . . . Sorry I brought it up. . . . It is doubtless for the best. . . . I suppose I must accept we are two people who, if I had not been born who I am" — another tactful reminder of the chasm between their stations — "might have been perfect for one another but are doomed to be nothing more than a short interlude in one another's lives. . . . More's the pity."

"I think I preferred my excuses." She wanted to leave. Or shout and scream and slap him for wounding her. "They sounded less depressing." Or callous. She turned away and stared back at the distant sea on the horizon. Even that had lost its magic. "We should go."

"But we are still friends, aren't we?" He sounded sad and she didn't care. "I never meant to hurt you."

"You haven't hurt me." *Just cut me to the quick.* "I am far too sensible to have ever expected promises from you or be deluded enough to want them." And she had too much respect for herself to agree to his debasing proposition. "Only a fool falls for a scoundrel, after all, and only an idiot would tie herself to him."

She thought he was different. Because with him, she was different. Happier, lighter, even younger. But not anymore. He had spoiled something she thought was lovely and turned it vile. Diminished her and all that she was, when she had fought so hard to be something.

Just never enough.

She swallowed past the lump in her throat and blinked the threatening tears away. It was never easy to hear you weren't quite good enough — an almost but not quite — but to hear it from Hugh, a man she had allowed herself to care deeply for, was somehow worse.

"Minerva . . ."

"There is nothing left to say, Hugh. You asked, I said no, let us leave it at that."

She would give him some credit for his honesty. He could have blithely seduced her with empty promises of more and cast her aside, as men of his ilk often did with women who were beneath them. But he had respected her feelings and been truthful about his intentions from the start. And that, too, was so typically Hugh.

"If it's any consolation, I am truly sorry I cannot promise you more today . . ." His expression was intense, more serious than she had ever seen it. "But I *will* promise you one thing today. I *will* be there for you, should you ever need me. Wherever, whenever . . . You can always count on me to come to your aid."

"My own personal knight in shining armor." The bitterness leaked into her tone.

"At best, my armor is tarnished, but the knight beneath is not all bad, I hope."

"Nor all good." More was the pity. She was too angry to look at him. Too disappointed and humiliated and hurt.

"I care for you too deeply to lie to you."

"I know." Just not deeply enough to want it all.

# CHAPTER TWENTY-THREE

"Where the hell have you been?" Diana met them at the stables as they pulled to a stop. "I have been tearing my hair out!"

"There was no need to worry. Hugh thought I needed a break so we went out for a drive. He did tell Payne to inform you we would be back in plenty of time for dinner."

In his misery, Hugh hadn't given any thought to the inevitable confrontation with Minerva's sisters. Perhaps he should have, but he was too preoccupied with the gravity of what had just occurred to care about anything else. He had bared his soul, offered himself to her as truthfully as he could, warts and all, and she had politely turned him down. He should have expected it, because even as he had offered it he wasn't entirely sure precisely what he was offering above an attempt to give deep affection and monogamy a go to see if they did have a future. But still, her calm, cat-egoric refusal had cut like a sword.

*I am far too sensible to have ever expected promises from you or be deluded enough to want them.*

He couldn't really blame her. He wasn't a good bet. The sorry truth of that unshake-able fact made his tainted Standish blood boil.

Diana's eyes swept the length of her, tak-ing in the disheveled hair, the sand stains on her skirt, and her kiss-swollen lips, then glared. "Oh, we shall discuss all that at length later, dear Sister, let me assure you, but right now we have a much bigger prob-lem on our hands. Come!"

With that she strode off, expecting them to follow. Diana took the servants' staircase behind the kitchen rather than enter the family part of the house, marching directly to Lucretia's door. She tapped it and whis-pered against the wood. "It's me."

They heard a key turn in the lock, then came face-to-face with a wide-eyed, harried Vee when it opened. "Oh, thank goodness! I'm at my wits' end. Thankfully she's sleep-ing again . . . for the moment, at least . . ." The youngest Merriwell stepped aside while Diana herded them all into the darkened room before locking the door again.

As his eyes adjusted, Hugh began to make out a Lucretia-shaped lump on the mattress. There was an odd smell in the air. A bit like spirits mixed with cheap perfume. "What's wrong with her? Is she sick?"

"She's drunk!"

Diana marched to the nightstand and turned up the lamp, and the full extent of the problem was shown in stark relief. Next to the lamp was an empty decanter. He recognized it as the one from the library. Another similarly drained wine bottle lay on its side, uncorked on the floor. A third was cradled in Lucretia's pudgy arms as she snored loudly.

"She pleaded another headache this afternoon before we went to the Ladies' Society and retired to her room. I didn't check on her, because Mr. Peabody suggested a ride, and by the time we came back she was in a right old state. Fortunately, she had dragged herself up here, so your family haven't collided with her yet — but she's been singing so enthusiastically it's only a matter of time before they do. Our dear, grieving, alcohol-averse *mother* has a substantial pair of lungs."

Vee stood nervously wringing her hands. "I've been trying to sober her up, I even asked Payne to send up some coffee, but that was over an hour ago and I haven't seen him since."

"Well, at least she's finally quiet. I didn't think I could take any more Mozart." Diana leaned over the actress's prostrate body and attempted to slip the wine bottle from her grasp. That apparently had the power to rouse the woman from her deep slumber, and she hugged it tight, blinking out of one bloodshot eye in the harsh light.

"Turn the lamp off! Devil child!" Her hand flailed around searching for the bed-covers, and when it found none, hoisted her skirt up to cover her face, rewarding them all with the sight of her garishly striped stockings. The sort worn by thespians on the stage. "I am trying to *sch-leep*!"

"There's no way she'll be fit for dinner. While that is bound to raise your mother's suspicions, it's probably just as well she avoids the dining room, as I doubt she even knows her own name at the moment — let alone the one she's supposed to have. But I have no idea how we are going to explain it without confessing she is too fond of the hard stuff." Diana shot daggers at the lump in the bed. "Because I'll bet that a few servants saw her wandering the halls as drunk as a sailor and they must have told Her Ladyship. Or if they haven't yet, they soon will. Gossip like this is priceless."

"Payne will deal with the servants." Hugh turned to Vee. "Can you go find him and ask him what the blazes he thinks he is about not fetching that coffee!"

Vee didn't need to be asked twice, utterly relieved to be able to escape the room. He couldn't blame her. The final minutes of the ride home had been pure torture, and Hugh had had plans to hide in his bedchamber and lick his wounds in private until he didn't have the overwhelming urge to rage at the heavens for cursing him with his father's blood, or weep because she confessed she had a deep affection for him, too, but was determined to leave him despite his tentative olive branch. "I'll think of something to tell my family and I'll get Payne to find an easily bribed maid to stay with her."

Hugh had no qualms about removing the wine bottle, prizing Lucretia's fingers from the neck when she attempted to hold on for grim death. He was going to wring Giles's blasted neck when he got hold of him. He should have known there was something peculiar about a brilliant actress from the London stage being readily available at the drop of a hat. The damn woman was a drunkard! An unreliable drunkard he was now well and truly stuck with.

"It's probably best to let her sleep it off for a few hours and then once she is coherent, I shall have some stern words with her." He strode to the window, opened it, and tipped the remaining wine from the bottle ceremoniously out of it. "Clearly I need to put the alcohol under lock and key!" He glared at Diana. "You shouldn't have left her alone all day!"

It was an unfair barb, but he was at the end of his tether, furious at fate, his father's bad blood, his suddenly yearning, needy heart, and Minerva's quick acceptance of his logical reasoning without putting up a fight. If she'd have taken a chance on him to be a better man than his ancestors, then he damn well would have been! For her! Because she was worth the effort. Hell — he would lock himself away with her in Hampshire, away from all temptation that might fire his wayward Standish blood, dedicate himself to their relationship until he was certain he could continue in that vein.

But she was too sensible to want anything from him, let alone the distant promise of marriage, and he was too unworthy to warrant the chance. Minerva had too much experience of unworthy men to waste another minute on one, and he hated both her wastrel father and the unreliable Romeo even more as a result. If it weren't for them, he might have stood a chance! But thanks to them, she would leave and he would never see her again. For her, goodbye would mean goodbye. A clean cut. A clean slate. A fresh start. Not at all what he wanted. Too final. Too painful.

Too tragic.

Beneath his ribs, his heart still hurt. If this was what affection did, he shuddered to think what actual love would do to his body.

"And you shouldn't have taken my sister off alone! I knew you were a despoiler! I warned Minerva you couldn't be trusted! But I let my guard down and at the first opportunity, you stole her away!" Diana's pointed finger jabbed him in the chest much too close to his battered heart. "If she's been ruined, you'll have to answer to me!"

"I have not been ruined, Diana . . ."

"Or so you think! There is more than one way to ruin a woman, Minerva, and this repugnant rake probably knows all of them! Did the blaggard promise you marriage in return for *favors*? I suppose he took you to some filthy inn somewhere so he could have his wicked way with you away from prying eyes!"

Hugh grabbed the jabbing finger before it

did more damage to the organ Minerva had already bludgeoned. "I did *not* ruin your sister!" He'd wanted to. Lord knows he had wanted to. Ruin her and make her his, then never let her go. "And I resent the implication."

"Resent it, do you?" The most confrontational Merriwell placed one hand on her hip and gestured to Minerva with the other. "Look at the state of her! Do you deny you never laid so much as a finger on her? A man like you? London's very own Don Juan!"

Hugh did not need another lecture on the sort of man he was. "We have better things to concern ourselves with than your scurrilous accusations, Diana. Can we focus on the problem in hand?"

*"Là ci darem la mano . . . Là mi dirai di sì . . ."* Lucretia's garbled warbling came from under her petticoat tent at a volume and pitch guaranteed to offend the ears, the choice of song farcically fitting in the wake of Diana's suspicions — the rake's infamous seduction scene from *Don Giovanni.* The one where he tries to lure a good girl away from her morals and her fiancé. Like his mother, Hugh was coming to loathe Mozart.

"I knew it! I knew you couldn't be trusted!"

*"Vedi, non è lontano . . ."*

"Stop singing, Lucretia!" He yanked the petticoats from the woman's face. "You need to be quiet!"

"Did I ever tell you I played Zerlina at Drury Lane? It was a triumph . . ." He yanked the petticoats back.

*Bloody Giles!*

The sister's finger jabbed again. "What are you going to do to rectify your grievous wrongs, Lord Fareham?"

"Nothing, Diana!" The woman he desperately wanted to be able to ruin finally found her voice above the cacophony. "Because *nothing* happened." Her eyes flicked to his, and he couldn't read them. "I wasn't ruined. Hugh hasn't despoiled or seduced me. We did some sightseeing! I saw the sea. That is hardly a crime."

"The housekeeper said Payne is in his quarters." Vee burst back through the door, looking distraught. "Apparently he has warned everyone on threat of death he is not to be disturbed, even in an emergency."

"What the blazes!" Hugh marched to the door himself, desperately needing to strangle someone, and that someone might as well be his insubordinate butler. "We shall see about that!" Clearly the whole world had gone mad today. Nothing had felt right since he'd waltzed with Minerva. He turned to her, and in fairness had to admit that thanks to his reckless curricle driving, *she* did look like she had been thoroughly ravished. "I'll be back."

She nodded, apologetic when she had nothing whatsoever to apologize for, aside from rejecting him, which added more fuel to the flames — when he wanted her to be as furious at fate as he was. Wanted her to fight for him — for them. To at least give it a chance.

"We will hold the fort until you do." What a typically selfless and utterly annoying Minerva thing to say.

"Of course you will." Better that than take a stand for something that could be wonderful if . . .

Bloody *what-ifs*!

Hugh slammed the door and took the servants' stairs two at a time up to the third floor and hammered his fist on the door to his butler's quarters. "Open the blasted door, Payne, or I'll knock it down!"

He heard a key turn in a lock, and the door opened just enough for his butler to squeeze through before he pulled it shut behind him. "Thank goodness you are home, my lord . . ."

"Don't 'thank goodness' me, you layabout! What the devil do you mean abandoning the ladies to deal with that drunken actress alone? Is this how you behave in my absence? You promised to fetch coffee and then came up here to rest on your laurels!"

"Something unexpected and urgent came up, my lord."

"Something unexpected! And urgent to boot? Here — in your comfortable *private* quarters well away from the crisis below?" Hugh folded his arms and blinked.

"We have a visitor. Or rather, you have a visitor. A most insistent one. Thank goodness he arrived after everyone had retired and I was able to intercept him. For the sake of discretion, I brought him up here, where I have been guarding him since. Patiently awaiting your arrival." Payne pushed open the door to reveal an older man lounging in a chair by the fireplace. Arrogant emerald eyes locked with his, and Hugh knew exactly who he was before his butler introduced him.

"Mr. Alfred Merriwell, my lord. Miss Minerva's father."

His first reaction was to pummel the wastrel to a bloody pulp. Instead, he set his jaw and walked calmly into the room, sensing trouble in spades. "Mr. Merriwell . . . an unpleasant surprise. To what do I owe the pleasure?"

"I came to visit my daughters." The man crossed one leg over the other and smiled. "Is this a bad time?"

"I suspect you know perfectly well it's a very bad time, else you wouldn't be here. Let's not beat around the bush, sir."

"I was in church yesterday and witnessed the strangest thing. My daughter pretending to be someone else as the banns were read announcing her impending marriage. To you . . . an earl . . . a renowned rogue . . ." Hugh's eyes narrowed in warning. He'd take that criticism from Minerva, he'd suffer it from her sister, but not this snake.

Alfred Merriwell shrugged, unapologetic. "Rather than object when the opportunity was given, I did the decent thing and thought I'd come speak to you. Man to man."

"You were in the church?"

"I rented a room at the inn. What a friendly place the village is. Everyone was very keen to talk about you and *my* Minerva. Your long engagement on account of her battle with consumption. The tragic death of her father in the Cairngorms, of all places. She also seems to have found a new mother now, too . . ."

"What do you want?"

"You're a rich man." Blackmail. Hugh wasn't surprised. "I am sure you can work it out."

"How much?"

"I'd be a fool to walk away for less than a hundred, now, wouldn't I?"

Hugh sat, calmly mirroring the man's pose while his mind was racing. "What do I get in return for my hundred pounds, Mr. Merriwell?"

"I shall go back to whence I came and you won't see me again." Hugh highly doubted that.

"And what about your daughters?"

"What about them?"

"Will you expect to see them before you leave? To tell them you have returned from your extended trip to who knows where? To share your newfound good fortune from your extorted one hundred pounds?" It was a test. One he felt in his bones Alfred Merriwell would fail.

"I don't see any reason why they need to know. The girls are better off without me. Especially as they are bound to be leaving with some of your money, too — what with there being plenty to go around. Am I right, Lord Fareham? Because we both know you and *my* Minerva aren't really engaged and

385

you certainly haven't known each other for two *long* years."

"You sound pretty certain of that. How could you possibly know we haven't been courting for two years when you abandoned them for pastures new five *long* years ago?"

"I've checked on my girls."

"You've checked on them?"

"Here and there. To satisfy myself they were doing all right." Which meant the scoundrel was never too far from London and must have seen them struggling.

"From a safe distance, I assume, seeing as those girls haven't seen hide nor hair of you since you disappeared?"

The man shrugged. "I never saw you once in Clerkenwell, my lord. Odd, don't you think? Seeing as everyone here claims the pair of you are madly in love and have been eagerly awaiting your nuptials for ages."

"A better question is why, if you were in Clerkenwell, you left Minerva to raise your children with no support — financial or otherwise?" His first image of her sprung to mind. The shabby, mismatched clothes, the down-at-heel shoes. The desperation for nine measly shillings and threepence.

"Minerva was a better parent than I ever was. She took to it right after her mother passed and so the other two were better off.

Some men aren't cut out to be fathers, Your Lordship. I did my time. And I did right by them until they were old enough to fend for themselves."

"She was nineteen!" All pretense of calmness disappeared in his bark. "She was nineteen and you ruined her life!"

"I taught her a trade. She had a steady income. The roof I put over their heads. What else was I supposed to do? I did as right by them as I could. You are a man of the world, Your Lordship. . . . We men have needs, don't we? Needs that won't be met when you come with three more mouths to feed."

"You left them for a woman . . ." It was a statement not a question. "One better situated than yourself." More images of Minerva working her fingers to the bone, struggling to make ends meet, feeding three mouths while her father ate his dinner elsewhere made his fists clench. "You selfish bastard!"

"It takes one to know one. Men like us do what we must to get what we want." Alfred Merriwell shrugged again, entirely unrepentant while Hugh felt sick to his stomach. "One hundred pounds, Lord Fareham — or I tell the whole village the truth." He stood and brushed imaginary lint off his tatty jacket. "I shall expect the money tomorrow. You can find me at the inn. Just ask for Mr. Smith."

# CHAPTER TWENTY-FOUR

A very different Hugh came down late to dinner that evening and remained for the next week. Not that anyone else would have noticed, because he was, on the surface at least, the same mischievous, charming fellow he always was. Perhaps more so. The life and soul of everything, constantly entertaining everyone and always laughing. But the special connection Minerva had always shared with him was gone, and while his blue eyes twinkled, they no longer twinkled for her.

By unspoken tacit agreement, they avoided one another unless they were in company, and she hadn't ventured to the portrait gallery. She was too angry, too sad, and too proud to listen to his oh-so-reasonable explanations again or to suffer a second insulting proposal to become his kept woman.

Even when a beautiful set of watercolors

arrived, complete with brushes, papers, and an easel, she chose to thank him over the breakfast table rather than do it in private. Each evening they bid each other a bland good-night, neither lingering in case the other uttered the dreaded words "my love" and they would be forced to be alone together with all the suffocating awkwardness such a meeting would now entail. Instead, they sent messages via Payne. Short, impersonal, painful messages that only imparted whatever pertinent detail was necessary to keep their interminable ruse going until Lord Bellingham returned to save them.

Worse, if indeed things could be worse, Minerva had to put on a show for everyone, including her sisters, constantly wearing the mask of cheerful normality when it felt as if she were dying inside. Nursing a newly broken heart in a house filled with jollity was exhausting, and she collapsed on her bed each night mourning the loss of him while sleep refused to come. When it did, he occupied her dreams until she woke up bereft and drained, only to begin the cycle again.

"The green or the red, miss?" In the mirror she listlessly watched Martha's reflection hold up two gowns. "Both are stunning."

Not so long ago, Minerva would have killed for dresses so fine and beautiful. She had been overwhelmed when those two evening gowns had arrived, and excited to wear them. Now neither held any appeal. Nor did the assembly. Especially as she wouldn't be waltzing. How could she waltz with him now? "You choose."

The maid smiled, then laid them both out on the bed. "Let's do your hair first and see which one looks the best once it's done. What sort of style do you want?"

"Whichever you think best." She handed over the brush she had been dutifully pulling through her hair at Martha's insistence, to make it shine, not that she had anyone to make it shine for. With a smile as false as the role she was playing, she settled back and suffered the maid's ministrations.

The light rap on the door was followed by Olivia's voice. "Might I come in?"

"Yes . . ." Hugh's mother had never visited her bedchamber before, or even this wing. "Yes, of course." She sat up straighter and pulled the thin robe closed, embarrassed to be in just her chemise and the low-cut tight stays Martha had assured her went with an evening gown.

The older woman entered smiling, already fully dressed in a glamorous peacock-blue silk gown and dripping in what Minerva assumed were real sapphires and diamonds. "Could you leave us, Martha?" Olivia clearly had something of great import to say. "I shall summon you again when we are done."

She tried to ignore the trickle of unease that skittered down her spine, and managed to conjure a welcoming smile. Despite her rift with Hugh, she had been getting on famously with his mother. The probing questions had stopped and, much to her surprise, they had started to become friends. Enough so, Minerva had stopped herself twice from confiding about her rift with Hugh.

"I hope you don't mind me barging in on your toilette, only I wanted to bring you this." Olivia produced a velvet-covered box from behind her back and held it out to her. "Open it."

Slowly, she reached for the box and lifted the lid, then blinked in surprise at the contents.

"My mother's rubies. She gave them to me as a wedding present and seeing as I never had a daughter, I should like to give them to you."

Minerva snapped the box shut and handed it back. "I really can't. . . . It's too much."

"Nonsense, my dear." Oliva opened the box herself and removed the heavy cascade of gems, which glittered in the lamplight. "I want you to have them and I simply will not take no for an answer." She undid the clasp and draped the necklace around Minerva's neck. The largest teardrop ruby rested above her décolleté, the matching collar of several fat rubies interlaced with diamonds rested heavily at her nape.

Like shame.

"I knew they would suit you! You have the coloring to carry them. Red favors dark hair. . . . And I see you have just the gown to go with them." She pushed Minerva's unbound hair to one side to fix the clasp. "There are matching earrings, a broach, and a bracelet — but we shall affix those once you are dressed."

Minerva sat frozen, lost for words. The weight of the lie she had told this kind woman was heavier than the gems she had no right to be wearing.

"Are you excited about tomorrow?"

The dreaded wedding dress day.

"Yes. Very." There was nothing more awkward than being measured for a beautiful wedding gown you knew you would never wear.

"I know it is a little unorthodox choosing bridal gowns and bridesmaid gowns on a Sunday, but Madame Devy is a very busy woman and I am sure the Almighty will forgive us as we will be attending the sermon in the morning, and choosing a gown in the afternoon is hardly work, now, is it?"

Church.

Minerva had forgotten about that dreadful ordeal, too. Tomorrow she would have to draw upon all her strength to sit through the second fraudulent reading of the banns followed by an entire afternoon trying to appear enthusiastic about her pointless trousseau. Unless the Almighty decided to put her out of her misery and smite her for perpetuating the falsehood.

"It will be fun." If your idea of fun was pouring vinegar into your eyes.

"Would you allow me to do your hair?" Olivia didn't wait for a response, picking up the brush and gently dragging it through her locks. "As a child, I loved to play with the hair of my dolls and couldn't wait to have a daughter to practice my skills on — but alas — the fates granted me just one child, and can you imagine the ruckus he would make if I attempted to do his?"

394

"Did you want more children?"

"I should have liked a larger family . . ." The twinkle in Olivia's blue eyes, eyes so like Hugh's, dimmed for a moment. "But I fear I was a little too old when Jeremiah and I married. It is such a shame, because he would have made a wonderful father. He has Hugh, of course, and since my first husband died, he has stepped into that role. They get on splendidly as you've seen . . . but I do wish I could have given him the joy of a baby. Never mind, he shall now have grandchildren to look forward to and doubtless spoil rotten. You shall be sick of the sight of us . . ." She rubbed Minerva's shoulder and grinned. "Because we have decided to stay. Isn't that marvelous?"

"Stay in England?"

"Yes. . . . We haven't told Hugh yet. But for a while now, Jeremiah has been talking about selling his business holdings in America."

"Isn't that a bit hasty?"

"If the last few years have taught us anything, it's that home is here. We both miss Hampshire dreadfully, and with you and Hugh finally getting married, and the promise of those grandchildren on the horizon, it seems like all the fates are aligned. Jeremiah has already sold his shipping company. He signed the final papers the week before we sailed. He's going to send a letter to his lawyers to instruct them to sell the rest and the house in Boston. It seems silly keeping a house we have no further use of."

Panic and remorse warred, making her gut clench with guilt. This was all getting out of hand.

It was one thing to allow herself to be measured for a ridiculously expensive gown she wouldn't wear, it was quite another to allow two innocent people to completely upheave their life to be closer to the grandchildren who would never come.

"Perhaps he should keep the remaining businesses and the house and simply extend this visit here? You never know, in a few months you might miss Boston, too."

"There is nothing holding us in Boston. Jeremiah was an only child and his parents are long dead. Besides, he spent so many years living here when he was a diplomat, most of his friends are here, too. Alongside a few canny investments he made along the way. He has always had a peculiar talent for speculation and can do that just as well here as across the Atlantic. No. . . . We are agreed. It is better to move on with a clean slate. You can help me look for a house!

Won't that be fun?"

"Olivia, there is something you should know. . . ." The words died in her mouth. As much as she didn't want to lie to his mother, she couldn't betray Hugh either. She owed him that at least. "We would prefer you to remain at Standish House."

"Good heavens no! As much as I love this place, a new bride needs to become mistress of her house and not have an interfering mother-in-law poking her nose in. Which obviously, I will not be able to resist doing. You might have noticed I am quite a bossy woman."

"Not at all . . ."

"You are such a bad liar, Minerva. It is one of the things I like most about you."

If only she knew.

But it wasn't her place to tell Olivia the truth — it was Hugh's and tonight she would tell him in no uncertain terms. "In fact, there is nothing I dislike . . . apart from your singing, of course."

"Diana says my singing sounds like a bag of cats being strangled."

Olivia chuckled and grabbed a handful of hairpins. "Hugh is such a naughty boy to have set us both up like that. But with hindsight, it was a funny evening. Your sing- ing . . . your mother . . . the sherry . . ."

Sharp blue eyes assessed her in the mirror. "How is your mother now that we are a house of temperance?"

Vee had saved the day over dinner that fateful day of the kiss on the beach, when it became apparent a servant had apprised Olivia of the inebriated Lucretia in her bedchamber. When Minerva was too emotionally drained and had nothing left in her to think of an excuse, her baby sister had stared down at her plate mournfully and said their mother had taken to drinking too much in the dark days after their father died but was working hard to control her habit. Miraculously, it worked, and both Olivia and Jeremiah had had nothing but sympathy for the woman and had bent over backward to support her since. All the decanters had disappeared, the spirits were locked away, and only water or elderflower cordial was served at mealtimes. They were such good people.

Another thing Minerva felt guilty about. Lies heaped upon lies. So many it took all her wits to keep up with them. She was starting to wish Lord Bellingham would return simply to bring an end to them. And an end to seeing Hugh every day and hurting.

■ ■ ■ ■

"You have such beautiful hair. I think that gown demands a loose style, don't you? But obviously piled on your head to do those jewels justice. It is long past time someone did. I was always too short to carry them off. They rather swamped my squat neck. I am delighted they have found a new home."

"I really cannot accept them . . ." A statement that would inevitably also lead to revealing the truth if Minerva dug her heels in. "But I shall be delighted to borrow them for tonight."

"Have it your way. We shall call them borrowed if that makes it easier for you to accept them, but I shan't be taking them back. They are my wedding gift to you."

"But we are not married . . ."

"But you will be and I am delighted about that, too. I confess I had my doubts. With Hugh's transient relationship with the truth and his reluctance to even consider marriage for so many years, I had convinced myself his engagement was a sham. . . . Even when I met you, I had grave suspicions. I think I was so convinced I was being deceived I saw fault in everything and perhaps gave you a hard time because of it.

I am ashamed of that now because it is obvious you and my son are deeply in love . . . and *lust.*" She paused, grinning, and waved the brush.

"Oh, don't look so surprised, dear! Did you think you were being subtle? I see the way he looks at you and the way you look at him when neither of you thinks anyone is watching. It is wonderful! Such devotion and passion cannot be forged. I am not surprised you have *anticipated your vows.*"

"We really haven't!"

"I am not a prude, Minerva. Such things are natural when a lady meets her soul mate. Why do you think I never made a fuss when the pair of you ran away the other day? I remember what it felt like to want to be alone with my man before I married him. The fizz of excitement . . . the utter perfection of it being just you and him. No pretense. No airs and graces or stifling politeness. A little taste of marriage and how it should be between two lovers . . . Although, in view of your little *lapse,* the pair of you are playing with fire delaying the wedding until Valentine's. Have you heard back from your father's family in Scotland?"

"Not yet."

"Then perhaps the letter got lost in the post? We shall draft another one tomorrow and have it sent by special messenger." Olivia pushed in a final pin and stepped back to admire her work.

"Beautiful . . . You shall be the belle of the ball and must dance with every young buck there to make my son horrifically jealous. Such things keep a besotted husband on his toes and will do Hugh good."

"I dance as well as I sing, Olivia, so it is probably best if I stick to watching."

"You don't dance at all? But Hugh said the pair of you waltzed. . . . It was such a lovely story . . ."

"I can waltz." Minerva smiled reassuringly in the mirror, not wanting to trample on another of this lovely woman's misconceptions. It had been Hugh's lie long before he had enticed Minerva to assist with it. She would be breaking her heart enough by running off with her son's best friend. "Just about." At least she'd had one lesson before that was ruined.

"Even better! Then you shall only dance with Hugh and the whole neighborhood can witness how much you adore each other!"

"Absolutely." There was no point in telling this grievously deluded woman not to hold her breath. There would be no dancing anymore, just as there weren't any private conversations in the gallery between them any longer either. Like the tide on that beautiful beach, Hugh had receded and not even the moon could influence that. "But please make excuses for me if I am pressed to dance with another."

"Leave it with me. I am a more convincing liar than you could ever be."

# CHAPTER TWENTY-FIVE

"But it is the last waltz!" His bloody mother would not be swayed. "Neither of you have danced a single dance all evening and I am sure nobody here will begrudge the pair of you one waltz." She pushed Minerva toward him. Despite sparkling in vibrant rubies, her green eyes were hardened emeralds. Cold and hostile. "And I'm sure they will all be delighted to have something to gossip about when you two lovebirds inevitably dance it scandalously too close." If just gazing at her made his heart weep, holding her would be pure torture.

"When you put it like that, how could I refuse?" He held out his hand and she took it, sending every one of his nerve endings spiraling out of control. But her touch, like her expression, was as detached as their now hideous relationship.

Hugh was in agony. Miserable, wretched, confused agony, and he had absolutely no clue what to do about it as he walked Minerva onto the floor. After enduring a week of her frigid avoidance, and the latent hostility he didn't fully understand, he had been dreading this. He would have to hold her again — knowing full well he would never properly hold her again. This would be the absolute last time.

It didn't help that she looked more beautiful than he had ever seen her, in a figure-skimming red silk gown that also, he noted with irrational jealousy, drew a great many admiring stares from the other gentlemen present. Or that she had been aloof toward him since the day he had confessed his feelings toward her despite claiming she felt the same way about him. Or that his blasted eyes had been drawn to her for every second of the never-ending two hours they had been here, enviously watching her laugh and chat with everyone who didn't have the misfortune to be him.

With him she was coldly monosyllabic. Disinterested. Distant. Even her fingers were stiff in his as they took their positions. He spun her into his arms and she smiled. It was a smile he was paying sixty pounds for, because it didn't touch her eyes.

He hated it. The pain felt like an anvil on his chest.

The orchestra played the first bars, and she stepped on his foot as her uncoordinated body fought the music. He could feel her frustration at herself beneath his palms and seriously considered leaving her to flounder because she had rejected him, before he remembered his part of this impersonal transaction. They had to put on a show even if he wasn't feeling particularly inclined to do so.

"Back, side, together — forward, side, together —" He felt her body relax in his arms as she finally found the rhythm, anticipating his movements rather than listening for the beats in the music her endearingly tone-deaf ears couldn't hear. He loved that imperfection. Almost as much as he loved holding her.

She was content to dance in silence. Probably just as well as he was out of meaningless things to say. They did a lap of the floor, managing to dance such an intimate dance like total strangers — bodies scandalously touching because she couldn't dance the steps otherwise, eyes averted and souls in completely different counties.

"You need to tell your mother the truth." Hugh fumbled the next step at the abruptness of her tone. "Things have gone too far. She's given me rubies."

Another thing to feel guilty about. "You can leave them when you go."

"Yes . . . that's exactly what I should do. Callous disregard when she has been nothing but kind to me. I hate lying to her."

"Giles will be back any day. I've written to him demanding he return so we can finally end this charade. Then you can stop lying." While he continued in her absence.

Although the heartbreak would be painfully real. After days of suffering it, the persistent pain in his chest was bordering on acute. He wanted to blame the dress, but knew it was her he missed. Them.

"It was never supposed to last this long. I agreed to stay for a few days once your mother arrived — a week at most."

"It cannot be helped."

"She thinks we are . . . lovers." *As if.* "And that I might be already with child . . . She's excited."

Hugh didn't reply, because oddly he was mourning the loss of that imaginary child now as well as Minerva. Another blasted *what-if* that would never come to pass.

To compound his misery, he could see Sarah and her husband had just entered the assembly room. Then behind them, Sarah's mother. Clearly fate or the Almighty wanted to make tonight the most god-awful of his life and send every possible bane to poke his open wounds.

Typically, she spotted him and raised her hand in a wave. He pretended he didn't see it but wasn't quick enough to disguise his discomfort from his dancing partner, whose gaze wandered to the spot his had just vacated, and widened.

"Mrs. Peters is here . . ."

"Is she?"

"You know she is. Why are you ignoring her?"

"We are dancing." It was easier to deflect than kick that hornet's nest. "And I am well aware of the fact you have gone above and beyond what you signed up for these last few weeks, but I promise you the day Giles drags his sorry behind back will be the same day you get to leave. In the meantime, leave my mother to me."

"Because that has all been going so well, hasn't it? The banns are being read for the second time in the morning and then directly after, I am being fitted for my wedding gown. As I said . . . this has gone much further than I ever anticipated."

"What do you want? More money? Name your damn price, Minerva, and let's be done with it!"

Her green eyes narrowed, hardening further. "Money will not right the wrongs we are doing to a generous and unsuspecting woman! Or to Jeremiah, who has been nothing but lovely. They are moving back here. Did you know that? Jeremiah is selling everything they have in America to be here with us! She is turning her life upside down for a lie . . ."

Hugh felt sick. This wasn't just going to leave him heartbroken — it would crush his mother, too. *What a hideous, seething mess!*

"It will all be over before anything undoable will be done." He would hunt Giles down and drag him kicking and screaming back to Hampshire if he had to. "There are just a few days left of this torture at most and then I shall repair the damage it has caused." If it could be repaired, which he doubted. He certainly wouldn't get over it, and that wasn't just the loss of Minerva. He had betrayed his mother when she had been betrayed quite enough already — how did that make him any better than his father?

"The *extensive* damage." Her gaze bore into his in accusation, and he mourned the loss of their easy friendship, too. How could one kiss and one short conversation so effectively kill all they had? "Very likely unrepairable damage. Tell me, Hugh, was it worth it?"

"No . . . of course not! I am not a fool, Minerva. I do know I have made a royal hash of things. With hindsight, obviously, I would have dealt with things differently." He wouldn't have invented a damn fiancée and then there would have been no possibility of kissing the siren on the beach and offering himself to her. Nothing had been the same since. Everything was spoiled. "I would have told my mother the truth before she sailed to Boston, told her I wouldn't be marrying anyone or giving her those longed-for grandchildren because I couldn't! I daresay the guilt of breaking her heart two years ago would've been better than all the hurt and pain this sorry debacle has caused me."

" 'Debacle'? A word which rather minimizes your part in it all. This is all your doing, Hugh. Every last bit of it. And it was entirely selfish."

*Oh, how he loathed his tainted Standish blood!*

"It was self-defense!" Agitated, he clumsily twirled her to the farthest part of the floor. Away from prying eyes, listening ears, and the newly arrived but timely reminders from the past currently standing at the refreshment table. "Selfish would have been to allow her to wear me down. To be dishonest and disingenuous. To marry some poor, unsuspecting woman then ruin her life as countless other men in my cursed family have done before me!"

"Because the Standish male makes for an exceptionally bad husband."

"At least I acknowledge my failings."

"Is philandering such a glorious pastime? Is that why you cannot make promises?"

"I've told you why I cannot risk promises." Vows were meant to last forever. "The Standish male has notoriously wandering eyes."

"So you keep saying . . . although I only have your word on the matter."

"Then allow me to enlighten you to justify my actions. My father was a philanderer, so was his father and his father before him." Baring the soul was meant to be cathartic, yet all Hugh felt was anger, frustration, and shame admitting it.

"Aside from you, I've never heard a cross word said about your father."

"That is because he could charm the birds from the trees, exactly as I can, and people only see what they want to see. Myself included. He used that dubious talent to his advantage but irrespective of the feelings of others."

"He wasn't a good man, then? Everyone

else is wrong?"

"He was a good father. A good landlord. An excellent politician. He was forward thinking and liberal. He did a lot of good. To the whole wide world he was a good man. A great one, even, and certainly better than his father, who was universally hated. But behind closed doors, in his personal life, he was different from the public façade he cultivated and not that much different from his own father despite regularly listing that callous bastard's many faults."

Fifteen years of distance did nothing to prevent the bitterness rising to the surface. "Like my hideous grandfather, my father was also a liar who pursued his own pleasures to the detriment of everything and everyone else. He was unfaithful to my mother before he had even walked her up the aisle and continued to betray her throughout their marriage. Something I only learned in the weeks before his death because they both kept it from me!" When they had ripped the floor from beneath his feet, they also tore the rose-tinted veil from his eyes, and ever since he had vowed to himself he would never allow his hereditary defects to wreak such destruction.

"That doesn't automatically mean you are of the same ilk."

"I spent my formative years trying to emulate a man who wasn't the man I thought he was! It is his voice in my head! His blood in my veins! By the time I realized I shouldn't model myself on him, it was too late. The die was cast. I am more him than not. . . . Two peas in a pod. Isn't that what everyone says?"

"They do, but . . ."

He didn't want to hear empty platitudes. "You've seen all the pictures in the portrait gallery, Minerva. If you take away the clothes, the years, and the name plaques, those Standish faces are one and the same. Interchangeable, intrinsically selfish, and entirely incapable of falling in love or remaining faithful to one woman." Deep affection wasn't love. The constant ache in his chest wasn't love either. The need to make her his didn't guarantee forever.

"Have you ever tried?"

She wasn't listening! "I know what I am, Minerva. Up until you came along, I avoided romantic attachments, knowing full well there was not enough within me to sustain them."

"That sounds more like a convenient excuse for untangling yourself from unsavory entanglements!" Her nose was in the air, and she deigned to look at him down it.

"Are you *not* in control of your own actions? Your own destiny?"

Her sudden resort to sarcasm galled. "I *am* in control of my own destiny." Couldn't she see that was the reason he was being so damn noble?

"Really? Then why do you continually fall back on your Standish blood to justify your terrible behavior?"

"While I am not justifying the huge mess I have made, this entire regrettably misguided charade came about because I absolutely refused to follow in my father's footsteps."

"Because you are incapable of falling in love or remaining faithful."

"I never believed I was capable of either." Although there was a good chance his deep affection might grow into love if nurtured, and he would have made a damn good attempt at remaining faithful if she had accepted his offer.

"What about Sarah?"

"*Sarah!*" He stopped dancing momentarily to stare at her, stunned.

"I have eyes, Hugh. Every time you see her, you behave peculiar."

"Then clearly you need spectacles if you cannot see what everyone in this room does."

"I see the way you look at her! Why don't you just admit it. She broke your heart and that caused you to harden it. Perhaps you still love her — or perhaps you still feel guilty for disentangling yourself from her, too? Another *unsavory* entanglement which could never sully the impressive house of Standish. Because heaven forbid a common woman should taint that illustrious, noble, and *tainted* bloodline."

Had she gone quite mad? "I don't love Sarah!"

"But you did!" She spat the words in his face. "For once in your life, tell the truth, Hugh!"

Several pairs of eyes were now watching them intently, so he took her elbow and steered her toward the alcove. The awful truth might well be common knowledge here but nobody ever said it aloud. Especially him.

"Sarah is my *sister,* Minerva!"

Her mouth fell open. Then she craned her head to look at his sibling, no doubt taking in the unmistakable similarities. The blond hair. The height. The blue eyes. The same features. All his father's. Peas in a pod. "I never knew you had a sister!"

"Neither did I until I turned seventeen! The woman over there with her was my

414

father's mistress." And once again, although for the life of him he would never understand it, his mother was chatting to the woman as if she hadn't stolen her husband and destroyed her marriage. "Probably one of many, I suspect — but he moved them both into our house when he found out he was dying . . ."

He could still remember his mother sitting him down and explaining it to him. That his father's other family had a right to be there, too, because they loved him just as much as he did. So calmly, as if the walls of Jericho weren't crumbling around his ears and everything he had believed about the man he had worshiped hadn't all been a flimsy lie.

Days later, Hugh had had to stand with those unwelcome strangers around his father's bedside as he took his final breath, holding the hand of the woman who wasn't his wife while his actual wife looked on like a spectator. His father had died without ever explaining how that horrific and, for Hugh alone apparently, sudden new reality had come to pass.

"I think this gives me the right to behave a little peculiarly on the odd and unavoidable occasions when I collide with them."

Behind them, people clapped as the waltz

came to an end.

"She didn't break your heart?" That was the single detail she cared about when he had just laid his blackened soul bare?

"No." Hugh screwed up his face in disgust. "I cannot believe you even thought such a thing."

"Perhaps if you had been open from the start, I wouldn't have jumped to conclusions."

"I have always been open with you."

"You allow me to know what you think only if it suits you to tell me."

"That is unfair."

"Is it? You are the master of deflection. Constantly making jokes and hiding behind a mask of charm or avoiding real honesty because it . . ." She threw up her hands. "Really, I do not know what causes you to behave like that — but I suspect you avoid genuine honesty at all costs because it frightens you."

"I have always been honest with you, Minerva."

No, he hadn't.

There had been pockets of brutal honesty spread amongst a great deal of deflection. He was uncomfortable being seen as anything other than what he was — a huge disappointment who couldn't be trusted not to let people down. "You know more of the real me than most do." That was closer to the truth.

"Maybe — but I've learned more about the *real* Hugh through your mother, Jeremiah, and Payne than I've ever heard from your lips. Tell me — would you have ever mentioned you had a sister unless I had made a mistake about the nature of your relationship?"

"How was I to know her husband's regiment was coming home? We do not keep in touch . . ."

"I shall take that as a no. Because talking about her would mean talking about your complicated emotions concerning your father, and why would you entrust anybody with anything meaningful when it's easier to keep everything superficial! Then blame your Standish blood for everything else." She exhaled slowly, shaking her head. "It makes me wonder what else you haven't told me?"

"Nothing of importance."

Bitter bile rose in his throat at the lie. He still hadn't told her about her father despite Payne's daily remonstrance. But how would it help her to know her sire had been within arm's reach at all times but had ignored them for his own selfish reasons? Or that he had uncovered more unsavory details on the wastrel since he had started digging? Besides, if he confessed he had paid the man off, she would assume he had done it to save his own skin, and admitting otherwise would involve having to tell her again he had done it out of his deep affection for her.

*Deep affection?*

Perhaps he truly was afraid of real honesty, because he knew in his bones affection probably wasn't this painful nor was it this all encompassing. He had a deep affection for Payne — it was nothing like what he felt for Minerva.

"You are exhausting, Hugh! And I am tired of it."

The floor tilted beneath his feet. "What are you saying?"

"That we cannot continue this awful ruse indefinitely. Not when it has run its course and it's making us both utterly miserable." She paused, her fingers going to the heavy ruby necklace as she glanced across the room to his mother and his father's favorite mistress. "The banns are being read again tomorrow. I shall sit through those but I will not allow them to be read for the third and final time next Sunday. Which gives us exactly a week . . . to either enact the final scene in your story or to face the music."

Her eyes were troubled, angry, the unfathomable green depths swirling with bitter regret that cut deep. But not as deep as her parting words. "Either way, by this time next Saturday, I shall be gone, Hugh. It is long past time we said goodbye. . . . In truth, I bitterly regret we ever said hello."

# CHAPTER TWENTY-SIX

Because her tears were about to imminently fall, Minerva excused herself and rushed to the retiring room. After ten minutes and the hasty repair of her face, she left it shaky — but outwardly calm at least. She took a deep breath, intending to return to the relative safety of Olivia's side, but found her feet taking her toward the door instead, craving fresh air for a few moments before she pasted on her mask again.

She hadn't lied. Being *his* Minerva was exhausting. Every day threw up new challenges she was ill equipped to cope with. Rubies, wedding gowns, drunken actresses, secret sisters, her own crushed heart. Was it any wonder she was at her wits' end? Or that tears were never far from the surface? She had been lured here by the promise of greener grass and had found herself waist deep in a field of nettles instead.

She embraced the brisk winter chill as she

wandered past the waiting carriages, toward the dark village square, needing to be alone.

"When did you learn to dance?" The voice chilled her more effectively than the December night could.

"Father?" Her head whipped around from left to right, trying to find him in the blackness, until a brief flash illuminated him leaning against a wall as he lit one of the foul-smelling cigarillos she had always hated.

"Landed on your feet, haven't you? Engaged to an earl no less."

She felt sick, knowing his convenient presence after such a long time could only signal one thing.

Trouble.

"What are you doing here?"

"No tearful reconciliation for your long-lost father?"

"I hoped you had died in a gutter somewhere years ago."

He took a long drag, then slowly blew out the smoke. "You always were a cold one, Minerva."

"Answer my question! What are you doing here?"

He shrugged, typically unfazed. "I'd have thought it obvious. I've come to rescue my daughters."

"We don't need rescuing." The acrid smell of the cheap tobacco took her straight back to Clerkenwell in the dark days before he disappeared. Hiding in silence while the rent collector, the debt collectors, or the occasional Bow Street Runner hammered on the door. That same door being pounded by the fists of whichever messenger had been sent to summon her in the middle of the night to fetch her drink-sodden sire from whichever fetid pit he had collapsed in. Hiding the bulk of her hard-earned wages under the loose floorboard so he wouldn't take them and drink himself unconscious rather than see food on the table. "How did you find us?"

"If your little con was a secret, you probably shouldn't have allowed Venus to leave a forwarding address at the Dog and Duck. I took that as an invitation. Not that I needed one. We are family after all and I am still head of the household."

"Something you have managed to conveniently forget for the last five years! I won't bother asking where you've been. I know already all I'd hear was the usual crock of lies."

"Talking of lies, Daughter dearest, I wonder how your earl's mother or this quaint little village would feel about the lie you and he are telling the lot of them?"

Icy tentacles of dread wrapped around her ribs and squeezed her chest. "What makes you think we're lying?"

"Him? Marry you?" Her father threw his head back and laughed. "Earls don't marry guttersnipes."

Wasn't that the truth! "I thought I was a gentleman's daughter? A blessedly *dead* gentleman's daughter!" Minerva turned on her heel. She would brazen it out and then talk to Hugh, let him know they no longer had a week. They had hours.

"I hear I froze to death . . . in the Cairngorms." She stopped in her tracks. "And I thought you always looked down your nose at me because you thought you were morally superior, when it turns out the apple didn't fall far from the tree, did it . . . Minerva *Landridge*?"

"Nobody would ever believe you over Hugh."

"Hugh, is it? Cozy . . . But we'll see? Or we could do this the easy way, and everyone remains none the wiser . . ."

"What do you want?"

"Whatever he's paying you."

"He's not paying me."

"Then I'll have those rubies. . . . They are rubies, aren't they? A toff like him would never buy paste."

Automatically, her hands went straight to her neck to protect Olivia's unwanted gift. "They aren't mine. They're borrowed."

"Then I shall expect the funds in cash, then. Shall we say a hundred pounds . . . by tomorrow?"

"He's only paying me sixty!" She instantly regretted the stupid outburst, born entirely out of panic, but couldn't take it back. The damage was done.

"Only sixty?" Her father looked her slowly up and down, making her feel sullied and dirty. "You sold yourself too cheap, girl. . . . Or do you think me a fool when your fancy man's pockets are lined with gold?" He blew smoke in her face and chuckled again. "I'll take seventy-five. I'm sure you can convince him to give you more. The poor fellow looks at you like a dog at a butcher's window. Use your wiles, girl . . ."

"I am not giving you a penny!" She turned, but he grabbed her arm and yanked her back.

"Happy to see your beloved's name dragged through the mud, are you? The locals here all think he walks on water. And what about that mother of his? Does she know her precious boy has hired himself a fiancée? Or a whole family of *Landridges* to go along with her? Betrayal like that cuts a mother deep . . ."

"Stop!" He knew too much — or he had pieced it all together too well — and thanks to her stupidity, he had confirmation she was being paid. "I can't give you seventy-five. I can't even give you the whole sixty . . . We have bills . . . rent . . . If we don't pay up, we'll be homeless." Mentally she rapidly added up everything, wondering if she could get away with more, then realized it wasn't worth the risk. "I can give you forty. By tomorrow. If you promise you'll go away . . ."

If she could remove her father for a few days, she could think of a way to terminate her pretend engagement swiftly and head back to London before her father ruined Hugh or hurt his mother . . .

What was she thinking? This was merely opening the floodgates. Her father was vile enough to continue his extortion, and he had never kept a single promise to anyone in his life. He would be back like a bad smell, and he would want more. Some things were as inevitable as night following day.

"Minerva?"

Neither of them had seen Hugh's stealthy approach.

"What's going on?" His eyes slowly turned to her father's and glared. She had two choices. Both were awful but only one felt right.

"My father knows. He's trying to blackmail me!"

Hugh took this shocking news with impressive calm, almost smiling as he folded his arms. "Is that so?" Bizarrely, his strength soothed her. "Was my hundred not enough, Mr. Merriwell?" The relief at having an ally was swiftly replaced by horror as the full weight of that damning statement sunk in.

Hugh wasn't surprised, because he had already met her father. Met him, paid him, and purposefully kept it from her. Another betrayal. Another reminder he wasn't at all the man she had believed him to be.

"You cannot blame a fellow for trying, my lord."

"I can. Especially when his duplicity reneges on the bargain we made."

Bargains? Blackmail? More secrets? So many lies she no longer knew which way was up. She must have shivered, because he turned to her and immediately shrugged out of his coat and wrapped it gently around her shoulders. The instant warmth — his warmth — should have comforted her, but it didn't.

"Go back inside, Minerva. I will handle this."

"No!" She wanted to slap him. "I have a right to hear everything said!"

"Get lost, girl! I'd rather deal with the organ grinder than the monkey . . ." The final word came out in a croak as Hugh's fist gripped her father's lapels and twisted. Hard.

"Do not speak to her like that!" With her father's boots scrabbling for traction on the floor, he turned back to her with gritted teeth. "Go back inside, Minerva! *Now!* The things I need to say to your father are not for a lady's ears and this is my mess to sort out!" And with that he frog-marched him farther into the darkness.

She simply stood there, glued to the spot like a statue, desperately trying to comprehend everything, before coming to the conclusion there were too many gaps for her to understand exactly. Too many questions now needing answers. Why had her father suddenly turned up? Where had he been? The intervening five years hadn't been kind to him. He looked older. Sicker. Colder than he ever had before. When had he approached Hugh? How long had Hugh been keeping this from her? And more importantly, why?

As her lungs burned from the frigid air sawing in and out of them, Minerva realized she already knew the answer to the last question. Hugh had done whatever was necessary to save his own selfish, shallow skin and hadn't given a damn how she would feel! Or how her sisters would feel . . . What in heaven's name was she going to tell them? Hurt made her want to run and tell them now, but common sense told her now was not the time.

Hugh emerged out of the darkness alone.

"He won't bother you again." He came to stand in front of her. "I'm sorry you had to suffer that. I thought I had fixed . . ."

Her hand shot out without her realizing, and slapped him hard in the face. He recoiled, stepping back, his expression wary.

"Let me explain . . ."

"There really is no need. Even a *monkey* like me can work it out!" She pushed his chest hard with flattened palms. "You looked after yourself, didn't you!"

"Minerva, it wasn't . . ." She pushed him again, putting all her weight into it.

"You did whatever you thought was necessary to maintain your convoluted and self-ish charade!" Another push. He made no attempt to defend himself. No attempt to stop her. "You are a liar, Hugh Standish! A lying, self-centered, untrustworthy, two-faced scoundrel! And I want nothing more to do with you!"

She ran then, not caring that his jacket fell from her shoulders into the mud, not caring that every carriage driver in the long line of them waiting outside the assembly rooms could see her in this state, dashing back to the sanctuary of the retiring room and bolting the door behind her in case he had the poor sense to follow, then sinking to the ground in a heap.

At least she expected no less from her father. He was a wastrel. Morally moribund and terminally hideous. She had hated him all her life but had always known where she stood. But Hugh . . .

He had manipulated her with charm and played her like a fiddle. She'd fallen for his story and agreed to lie for him. Fallen for every supposedly well-meant good deed. Fallen for every honeyed falsehood that had dripped out of his practiced seducer's mouth. Fallen for him. All of him. Completely.

Fallen in love.

With the worst sort of scoundrel.

What the hell was she going to do?

# CHAPTER TWENTY-SEVEN

"She said to put it in writing, my lord."

Hugh gaped at his butler. "Writing?"

"Yes, my lord. I am sure you are familiar with it. It requires pen and ink and paper. There is some in your dressing room. Shall I fetch it?" Payne deposited the glass of brandy on his nightstand. "I did tell you to tell her about her father."

"Thank you, Payne. What I really need at this moment is another sanctimonious 'I told you so.'"

"You are most welcome, my lord. I do try my best. Will there be anything else?"

"Go back to the blasted woman's bedchamber and tell her I demand an audience!"

"Of course, my lord. I am sure my knocking for the third time at this late hour will garner more a favorable result than the previous two." The outspoken servant bowed with little enthusiasm and disappeared again out of the door.

A blasted letter! Outrageous. When he had tried repeatedly to apologize to her and explain his reasoning. He had tried last night, when a stony-faced Minerva had finally emerged from the ladies' retiring room, where he had been waiting, but she had glided past him into the ballroom as if he were invisible. Then she proceeded to attach herself to his mother's side for the rest of the evening. Back home, she used her sisters as her bodyguards.

He had said "Good night, *my love*" at the top of the stairs.

"Sleep well, *my love.*"

He ensured that the "my loves" were enunciated with particular emphasis in case she had forgotten their code, yet she left him to pace the length of the portrait gallery for two painful hours before he accepted she wasn't coming.

Nor did she appear the following morning either. He could say that with absolute certainty because after a night of torturous insomnia he had returned to the gallery promptly at five, watched the sun rise, and heard the house wake, only to be greeted by the deadpan face of Payne, who had been sent by his mother to tell him if he didn't eat breakfast in the next fifteen minutes, he could go to church on an empty stomach.

Church had been another delight. She had ignored him in the carriage. Ignored his attempt to trail behind the others as they arrived, and then sat next to him stiffly. Exactly like an iceberg. Staring resolutely at Reverend Cranham as the banns were read again before bolting out the door on Jeremiah's arm.

Hugh had tried again in the afternoon, only to be shooed away by his mother because Minerva was in the midst of being measured by Madame Devy for a blasted wedding gown and trousseau. A task that apparently took several hours and one that caused him to watch the sun go down as he paced his study, and any plans he had had to intercept her before or after dinner were thwarted because she never bothered to arrive. Minerva had been struck down by a sudden headache, and thanks to her hawk-eyed, hovering sentry Diana, he'd had to abort his forlorn attempt to lay siege to her bedchamber.

Clearly she was determined to make him suffer. And it was working. He'd never felt more wretched in his life.

Listlessly, he stared out the window, swirling the amber liquid in his glass. Maybe he *should* write her a blasted letter. As much as she didn't want to hear him, he had much to say. Most of it groveling. He was sorry for practically everything. For dragging her into his mess, shamelessly using her obvious need for money for his own gain. He was sorry for upending her life and dragging her across the country, making all his problems her problems, foisting Lucretia and his mother on her, causing friction between her and her sisters, hiding her father's return, hiding his unpalatable truths from her and . . .

And most important of all, he was sorry for not being good enough.

Because he absolutely understood all the reasons she was furious at him and why she wanted to be permanently shot of him.

The sad truth was, he could probably write all that much better than he could say it. He did have a way with the written word. It was his innate talent at letter writing that had got him into this predicament in the first place. But a letter was so impersonal, and he needed the personal now more than he ever had before. He needed to look into her eyes. Needed to see if she felt as wretched as he did. To see if she cared enough to gift him with just a kernel of hope.

Payne came back in without knocking. His

bland face said it all.

"I am to tell you that you are a brute. A beast . . ." He ticked the insults off on his fingers. "A big fat liar. A child who needs to grow up. A vile, sweet-talking seducer." The butler scowled at that. "If you will excuse the interruption in the message, my lord — shame on you!" He skewered Hugh with a glare, his lip curled in distaste. "Have you no morals?"

"I didn't seduce her . . . not completely. We kissed . . . twice." Not that it was any of Payne's bloody business! "And, for the record, on both occasions she kissed me back."

"Did you give her a choice?"

"Do you want me to kick your insubordinate arse down the stairs? Of course I gave her a blasted choice! What do you take me for? Get back to reciting your bloody message. I could see you were enjoying it."

"A vile, sweet-talking seducer . . ."

"We have established that."

"A coward."

"That's a bit harsh."

"Who is not very nice." That one hurt. "And a snob."

"*'A snob'?* Are you sure?"

"I queried it myself, sir, as there is no denying you are many, *many* dreadful things . . . but I have never once known you to resort to condescending aristocratic airs and graces with anyone."

"I do believe that is the most gushing praise I have ever received from you, Payne."

The butler acknowledged this with a curt nod. "But she was adamant. She said you were — and I am directly quoting here rather than paraphrasing — 'a cowardly snob who shamelessly uses his dead ancestors to untangle yourself from unsavory entanglements.' "

The familiarity of the unusual phrase sparked something in his memory. She'd said exactly the same thing last night — but he had been too stunned she thought he had romantic feelings for Sarah, of all people, to pick up on it.

"What does that even mean, Payne?" Because clearly for Minerva it mattered enough to warrant repeating.

"I couldn't hazard a guess, my lord, but she had tears in her eyes as she said it and she choked the words out."

"Choked?"

"She was most upset, my lord. *Most* upset."

"*Most* upset? Or crying upset?"

"It certainly sounded as if she was crying after she slammed the door in my face.

Which, of course, was really your face as I was there in your stead." The butler frowned, troubled. "She had that drawn, pinched, and puffy look about her features which women get when they are in utter despair. I thought she had been crying prior to the door slamming, too." He pointed to his eye. "She was very bloodshot."

Hugh hadn't thought his suffering could get any worse. Once again, he was proved horribly wrong. Minerva was crying — brave, tenacious, resourceful, selfless, all-round wonderful Minerva was crying — and it was all his fault.

"Oh yes . . . and she told me you weren't worth the money nor the time nor the effort she's put into you and she hopes, with every fiber of her being, you rot in hell."

"Well, you can inform her that her wish has come true. I am in the deepest bowels of hell already."

And he hated it. He'd never felt so ill without actually being ill. His vocal cords felt strangled, his head was all over the place, he couldn't sleep, couldn't eat, and something hard, heavy, and bony was jumping mercilessly on his heart. "I'm sure it's only a matter of time before the rot sets in." Hugh let out a long, self-pitying sigh. "What am I going to do, Payne? I am utterly miserable."

"If I might be so bold, my lord, you have been utterly miserable for at least a week. Ever since the day the pair of you escaped, when I assume you kissed her — and she foolishly kissed you back."

"You are very astute, Payne. I have been. I cannot seem to shake it."

"Perhaps it is time to face facts."

"That she hates me and wants nothing more to do with me?"

"That you have fallen in love with your fiancée and you need to tell her."

The queasiness was immediate, and he wanted to deny it, but the feelings he had for Minerva were just too strong to deny what they truly were any longer.

"I do love her." All the air escaped from his lungs in a whoosh. The unthinkable had happened. "I *love* Minerva. . . ."

"Then tell her."

"I have." That was the root cause of his misery. The thing that ate away at him mercilessly. "She didn't want to know."

"I must say that surprises me, as I thought her quite smitten with you, although heaven only knows why."

"She said she had affection for me, too. Then turned me down flat."

"You proposed?"

"I proposed we conduct an experiment to see if I *should* propose one day. Sort of."

"Sort of?"

"Well, not in those exact words."

"Might I ask which words you used?"

"It wasn't so much a proposal, really, as a declaration of sorts that I might well be amenable to pursuing a serious attachment if she was. Although obviously, given my history I was not in a position to ask outright . . ." Payne watched his gesticulating left hand with interest. "Because I am well aware I am not a sound bet. I certainly recall telling her I felt attraction, passion, and a deep affection for her. And I definitely suggested in *the strongest possible terms,* whilst I couldn't make cast-iron promises I wouldn't return to my old ways — because let's face it, the Standish male makes a notoriously bad husband and all that . . . but I would certainly endeavor to do my damndest to be worthy of her affections and eventually . . ." Payne held up his hand and shook his head.

"That *is* a lot of words."

"I was thorough."

"Not necessarily clear words."

"They were as clear as crystal, Payne. I laid all my cards on the table. Bared my soul. Warts and all."

"But did you say *the* word, my lord? The actual word? The one which would have made all those other words quite superfluous?"

"If you mean the dreaded 'L' word, then not exactly."

"Not exactly?"

"I used the words 'deep affection' rather than the dreaded 'L' word. It had all come on so suddenly, you see. I suspected it but I wasn't entirely sure I was ready for it at the time." Was he ready for it now? Love was a huge commitment. A much bigger commitment than deep affection. He took a big slug of his brandy and plopped heavily on the mattress, because the solid oak floor felt oddly unsteady. "But it was certainly implied."

"I see." Payne shook his head again and walked to the door. "It's a miracle you haven't driven me to drink."

"Is that it?"

"It's midnight. I am going to bed."

"Is that all the counsel I am to receive in my hour of need? I am a broken man, Payne!"

"You are an idiot, my lord." His more-annoying-than-usual servant turned the handle and smiled. "But I am sure you will work it all out in the end."

Hugh nursed the brandy for a few minutes, trying to work it all out, and then decided he couldn't. What was there to work out? Because once you scraped back all the other complications, it all boiled down to one depressing thing.

He wanted her and she didn't want him.

It was that simple and that tragic and he couldn't change a damn thing about it.

But she was miserable, too, for entirely different reasons, and he could at least apologize for everything he had done to cause it. And if she wouldn't talk to him, he might as well write it down because, if nothing else, a heartfelt and genuine apology would go some way toward letting her know he wasn't entirely the selfish and callous brute she accused him of being. If she didn't accept it, so be it, but she would read it, and that would have to do.

He strode to his dressing room and grabbed the stationery, then sat at his dressing table only to stare mournfully at the blank sheet. He needed a good opening sentence. Something strong.

My Dearest Minerva,
    I am in torment. I wish you would speak to me, but in the absence of conversation

I am forced to justify my actions concerning your father . . .

He scribbled out the words, then screwed
up the sheet into a tight ball, which he
threw.

My Dearest Minerva,
    I am an arse.
    I suspect I have always been an arse,
but since I met you, I keep seeing myself
in the mirror and wishing I wasn't an arse.
I realize to you my behavior seems bizarre
at times, probably childish and definitely
selfish. You called all those things correctly, my love.

My love.
Not a code word or a call to arms. But a
fact. An irrefutable, undeniable, and ir-
repressible fact. Some things just were.

> But the truth is, I love you
> and it terrifies me.

And for some inexplicable reason, he
didn't feel queasy anymore. Why was that?
Had he finally accepted it? Was he finally
prepared to take the risk?
As a test, Hugh closed his eyes and pictured Minerva in a wedding gown, coming

toward him down the aisle. He smiled at the image, as it wasn't anywhere near as abhorrent as he had always assumed such a thing would be. He mentally took her hand and listened to the ghostly voice of the fantasy Reverend Cranham recite the vows . . . *"Wilt thou have this woman to thy wedded wife? Wilt thou love her, comfort her, honor, and keep her in sickness and in health; and, forsaking all others . . ."* The queasiness returned with a vengeance. *"Keep thee only unto her, so long as ye both shall live."*

The biliousness was accompanied by palpitations so erratic he had to take several deep breaths to bring them under control. He knew exactly what had caused this extreme reaction. It was his tainted Standish blood rebelling.

It was just too damn strong.

# Chapter Twenty-Eight

The tap on her door woke her up. She must have cried herself to sleep again. "Who is it?"

"Me . . ." The door opened, and Minerva cursed herself for not having had the good sense to lock it. "I really need to talk to you." She could see only his outline in the dark room.

"Go away! How dare you come into . . . Do not *sit!*"

But he had. Directly on the mattress next to her. Instinctively, she shuffled as far away as she could, clutching the bedcovers tightly around her, acutely aware of his presence in her sanctuary. "Get off my bed!"

"I wrote you a letter like you asked." His voice was flat and sounded thoroughly miserable.

She blinked into the darkness, hardening herself against the flash of pity she felt for him. "And you expect me to read it now?"

"No . . ." She heard the whisper of paper as he deposited it on the nightstand. "But what I have to say cannot wait." Her eyes were slowly adjusting to the dark, enough she could see his broad shoulders weren't draped in a jacket, and they were decidedly slumped. As if they carried the entire weight of the world. "It is about your father, and you have the right to hear it."

She would not feel sorry for him.

"Then say it and go."

"He turned up here unannounced last week while we were at the beach. Fortunately Payne intercepted him and I was alerted to his presence later that evening. He demanded money straightaway and I played along, knowing full well he was unlikely to remain out of sight. I gave him fifty pounds and informed him he could have the remaining fifty once everything was done if he adhered to the terms of the bargain. I also offered him the chance to meet with the three of you that night — he declined, stating you were all better off without him. My keeping it from you was my foolish way of attempting to minimize the hurt his curt dismissal would have caused."

"That wasn't your decision to make."

"I know and I am sorry. . . . Truly I am,

but it was well meant if clumsy. Your father admitted he has been living in London since he abandoned you, with some woman who wouldn't take him with three daughters, as if that was a good-enough excuse. He was entirely unrepentant, in fact. But something about that story didn't ring completely true, because I remembered your own suspicions about him and that Bow Street had knocked on your door looking for him. I escorted him to the inn, supervised his packing, and had my carriage take him to Southampton to catch the morning post to London. My man watched him board that carriage and leave. That same morning I dispatched a letter to my solicitor instructing him to hire a Bow Street Runner to investigate your father further." He sighed and rested his head back on the headboard.

"I realize I should have told you all that then — but things were awkward between us and, in my defense, I didn't want to worry you until I was in complete possession of all the facts. Two days ago, I received the Runner's preliminary findings and they are not good."

"What has he done?"

"Quite a bit, it turns out. Your father hasn't used the name Merriwell in five years. He goes by Smith now — or occasionally Jones. There was a woman. In fact, there have been several, but none have lasted longer than a few months and he changes them as regularly as he changes jobs."

"He's working? Good heavens. There's a turnup for the books."

"I suppose that depends on your definition of working, for it seems your father has been putting his talent for woodcutting to good use. . . . He's been counterfeiting money, Minerva. . . . And in case you didn't know, that's a capital offense."

"Oh dear . . ." She blew out a strangled breath. The weird thing was, she wasn't the least bit surprised. "He cannot be very good at it, else he wouldn't be resorting to blackmail."

"The people he works for aren't particularly discerning or diligent about the quality of their counterfeits. The Runner said they have proof your father has been involved in the practice for over eight years off and on — which meant he was doing it when he still lived with you in Clerkenwell."

Certain things now made sense. The irregular hours, the unsavory characters knocking at the door, his keenness she develop her talent for the trade when he had never taken any interest in her little drawings before. "I suppose I should be thankful he left when he did. I am sure it was only a matter of time before he tried to rope me into it. He never did have a particularly keen eye for detail or half my talent for drawing."

"Yesterday, I threatened him with the authorities myself unless he stuck to the terms of our bargain."

"That was undoubtedly very wise. He daren't expose you now."

"I didn't do it for me. I don't blame you if you don't believe me, but I did it for you. I couldn't bear the thought of him barging in on you in the future and ruining the new life you will make for yourself. Because he was right about one thing — you are better off without him."

Minerva said nothing. The weak part of her wanted to believe him. Common sense told her he was spinning her a yarn. "My own knight in shining armor . . . Of course, your selfless bravery on my behalf would also make me feel naturally beholden to you."

"I knew you wouldn't believe me."

"What do you want? Thanks? For getting rid of a man who likely wouldn't be back in my life if I had never met you?"

"I didn't come here for your gratitude. I

came here because I wanted to ask you what you wanted me to do about him."

"Do?"

"Your father is a wastrel and a crook, Minerva. And you're right, he is also back because of me and to a much greater extent because of my money. I am also under no illusions he won't turn up again like an ironic bad penny — either here or later when you are gone, wanting more money. I have the power to stop that if you want me to. All I have to do is pass over my information to the authorities and he'll never bother you or your sisters again."

"They'll hang him."

"If they catch him. But if I tip him off, then the snake will run in another direction, head to a new town, give himself another alias, and we can leave his future to fate. I wasn't foolish enough to allow him to leave a second time without putting him under watch. A man who would gladly make his daughters destitute for a measly forty pounds, blackmail one of them and suggest she uses her wiles to make it seventy-five, is not a man who can be trusted."

"You overheard our conversation?"

"By accident. I wanted to talk to you. . . . I never meant to make you cry. I feel wretched . . ."

"Please go."

"I care for you, Minerva . . ."

"Get out!" She had thought there were no tears left. "Just leave me alone, Hugh."

"Can't we talk about it? About us?"

"Us? What 'us' would that be, Hugh? The 'us' where I get to be used while you retain your precious freedom?"

"I don't follow . . ."

"I am grateful for your help concerning my father but I still won't be your mistress!"

"Mistress?"

Emotion choked her. "I might not be a genuine gentleman's daughter, but I was brought up to believe I was. I have the same values as any gentleman's daughter, the same morals and I will not debase myself by . . ."

"Mistress!" He grabbed her upper arms, his knees now touching hers as he knelt on the mattress. "What the blazes are you on about? I don't want a mistress! I've never had a blasted mistress! Where in God's name have you got that mad idea from?"

"You asked me outright . . . last week . . . on the beach!"

She could see his mouth was slack as he stared at her in total silence. When he finally spoke, it was tentative, as if he was choosing his words carefully.

"I might not have said it articulately last week, because I was still in a state of shock about the strength of my feelings, but I know I never asked you to debase yourself. I certainly never said the word 'mistress'!"

"It was implied."

"It most certainly wasn't. I bared my soul to you. I offered myself to you. Warts and all!"

"Offered yourself? You said you were not in a position to offer marriage — just yourself!"

"For enough time as it took for me to be certain I could make a decent go of it! I can't ask you to shackle yourself to me until I can be sure I won't behave like my father and his father before him. I said *that*. I know I did."

"You most certainly did not say that!"

He was silent again, apparently bemused.

"Then blasted Payne was right and I really did make a mess of it." He sat back on his heels, and she felt his warm breath on her face as he huffed out a sigh. "Untangling myself from another unsavory entanglement . . . I never picked up on it. You said it twice and I never picked up on it. What a fool I am. . . . You think *you* are the unsavory entanglement."

Minerva was beginning to think she might

have got the wrong end of the stick. "You are an earl . . ."

"I am an idiot." His palm came to rest on her cheek. "A blithering idiot! For a man who supposedly has a way with words, I've certainly made a complicated situation nonsensical if you think I only want you as my mistress."

"You don't?"

"I just want *you,* Minerva." His thumb found one of her tears in the darkness and brushed it away. "All of you and everything that entails. Forever . . . I love you."

"You . . . love me?"

"Don't sound so surprised. . . . You are inordinately nice." He let out an odd sound. Part laughter, part relief. "And when I offered myself to you . . . very badly as it turned out . . . it was only in so much as I needed time to adjust to things, to make a concerted effort to be the man I want to be for you, the faithful and trustworthy man you deserve. Before I saddled *you* with *me* and *our children* to my Standish blood for life."

Inside her chest, her heart melted. "That's actually rather sweet . . . and noble . . . and nice."

"That's what I thought at the time, but . . . No wonder you've been so angry with me. I would never, ever suggest taking you to my bed without proper commitment. I thought I was proposing an extended courtship. So that when I did propose . . . if I *could* propose . . . I would do so in the knowledge I would keep my vows. Once I'm sure, completely sure, I'll ask for your hand but not before, because I believe vows should be forever. I don't want to be my father. I couldn't bear to hurt you that way."

"I'm afraid I didn't hear any of that."

"And that's why you said that curt no. Will you take a chance on me now?"

She nodded. There was no indecision. No need to weigh it all up in her mind. The tormented man in front of her wasn't cut from the same cloth as either her father or the sweetheart who had abandoned her. He was her knight in shining armor. A true gentleman in every sense. He might not see it himself, but he was honorable, decent, and noble to his core. A man with tainted blood wouldn't care so much about others that he would sacrifice his own feelings to avoid hurting the feelings of others. Yes — he went about it in completely the wrong way, but his heart was so big it made hers want to burst and weep for him at the same time. If ever a man needed a sensible woman to guide him through life, it was

Hugh. And if ever a man needed loving and saving from himself, it was Hugh, too.

"I am going to need the words, Minerva. The actual words . . ."

"Yes."

"And you won't leave me when Giles comes back? Because I'm going slowly mad with the stress of it all. I've never been in love before. It's all new and it's petrifying. I never imagined I was capable of it, so to find it had happened without me knowing completely threw me. I tried to fight it and I can't. Tried to call it lust and affection and make excuses for it, when the truth is, I've not been myself since that day I met you in London. It's like something missing fell into place and I've been dreading the day you leave me. I thought I'd told you all that and you just didn't want me. I've been trying to accept it, but it's felt like a death." He rubbed his chest. "I have this constant pain here. I can't eat. I can't sleep. I have been entirely miserable and . . ." She kissed him. She couldn't help it. Poor Hugh, and how sublimely wonderful that he was in utter turmoil!

"I love you, too."

He replied with a kiss so perfect, so honest, and so heartfelt she never wanted it to end. But it did end. Not by either of them pulling away, but because the timbre of the kiss changed as they both poured their entire souls into it.

His arms wrapped around her, dragging her against him, and she discovered that after a miserable week apart, that was exactly where she wanted to be. Passion ignited instantly, as it had with their previous kisses, but the intimacy of the darkened room, the bed, and their newfound understanding of one another brought another dimension to it.

When he gently lowered them both down to the mattress, she went willingly, reveling in the feel of his big body over hers, feeling safe and adored and oddly powerful at the same time.

He loved her.

Wanted to commit to her. Take vows. Have children. And he was petrified. Of spoiling it. When she knew in her heart he could never spoil it. Whatever he misguidedly thought, he just did not have that in him.

His honesty, trepidation, and the darkness made her bolder, and she allowed her hands to explore his body, over the thin covering of his shirt, marveling at the muscles under his skin, the way they bunched beneath her touch. As his tongue and lips danced with hers, she slid her hands beneath the soft linen to explore him, the warm feel of his body beneath her palms, the bristle of the scattering of hair across his chest, the taut, flat planes of his stomach, and his overburdened broad shoulders before her arms wrapped around his neck.

He sighed into her mouth as she arched against him in invitation, smoothing one hand down her hip and thigh with aching slowness until he found the hem of her nightdress, and retraced his path back up on her bare skin, lingering momentarily to rest on her hip before it snaked up to cup her needy breast.

She felt him smile against her lips as her nipple pebbled beneath his palm and a guttural moan escaped her lips, and despite her pushing the sensitive flesh shamelessly into his hand, he made her wait before his index finger traced the shape of it. The strange new sensation was so intense, Minerva shuddered, then moaned as he replaced his finger with his mouth above the filmy fabric. Sucking the sensitive tip into his mouth and laving it with his tongue.

That proved her undoing, as suddenly her nightgown became an unwanted barrier while her other breast demanded attention.

She grabbed the fabric and began to pull it up before he stopped her and took over, patiently unwrapping her like a delicate gift until she was completely bared, her modesty veiled by nothing but the night.

She could see his eyes in the blackness, intense and focused as he gazed upon her with a reverence that fired her passions further.

"You are beautiful . . . so beautiful . . ."

Simple words, honest words. Flippant and mischievous Hugh had been replaced by a man who seemed to exist only for her. Only in this moment.

"I've dreamed of this . . . wanted this for so long." He traced his hands over her body, his breathing shallower and more erratic than she had ever heard it. "If I survive these next few months without dying of the wanting it will be a miracle."

The next time he kissed her, she felt his need and his restraint, realized he was holding back for her, and loved him all the more for it.

He *did* intend to wait. Never intended to ruin her — although now it did not feel like ruination, more an affirmation of the love they shared.

"Do you want me?"

"Always. Since the very first moment I saw you."

"Then have me, Hugh."

He pulled back, stared down at her face. She watched his features change as he went to war with himself. "I can still love you thoroughly without that."

"But I want *that.* I want it all. All of you."

"Even though I still cannot make any firm promises? Not until I'm sure I won't hurt you."

He wasn't capable of hurting her. He felt things too keenly. Cared too much. Why couldn't he see that? "Because you are too noble to make empty promises. And because you love me and I love you and sometimes things just are."

"And that is enough?"

"It is enough for now." She knew in her heart his reluctance was born out of nobility, but with her by his side it wouldn't take him long to realize he wasn't his father. "Make love to me, Hugh."

He seemed oddly clumsy as he dispensed with his shirt, yanking it over his head and swearing impatiently as he fumbled with the buttons on his falls.

"I can do that." Minerva took over, and he lay back and let her.

"I'm nervous."

"Whatever for? I'm the novice. You have done this before."

"Not like this. That was purely physical

457

and never involved my heart. I've never *made love* before, Minerva. I've certainly never deflowered a virgin. It is a big responsibility." He lifted his hips as she dragged the fabric down, then watched her face when she saw what lay beneath it silhouetted by the shadows. It was big and hard and totally male. He tipped her chin up to look deep into her eyes. "Don't be scared, my love, I won't hurt you . . . at least not intentionally."

"I am not scared. I am familiar with the mechanics." "Scared" was the wrong word. Apprehensive. Curious. A little overwhelmed. But desperate for him.

"The mechanics?" His eyes were dancing again. "Mechanics do not begin to explain what is about to happen. But if I do it right, then you will soon be a boneless puddle on these sheets and I will be the happiest and smuggest man in the world."

"A bold claim, sir . . ." He grabbed her, and she giggled as he rolled her beneath him.

"Not a claim. A fact." He kissed her again, his big hands easily spanning her waist before he filled them with her bottom. "But it could take hours." She could feel his hardness against her abdomen, insistent and hot.

Minerva lost herself in his kiss, wanting

more, but happy to continue just as they were until Hugh nuzzled her neck, trailing shot, fevered kisses over her shoulders then downward to worship both breasts again. He taught her how to touch him, encouraging her to learn his shape and size while sighing his appreciation of her unschooled hands. She was writhing on the sheets like a wanton just before his lips nuzzled the top of her thighs and she stilled as he paused and smiled up at her, questioning.

"What are you doing?"

"I thought I'd kiss all of you . . . out of principle . . . if that is all right with you."

"Yes . . ." Because that sounded sinfully delicious and suddenly felt unbelievably necessary. "It is important to be principled."

"Indeed it is . . ." His warm breath whispered over the sensitive skin a second before his tongue did, and the pleasure was so exquisite, it robbed her of air. Then the entire universe shrank, and nothing else existed except him, her, and his clever mouth.

Hugh had promised her she would be a boneless puddle by the time he was finished with her, and he absolutely intended to make good on that promise. Not out of arrogance or to fuel his ego but because she deserved it. Although she had the love of her sisters, she was the one who looked out for everyone. She was selfless and trusting and never asked for anything for herself. He was determined to fill that void and be the person who she could lean on and rely upon to always put her first. And that would start right now. Tonight, his needs were inconsequential because she was the one taking all the risk, and her trust in him was humbling.

He could feel her climax building as he lapped at her core — nobody else would ever see her thus, or kiss her or make love to her. Minerva was his.

He would be her first and her last. Just as she was his first and his last. Because he would make sure of it. Some things just were.

He could feel the tension in her long limbs and her own frustrations. Knew she was close. Wanted so much to be buried deep inside her body, but not yet. Not yet.

"Relax, my darling . . ." Her hands were twisted in the sheets, her head thrashing from side to side. The carnal moan she made when he dipped his fingers inside to stroke the inner walls of her body was the singularly most erotic thing he had ever heard. Then he felt her body clench as the glorious pleasure took her over the edge, her hips bucking, every muscle in her body taut before she exhaled on a guttural sigh and every single one of those muscles relaxed.

"What was that?"

"The first of many, I hope." Her eyelids had fluttered closed, her hair was a wild tangle, her limbs thrown across the rumpled sheets with abandon. "But perhaps we should leave it at that for tonight." He kissed her mouth tenderly.

"But we haven't . . ."

"I can wait." He would wait for her forever if he had to.

"I don't want to wait." Her fingers plunged into his hair and tugged him down to her mouth again. "I want it all."

She kissed him with unbridled passion, something that surprised him when he had assumed her passion spent. She hooked one of her long legs around his, twisting until his erection rested against her womanhood, pushing her body against his in invitation. Her greedy hands smoothing down his back to his buttocks. "I want you . . . inside me."

Fresh nerves plagued him, and he marveled at what it was about this woman that made him feel like an anxious virgin. "If you're sure . . ."

Her teeth had found his ear. "I'm sure." She adjusted her legs in invitation and his own body betrayed his attempt at resistance by hardening further and finding its way to her entrance. "I've never been more sure of anything in my life."

As slowly and gently as he could, Hugh edged inside, intending to give her time to get used to his size and shape, but Minerva would have none of it.

Just the touch of her against his skin, her soft, warm, wet heat, sent him mad, and he gritted his teeth, holding back, continuing in the aching slow vein he had started until he came against the barrier of her virginity. She seemed to understand his hesitation and smiled, kissing him deeply as he pushed past it. She tensed briefly and then sighed as he filled her, and he knew the worst was over.

When he began to move, again, his pace was gentle, but Minerva deemed it too gentle, and as he plunged into her, any chance of further restraint died as his own body craved release. She matched him thrust for thrust, calling his name and announcing her pleasure until he felt her tight body contract and pulse around his and he could hold back no more and she took him to a place he had never been. A place of stars and rightness and ecstasy he knew he never wanted to leave. A place that just was and was always meant to be, where there

were no what-ifs.
  Only love.

# CHAPTER TWENTY-NINE

"I've made sure the servants are scarce, Miss Minerva." Payne deposited the tea tray on the table in the morning room. "Will there be anything else?"

"It might be prudent to remove the breakables." She smiled without humor, dreading two conversations that were destined to be difficult, though for decidedly different reasons. She had decided to talk to Diana first, knowing she would take the news of their father much better than Vee, but also knowing she would take the news about Hugh worse. Usually they were so close, the bond between them unbreakable as they battled the world together, but things had been strained between them since the day she had escaped to the beach. Now Minerva would have to admit she had lied about her relationship with Hugh while simultaneously trying to convince Diana to find the grace to accept it. "And if you hear screaming, try to ignore it — unless it's me, in which case, send in the cavalry."

"I already have the militia standing by. Men with muskets are just one bloodcurdling scream away." He patted her on the shoulder as her sister arrived. "I'll be down the hall if you need me."

"What is going on?" Diana was never one for unnecessary preamble. "Because something clearly is if we need to have an emergency meeting in secret."

"Our father is back."

"For money, I suppose?"

Minerva nodded. There had never been any flies on Diana. "He has separately tried to blackmail both me and Hugh."

"Separately?"

She winced, knowing this next bit would not be easy. "He approached me at the assembly, demanding seventy-five pounds for his silence."

"And it didn't occur to you to tell me this Saturday night?" Diana shot out of the chair to pace. "I wish you had! What a nerve that wastrel has! I'd have sent him off with a flea in his ear and a couple of black eyes for his trouble!" Then anger turned swiftly to suspicion. "Why have you kept it from me for so long?"

"Because things have been" — Minerva

huffed out breath — "complicated."

Her sister paused, her eyes narrowing in suspicion. "Because of Hugh?"

"Yes . . . no — not just because of Hugh. There's Olivia and Jeremiah, too, and a whole host of other things to consider, but . . . you see the thing is, Hugh and I . . ." She watched Diana's fists clench and realized it was all about to explode in her face unless she handled things properly. "Could you sit down? Please? I have so many serious things I need to talk to you about, I'd rather tackle it in order because I have some important and pressing decisions to make, then I promise you can shout at me once it's all done."

Because it was easier, she told Diana all about her father first, from the day Payne had hidden him to the Runner's discovery of the counterfeiting, to Hugh's timely interference two nights ago alongside the discovery it had all been kept from her, too. Being more cynical about their father than even Minerva, Diana took it all in stride — it was Hugh she had the most issue with.

"Why didn't he tell you our hideous father was back a week ago?"

"Hugh thought he was protecting us by keeping it quiet."

"Hogwash! He was protecting himself!"

"That's what I thought when I found out at the assembly. . . . But we had a dreadful argument that day at the beach and I refused to speak to him and . . ." Her face must have given her away, because Diana's mouth gaped.

"Oh God . . . I was right, wasn't I? You did have your head turned. . . . There was something going on between you."

"Not then . . . or, not exactly. We had only kissed twice at that point . . ." At Diana's horrified expression the words tumbled out because she had to defend Hugh, and if she didn't take her portion of the blame from the outset, her protective sister would assume the worst of him. "There's always been an attraction between us and we both have tried to deny it, but these past weeks have . . . well, they have mostly been rather wonderful, if you must know." Minerva clasped her hand across the table. "I love him, Diana, and he loves me."

"He's a scoundrel, Minerva. A charming one, I will grant you — but still a scoundrel who will only break your heart again." Her sister had been her rock and only confidante in the dark days after both their father and then Minerva's sweetheart abandoned her in quick succession. "Can't you see that?"

"He isn't. He only thinks he is. If you only

knew him the way I do . . ."

"What, clandestinely? Behind everybody's backs — including your family's?" Diana tugged her hand away. "Stop being so naive, Minerva. If his affections are genuine, he would have no cause to keep them secret. Yet instead he's had you sneaking around, running away on day trips so he can have his wicked way with you, convinced you to keep secrets."

"It's not like that."

"Isn't it?" Diana folded her arms. "Has he proposed?"

Explaining Hugh's darkest fears felt too disloyal now that she understood them. "Not yet. But he will." Minerva had seen the love in his eyes. Seen it and felt it everywhere. "Once he sees what I see . . ."

"You won't change him! Leopards don't change their spots."

"I know." Hugh's spots were perfect. She knew that now. "Just as I also know he is loyal and kind, generous, good-hearted." All obvious traits that even the cynical Diana couldn't deny. He had never let her down, and she knew in her heart he never would. "He loves me, Diana."

"And that's enough?"

Minerva smiled and nodded. "It is enough for now."

"But . . ."

"I love him, too, Diana. So very much. And I trust him to do right by me, which is staggering all things considered, but the truth. Hugh makes me happy."

Her sister took her hand and sighed. "Then I shall be happy for you, too, because you deserve all the happiness in the world, Minerva, and I will give Hugh the benefit of the doubt for now because I trust you." She smiled, then narrowed her worried, wary, still-so-cynical eyes in mock affront. "But be warned, if he doesn't propose to you soon, he'll have me to answer to."

"Hugh is lying! Papa is not a blackmailer!" Angry tears coursed down Vee's face. Unlike Diana, she took the news of Minerva's relationship with Hugh in stride but was devastated about their father.

Minerva would be as tactful as she could, but no amount of tact in the world could lessen this awful truth. "There is a warrant out for his arrest, dearest. He is officially a wanted man."

" 'Wanted' isn't the *same* as 'guilty,' though, is it? There would have to be a proper trial. The Runner could have lied. Hugh could have paid him to lie . . ." Vee's face was ashen as she racked her brain for excuses for the inexcusable. "How do you know your precious Hugh is telling the truth? Who appointed him both judge and jury?"

Minerva stayed Vee's outburst with her hand.

"Hugh wants to do whatever we decide. As far as I see it, we have two choices. If he comes back, we alert the authorities . . ." She tried to ignore her little sister's sharp gasp at that implication. "Or we threaten him with the authorities and send him running, making it clear he can never return to London to bother us again."

"As much as I know he deserves the former, I cannot willingly send him to the gallows. But I *do* want him out of our lives, so I shall vote for the second option." Diana's pragmatic answer was assertive, echoing her own thoughts.

"I agree." Minerva had had much longer to think about it and didn't have a cold enough heart to hand him over to the authorities either. "In a strange sort of way, I'm glad I finally know where he has been and what he has been up to, as it removes all residual doubt."

Diana gave a half-hearted shrug. "By that you mean it justifies hating him, when I confess I had reached that point long before he left. I was quite happy to never see or hear from him again."

"I do not believe what I am hearing. . . . He's our father! Does he deserve no sympathy?" Frustrated tears coursed down Vee's face as she clutched at Minerva's arm. "No understanding?"

"What is there to understand? He's a crook . . . a forger. A man who would sell his daughter for his own selfish gain. He left us because he had no morals and never looked back." Diana said exactly what Minerva was thinking as she tried to comfort Vee. "You were a child. We protected you from the worst of it, but he was *not* a good man. He was a drunkard and a wastrel and . . ." There was an odd look on her face, one that suggested she could say more, but was holding back. "And I, for one, rejoiced when he went."

"If you send Papa away, then I shall go with him!"

"He won't take you."

"He will! And you cannot stop me!"

There was no point in arguing with her baby sister's misconceptions. Vee would have to learn for herself exactly how cold and calculating their father was, and doubtless she'd be the one to pick up the pieces. But Minerva would cross that bridge when she came to it. Because it would come to it. "So we are agreed?" Minerva took both of her sisters' hands, keen to stop them going round and around in ever decreasing circles. "I shall tell Hugh we will not report our father to the authorities but let him know in no uncertain terms his presence here is unwelcome." Diana instantly nodded. Vee's agreement took longer and was begrudging, but at least they had her confirmation. That was one thing off Minerva's mind. "In the meantime, keep your wits about you in case he approaches you. If he does, speak to me or Hugh immediately."

Now all she and Hugh had to do was work out a way to tell his mother the truth. They had agreed to do that together this afternoon but still hadn't worked out exactly how to do it. They would discuss all that as soon as Hugh came back from his ride — if Vee ever stopped crying.

As she wrapped an arm around her sobbing sister's quaking shoulders, the butler poked his head around the door, looking worried.

"I am really sorry to interrupt at such a difficult time." He looked at Minerva with a pained and entirely put-upon expression. "But I am going to need some help with the actress . . ."

# CHAPTER THIRTY

As soon as they turned the corner, blasted Sarah, her husband, and her mother had all turned to wave a cheery hello as they also made their way down the drive. *His* drive. Which only led to *his* house.

"What are they doing here?" Because frankly, the Peterses were the last thing he needed today. He dragged everyone out for a long ride to give Minerva the privacy and space to talk to her sisters, but had been on tenterhooks the whole time wondering how Diana and Vee had taken the news of their father and, more importantly, how they felt about him courting their eldest sister.

"I invited them for tea, dear." His mother waved back, and Hugh realized why she had been so determined to be back home before two. "I thought it was high time they met Minerva and her family properly. Sarah says she's hardly seen you these past few years. I take it Minerva knows you have a sister?"

"Of course she does! Minerva and I have no secrets." Or at least they didn't anymore . . . apart from the big one they were keeping from his mother. "But I haven't apprised her family of the connection, so your little impromptu tea party is insensitive. It's really not the sort of conversation one should have over tea."

"Nonsense . . . The Landridges are not the least bit judgmental. Why would they be when they've had their own fair share of scandals? It's not as if Sarah is a deep, dark secret." More was the pity. "The whole county knows she is Hugh's daughter. The pair of you are two peas in a pod." Oh, how he hated *that* term. "And besides — it is much too late to change plans now. We can hardly turn them away from the front door. Not when they were so thrilled to receive the invitation."

She kicked her horse into a trot and went off to greet them.

"Did you know about this?"

"Do I look as if I knew about this?" Jeremiah did seem a little confused. "Your mother is a law unto herself. Heaven forbid she tell me what's afoot. I know they chatted at the assembly the other night and your mother has always gotten along well with Charlotte and Sarah . . . but did I know she had orchestrated a quaint English tea to enlighten the Landridges with the unorthodox peculiarities of the Standish family? No." He shrugged in a what-will-be-will-be sort of way. "It will be all right. Minerva's family are good people . . . or, at least her sisters are. The jury is still out on the mother — although between you and me, I much prefer her drunk than sober. . . . Come on. Let's make the best of it."

Hugh had no choice but to grin and bear it. As the groom relieved him of his horse, he offered pleasantries to his father's favorite mistress, marveling at how his mother could natter away with her like they were old friends rather than bitter rivals. He stiffly greeted Sarah and Captain Peters, then trailed after them all as they wandered back toward the house.

It was surprisingly quiet inside, thank goodness, which made him hope the revelations hadn't been too traumatic. A maid, rather than Payne, hurried forward to take their coats, and was swiftly dispatched by his mother to fetch tea. "Shall I bring it to the *morning room,* my lady?" There was something about the maid's fraught expression as her eyes flicked nervously between his mother and him that made Hugh a little anxious. They rarely sat in that room in winter.

"Oh no . . . It's always much too chilly in there even with the fire. We shall have it in the drawing room. Can you also send word to the ladies we have company?"

The maid bobbed a curtsey and dashed off, and always the perfect hostess, his mother led the way to the drawing room and ushered them all in.

Too late, Hugh saw the unmistakable shape of Lucretia DeVere fast asleep in the chair by the roaring fireplace, her mouth wide open and her silly riding hat at an odd angle. As if she sensed she had an audience, her eyes blinked open and slowly focused, then she shuffled to sit straighter and failed miserably.

"We are so sorry to disturb you, Mrs. Landridge." Like him, his mother was looking for any damning evidence that might suggest their rotund and theatrical houseguest had partaken of a little nip of spirits unsupervised.

"I apologize profusely. I must have fallen asleep. . . ." She certainly sounded lucid enough. "This chair and fire are much too cozy."

"I am just glad you feel at home." Nothing fazed his mother, who beamed. "Mrs.

Landridge, might I introduce you to Mrs. Edgerton, her daughter, Mrs. Peters, and Captain Peters, her charming husband. They are *particular* friends of our family." She glanced at Hugh, her expression letting him know she was being subtle so he could break the truth his way.

"Mrs. Edgerton . . . Mrs. Peters . . . Captain . . . What a pleasure to make your acquaintance." As regally as any duchess, the actress greeted the new guests from the comfort of her wingback. "Has somebody summoned my daughters? Only I have three girls, Mrs. Edgerton. The eldest, Minerva, is betrothed to darling Hugh here."

Beside him, he felt his mother relax, too, just in time for a flustered Minerva to skid into the room with Diana.

"You are back . . . and with guests." Both ladies had overbright smiles pasted on their faces. "How lovely . . . *my love.*" She squeezed out the endearment through impressively gritted teeth, her expressive emerald eyes boring into his. He instantly picked up her cue but was powerless to act upon it while the introductions were about to be made.

He smiled weakly.

"Minerva . . . Diana . . . meet Mrs. Edgerton." They bobbed a polite curtsey. "And as Minerva has already had the pleasure of meeting Sarah and her husband, Captain Peters, it is only you who needs to be introduced, Diana. And Vee, of course." He looked to his intended. "Is Miss Vee on her way?"

"She was finishing the chapter in her book but will doubtless join us shortly. In fact, I shall check on her now."

She spun on her heel and disappeared back through the door. Hugh left it all of twenty seconds before he could think of a lackluster excuse to follow while the others took their seats.

"I think I will just chase the tea tray. Riding is such thirsty work . . ."

Thankfully, Minerva was waiting for him, appearing from behind a suit of armor as he was about to dash up the stairs. She grabbed his hand and dragged him into the closest room. "Lucretia is intoxicated! What possessed you to allow her to ride home alone?"

"She said she felt ill and needed to go back to bed."

Although, she hadn't looked particularly ill. Hugh had let her go because it seemed like the ideal opportunity to speak to his mother and inform her of the truth. Get it over with and return home unburdened of all the lies and ready to start a new chapter with the angel who had stolen his heart and didn't deserve to share the blame for all his stupidity.

Except he hadn't. He'd procrastinated like a coward, couldn't find the right words, and felt thoroughly wretched as a result, convinced he was doomed to be a disappointment forevermore if he had fallen at the first furlong. Then the appearance of Sarah and her mother had plunged him into a considerably worse mood.

"Well, she managed to avoid her bedchamber and wandered to yours, where she found brandy and drank the lot. We couldn't budge her from the drawing room and left her to sleep it off."

"How long ago?"

"Two hours — or thereabouts. Not long enough for her to be entirely sober! That's for sure. She demolished an entire decanter of brandy in a very short space of time."

"Oh dear."

"And Vee has locked herself in her room and refuses to come out."

"She didn't take the news well, then?"

"Neither of them did. Vee is in a state because she's convinced we're all out to unjustly sully our father's name and has declared her intention to leave with him as soon as he comes to fetch her. She hates me for betraying him and Diana for backing me. But while my dear sister has never had any illusions concerning our father, I've had the devil of a job convincing Diana that you are not the vile seducer she has always suspected you of being. It has been a *very* trying morning and clearly, the ordeal isn't over."

He took in the taut, pinched expression and pulled her into his arms, unable to resist kissing the top of the dark head he adored so much. "Alas, it isn't. My mother apparently invited them over for tea without telling anyone after she discovered I haven't kept in touch with Sarah — and decided to remedy that. I am livid at her and I tried to get us out of it — but you know my mother."

"I suppose it's nice she wants to encourage your relationship with your sister. It cannot be easy on her knowing her husband had a family with another."

"It seems easier on her than on me. I'll never understand why she tolerates them."

"Have you ever asked her?"

"Not exactly . . ."

He hadn't.

In the past she had tried repeatedly to talk about the betrayal, and he had refused to hear it, let alone condone it. But Minerva raised a good point. Why did his mother tolerate his father's mistress? Why didn't the existence of Sarah — a woman the exact same age as Hugh — hurt her like it hurt him?

"Then perhaps you should?" Her head burrowed against his chest, and he liked the feel of it there. "Ask her when we tell her the truth. It strikes me as the most fitting time. We might as well get it over with in one totally hideous, unswallowable lump."

"I tried to tell her this morning . . ." He sighed and held her tighter. "But not very hard. I was in too fine a mood and I selfishly didn't want to spoil it."

"I wonder why?" Just from the tone of her voice, he could tell she was smiling. He tipped up her chin so his eyes could confirm it. He loved her smile. It had the power to turn every dire situation, like the one currently awaiting them in the drawing room, into something not quite so dire.

"I wonder?" Because he no longer had to restrain the urge to kiss her, he did, and just like her smile, it miraculously made the drawing room and the buzzing hornet's nest within it disappear from the face of the earth.

"Hugh, what are you . . . Oh! . . . *Oh . . .*" They guiltily broke apart only to see his mother grin from ear to ear. "Never mind. I thought you two were merely avoiding the Peterses. Silly me! I should have known you two lovebirds would need to say a *proper* good afternoon after I deprived you of each other all morning." She pulled the door back. "Don't be long."

Minerva's vibrant blush was charming, so he kissed her quickly again. "Look on the bright side, at least she now knows our affection is genuine, if nothing else." He took her hand and laced her fingers in his. It felt utterly perfect. "Once more into the breach?"

"I'm not sure my nerves can take much more. I wish it was over."

"It will be very soon — but now is not the right time."

They returned to the drawing room hand in hand, where Hugh was greeted by the full force of Diana's scowl. He supposed he couldn't blame her, it came out of deep love and loyalty for her sister. Anyone who loved Minerva was all right by him, and he resolved in that moment to make a concerted effort to win the crotchetiest Merriwell over.

"Where do you all hail from?" The dreaded Mrs. Edgerton, who almost everyone in the room knew had never been a "Mrs." at all, smiled at Lucretia, who still seemed coherent despite listing slightly on the wingback.

"Oxfordshire. It's such a beautiful county. I'd argue its beauty rivals Hampshire."

"It does indeed." Captain Peters smiled as he sipped his tea. "Rivals it *and* exceeds it."

"But he is horribly biased," added his wife, looking exactly like their father used to when he was amused by something. "Teddy hails from Oxfordshire, too. His family still resides there."

"Really?" His mother helped herself to the plate of biscuits Payne was holding out. "Isn't the world a small place? I wonder if you ever collided before today?"

Despite Minerva's hand in his, Hugh began to feel uneasy at the turn the conversation was taking. "How are you finding life at Aldershot?" Sarah turned to him amazed, as if such a chatty question had never come from his lips before. Which he conceded it probably hadn't.

"It's a lovely town. One well used to and tolerant of the militia."

"I suppose it is highly likely we have collided." Clearly Captain Peters was still eager to reminisce. "Which part of Oxfordshire do you hail from?"

"Chipping Norton." Lucretia's tea sloshed over the rim of her cup as she spoke.

Captain Peters beamed from ear to ear. "By Jove, it really *is* a small world! Whereabouts in Chipping Norton? My father has his practice in Goddards Lane just off the market square. He's the local physician."

A huge gust of wind suddenly wafted much too close to Hugh's suddenly flimsy house of cards. "And how are you liking having your grandchildren so close, Mrs. Edgerton?" In his experience, older ladies were obsessed with their grandchild — or their need for grandchildren, so perhaps she wouldn't notice his voice was suddenly wobbly.

"Oh, I love it, Hugh! Priscilla is an absolute joy and now that little Hugh is walking, he is a handful. The scrapes that child gets himself —"

"Little Hugh?" Diana stopped glaring at him long enough to look perplexed, making Mrs. Edgerton's mouth close like a frightened clamshell as she blinked at her, embarrassed.

"After his grandfather," offered his mother helpfully. "He was a Hugh, too."

"There are suddenly so many Hughs, it's hard to keep up." She resumed glaring at him again. "Is 'Hugh' a Hampshire name?"

He felt Minerva's fingers tighten in his, but before either of them could say anything, his mother did.

"It is a Standish name, Diana dear. Little Hugh is Hugh's grandson."

"Hugh has grandchildren!"

"Not *my* Hugh, dear. *He* is named after his father. Little Hugh is *his* half nephew." Brazen, blatant, as if such a bombshell was of absolutely no consequence at all. Diana's cup paused midway to her mouth as she looked from him to Sarah and back again. "And that is absolutely right, dear. . . . Sarah is indeed Hugh's half sister."

"I see."

"So you see, Diana, your father marrying an actress is nowhere near as scandalous as *this* family." Then, as if she hadn't done enough damage, his mother turned to Captain Peters. "I suppose you know all about the scandalous Landridges, don't you, Captain Peters? I suppose juicy titbits of gossip fly around Chipping Norton as quickly as they do here in Hampshire. I should imagine the tale of a country squire marrying an actress fresh from the stage of Drury Lane made quite a stir in sleepy Chipping Norton?"

"I confess, up until today, I've never heard of the Chipping Norton Landridges."

"We live in one of the outlying villages." Minerva spoke for the first time, and Hugh loved her all the more for loyally trying, but the putrid stink of the end was in sight, and he knew it would take a miracle at this stage to stop it. "It's . . . um . . . quite remote."

"Which one? Being one of the only physicians for miles, my father knows them all well. I used to accompany him on his rounds as a boy. Heythrop? Swerford? No . . . don't tell me . . ." Suddenly, "Guess the Remote Village" was a diverting game. "Adlestrop? Churchill? Enstone? One of the Tews?"

"Oh!" Diana slipped off the sofa into a heap on the floor, wafting her hand around like Lucretia. "I feel faint . . . so dizzy . . ."

"Fetch the smelling salts, Payne!" Jeremiah jumped to attention and immediately went to her aid.

The reprieve galvanized Hugh. "Open the windows! Let in some air!" He was sorely tempted to throw himself out of them. But alas, the fickle finger of fate was not done with the surprises, because Giles chose that exact moment to appear in the doorway.

# CHAPTER THIRTY-ONE

"What the blazes is going on?" Lord Bellingham blinked as he took in the scene.

"Diana fainted." Although, it had been a shockingly poor performance as far as Minerva was concerned. It was patently obvious Jeremiah knew something was afoot, because each time he glanced at Hugh kneeling next to Diana, his eyes narrowed.

"Does she need me to loosen her stays? I'm an expert on loosening stays."

"Giles! How lovely to see you!" Hugh's mother enveloped him in an enormous hug, her smile overbright and her welcome too effusive. "But if any stays need loosening, it most definitely won't be by you. Allow me to introduce you to everyone."

In a surreal spectacle she couldn't quite believe, Minerva watched Hugh and Jeremiah lift her sister back onto the sofa while Lucretia began to snore again and Olivia paraded Lord Bellingham around the room, blithely introducing him to everyone. "Mrs. Edgerton . . . Captain Peters . . . Mrs. Sarah Peters" — she briefly glared at her son — "Hugh's half sister . . ."

"What? I go away for a few weeks and he suddenly gains a sister?"

"He's had one for thirty-two years, dear." She patted Lord Bellingham's hand and scowled at her son again. "I thought he might have told you. But alas, he is one for secrets — and the occasional *lie.*" Blue eyes so like Hugh's swiveled to Minerva's, and in that moment she realized Olivia was beginning to smell the rot.

"He is indeed. . . . Is that biscuits I see? I'm famished . . ."

To keep the woefully leaky boat afloat, Olivia and Jeremiah commanded the conversation, keeping it off the rutted road to Chipping Norton and on to safer topics, leaving Hugh to ferociously waft a lace fan at Diana's face for much longer than was necessary. At a loss as to what else to do, Minerva poured everyone more tea while her heart threatened to beat out of her chest, then she sat and tried to fade into the upholstery.

A few seconds later, Hugh's best friend decided to sit next to her, clearly still laboring under the misapprehension they were about to elope.

"You look ravishing, Miss Minerva." He kissed her hand and lingered over it, winking. "I missed you."

"That's nice." She tried to tug her hand away.

"How have you been?"

"Good . . . *busy* . . ." She could hardly drag him off for an urgent conversation.

"Did *you* miss me?" Minerva rolled her eyes, hoping that would convey her message.

"Stop flirting with my future daughter-in-law, you rascal! Can't you see your advances are falling on deaf ears?"

"You cannot blame a fellow for trying, Olivia. I still hold out the forlorn hope *dearest* Minerva will see sense and run away with me." He stared deeply into her eyes, every inch the Casanova he had been charged to play. "Just imagine how much better life will be with *me.*"

"The wedding gown is being made and the banns have been read, Giles. *Twice.*"

Lord Bellingham glanced over at Hugh, who seemed to be jealously scowling at the pair of them, or rather at Minerva's hand still grasped within his friend's. "Then thank goodness I came back just in the nick of time. Everyone knows they are not official until the third one." He kissed her hand again. "Did I ever tell you I will become a duke one day?"

"Did I ever tell you about the time I played Cleopatra at Drury Lane?" Lucretia had awoken.

"Did the critics call it a triumph?" An uncharacteristically belligerent and sarcastic Hugh had abandoned Diana and decided to wedge his bottom on the small settee between Minerva and Giles. "And welcome back, my friend. Do I have some *interesting* things to tell you . . ."

Apparently oblivious to the odd atmosphere, Sarah and her family stayed another half an hour, by which time everyone except Olivia and Giles, and the actress who was dead to the world, had quite run out of polite things to say and were willing the guests to leave. When they did, they all waved them off at the door with tight smiles. It had barely shut when Jeremiah's smile slipped off his face and his fists went to his hips.

"What the hell is going on!"

"My sentiments exactly, my dear — although let us take this back to the drawing room rather than cause a scene in front of the servants." Olivia glared at the hovering

Payne, who was doing his best to blend in with the oak paneling. "I suspect we shall need more tea."

"And a big plate of biscuits . . ." Giles unapologetically shrugged at Hugh's disbelieving stare. "Surely you cannot expect me to spectate on an empty stomach?"

"Bring back some damned brandy, too, while you're about it!" Jeremiah was openly seething. "And as God is my witness, if so much as one drop goes near Mrs. Landridge, heads *will* roll!"

One after the other, they traipsed back into the room on leaden feet. Oliva sat, as cool as a cucumber and every inch a lady, and gestured for them all to follow suit as if this were just any polite afternoon tea and not the complete end of the world.

"Well, that was embarrassing." She slowly scanned all the faces. "I am intrigued to hear what you all have to say for yourselves." Her eyes settled on her son. "Experience tells me I should start with you, Hugh — as this ridiculous debacle bears all your hallmarks."

Minerva heard him exhale, and she slipped her hand in his for support.

"Where to start? You see, the thing is . . ." The sound of muffled voices in the hallway momentarily distracted him. "Two years ago, in an act of complete desperation, I . . ."

"Let me in, I say!"

It sounded as if someone's fist was hammering on the front door.

"This is official business!" The sound of the strange raised voice in the hallway had them all turning.

"The family are not at home, sir. If you could come back later." Payne's voice was agitated and strained, as if he were wrestling with the caller.

"I demand to see Miss Merriwell! This man is her father!"

By this point, all Minerva had the strength to do was swallow while Hugh groaned and dropped his head in his hands. "I suppose there is always still that beach in Italy. . . ."

In manacles, Alfred Merriwell was instantly brought in by two burly men while the waiting constable twisted his hat in his hands.

"We arrested him drunk in Winchester, my lord, after the innkeeper accused him of passing fake coin. On his person we found this." He deposited two piles of banknotes on the table. "Most of these are real, to be fair." Only because Hugh had given them to him. "But these ones here are blatant forgeries. Mr. Smith here *claims* you gave him the lot and says you will vouch for his innocence, what with your being betrothed to his daughter and all."

No doubt after hearing the kerfuffle, Vee finally deigned to make an appearance. Her face was white with fear behind her spectacles as she took in the damning scene, but to her credit she said nothing. Still, her heartfelt glances toward her feckless father were tragic to witness.

Hugh looked toward Minerva for any sign how best to proceed, and she squeezed his arm. "That is true, sir. Hugh gave him the money to . . . er . . . purchase things for the wedding."

"Were you aware you were passing off counterfeit money, my lord?"

"Of course I wasn't! My man of business gave me the notes at our last meeting, and he procured them directly from my bank in London as he always does." Sometimes being an aristocrat had its advantages. One of them was the law for the rich and the law for the poor were unfairly different. Alfred Merriwell would have to prove his innocence. The authorities would have to prove Hugh's guilt. Powerful men had people to withdraw their money for them while they did more important things. Like sit in wingbacks at White's and complain about the state of the world. "Somebody there must have failed to notice they were forgeries."

"Then whoever that was, my lord, might want to consider investing in spectacles, as they were *very* poor forgeries indeed." But the constable smiled and clicked his fingers at his burly minions. "Let him go. And thank you for your time, my lord." He bent and picked up the smaller pile of banknotes. "I am afraid I will have to take these. All counterfeits must be destroyed. It is the law."

"Perfectly understandable."

"Perhaps the bank in London will compensate you for your loss?"

Hugh waved away the helpful advice. "It's just money. I have plenty of it."

After a patronizing and interminable lecture on what to look for in a forgery in case Hugh was inadvertently duped again, the constable and his men thankfully refused his mother's polite offer of refreshments and left. As Payne saw them to the door, the rest of them sat like statues. It was a brittle, awkward silence, finally punctuated by Vee.

"Papa!" She ran into her father's arms. "I've missed you."

Diana, on the other hand, couldn't hide her disgust. "Would you look what the cat dragged in."

The butler returned, glared at Hugh, and then stalked to the fresh decanter of brandy he had only minutes before placed on the sideboard. He gripped it by the neck, yanked out the stopper, and swigged directly from the bottle.

"Payne?" His mother took a regal sip of her rapidly cooling tea as if such a sight was commonplace. "When you have finished with that, can you instruct Cook to prepare the fatted calf? Such a feast is traditional, I believe, when a miracle occurs and a dead, frozen parent defrosts in the Cairngorms?" She smiled without humor at Minerva. "You should wake your mother, dear. She will be *delighted* to have him back."

Out of the corner of his eyes, Hugh watched Minerva's wastrel father subtly reach for the remaining banknotes on the table. "Don't you dare!" No longer caring, because frankly, there was nothing left to salvage, he marched over and snatched them up. "These are mine. You are not getting a farthing and I invite you to do your worst."

"Let's not be hasty, my lord." The wretch had the cheek to smile.

"Hasty?" He grabbed him by the lapels and hoisted him in the air. "*Hasty!* Thanks to the generosity of your daughters and my high esteem of them, I did not hand the constable my extensive dossier on your illegal activities, nor did I apprise him of your real name, *Mr. Merriwell* — but I promise you this! If you dare come within a hundred miles of one of those girls in the future, I shall hand it all over and tell them to throw the book at you!" Hugh deposited him back on the ground and pushed him away. "Get out of my house before I throw you out!"

Despite clearly wanting to wring his neck, Jeremiah came to stand loyally beside him, looking menacing. But like the snake he was, Minerva's father made a beeline to the door to save his own skin, not caring what carnage he left behind. He paused only when he gauged he had enough distance to avoid Hugh's fist. "You'll live to regret this, Fareham! Mark my words!"

"Papa!" The youngest Merriwell rushed after him and clutched his sleeve. "Wait . . . I'm coming with you."

Callously, he ripped his arm away. "Perhaps another time, Venus."

"But I want us to be together . . . to be a family again . . ." He stalked toward the front door, unmoved. Tear-filled eyes looked back at her sisters. "Tell him we want to be a family again. *Tell him!*"

It was Minerva who went to her first in

the hallway, closely followed by Diana. "Darling Vee — our family was always just the three of us." The front door closed with a bang, and the pair of them spirited her away so she could cry her heart out in private.

# CHAPTER THIRTY-TWO

Hugh hadn't noticed his mother had left her seat until her hand whacked him around the head. *"Merriwell?"*

He nodded. "There are no Landridges. Not here and not in Chipping Norton either."

"And if it's only ever been the three of them, who, pray tell, is that?" A quaking finger pointed at Lucretia, who had failed to wake up once during the entire ruckus or the constable's long visit.

"An actress I hired to play their mother."

"Oh, I am *so glad* I arrived in time for all this." Giles's voice was muffled by the big mouthful of biscuit he had just taken. "Didn't I tell you, Hugh, this sham was doomed to fail from the beginning?" He nudged Jeremiah, grinning. "I do so love to be right. There is nothing better than a good old-fashioned 'I told you so.' "

"And Minerva?"

"When I met a woman by chance who happened to be called Minerva, I offered her forty pounds to pretend to be my fiancée for as long as it took to terminate the engagement. She was supposed to elope with Giles on the second night — but he was unexpectedly called away, so we had to keep the ruse going until he returned."

"It was all a fabrication?"

Hugh nodded mournfully.

"But I just caught the pair of you kissing!"

"All part of their charade, Olivia." His stepfather's voice was flat. "Hugh's twisted way of remaining a merry bachelor."

"But that kiss was real, Jeremiah! I witnessed it with my own eyes!"

"It was." Hugh ignored his friend's suddenly widened eyes. "Against all my better judgment, I've inadvertently fallen in love with her."

He watched her sag in relief. "At least there will still be a wedding . . ."

"No, there won't." He couldn't have the conversation that he had avoided for fifteen years in front of anyone except his mother. "Can we talk in private?"

He took her to the dining room, and they sat opposite each other at the table — his mother stony faced, Hugh riddled with guilt yet oddly relieved to be able to finally tell the truth.

"I suppose you are going to blame me for all of this, aren't you? Some silly rebellion for my subtle attempts at matchmaking."

"They were never subtle, Mother." That sounded like blame, and Hugh huffed out a breath. "But I do not blame you — because I am sure your interference was well meant. I blame myself entirely. It was a silly, thoughtless, and hurtful thing to do but it was never meant to last this long or become so complicated. But I was seduced by the freedom and . . ." He sighed and shook his head, more for himself than her. All the lies had to stop here. "There is no excuse other than I couldn't bring myself to hurt you with the truth. Yet in trying not to hurt you I've ended up hurting you more. Something I certainly never intended to do after everything my father put you through. Which is ironic, really."

"For the love of God, speak plainly, Hugh! I am all done with your nonsense. If you love Minerva as you claim, I fail to see why you cannot marry her."

"Minerva understands and accepts my predicament and has agreed to wait until I am sure I won't repeat my father's mistakes."

"I don't follow?"

"The philandering? The mistresses? The bastard children? I saw how it devastated you when he died. I cannot imagine how long you suffered in silence alone before I was let in on his dirty secret."

"Hugh wasn't a philanderer."

"Yet the fruit of his loins was just in our drawing room drinking tea! I knew about grandfather's mistresses, of course — because Papa often told me about them — and not once did he give any indication he was cut from the same cloth. Which is the exact same cloth I am cut from. Two peas in a pod . . . I never wanted to put a wife or children through all that. I never want to be that man. I couldn't bear it."

"And that's what all this is about?"

"I never understood why you were so hell-bent on me marrying for love when you married a man who had scant regard for it. Nor do I understand why you tolerate the evidence of his infidelities."

"You think you are destined to follow in their footsteps?" She sunk back on the chair, shaking her head. "Oh, Hugh . . . What a pointless and wholly avoidable mess." Tears swam in her eyes. Pitying tears instead of the sad ones he had expected at the reopening of such old wounds. "When I tried to talk to you about it all those years ago, I thought you understood." She reached for him and gripped his hand across the polished mahogany. "But then, you were still very much a child and perhaps I am guilty of censoring those conversations, and too readily accepting your assertions you understood the situation and were at peace with it.

"Your father wasn't a philanderer. In fact, he was the exact opposite. He fell in love with Charlotte when he was young and was still deeply in love with her when he took his last breath. She was *always* the only woman for him and apart from the first weeks of our marriage, he was *always* faithful to her."

"Now it is me who doesn't follow."

"She was a farmer's daughter. They grew up in the same village. Played together as children. As time went on, their friendship turned into love and they wanted to marry. But Hugh's father wouldn't hear of it. Future earls didn't marry beneath them, and you already know what a horrid tyrant your grandfather was. To cut a very long story short, he went behind Hugh's back to her father, threatened to turn them off their land and completely ruin them unless Charlotte terminated the engagement and promised never to see your father again. He had also brokered an arranged marriage with me. My father was a duke, so I was considered the more suitable and advantageous match. That was the way of things in those days . . . I was young, barely seventeen and much too cosseted to go against the plan, and I married a stranger not much older than me. Newly heartbroken, barely twenty, and always one to do his duty, Hugh did as he was told — but only because he had failed in his attempts to win Charlotte back."

"She turned him down." Suddenly it all made sense.

"She couldn't see her family thrown out on the streets, and your grandfather was a cruel and vindictive man exactly as you have always been told. She didn't tell Hugh all that, merely saying she did not love him enough, which must have destroyed them both. But on his final attempt to change her mind, the night before his wedding to me, as they said their final goodbye, Sarah was conceived. To be fair to your father, he never would have married me if he'd known, and they were much too young and green to truly understand the consequences of their actions."

She looked suddenly wistful. "When your

father said his vows to me, he meant them and he tried to be a good husband. He discovered Charlotte was with child the same week I discovered we were to have you and then the whole sorry tale came out. I ranted and I raved at the stranger I married and we were both miserable for the longest time — until I realized it wasn't his fault. Any more than it was mine. It just was."

"Because some things just are."

Would he have understood all this at seventeen? Of course not. He was too busy being outraged on his own behalf and heartbroken at the perceived betrayal to consider the reasons behind it. The weight Hugh had always carried on his shoulders suddenly felt lighter.

"Hugh being Hugh, he couldn't abandon them, and honestly, I never could have grown to love and respect him as much if he had."

"You loved him?"

"As a friend, darling. We were stuck together for all eternity, there was no point in spending all that time miserable. But it was a marriage in name only. He kept his vows and quietly supported Charlotte and Sarah in case your grandfather got wind of it. We all muddled along as best we could for the sake of appearances for ten whole years, until your grandfather died. Then I gave Hugh permission to be with her, and in return, he introduced me to Jeremiah. . . . And we both finally got to enjoy being with the person we loved without having to pretend. Except, for Hugh, that wasn't for very long."

He felt a rush of emotion for his father almost as painful as when he had first died, except this was tinged with regret.

"Before he died, he made me promise to ensure you only married for love. I suppose I did take that promise a little too literally. Your father always did despair of my meddling. He would have left you to find your own love . . . which ironically you did, albeit with a little push from me. If it hadn't been for my meddling, you never would have lied. And then you never would have met Minerva. Your father would have approved of your choice."

For fifteen years he'd been angry at the man who had shaped him — unfairly. His father hadn't deserved that.

Had it shown in those final moments?

His concern must have appeared in his expression, because she shook her head and came to stand behind him, wrapping him in a motherly hug and stroking his hair. "You were a good son, Hugh. The best. Just as he was a wonderful man. A great father to both you and Sarah — but I always thought he had a special bond with you. You are so like him. In every conceivable way — aside from your mischievous streak and outstanding sense of humor, which I like to think came from me, of course. And because you are so like him, all he saw was your love at the end and so did I. I never knew you despaired of being his exact image."

"Well, I suppose that explains why I've tired of the bachelor life."

"And while you were trying so desperately to do the right thing, you did the absolute worst thing in the end. He couldn't bear to hurt anyone's feelings either." The hand that had just lovingly stroked his hair clipped him around the ear. "You have some serious amends to make!"

"I know."

"To me, to Jeremiah, to that lovely young lady who is miraculously prepared to wait for you despite your total idiocy . . ."

He was an idiot. Because she didn't have to wait!

Neither did he! The Standish blood that ran through his veins wasn't tainted. It was his father's blood, not his grandfather's. Therefore it was loyal and decent and capable of lifelong, deep, and abiding love!

What a wonderful revelation!

". . . to Reverend Cranham, the entire congregation of Saint Mary's, Madame Devy . . ."

Hugh knocked the heavy oak chair over in his hurry to get up.

"Where do you think you're going, Hugh! I haven't even got through the half of it yet . . ."

But he wasn't listening. He dashed across the hallway and back into the drawing room and skidded to a halt.

Jeremiah was still seething. Lucretia still snoring. Vee sat on the settee. Eyes red, swollen, sad, and remorseful behind her spectacles. Diana next to her, her gaze instantly narrowed at the sight of him, looking out for her sister. Giles munching on a biscuit, waiting for the next gripping installment in Hugh's epic farce to unfold. Payne hovering while still doing his best to merge into the woodwork.

And Minerva.

Rushing toward him, concerned. Wonderful, selfless, passionate, uncoordinated, outspoken, and perfect Minerva worried entirely about him. Because she loved him.

"Is everything all right?"

"It is better than all right. It is . . ." Frightening, exciting, unexpected, mind-boggling. The floor was tilting and his head was spinning — but he was free. "Truly . . . *excellent.*"

Hugh grabbed her hand and dropped to his knees.

"Do you remember when I said I believed vows should last forever?"

She nodded, confused.

"Well, I still believe it! Marry me, Minerva. Not next year or next month or even next week. Marry me *now* because I cannot wait another day to spend the rest of my life with you."

"But you said you wanted to wait . . ."

"All the more reason to ignore it! Look at the mess I've made. I've been a blithering idiot! I'm a menace to myself and those around me. I can't be trusted to make important decisions all by myself."

"That's true." His mother sailed into the room, grinning. " 'Marry me today' indeed — when the banns still need to be read on Sunday and Madame Devy won't be able to get Minerva's beautiful wedding gown here on time! No indeed!"

"But I don't understand . . . last night . . ."

"Last night I believed I was just like my father, and I assumed that was a bad thing, but now I know it wasn't. It isn't." It was wonderful. Truly excellent in every way.

"You see, it turns out he wasn't a philanderer at all — that was just my grandfather." He could see she was struggling to keep up — and no wonder; he was making no sense. "What I mean is, I was wrong, Minerva. About him. About me. About us. About everything. I will never let you down because you already know I'd rather die than hurt you. So marry me and you have my solemn vow I'll spend eternity proving it."

Minerva smiled, her beautiful eyes brimming with love, but before she could respond, his meddling mother decided their nuptials were a fait accompli.

"A Christmas wedding is better, I think. Don't you, Minerva? Valentine's is such a long way off. Besides, I've already ordered the musicians and sent out the invitations, although I am a bit annoyed I shall have to redo the table plans, now that your nonexistent relatives from the Cairngorms won't be coming." Then she rolled her eyes as Lucretia began to snore again. "Although at least we'll be spared the Mozart — so every cloud . . . What music would you like, Minerva dear?"

"It will make no difference . . ." She laughed and tenderly stroked Hugh's face. "I cannot hear it."

"Is that a yes, Minerva?"

"And once again, I have been proved right." A smug Giles addressed nobody in particular. "I warned him. *Actually* falling for his fake fiancée would only end in catastrophe. And here he is, stumbling headlong into the parson's trap like a man possessed! The biggest catastrophe of them all. If I wasn't so delighted to have been so prophetic, I'd be devastated for him."

His mother sighed. "He's a man in love, Giles dear. You should try it. In fact . . . Diana's awfully pretty. I've seen you watching her when you think nobody is looking . . ."

Diana was outraged. "I wouldn't have him if he were the last man on earth!"

"And I wouldn't touch that harridan with a barge pole!" Poor Giles looked absolutely terrified.

"Can you all just shut up so the lady can answer!" Jeremiah's bellow brought a welcome silence to the room. "Unless you want to run from all this madness, Minerva? In which case, I'll have the horses saddled."

"She can't ride either." Jeremiah glared at Vee, and she set her jaw stubbornly. "Well, as we are all suddenly telling the truth, I thought I should mention it . . ."

Hugh felt his lips twitching at the ridiculousness of it all and saw Minerva's do the same. What bizarre stock they both came

510

from. So much so, life was never destined to be dull. Their children would be interesting. He had never considered them before but suddenly couldn't wait to meet them all. A house full of adorable green-eyed troublemakers to make their happiness complete.

"So what's it to be, my love? A wedding followed by a life of nonsense with all of these escaped lunatics or the blissful quiet of a life of delirious exile on a beach in Italy?"

"I've become rather accustomed to the chaos these past few weeks. . . . And Madame Devy's design was rather wonderful . . ."

"I am going to need the words, Minerva. The *actual* words."

"Then, yes. I'll marry you."

He kissed her, and all the chaos receded temporarily into the background. That was something he decided to do whenever life got out of hand. He would kiss his wonderful wife and she would make it all better exactly as she was doing now.

"Then all's well that ends well. And I promise that is the absolute last theatrical reference I ever use, *my love.*" Two words that felt perfect on his lips and that he would use wherever possible.

*My love.*

His. For all eternity.

"Did I ever tell you I played Helena at Drury Lane . . ."

The unanimous and heartfelt noisy groan said it all.

# ACKNOWLEDGMENTS

As the old saying goes, it takes a village to raise a child, and as each story feels like my baby, it also takes a village to write a book. This book is one I have wanted to write for a long time, because it has bubbled away in the back of my mind for years. It would still be there, waiting patiently behind my other writing commitments, if my wonderful husband hadn't nagged me weekly to ignore everything else and just write it. I have also been blessed with the two best kids in the world, who have been very forgiving of the fact that their weird mother lives most of her life in her own imaginary world. So thank you, Katie and Alex, for being wonderful, for your encouragement, for growing up to be amazing adults, and for making me laugh. Words cannot say how proud of you I am.

I would also like to thank the writing community, especially my two little "tribes,"

513

who have been there for every step of this journey. The Harpies, my fellow historical romance–writing friends and support network — Nicole Locke, Laurie Benson, Lara Temple, Janice Preston, Jenni Fletcher, Harper St. George, Catherine Tinley, and Elisabeth Hobbes — you rock, ladies! And my exclusive little local writing group, Essex Writers United, who diligently critique my chapters and lead me astray — Liam Livings, Alison Rutland, Lucy Flatman, Kelly Stock, Sophie Rogers, Karen Osborne, Zeba Shah, Andrew Willmer, and Sarah Dorrian — my comrades in arms and my friends for life. Also thanks must go to Linda Fildew and Mills & Boon, from whom I have learned so much.

Finally, a special thank-you to my tenacious and wise agent, Kevan Lyon, for believing in me, and my editor, Jennie Conway, for her unfailing enthusiasm for this story. You are a joy to work with, ladies, and I couldn't have done this without you!

# ABOUT THE AUTHOR

When **Virginia Heath** was a little girl it took her ages to fall asleep, so she made up stories in her head to help pass the time while she was staring at the ceiling. As she got older, the stories became more complicated, sometimes taking weeks to get to the happy ending. Then, one day, she decided to embrace the insomnia and start writing them down. Now her Regency romcoms (including the Wild Warriners and Talk of the Beau Monde series) are published in many languages across the globe. Twenty books and two Romantic Novel of the Year Award nominations later, it still takes her forever to fall asleep.

The employees of Thorndike Press hope you have enjoyed this Large Print book. All our Thorndike, Wheeler, and Kennebec Large Print titles are designed for easy reading, and all our books are made to last. Other Thorndike Press Large Print books are available at your library, through selected bookstores, or directly from us.

For information about titles, please call:
  (800) 223-1244

or visit our website at:
  gale.com/thorndike

To share your comments, please write:
  Publisher
  Thorndike Press
  10 Water St., Suite 310
  Waterville, ME 04901

PV 01/23